The former deputy editor of *Tatler,* WENDY HOLDEN has worked at the
Sunday Times and the *Mail on Sunday.* She is the author of the inter-
national bestsellers *Simply Divine* and *Bad Heir Day* (both available in
Plume editions). Ms. Holden lives in London and Derbyshire.

D0057300

Bad Heir Day . . .

"A satiric field guide to the trust-fund twentysomethings, social-climbing parents, and gold-digging singles of London . . . *Bad Heir Day* neatly skewers its targets."
—*People* magazine

"Sparkling . . . If you liked *Bridget Jones*, you'll *love Bad Heir Day*."
—*Romantic Times*

"Very funny . . . The whimsical ingenuity of P. G. Wodehouse meets the sex-o-matic action of Jackie Collins. Holden stays in control of her supercharged farce all the way, even when a host of hysterically funny secondary characters almost steal the show."
—*Kirkus Reviews*

"Holden not only dissects social trends but also restores the pun to literary respectability—an amazing feat."
—*Esquire* (UK)

"A romp of a novel."
—*The Mail on Sunday*

"Savagely amusing . . . The satire is deadly, the plot addictive and the pace exhilarating."
—*Metro London*

"Laugh-out-loud funny . . . A treat."
—*The Express*

. . . and her debut novel *Simply Divine*

"*Simply Divine* uses lively, punning prose . . . in Holden's tartly rosy world, Cinderella gets both the prince and the kingdom. Now what could be more absolutely fabulous than that?"
—*The New Yorker*

"A funny, insider sendup of celebs and tabloid values . . . A wry romantic comedy with a twist."
—*New York Daily News*

"Delightful . . . A pun-a-minute read . . . Consider Holden's first novel a cool, iced caffeinated latte in book form, ideally consumed while lolling in a beach chair."
—*Entertainment Weekly*

"The literary equivalent to a box of chocolates."
—*Marie Claire*

"Saucy."
—*Cosmopolitan*

"Witty . . . Clever . . . Intelligent . . . Holden is a writer of serious wit who puns with aplomb and balances her Manolo Blahniks on the line between woman-as-Cinderella and woman-as-self conundrums."
—*Fort Worth Star-Telegram*

"Wonderfully high-spirited . . . A writer poised to become formidable in her field."
—*The Sunday Telegraph* (London)

fARM fATALE

A COMEDY OF
COUNTRY MANORS

WeNDY HOLDeN

A PLUME BOOK

PLUME
Published by the Penguin Group
Penguin Putnam Inc., 375 Hudson Street, New York, New York 10014, U.S.A.
Penguin Books Ltd, 80 Strand, London WC2R 0RL England
Penguin Books Australia Ltd, Ringwood, Victoria, Australia
Penguin Books Canada Ltd, 10 Alcorn Avenue, Toronto, Ontario, Canada M4V 3B2
Penguin Books (N.Z.) Ltd, 182–190 Wairau Road, Auckland 10, New Zealand

Penguin Books Ltd, Registered Offices:
Harmondsworth, Middlesex, England

First published by Plume, a member of Penguin Putnam Inc.
Previously published in Great Britain by Headline Books Publishing, in somewhat different
form, under the title *Pastures Nouveaux*.

First Plume Printing, March 2002
10 9 8 7 6 5 4 3 2

Ⓟ REGISTERED TRADEMARK—MARCA REGISTRADA

CIP data is available.
ISBN 0-452-28302-7

Printed in the United States of America
Set in Adobe Garamond
Designed by Eve L. Kirch

PUBLISHER'S NOTE
This is a work of fiction. Names, characters, places, and incidents either are the product of the
author's imagination or are used fictitiously, and any resemblance to actual persons, living or
dead, business establishments, events, or locales is entirely coincidental.

To Noj

fARM
fATALE

CHaPTER I

Bang on 8 A.M., the car alarm that had been shrieking all night finally stopped. After a two-second pause, the road drills began. Rosie could hold back no longer.

"Mark? You know we've been talking about moving to the country-side . . ."

"*You've* been talking about it, you mean," corrected Mark, hunched over his bowl of Cheerios and flicking rapidly through the newspapers. "I don't believe it." He groaned.

"I know." Rosie pressed her hands to her ears. "They only dug up that patch a week ago. Something to do with cable TV . . ."

"Not that," said Mark, his spoon dripping milk as he shook it at the center spread of a tabloid. "This. The *Mail*'s got Matt Locke. We've been trying to get him for ages."

"Who's Matt Locke?"

Mark looked at her, exasperated. "Honestly, you're like that judge who asked 'Who is Gazza?' Don't you ever *read* the papers?"

"You know I don't. Apart from the horoscopes." No doubt, Rosie thought, she was missing something, but she failed to share the awe with which Mark regarded newspapers in general and his job on one in particular. After all, it wasn't as if he was setting the national agenda, exposing Nazis, or bringing corrupt politicians to book. As far as Rosie could make out, Mark's job as assistant editor on a Sunday lifestyle section mostly involved rewriting other people's articles—"tickling up" as he called it—and attempting to persuade celebrities to give interviews about everything from their cystitis (for "Disease of the Week") to the contents of their refrigerator (for the "Chillin'" slot).

"Matt Locke, m'lud," Mark explained with elaborate patience, "is an extremely successful singer. The chisel-cheeked champion of howling rock 'n' roll angst, he burst on the scene two years ago with the number one platinum album *Posh Totty,* an epoch-making elegy to soaring strings, gutsy guitar, melancholy blues, and a touch of country and western, following it up with the even more successful *What Did Your Last One Die Of?* Then, at the height of his fame, he crashed and burned amid claims that the stress was too much."

"Oh," said Rosie, peering at the newspaper photograph of a girlish-looking youth with elaborately tousled hair and huge lips. He did not look particularly stressed. Actually, he looked half asleep.

She winced as the road drills outside changed to an even more brain-penetrating key. "Darling, you know you said you'd think about it. The countryside, I mean."

"Recycled interviews, of course," Mark muttered, pressing his nose almost against the newspaper. "Nothing that's not been printed before. Apart from these aerial pictures of Matt in his garden, although they're so blurry it's probably one of the gnomes."

"Two-thirds of people living in cities want to live in the country," Rosie persevered, hoping she'd remembered the figures properly. "Thousands are migrating every month."

"So if we stay in London," Mark said flippantly, "everyone else will eventually leave, house prices will go down, and we'll end up with a mansion on Regent's Park Road."

"Oh, *Mark.*"

"Look," Mark said, putting the newspaper down at last. "I know I said last night that I'd think about it, but it was the wine speaking. I don't want to leave London. I'm a townie born and bred. Crowds and noise are my lifeblood; filth is my friend. I can't breathe anything but carbon monoxide. A landscape of brutalist shopping precincts, down-at-the-heel Tube stations, and municipal concrete bunkers is the only sort of scenery I have time for. Besides," he added, stretching with satisfaction, "I'm going to be promoted. At long last, the paper's going to give me a column of my own."

"It *is*? But you never mentioned that last night."

"Well, it's not quite sorted out yet."

"So it's still 'Driving Miss Daisy' for the moment?"

The main column in Mark's section, "Driving Miss Daisy," recorded the adventures of Househusband, a stay-at-home father who looked after his infant daughter, Daisy, while his wife, a successful futures trader, went to work. Desperate for a column of his own, Mark despised the weekly chore of extracting the material out of Househusband and writing up the results himself. The fact that Househusband was incapable of stringing a sentence together, much less coming up with ideas, was, as Mark often savagely pointed out, not unconnected to the fact that he was the brother-in-law of the paper's editor.

Mark's brows drew together crossly. "For the moment, yes. But they've obviously given me that to train me for better things." He raked a hand through his rumpled golden hair. "Rosie, I can't leave. I'm on the brink of a promising career."

"Look," she said persuasively. "Why don't you ask the paper for a writing contract? Or go freelance, if they won't do it. You'd enjoy it much more. We could live anywhere we liked then. You can't really want to stay here." The hand she waved at their rented flat's dust-bloomed windows jerked involuntarily as a backfiring car joined the shrilling symphony of drills. "Imagine. Clean air. Cottages with roses round the door. Sun-dappled country lanes, empty of traffic."

Mark merely shrugged at this. Her dreams, Rosie realized miserably, were not his. In which case she'd target his nightmares, namely the dentist and going bald. "Water that doesn't cause tartar buildup behind your teeth. Rain that's clean and doesn't poison your hair follicles." As he still looked unimpressed, she added desperately, "Struggling into the office on the crappy, broken-down old Tube with your face pushed into someone's bottom. Or armpit."

"You don't have to struggle on the Tube anyway," Mark cut in self-righteously. "You're a freelance illustrator. You can lie around all day if you want."

Rosie rolled her eyes but refrained from pointing out that the endless illustrations for the food and horoscope pages of various glossy magazines in which she seemed to have become a specialist left little time for bon-bons on the couch. The fact that paintings of scallops and Scorpio were relatively poorly paid was, Rosie thought, another argument in favor of the move. Her fees would go further in the country.

"But what about everything we'd leave behind?" demanded Mark. "Restaurants, the theater, the cinema, and all that."

"But you decided a while ago we couldn't afford to eat out anymore," Rosie said gently. "We never go to the cinema and I can't remember the last time I saw the inside of a theater." In fact, she added silently, the most cultural thing we've probably done all year was eat Marks & Spencer's ravioli in front of *The Charlie Rose Show*. "We don't really make use of London these days," she pressed. "If you went freelance, we could live anywhere in the country. So why not live somewhere that's nice?"

Mark's handsome face was preoccupied. He was, Rosie knew, searching for the defining argument against, the ultimate no.

"But I'm on the fast track. The managing editor told me the other day that anything could happen. Which can only mean one thing. They're seriously thinking about giving me my own column."

"But wasn't he just saying anything could happen now that everyone's combining jobs because of the cutbacks? I mean, now the fashion editor's the foreign editor, too, so he's got a point."

"As I believe I mentioned," Mark said defensively, "the only reason Tallulah covered the military coup in Zwanwe was because she was doing a bikini shoot in the disputed border area at the time. Getting her to do a few interviews while she was there was only sensible."

"Even if her scathing criticism of the local warlords' dress sense wasn't," muttered Rosie, suddenly tired of arguing. "Darling, listen to me," she pleaded. "Moving out's not a mad idea. A recent survey said seventy-one percent of all people thought the countryside was more peaceful than the town. Fifty-four percent like the feeling of space and, um, fifty percent like the trees and forests." She was gabbling now, she knew.

"Fascinating," said Mark. Rosie looked at him sharply. Was he being sarcastic? The smooth dips and planes of his face, however, expressed only thoughtfulness.

Rosie waited, stiff with hope, watching Mark anxiously. Odd how, straight from bed, clad only in crumpled boxer shorts and an ancient T-shirt, he still managed to look devastating. She drew her toweling robe around herself, conscious of gray calves so long unshaved they probably needed a combine harvester by now. "So what do you think?" she ventured.

"I think," Mark said, slinging the spoon back into the pool of milk in his bowl, "that I might suggest it to the editor as a features idea."

Rosie ground her teeth and decided to drop the subject of the countryside. For now.

"Don't forget we're going to Bella's for dinner, will you?" she reminded him.

"Oh, Christ. Do we have to?" Mark groaned; he had little time for Rosie's best and oldest friend.

"Yes. Half-past eight. You know Bella. Starters timed to the nanosecond. We can't be late."

"Well, I will be." Mark returned with a pile of clothes from the bedroom, which he proceeded to put on in the hallway. "I'm working late. I'll be very late. Anyway, the last time Bella came here she was at least an hour late."

"She did get lost."

Mark was zipping up his gray suit trousers. "She was horrified to discover we lived in the one part of east London without a single Britart studio, Alexander McQueen atelier, appearance in a Guy Ritchie film." He shrugged on the crumpled jacket. "Look, do we have to go, seriously? Can't we stay in and have a curry? I got a new video yesterday—*Scream If You Know What I Did Last Friday 13th*."

"Sorry," Rosie said firmly. "We've been booked for ages. We can't put her numbers out."

After several attempts at slamming it, Mark finally succeeded in shutting the flat door behind him. Rosie struggled upright from the bean-bag chair. The unenticing prospect of a long day bent over her drawing board painting Pisces and plum tomatoes stretched ahead. But it wasn't really the work that was the problem. It was the surroundings. Rosie looked glumly around at the sitting room, at the rumpled, crummy, paisley cotton throws that somehow hinted at the cheap and nasty floral-print sofa they were meant to be disguising. She contemplated the plants, their dusty leaves accentuating the dark foliage snaking across the disgusting seventies' wallpaper. Through the grimy windows, the surrounding tower blocks pressed in like bullies on a playground.

Moving into the wardrobe-size kitchen, she looked up at the strip-lit ceiling, where yellow stains represented decades of cooking that owed nothing to Delia Smith. Once upon a time, she remembered, there had been talk of repainting. Probably around the same time that there had been talk of removing the hideous wallpaper and of replacing the hairy orange floor tiles with sisal from a John Lewis store. None of which had ever come to anything.

How easy it would be, Rosie thought, if she could simply pick up her things and move away on her own. But that was impossible. Difficult though Mark often was, she loved him.

"Although God knows what you see in him," Bella, who was no fonder of Mark than he was of her, would say. "I suppose he's good-looking," she would grudgingly admit.

And passionate, Rosie would silently add, even if sometimes it did take the form of bad temper. *And* funny, although he could be acerbic at times. *And* enthusiastic. *And* ambitious. *And* . . . well, that would do.

As she ran hot water over the pots in the sink and squirted in the shampoo standing in for dishwashing soap until someone—no doubt her—remembered to buy some, Rosie tried not to think of Bella's wengewood-fronted dishwasher, not to mention her gardener, housekeeper, hot and cold running nannies, and brace of cleaners. Or the fact that, despite a supposed full-time job as a stylist for a fashionable interior-design magazine, Bella had so much time and money on her hands that she could change the inside of her house almost as often as her clothes. Rosie had picked up the telephone only the day before to find Bella wondering where she could get Bakelite light switches for her downstairs loos.

Rosie sighed. That Bella had been at the front of the queue when good fortune was dispensed was indisputable. The lucky star that had, throughout her teens, ensured that Bella never went short of boyfriends, money, or the latest clothes had more latterly ensured that she never got parking tickets, failed to catch a waiter's eye, or hung about more than five minutes for a taxi. In the fullness of time, this obliging planet had also delivered Simon, heir to a brewing fortune, who had fallen for Bella at a Chelsea dinner party.

Six months of weekends in Paris and Venice later, Bella had walked up the aisle in a Ben de Lis dress, having arrived in a landau driven by four of the brewing company's shire horses. Following a honeymoon in Porto Ercole, she had arrived back to a white-stuccoed slice of North London real-estate splendor. Number 28 Campbell Crescent boasted an original fanlight, four lavatories including two en suite, an upstairs sitting room the size of a ballroom, a porticoed entrance flanked by sculpted bay trees in pots of impeccable plainness, and a gleaming period bootscraper. The whole ensemble drove Mark mad with jealousy.

As she rinsed a sequence of chipped mugs under the tap, Rosie anticipated the approaching evening with dread. Shy, gauche, and gentle, she always felt more like a waitress than a guest at her friend's loud and competitive dinner parties. Odd, really, considering how well she knew the territory. Not to mention the conversation, which rarely varied. School fees (the ruinous nature of), Property prices (the completely justified/obscene rise of, depending on whether one was selling or buying). Cleaners (the cheek of). Beach holidays in Norfolk (the wonders of). *The Naked Chef* (ditto). The children's television of the early 1970s (ditto). Exotic foreign circuses (ditto). Organic delivery boxes (ditto). Ralph Fiennes (ditto) whom someone had always spotted in their local cheese shop (ditto). Rosie's heart sank at the prospect.

The thought of seeing Bella was the only saving grace. She desperately needed to talk to her about the countryside, with particular reference to ways of persuading Mark to move there. Bella, while a committed urbanite and unlikely to support the idea in principle, would certainly rise to the challenge of forcing Rosie's boyfriend to do something he didn't want to. And in any case—Rosie grinned as the thought struck her—Bella's competitive North London neighbors were an anti-urban argument in themselves. Usually. Her heart beat fast with fear at the thought that her friend might, just this once, have invited someone reasonable.

Luckily, she hadn't. That they were worse than ever was made obvious in the first five seconds.

"Sorry I'm late. Someone under the train at Aldgate East," Rosie gasped, noticing that Mark wasn't there yet either.

"Really," said a hard-bodied blonde whose sticklike arms rattled with bracelets. "People are so bloody inconsiderate, aren't they? Don't they realize some of us have dinner parties to go to?"

"This is Xa." Bella pushed the blonde in Rosie's direction. "Short for Xanthippe. She's in fashion PR."

"Hi," rasped Xa. "We were just discussing this *fabulous* French circus, Cirque du Soleil. Have you heard of them?"

Here we go again, thought Rosie.

Just how was it, Rosie wondered, that Bella, her large-eyed Italianate face framed by a chin-length bob of glossy black, had managed to be at the front of the looks queue as well as the luck one? Rosie had always felt herself vague and smudgy-looking beside the strong and definite lines of her friend. Bella, however, disagreed. She had a theory about what certain men found attractive about Rosie. "They adore you because you remind them of that blond choirboy in the fourth form that they always wanted to roger behind the bike sheds." Rosie had never been entirely convinced about this; certainly she had failed to have an electric effect on either of the men present tonight. After a cursory glance following her entrance, they were now talking to each other with their backs turned. And Mark, of course, was in thrall to her to such an extent that he had as yet failed to turn up at all.

"This is Florian. He's married to Xa. Works in television." Bella handed her a glass of champagne and pulled at the sleeve of a tanned man with prosperous hair and aspirational glasses chatting animatedly to the fat, red-faced Simon.

Bella suddenly gave an excited squeal and nudged Xa. "Oooh. Almost forgot. How was the *wedding?*"

"Fabulous. The Naked Chef was there, as well as Ralph Fiennes."

"*No!*" exclaimed Bella, clasping her hands in ecstasy. "How *amazing.* I bumped into him in the cheese shop only the other day."

Rosie shifted from foot to foot, wishing desperately that Mark would come. And even more desperately that they had stayed at home after all and watched *Scream If You Know What I Did Last Friday 13th.* She disliked horror films but preferred them to horror dinner parties. This showed every sign of being Bella's worst yet, and Mark wasn't even here to appreciate it. Nor had there been any opportunity to have the longed-for word with Bella.

"Went to a rather glamorous wedding yesterday," Xa informed Rosie in a throaty bark. "Friend of mine who's a successful fashion designer."

Florian snorted contemptuously. "So why the hell couldn't she afford better church decorations? Bloody candleholders were baked-bean tins without the labels on."

"Baked-bean tins are *tremendously* chic," returned Xa crushingly.

"What about those ketchup bottles with the roses in, then?"

"HP sauce bottles, *actually.*"

"It sounds wonderful," croaked Rosie valiantly.

"Oh, it *was,*" gushed Xa. "The vicar had a tan and Gucci spectacles. And the organist was a woman who apparently used to play with Prince."

"How *terribly* glamorous," Bella said admiringly.

"You thought she was some newscaster at first," Florian said accusingly to Xa. "Though God knows how you know what any of them look like. You haven't watched the news since Princess Di died."

The doorbell rang. Mark, thought Rosie in relief. Bella disappeared behind the old-gold sitting-room door. "Mark, darling!" Rosie heard her exclaiming rather too brightly.

"I wasn't sure about Jerry wearing that turquoise and orange though . . ." Xa remarked. As Florian began to stare pointedly at her pink cardigan and lime-green skirt, Xa flared her nostrils furiously. "What exactly is it you don't like about this outfit?" she demanded. "The shop said I looked like a million dollars."

"Couldn't they have made it pounds?" drawled Florian. "Worth more. Still, I suppose we should be grateful they didn't say euros."

Mark, Rosie noticed, as he trailed into the sitting room after Bella, had made even less effort than usual. His hair was a mess, he had tired brown shadows beneath his eyes and ink stains all down his suit. She also noticed, feeling gratified for the first time that evening, that even in that state he was at least ten times better-looking than any other man in the room. Xa had apparently noticed the same. Her face suddenly lit up and she began buzzing around him like a particularly chatty bee. The words *Cirque du Soleil* came floating over to Rosie. "Sweetie, I'm just going to check on supper," Bella announced to Simon as she descended the Kandinsky-inspired spiral staircase down to the basement kitchen. "Put something a bit more lively on, will you, angel?"

As Simon fumblingly replaced the *Buena Vista Social Club* with *Ibiza Club Anthems Vol. 20,* and Mark was finally stung into replying to Xa, Rosie slipped gratefully down to the kitchen after Bella.

Bella's kitchen was cutting edge in every sense of the word. An expanse of sandblasted glass, industrial stainless steel, and with hundreds of recessed lights on the brilliant white ceiling, it looked like a submarine control room. There was no sign of Bella at the vast, eight-ringed, catering-standard stove. Following the faintly discernible scent of cigarette through the open French windows, Rosie found her friend on the deck outside, cheeks concave with the ferocity of her smoking. Bella started in surprise and coughed violently. "Damn, you caught me."

"Bel, you're supposed to have *given up.*"

"Darling, I work on a glossy, remember. Two packs a day are the legal minimum for appetite-suppressing purposes. Speaking of putting one off one's food," she said, grinning, "how's it going up there?"

"Great." Rosie smiled back. "Xa was just explaining to Mark as I left how pews were a really fantastic place for Pilates. Said she'd done forty buttock clenches by the time the bride arrived."

Bella snorted. "Unspeakable, isn't she? Only had them round because Florian's apparently interested in doing some hideous-sounding fly-on-the-wall documentary about the barmaids in Simon's pubs or something."

She stepped back into the kitchen, her metal heels clacking across the hand-polished slate floor tiles, and returned to the stainless steel–topped counter. This was dominated by a large earthenware bowl filled with an arrangement of feathery new carrots, frilly lettuces, bundles of magenta radishes, pearly potatoes, and gleaming tomatoes. Rosie gazed at it in admiration, thinking that it looked like something by Arcimboldo, the Renaissance painter par excellence of over the top fruits and vegetables.

"Gorgeous, isn't it?" Bella smiled. "Field of dreams.com does a much better organic delivery box. I'm so glad we changed from Heart and Soil. Their apples were always a bit wormy and the tomatoes all had blossom-end rot. Although I must say I was quite tempted by Rocket Man. Dido at the office uses them and apparently the deliveryman is gorgeous. His knobbly russets are to die for."

Rosie nodded vaguely, wondering if the earth on the potatoes was real. It looked so rich, so brown, almost edible itself, in fact. Bella picked out a lettuce and began a prolonged session of rinsing it under the state-of-the-art tap.

"Yes, it's organic all the way from now on," Bella said, shaking the lettuce energetically around her head in a wire basket and splattering Rosie with water. "I mean, how could anyone put any of those other ghastly things into their bodies?"

Rosie, who had always wondered how Bella could put a ghastly thing like Simon into her body, did not reply. But evidently she had, with the result that their staggeringly spoiled son, the unspeakable Ptolemy, now walked the earth. Rosie's attention returned to the display of nature's bounty and the countryside longings it provoked. Growing your own organic vegetables in your own garden, she thought, would be infinitely better than having them dumped on your front step in a sack by someone gorgeous from Rocket Man. However knobbly his russets.

"Darling, are you all right?" Having arranged the lettuce, Bella was snipping parsley over a gleaming silver baking tray in which were arranged six prime halves of lobster. "If you're wondering about the lobster, they're free-range and reared in happy seas. I checked. So don't come over all animal welfare on me."

"It's not that." Rosie blushed. The fact that she could not bear even to swat a mosquito was the source of endless teasing from both Bella and Mark. "After all, it's not as if they're very grateful," Mark would observe as, whenever the temperature rose, the mosquitoes responded by biting every exposed inch of Rosie's pale skin.

"What is it, then? Tell Auntie Bella. Is it Mark?" Hope flickered in Bella's black eyes.

"Sort of."

Bella put down her scissors momentously. "Oh, darling, I told you he was hopeless from the start. Good-looking but deeply *not worthy.*"

"No, it's me," Rosie said sharply. "I want to move."

"Well, I do think you could be a *bit* more central. I hear City Road's a good bet. And King's Cross is apparently the new Belgravia, though admittedly that's stretching it a bit."

"Not in London. Out. To the country."

"The *country?*"

"Yes. I've been thinking about it for a while, actually. But I mean it now. I'm dying to live there."

"You sound," Bella said shrilly, "like Chekhov's *Three Sisters.* Except in reverse." She slammed the lobsters into an oven big enough to roast an entire sheep. "Darling, the country's ghastly. You never know what you're standing in, for a start."

"How can you say that?" gasped Rosie, gesturing at the Arcimboldo bowl. "You buy organic vegetables, don't you? They're grown in the countryside." She decided to give the earth on the potatoes the benefit of the doubt.

Bella shuddered. "Not mine, darling. Field of dreams.com grows everything on an allotment in Tulse Hill."

Rosie tried another tack. "Bel, as far as I'm aware, you've never been to the countryside. How do you know what it's like?"

"I have so. Not *here,* admittedly—I'm always terrified that if I ever leave London they'll close the gates and not let me back in. But I've been to it in France. *Dreadful.* The ducks quacked all night."

"Are you sure they weren't toads?"

Bella reflected on this and went slightly red. Then she relaunched the attack. "But it would be awful. There wouldn't be anyone you know, it would be horribly quiet, pitch black at night . . ."

"Yes," said Rosie, smiling. "*Exactly.* It would be perfect to work in. So peaceful."

Bella's elegant shoulders slumped. "Can't you just go to Hampstead?"

"So you think it's a terrible idea. I thought you might."

"We-ell, yes." Bella tested a strand of spaghetti with her perfect white teeth. "And I'd miss you *horribly,*" she added petulantly.

"Oh, Bel. You could always come and stay. Bring Tolly if you want. He's probably never seen a real cow."

"Darling, you haven't met his headmistress." From her bright black eyes, Bella flashed Rosie an assessing glance. "You really want to do it, don't you?"

Rosie nodded. "If only Mark could land himself this column he's always talking about, we could go straightaway. It would be bliss."

Bella vented her feelings by tossing the spaghetti furiously around in the pan.

"Well, I suppose there is one thing to be said for the countryside," she said eventually, sighing.

"There *is?*"

"Well, it *is* rather fashionable at the moment, darling. The new sex, the new black, the new gardening, and all that."

"Oh, surely not," faltered Rosie, faintly alarmed. "People want a better life, that's all. Seventy-five percent—"

"No, darling," cut in Bella, "they want better publicity. Surely you've noticed. You can hardly open *Vogue* at the moment without reading about some Oscar-winning actress making nettle jam in a converted cow shed, free-range chickens clustered round her ankles."

"Oh." Rosie was not a big *Vogue* reader, despite having once painted some chard for their cookery page.

"Dog kennels, barns, sheep dips, you name it, some hipster's put sisal down and is living in it," added Bella. "I had to style some obscenely trendy producer's former flour mill turned living space for *Insider* only last week. Amazing place. All the chairs were shaped like teeth and the coffee table was an elephant's head made of chicken wire. All the work of this terrifically happening designer called Basia Briggs, who even you must have heard of, darling."

Shaking her head, Rosie suppressed a shudder. She made a mental note to get a copy of the latest *Insider* and look in areas as far removed as possible from models who liked to sit on molars. On the other hand, Mark might be more interested in the whole moving-out idea if he thought famous people did it, too.

"To put it at its simplest," Florian was saying as Bella and Rosie, bearing steaming plates of lobster-topped pasta, reentered the dining room, "the idea my company's currently working on is, quite simply, a vintage television station. One channel, as I say, is aimed at middle-class mid-thirtysomethings and devoted entirely to seventies' children's TV. Another will screen footage of the Second World War. Another, and this is the one we're really banking on, will be devoted to Princess Diana . . ."

"My idea," Xa said proudly, the brilliant beam she directed round the room marred only by a smudge of lipstick on her teeth. She caught Rosie's eye. "Your very charming boyfriend's just been telling us that *you* want to move to the countryside," she announced. "And that he doesn't."

Rosie flashed a furious look at Mark. How dare he discuss their disagreements in public? He gave her a glazed look in return; his bleariness, she suddenly realized, was actually inebriation. His late arrival was no doubt due less to excessive working hours than to excessive after-hours consumption of gassy lager with his colleagues.

"But I think the country sounds rather fun," slurred Xa. "We once thought about buying a beach hut in Norfolk. Simply brilliant for bucket and spade holidays."

She looked wistful. At least, Rosie thought, that was the charitable interpretation of her rolling eyes and slack mouth. "I'd love to live in a village," she drawled.

Across the table from Rosie, Mark's face was expressionless. He was either drinking everything in or had drunk everything already.

A muscle twitched in Florian's cheek. "We *live* in a village," he said through gritted teeth. "It's called Blackheath. And what about Orlando, anyway? Where the hell would he go to school?"

"I'm thinking of taking Orlando out of St. Midas's, actually," Xa retaliated. "There are at least ten other Orlandos in his class and it gets very confusing. Bloody headmistress is always bloody ringing up complaining how ginger Orlando has beaten up curly Orlando or run off with small Orlando's Pokémon cards."

"Oh, dear," said Rosie. "What an awful bully. How worrying for you. Which Orlando is yours?"

"Ginger."

"Oh."

There was a silence.

"Thought of the pub market?" Simon suddenly barked at Rosie, the long hairs on his eyebrows bristling. These, along with his stubby, snouty nose and pink face, always reminded her of a wild boar.

"Rosie wants to paint peacefully in the country, darling," said Bella, rolling her eyes at Rosie. "Not pull pints and dole out pork scratchings while everyone stares at her arse."

"Realized that. Actually meant the buildings. Hundreds closing every week now, and don't I know it. Quite nice old places, some of them."

"Oh. Shame," said Bella.

"Well, they're there to make money for pub companies first and foremost," Simon said thickly as he drained his red wine. "Don't run them as bloody charities."

There was another silence.

"Abattoirs," said Florian suddenly.

"I beg your pardon?" said Xa.

"Abattoirs," Florian repeated. "New rock 'n' roll, propertywise. *Thousands* gone into receivership since the mad cow thing. Did a program about it not long ago."

Rosie shuddered.

"Creutzfeldt-Jakob's apparently the best thing that ever happened to the rural property market," Florian added. "Specially now that the bottom's fallen out of chapels."

"Has it?" said Bella, watching Florian help himself to the Margaux.

"Oh, ya. Used to be ten a penny, but you can't get a Primitive Methodist this side of a hundred thousand these days. There was one on the moors outside Halifax going for one hundred twenty-two thousand last time I looked. But it *has* got planning permission for a swimming pool."

"Well," Bella said after a pause, "that doesn't sound very Methodist. Certainly sounds primitive though."

Rosie looked at her plate, wishing they would change the subject. It had obviously never crossed either Simon's or Florian's mind that one might wish to move to the countryside for any motive other than profit. Assistance came in the unexpected and inebriated guise of Xa.

"Let's play charades now, anyway," she yelled suddenly. "The one where we have to guess London restaurant dishes. What's this, everyone?" She immediately launched into a series of impressions of Donald Duck, someone wearing a crown and the frantic mixing of something in a bowl.

"Two Fat Ladies," bawled Florian, so loudly Rosie saw Bella shoot an involuntary glance upward to where, three floors above, Ptolemy lay in state in his *Terminator*-theme nursery.

Xa flung him a contemptuous stare. "It's got to be something off a *menu*, you moron. Who's this?" She mimed the crown again, then someone at the wheel of a car that then apparently twisted out of control. By the way of finale, Xa threw herself violently into Bella's mantelpiece-free chimney breast, whose fireplace was so minimal it was merely a square hole in the wall.

"Princess Di!" shouted Bella in sudden triumph. "Princess Di, a cake, and a duck . . . *oooh, oooh* . . . it's got to be the foie gras on a sweet-corn pancake from Kensington Palace!"

"I take it all back," Mark slurred as, what seemed like years later, they waited for the night bus in Upper Street.

"You do?" Rosie's heart almost stopped. She had spent the whole of the walk to the stop propounding the countryside-is-stuffed-with-celebrities argument. Had she got through at last?

"Yes," Mark hiccuped as the N73 rounded the corner, packed to the gills. "Much better evening than I thought. Quite interesting." He heaved himself on as the bus doors sprang open. "You'd miss all that sort of thing in the countryside. Nothing to do there."

Almost violent with disappointment, Rosie shoved him determinedly on board the reeking vehicle, then, thanks to his lack of coordination, she paid the inevitable price as it tried to move off.

"When a woman is tired of London, Mark," she said sighing, once she had struggled free, "she is not necessarily tired of life. Just sick of getting trapped in the closing doors of the night bus."

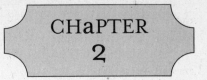

CHaPTER 2

Rosie awoke the next morning with a fuddled head and the pressing memory of an illustration of a member of Parliament she needed to do by the afternoon.

"William Hague!" she gasped. "I need William Hague."

"Well, that's something you don't hear very often." Mark groaned from under the duvet. During the night Rosie had been dimly aware of him rushing out of bed and making buffalo-in-agony noises in the bathroom.

"I'd better go and get the papers. There's bound to be a picture of him I can copy in one of them."

Craster Road, East Ham, looked its usually unlovely self as Rosie tramped down it. A collection of upturned wheelbarrows, odd socks, and plastic containers festooned the few front gardens not covered in concrete paving to provide a berth for a large mustard-colored car at least ten years of age. At the end of the road, Rosie turned toward the Tube station and its adjoining newsagent. Walking past the green wire fence dividing the pavement from the soggy park and children's zoo, she remembered how, six weeks ago, a gang of thugs had broken in and terrorized all of the little animals. Her urge to leave the city, Rosie knew, had crystallized from that moment.

The tiny Asian newsagent looked up from his high stool in front of the register and smiled faintly as she approached. He was, she saw, reading the etiquette page of *Good Housekeeping*.

"How are you?" Rosie deposited a sheaf of newspapers on the counter.

"Bearing down," replied Mr. Jayhind, adding up her bill on the keys with elegant fingers and a lugubrious air.

"You mean bearing up."

"No. Bearing down."

Her head still throbbing slightly, Rosie smiled at him. "I know what you mean."

Mark had left for work by the time she returned. Spreading the papers out so that they almost entirely covered the hairy orange floor tiles (an enormous improvement in the decor), Rosie eventually found a picture of William Hague with one of his constituents. "Barn Stormer" read the headline above the picture of an ancient structure standing in the middle of a moor not so much desolate as anguished. A man was standing next to it, receiving the congratulations of the Tory leader. Rosie peered closely at William Hague's face. Could she use it?

Her eye flicked through the story. Mr. Brian Stormer, a former driving instructor from Neasden, had, it explained, rebuilt his barn's entire fifteenth-century structure using wattle and daub techniques he had taught himself. What had particularly caught the Opposition leader's attention was the fact that Mr. Stormer had sourced his own yak hair for the daub; a feat that prompted unkind speculation on the part of the paper that Hague was planning to address his own follicularly challenged condition via this ancient means. Rosie, however, noticed only the barn-restorer's remarks on rural life: "Moving to the country was the best thing I ever did. I've got my peace of mind back."

Rosie sighed with envy. Little as the idea of mixing animal hair with lime, soil, and aggregate appealed to her, it looked more fun than spending the afternoon in East Ham drawing a dome-headed politician while the floor shook with the force from the downstairs neighbor's TV.

Still less appealing was going to the supermarket afterward, a chore that Rosie had been putting off for days. But it was her turn this week, as so often, despite the alternate-week system they had, it seemed to be. Damn. She didn't have a pound coin for the trolley.

Rosie miserably anticipated Mark's reaction to the lack of supper. They'd just have to fall back on the Shanana Tandoor Palace. She fought the urge to cry. How much longer could she bear this wretched city? But if leaving London meant leaving Mark . . . ? With a sinking heart, she slid her key into the flat's lock.

To her amazement, she entered the hall to Mark singing in earsplitting style. He had apparently come home early and was fiercely whistling in the kitchen, where, to judge from the accompanying billows of bacon-scented smog, he was making himself a sandwich. Rosie's repeated attempts to slam the door brought him shooting out into the hallway.

"Guess what!" he yelled ecstatically.

"What?"

"Something fantastic." He was grinning so hard and wide, she feared his face might split. "Househusband. His wife's run off to Monaco with an investment banker."

Rosie looked uncomprehendingly at him. Then enlightenment dawned. "Oh. I see. Something's happened. He's got some material for a change, you mean?"

"What? No, you chump. Househusband's wife left him for a capitalist pig. Slightly defeats the object of the column, the New Man role-reversal thing, wouldn't you say?"

Rosie shrugged. After the afternoon she'd had, Househusband officially ranked at the bottom in her list of concerns.

"As a result of which"— Mark was now capering gleefully round the hallway—"Househusband went on a drunken bender in his car, had an accident, and lost his license. So he can't drive Miss Daisy anymore. Even if his wife hadn't taken her to Monaco with her, which she has. So guess what's happened now?"

"Can't imagine. Wife and Forex dealer writing the column between them, are they?"

A slightly scared expression, as if the idea hadn't actually occurred to anybody, briefly crossed Mark's face. Then the grin returned. "No. They've given me a column. At last."

Rosie swallowed. This was it, then. All of Mark's dreams had come true. They'd never leave London now. At least, he wouldn't.

"This is my chance," yelped Mark. "The big break I've been wait-ing for."

"Good for you," croaked Rosie.

"Well, don't you want to know what I'll be writing about?"

Rosie bulldozed a smile across her face. "Tell me."

"You'll be thrilled."

"Will I?" Rosie doubted it.

Mark nodded. "Now that Househusband's collapsed, they need to start a weekly column about something else. Some other current topic. So I had this idea of doing something about people who've moved from the city to the country. The editor agreed it would be the perfect subject."

Rosie stared. Funny, but there was something familiar-sounding about that.

"Very keen, he was," Mark continued, "especially after I'd thrown in all that stuff you said about the countryside being the new rock 'n' roll and how every supermodel worth her Wonderbra contract is chop-ping wood and making chutney. Loved all those statistics, too—seventy-five percent of actresses converting abattoirs or whatever it was you said. The editor's got this idea that moving from the city to the country is the millennium dream and he wants me to write about what it's really like to swap the city for rural heaven. Thinks that will wow thousands of readers dying to leave loft apartments in Docklands for sweeping acres of Derbyshire."

"But how are you going to do that?" asked Rosie. "How can you write about what the countryside's really like from East Ham?"

"Well, we won't be living in East Ham obviously."

"You mean . . . ?"

Mark nodded. "We'll move to the country. I'll go freelance. Write it from there. We'll leave London."

As tears of joy and relief sprang to her eyes, Rosie leaned back against the wall. That the afternoon from hell had mutated into the evening in which all earthly desires were granted was all a bit too much to take in.

"I've finally got a *column*!" Mark's eyes were shining. "I can't tell you how much it means to me. Rosie!" He flung his arms about her and whirled her round in the air. "I love you, I love you. *I love you.*"

"I love you, too." Rosie giggled. There was no one quite as ebullient as Mark when he was happy, just as there was no one quite as miserable when he wasn't. She suddenly felt exhausted, as if she had fought a long and losing battle and then suddenly and unexpectedly won. Yet in the sunny blue skies of her happiness there hung a tiny cloud of concern.

"Will they pay you well? I mean, will it be enough to live on?"

Mark dumped her unceremoniously back on the carpet tiles, a cagey look on his face. "We're still discussing that. Cuts, you know. They're being their usual difficult bastard selves about it." He grinned devastatingly at her. "But hell, Rosie, what does it matter? I've got my byline at last. Picture byline if I can swing it. Or find a reasonable passport one."

Rosie tried not to dwell on the fact that the paper's refusal even to fund a proper photograph hardly promised wealth beyond the dreams of avarice.

"Anyway," Mark enthused, "houses will be much cheaper in the country. We'll never be able to afford to buy anything in London, not with property prices the way they are. We can't afford *this* disgusting dump, even," he added, swinging an arm round the flat he had so recently defended against all of Rosie's criticisms. "But we'll definitely be able to manage a deposit on something small somewhere in the country."

Rosie nodded. It was what she had been saying for weeks.

"And you can illustrate from anywhere. All you need is a drawing board and a few paints. All I need is a PC with E-mail. Which the paper is supposed to be providing." He beamed at her. "Along with a mobile."

Rosie smiled. He was repeating her own words back to her. With the exception of the paper providing the laptop and mobile. That *was* a surprise.

Following the announcement of the great news, Mark rushed out and bought a bottle of wine from the liquor store while Rosie called the Shanana Tandoor Palace. They spent the evening lying happily on the floor perusing an old map book. Wrapped warmly in a sense of shared purpose, they turned the pages, laughing at names like Slack Top and Tingley Bottom. "I'll start ringing the agents tomorrow," Mark said. "We should probably buy up north. It's cheaper."

As well as, Rosie thought, nodding enthusiastically, being the least likely place to be stuffed with the kind of people Bella puts in *Insider*.

Mark caressed the Cotswolds with a lingering finger. "Plenty of time to join the Jag and paddock set once 'Green-er Pastures' takes off."

"Is that what you're calling it?" Rosie clapped her hands. "Clever you. Mark *Green*. Of course."

"Yes, and the subtitle's 'The Good Life for the Millennium.' "

"What does that mean?" Images of digging up potatoes in the rain sprang alarmingly to Rosie's mind. "We won't have to lift leeks or anything?"

"Course not. Just something to press all of the readers' middle-class organic buttons, that's all. I can write about what I like. Guess what the subject of the first column's going to be?"

"Tell me."

"The hunt for the perfect cottage, obviously."

"Oh, Mark." She leaned over and kissed him, feeling that she had never before been so content with him. The good life, after all.

Mark's face was as happy as it was handsome, glowing with pleasure as well as the heat from the electric fire. As slowly, lingeringly, he removed his lips from hers, she saw his eyes had narrowed slightly as they always did when sex crossed his mind. Rosie inhaled the faint salty scent of his sweat; he pushed up her shirt and fingered her stiffening nipples and she gasped with anticipated pleasure. Lowering her hand to his crotch, she felt the familiar, delicious tension within her as her fingers caressed the familiar, delicious hardness.

The phone chose that moment to shrill in the hall.

"Damn," Mark snarled. "Who the hell rings up at this hour?"

"You don't have to answer it." Rosie, lifting herself on her elbow, had a distinct sense of missed opportunity.

"Might be work." Mark scrambled up.

"It's Bella," he said, loping back into the sitting room almost instantly. "Says it's an emergency."

"An emergency?" Rosie rushed to the phone, images of Simon in a coffin and Ptolemy attached to an IV racing through her mind.

"Bella?"

"Darling, you *are* there. So sorry to bother you this late."

"Are you all right?"

"Well, yes and no, darling."

"What's the matter? Is it Simon?"

"Simon?" Bella sounded astonished. "No, darling, this is a real emergency."

"Ye-es?"

"My assistant Lulu's gone down with the flu—or on some Guardsman, more probably—and won't be able to help me style a *terribly* important shoot for *Insider*. House in Roland Gardens, done by this *incredibly* hot interior designer called Basia Briggs . . . whom I think I mentioned the other day. Darling, I'm perfectly desperate . . ."

"Bella wants me to help her shoot someone called Basia Briggs," Rosie announced to Mark as she came back into the room.

"Basher who?" asked Mark, pulling her down again. "Sounds pretty bloody dangerous to me."

Seconds later, pinned against the floor, Rosie forgot the hairy orange carpet tiles and the danger of friction burn. "Thank God for 'Green-er Pastures.' " She giggled. "In every sense of the word."

Samantha finished the single tahini-smeared cracker that constituted lunch, looked at the slender sliver of watch on her wrist, and permitted herself a rare wrinkle of the brow. Where were those wretched magazine people who were coming to photograph the house? She'd been up at the crack of dawn getting the place ready—well, Consuela had, anyway.

She scrutinized her surroundings with a gimlet eye. Her impeccable sitting room was, she knew, the epitome of urban good taste; no less an authority than designer to the stars, Basia Briggs, had proclaimed it so. Although not until Samantha had paid her a sum Guy claimed equivalent to the gross national product of a small African country to redesign it.

Samantha's husband, Guy, had not been impressed with the celebrity design guru's unique vision. "Looks like bloody Lenin's tomb," he complained, waving a tanned, manicured hand at the vast vase, more than a meter square, which Basia had placed in the center of a coffee table the size of a double bed.

"Vase fascism," Samantha had hotly retorted, "is a central tenet of Basia's design philosophy. She wanted to challenge the fact that I filled the same vases in the same place with the same flowers every week."

"And what the hell's *that*?" Guy had raged at the next item to incur his displeasure, a beige object as big as a Labrador dominating the dining-room mantelpiece.

"The fossil, you mean?" In her heart of hearts, Samantha wasn't entirely convinced that the colossal, curved ammonite Basia had placed in the spot formerly occupied by the candlesticks and the Staffordshire dogs was one of her more successful innovations. Not the least because Samantha was now obliged to tiptoe about the sitting room as too hasty or clumsy a step might cause the heavy object to fall off. The thought of watching four million years of evolution (not to mention several thousand pounds of hard cash) smash into the grate was too great a risk to run.

"Lost a bit of one of your necklaces again?" Guy said next, producing what looked like a large piece of glass from under a cushion. Samantha snapped that it was a crystal, one of the many placed about the house by the shamanic-energy consultant Basia insisted she engage at a fee entirely separate from Basia's own. "Basia says it's all about balance," Samantha finished, in as dignified a manner as she could manage.

"Quite. Her bank balance," Guy said drily, hastily erecting a wall of newspaper between himself and Samantha as she continued her passionate defense of crystal therapy.

"Can't you feel the difference?" she demanded. "I've slept better than I've done for bloody years."

Guy lowered his paper again and stared directly at her undereye area, purple beneath its Touche Eclar concealer. "Darling, you're a terrible actress," he informed his fuming wife. "Considering you *are* an actress, that is."

Guy, not one of the City's most ruthless financiers for nothing and as accurate at pinpointing vulnerability in people as in companies, had been quick to spot that Samantha was less than thrilled with some aspects of Basia's unique vision. Determined not to admit this was the case, however, Samantha had employed every trick in her professional book to conceal the truth.

She had, for example, reacted with the utmost composure when Guy had homed straight in on the problem with the pared-down bathroom with its square Jade Jagger tub of thick Burgundian limestone. "Where the hell are the taps?" he had demanded.

Samantha had simply pointed to the single verdigris tube, curved on its end like an umbrella handle, that rose through the flagstones by the bath and explained that a powerful stream of water was released by pressing on the floor with one's foot. "It's a triumph of maximum minimalism," she added, frowning slightly. Or had Basia said minimal maximalism?

"It's like the bloody handbasins in train bogs" had been Guy's withering conclusion.

Similarly, on the day the Bolivian rush matting, dyed to the precise shade of beigish burnt sienna guaranteeing best feng shui, appeared, an aspect of glacial calm had disguised Samantha's thwarted desire for something more sort of floorboardy. Nor had she batted an eyelid when Basia, riding roughshod over her plans for big mirrors in the sitting room, had insisted on the only decoration being a wire-wood goat sculpture in front of the window and a screened print of two naked women daubed in mud over the fireplace. By the time Basia announced that the only furniture permitted in the bedroom was a futon and an illuminated clock projecting onto the white-painted wall above it, a mere twitching muscle in Samantha's well-rouged cheek hinted at the pain with which she had parted from thoughts of Provençal four-posters with billowing muslin curtains.

The only things Basia had allowed to billow anywhere in the house were the large canvas blinds hung in the lopsided manner the great designed proclaimed to be "fashionably askew" over the sitting room's huge bay windows. They were held in position with creosoted rope tiebacks especially sourced from the docks at Felixstowe. And, Samantha thought, they smelled like it. She had privately vowed to replace them with nice clean rope from the hardware store as soon as Basia had swept out of the house on a cloud of burning sage smoke for the last time.

Yet Samantha would not hear a word against Basia, particularly if that word was Guy's. "She's the interior designer to the *stars*," Samantha raged as her husband hooted with derision at the decapitated gerbera heads floating in identical trays on the dining-room table. "And she fitted me in first. Half of Knightsbridge is waiting for her."

"Sounds like the number ten bus," muttered Guy. He had failed to take to Basia after she had asked him whether, as a desk-bound suit, he had ever considered the benefits of a creative-drumming workshop.

Still, Samantha thought now, there were compensations in this life. She had been intensely gratified by the fantastically trendy interior-design magazine *Insider* wanting to photograph Basia's completed vision for a series about Urban Sancta.

But where were they? Samantha slammed her delicate white cup of Japanese green tea back into its saucer and forced the corners of her mouth, turned firmly down in annoyance, to turn back up again. She pressed a finger to her forehead to massage out the incipient wrinkle plunging like a dagger between her eyebrows.

Christ. The sage sticks. Oh my God. "Consuela!" screeched Samantha. "Get in here and do the sage sticks. Now." Basia's insistence that lighted sage sticks be waved around the house in order to combat the negative energies unknown visitors to the house might bring with them was central to her design philosophy.

"Con*sue*la!" bawled Samantha. "*CONSUELAAAA!* Oh, *fuck*."

The bell rang so suddenly and with such ferocity that Samantha's cup and saucer leaped out of her hands with shock and descended with disastrous results all over the outfit she had with great care and after much agonizing chosen for the shoot. She gazed in despair at the soggy green stains. It was thus, contemplating her tea-soaked breasts, that Bella and Rosie found Samantha when they walked into the sitting room.

CHAPTER 3

As she threaded cornflowers through the rope tiebacks on the curtain, it occurred to Rosie that helping Bella on a shoot wasn't the easy alternative to a day bent over her drawing board she had imagined. Placing her face close to the rope, as was necessary for the fiddly business of threading, Rosie found the powerful smell of creosote and fish overwhelming.

She jumped as Samantha stalked back into the room. Previously dressed to the nines, she was now clad to the tens in a restrictive black leather skirt and a tight pink cardigan that exposed a generous portion of her curiously shaped breasts. Breasts that, Rosie was interested to see, rose from the flat in separate domes with at least an inch of flesh between them, like a couple of pills in a packet. Although not aspiring to Samantha's air of rather contrived sexiness, Rosie nonetheless wished she had put on something smarter than paint-stained jeans and an old gray Gap T-shirt with obvious moth holes around the neck. Brushing her hair instead of bundling it back in a scrunchie might have been a good idea as well.

Rosie had seen so much makeup in only one place before and that had been in Selfridge's cosmetics department. Samantha had selected different shades of eye shadow for her brow and eyelid, plus a thick slick of eyeliner, bright purple lipstick, and eyebrows that, penciled in thickly nearest the nose, dwindled to thin lines at the temples like the legs of a bee. She tossed her long, bouffant, and suspiciously bright auburn hair back over her shoulders and demanded to know what Rosie thought of her sitting room.

"Um, great," said Rosie.

"Well, once I saw how *wonderful* these blinds looked in *dear* Hughie's flat in Manhattan, I was on the phone to Basia as soon as the Concorde hit the tarmac. Sorry, shouldn't put it like that after the crash, I suppose. Anyway, I got her to come straight round and put some up that looked just like Hughie's." Samantha paused as if waiting for something. "I'm talking about Hugh Grant's flat, obviously."

"You went to Hugh Grant's flat?" The floppy-haired thespian was one of the few celebrities who had penetrated the blanket of vagueness and indifference between Rosie and the famous. For Mark's sake, Rosie was determined to take an interest.

Samantha's small, heavily outlined eyes looked directly into Rosie's large gray-blue ones. She nodded, basking contentedly in reflected glory. There was no need whatsoever to admit that the closest she had been to the interior of Hugh Grant's apartment was a recent issue of *Hello!*

"How do you know Hughie—I mean Hugh?" Rosie asked.

"When did I meet Hughie?" Samantha laughed tinklingly. "It seems I've known him *forever* . . . but, no, it *must* have been that wonderful summer of the movie. Not—"

"*Notting Hill*?" interrupted Rosie excitedly. Mark would be thrilled at this. She peered at Samantha. The kooky redheaded sister? Too old for that, surely. The bossy press officer in the *Horse and Hound* scene?

"I was about to say 'not anything very recent,'" said Samantha icily. "I actually met Hughie on an earlier film."

Rosie racked her brains. Duckface in *Four Weddings*? But too old again, surely. Despite her obvious attempts to stem the tide of age, Samantha was clearly on the wrong side of forty.

"I'll give you a clue." Samantha raised a bee-leg eyebrow. "It was a period drama. Sort of Merchant–Ivory."

Rosie blushed, wilting under the wattage of that expectant purple smile. "I'm so sorry," she hedged. "I don't know . . . I'm hopeless on films."

"Punkawallah."

Rosie racked her brain frantically. Was that the film about Sid Vicious and Nancy Spungen? That would at least explain the makeup. "I'm sorry?"

"Punkawallah," Samantha repeated crisply. "You *must* have heard of it. Based on the novel by R. K. Stanborough, it's the dramatic true-life tale of a repressed maharajah and a viceroy with homosexual tendencies, set against the background of the crumbling Raj? No?"

Rosie shook her head apologetically, wondering as she did so how anything could be based on a novel and yet be a true-life tale.

Samantha looked thunderstruck. "But that's impossible," she declared. "It was an absolute landmark. The first of its kind. Ran for three hours."

Rosie, embarrassed, shoved a handful of cornflowers furiously into the canvas.

"It's always the bloody same," fumed Samantha. "The problem with that film is that it was the *first* period drama. Ahead of its time."

Rosie continued stuffing flowers in the curtains.

"As soon as *Punkawallah* came out," Samantha was in full furious flow now, "Merchant–Ivory stole the whole sodding idea. Suddenly, you couldn't find a beach *anywhere* without Maggie Smith in corsets having a picnic or Simon Callow drawing vaginas in the sand. Or someone in a crinoline dragging a bloody *piano* up it . . ." She fumbled for a cigarette, took a long, shuddering drag, and looked angrily at Rosie. "Worst of all," she announced, "my seminal performance in *Punkawallah* as the viceroy's daughter meant that, as far as every director was concerned, *I'd been there and done that.* For years after the film, I couldn't get bloody arrested. And all because I'd set the standard they now wanted others to reach."

Rosie tried to think of something comforting to say, "But why? I mean, Emma Thompson has been in loads of period films . . ."

"Precisely," snarled Samantha. "If it wasn't for *me,* people like Emma bloody Thompson would still be doing bloody fish-bloody-finger ads."

Another silence.

"Hughie, of course, didn't *get* typecast," Samantha ranted, sucking on her cigarette. "Being a *man.* The film industry's so bloody *sexist.*"

Rosie tried to change the subject. "Very sad he split up with Liz Hurley," she ventured, hoping she'd got it right and they hadn't gotten back together. "Was he with her when you knew him?"

"*Liz Hurley?*" Samantha's thin nostrils flared like a flamenco dancer's skirt. "At the time I was starring in *Punkawallah,* Liz Hurley was nothing but a fat little punk from Peterborough."

Rosie stared at her, puzzled. "Basingstoke, wasn't it?" she asked as a flash of inspiration struck her. Mark, she remembered, had once had to go there to do Liz Hurley's mother's fridge for "Chillin'."

Another silence. If only, Rosie thought desperately, I could place this woman in *one* film.

"I'm sorry, but what did you say your name was again?" she asked.

"Samantha Villiers," declaimed Samantha resonantly.

"Sorry, I meant the name you act under."

"That," Samantha said furiously, with as much dignity as she could muster, "*is* the name I act under."

"In the Villiers kitchen"—Bella, pacing around, was murmuring into the handheld Dictaphone that served the purpose of a notebook, "the key is simple angularity. Solidified space creating a serene environment . . . oh, *no no no,* Freya," she suddenly chided the photographer's assistant who was arranging an orange on a plate. "Only *tidy* peel. *Please.*"

As Samantha came storming in from the sitting room, Bella turned to her brightly. "It's crying out in here for rustic coffee bowls," she declared. "And some comb honey would be *lovely,* sort of *crushed* into a torn-off hunk of freshly baked bread with the steam rising out of it . . ."

But Samantha was not listening. "What are you *doing*?" she shrieked at the hapless Freya.

Terrified, Freya dropped the gerbera head she was pulling apart. Bella had asked for flower petals to scatter among the cups and saucers.

"Where did you get those from?" demanded Samantha.

"Um, the room next door," gulped Freya. "They were lying on the floor . . ."

"Floor? *Floor?*"

"Well, sort of a big box on the floor. With sort of plastic trays on it. Had some cushions round it."

"The *dining-room table,* you mean," hissed Samantha. "That's the whole bloody design concept you've ruined."

"Er, I'd just like to take a few biographical details now, while Jorgen's setting up the next shot," Bella interrupted with a dazzling smile. "Could I just ask you, Miss Villiers, where you met your husband? Did I hear something about the foyer of his bank when you were working as a receptionist?" She held out the Dictaphone in Samantha's direction.

Samantha looked thunderous. "Certainly not. We met on a film set."

"How tremendously exciting. What was the film, Miss Villiers?"

Samantha paused. This was a tricky one. It had been undisputedly a masterstroke, while sitting behind the reception desk of his bank, to tell the recently divorced vice president that she was an actress and had taken the job to research a role about a receptionist who rises to become the bank's first female president. Guy had been so captivated by this explanation—as well as Samantha herself—that the film's continuing failure to materialize had never seemed to occur to him.

"I can't recall it immediately," Samantha said eventually with a tinkling laugh. "One learns as an actress to—as Hamlet put it—shrug off the mortal coil of each part as it is finished in order to don the new. At the moment, I'm so utterly consumed by my latest challenge, the part of Christabel, that I have no emotional space for anything else. . . ."

"How terribly interesting, Miss Villiers," Bella gushed. "And who exactly is Christabel?"

"A femme fatale." Samantha tossed her hair. "Helen of Troy, Anna Karenina, Cleopatra. An irresistible siren who unleashes the forces of uncontrollable lust everywhere she goes. With far-reaching consequences."

As Bella opened her mouth, Samantha held up a commanding hand. "I'm not at liberty to reveal any more about it, I'm afraid. The part is in development."

Bella picked up her Dictaphone again.

"In the Villierses' hall," she murmured, "one table is almost hidden by a bowl of polished Chinese stones, a vulture's feather, two porcupine quills, and bunches of tiny dried lotus-flower seeds tied with a ribbon of steel beads. Intricate? Yes. Affected? No. Original and interesting? Absolutely . . ."

"My God, *those people.*" Rosie shook her head and stared disbelievingly out the window as, shoot finished, they sped away from Roland Gardens in Bella's vast black four-wheel drive.

"Par for the course, sweetie." Across the black leather–swathed gear lever, Bella's profile was tranquil. "Judging from the Polaroids, the shoot will be a great success. I'm sure the editor's going to want to use it as soon as possible, given that the Radical Minimalist look's probably not going to last long."

Rosie looked at her watch. The shoot had taken eight hours. Her nerves felt as frayed as the deliberately unfinished edges of the hessian cushions she had spent the afternoon arranging in piles meant to look as if carelessly tossed by someone with an unerring sense of style. Unfortunately, with every toss, the cushion pile had looked more erring, less stylish, and increasingly frayed at the edges. Still, at least she would get paid for helping, and, infinitely better, she would soon be in the country and hundreds of miles from Samantha Villiers and anyone remotely like her.

There had been neither time nor opportunity to discuss the great news with Bella until now. "Mark's agreed to move to the country," she told Bella triumphantly.

Bella swerved to avoid a meandering drunk on the Cromwell Road. "Really? He didn't seem all that keen on it at dinner, I must say."

"Things change," said Rosie enigmatically. She didn't have the energy to go into detail about the column. Nor, for the moment, did she have the details. "We're about to start the hunt for the perfect cottage," she added.

"Oh, well," said Bella reassuringly. "Never mind. Just think of all that lovely tweed and cashmere you can wear."

"Or *fur.*" Rosie cast a meaningful glance at Bella's coat. "I just don't know how you can wear it." Her friend's relaxed attitude to the fur trade had long been a cause of anguish to Rosie.

"What, this?" Bella looked down at her coat. "When literally thousands of acrylics have died for it?" She grinned teasingly at Rosie. "Of course it's not real, silly. It's my *work* coat. I keep my sables for the best."

The perfect cottage was taking some finding.

"Poor Mr. Dibble." Rosie sighed as, some days later, the postman's hunched, resentful figure trudged back past the kitchen window after depositing yet another avalanche of envelopes through the front door of the flat. Since Mark had registered with what seemed like every estate agent in the country, they got more mail than anyone else in the street.

Following the sound of frenzied ripping in the sitting room, Rosie, piece of toast in her hand, wandered in to find Mark sprawled amid a sea of paper.

"Former asbestos mill with planning permission in Blackburn." Mark waved a clipped-together piece of paper at her. "*Great* potential."

"Mill?" Rosie's toast fell facedown onto the carpet tiles. She picked it up, trying not to think how long it had been since she last vacuumed. Months, certainly.

She glanced at the photograph of the vast and ruined building stapled to the agent's details. Even with a blazing sun and a suspiciously Mediterranean-blue sky, the place was obviously barely standing. Nothing could be further removed from the cottage with roses round the door she had imagined. "What would anyone do with a mill?"

"*It up,* obviously. You could get about twenty executive flats in there. Not to mention a swimming pool, gym, parking for forty cars and quite possibly a helipad as well." Rosie looked at him in horror. "Not that we're going to, obviously," Mark added, "it's hardly the sort of thing *we'd* want."

"No," said Rosie emphatically. "We want a little cottage. With roses round the door." And a lavender-bordered path, she added silently. And a springy lawn spattered with daisies . . .

"Cottages are quite expensive," Mark cut in. "We might have to settle for something we can do up." Rosie nodded. No problem. Painting was her job, wasn't it? Mark shook the pile of particulars between both hands. "Quite a few things here, actually. A former butcher's shop near Derby . . ."

"Ugh!" Rosie grimaced.

"We're not looking for a manor house in the Cotswolds, you know."

"I know. It's just—a butcher's shop?"

Mark sighed extravagantly. "Buying something with fifty acres might be a bit beyond our budget."

"It's not where it is," Rosie said, sighing, "but what it is. I'm *vegetarian*, remember?"

CHaPTER
4

Samantha, perched perilously on one of the six blasted-granite disks that served as kitchen stools, looked up from her magazine and sighed. Her dissatisfied gaze lingered on the glass bricks of the walls, dazzlingly illuminated by sunken-floor uplighters. Held gingerly between her fingers was one of the thin porcelain cups Basia had decreed as the only type of china permitted in the house. As usual, it contained Japanese green tea, the only permitted beverage besides Evian.

She resumed her reading of the magazine.

It is here, in the rustic dream that is her thick-walled, fifteenth-century manor house, that society potter Carinthia D'Arblay Sidebottom goes about her exquisite and distinctive craft. In the hall, a lavender-scented silence pervades; brilliant sunshine floods the stone flags and glances off the glittering diamond-pane windows. Presently, Carinthia brings in a hand-painted tray on which everything, from the colorful mugs of steaming coffee to the thick rounds of shortbread biscuit, is homemade. . . .

Suddenly, Samantha longed with all her soul for a homemade shortbread biscuit, but these did not figure on Basia's list of Ayurvedically balanced foods for Pita personalities. This list, the legendary designer had insisted, should never be deviated from if Samantha's energies, both spiritual and physical, were to harmonize perfectly with those of the house. Judging from the permanent bad temper she had been in since Basia left, her energies still had some way to go.

Samantha groaned. As if the turbulent state of her chakras was not enough, there remained a mere *four weeks* before filming started to get inside the head of Christabel. She simply had to research Christabel's location, motivation, personal conversation, the *lot*. And today was location.

"CHRISTABEL: LOCATION," Samantha had written on the first sheet of her fat new pad. Underneath it she had written "THE COUNTRYSIDE." Christabel, Samantha knew from the production notes, lived in the countryside. But what she didn't know, had no idea about, in fact, was what the countryside was actually like. She was far from sure she had ever been there. After a few minutes more of pondering on this, Samantha had yelled for Consuela and sent her out for the latest editions of *Country Life, Country Living, Which Gazebo?, Charming Castles, Cottage Beautiful, Country Homes and Interiors,* and *Period Living.* It was in the glossy pages of *Cottage Beautiful* that she had stumbled across the wonderful world of Carinthia D'Arblay Sidebottom.

Samantha read on: *As one approaches the imposing yet romantic building, a panoply of textures asserts itself: lichened tiles, herbaceous borders, Carinthia's sparkling-white washing fluttering in the lavender-scented breeze, old stone the rich gold of digestive biscuits . . . .*

Samantha's fingers tapped on the zinc-topped table. Why did she feel so discontented all of a sudden? It wasn't as if she was lacking a panoply of textures herself, even if, sadly, digestive biscuits did not feature among them. Basia had been extremely keen on textures, as the Neolithic ax head, Maserati connecting rod, and carefully arranged pieces of broken glass currently festooning the windowsills attested. Admittedly, the textures, like the colors, weren't quite the ones Samantha had originally had in mind. Had it really been a good idea to allow Basia to paint all the outside brickworks a shade midway between khaki and brown? Guy had already forcibly expressed his doubts that explanations about fantastic chi would wash with the royal Borough of Kensington and Chelsea's planning department.

Forcing these unpleasant reflections aside, Samantha returned to

Carinthia's sparkling-white washing. *Inside, deep-silled windows painted simply in white provide a natural setting for garden flowers in hand-made jugs. Elsewhere, Carinthia's use of bold color, antique printed textiles, and reclaimed timber gives the tiny cottage a Tudor Mediterranean feel. . . .* Tudor Mediterranean, well, *yes,* thought Samantha, *that* sounded much more the sort of thing she'd originally been after with Roland Gardens. *Upstairs, gingham throws, rose-stencilled loo seats, and toile de Jouy abound . . .* The words stabbed Samantha to the heart. The thought of Basia's spartan futon muscling to the front of her mind, she stared jealously at pictures of white-painted Victorian iron bedsteads piled high with vintage eiderdowns and crisp white sheets (no doubt fresh from the line) whose lavender scent seemed to billow from the very page.

Outside, in Carinthia's vegetable patch, leeks, potatoes, and onions are encouraged to go to seed for aesthetic reasons, while in a corner of the "wild garden," Carinthia's bower stands wreathed in tantalizing whiffs from the honeysuckle winding elegantly round the weathered pillars of an eighteenth-century temple of Diana . . . .

Emitting a snarl, Samantha jerked her head up. Out of the single-pane kitchen window, its frame painted not crisp white but battleship gray, Basia's zen garden was all too visible. An untantalizing pile of sand, wet pebbles, and a verdigris turtle, it was raked daily, amid much muttering, by Consuela, whom Samantha had to forcibly discourage from polishing the turtle. This, on Basia's explicit instructions, had to be left to weather naturally. Even the *Insider* people had stopped short of photographing the zen garden, although they had been very excited and complimentary about the rest of the place. It had apparently been given six pages in the forthcoming issue of the magazine. That, at least, was *something.* Yet the faint glow of comfort in Samantha's breast faded as a cursory examination of the Carinthia article revealed it to be ten pages long.

Carinthia leads me to the kitchen, where she motions me to a roomy shepherd's chair at the deep-grooved farmhouse table where generations of families have broken bread. She crosses the delightfully uneven Elizabethan baked floor tiles [on which generations of families have broken their legs? Samantha imagined viciously] *and stirs something savory and satisfying in a vast iron pot on the shining stove. Lunch is imminent . . . .*

Samantha ground her teeth, remembering without enthusiasm her own lunch of a single slice of rye bread topped with olive oil and thyme. She closed her eyes as, utterly without warning, a mighty wave of shuddering envy of society potter Carinthia D'Arblay Sidebottom crashed over her. Samantha was aware of a violent longing for an exquisite little cottage—as long as it wasn't *too* little—and a glamorous garden with a delicious touch of wildness and without a verdigris turtle in sight. Suddenly, Samantha felt she hadn't wanted to be *anybody*, not Nicole Kidman, not even Catherine Zeta-Jones, quite so desperately as she now wanted to be Carinthia D'Arblay Sidebottom.

She looked round Basia's minimalist kitchen with loathing. Had generations of families broken bread here? Of course not. For a start, no bread, not even of the pita variety, was on the list of Ayurvedic foods for Pita personalities. Families, in any case, were not encouraged—particularly Guy's.

His former wife, Marina, and daughter, Iseult, were emphatically personae non gratae in Roland Gardens. The entire point of Samantha's designer overhaul had originally been to expunge any reminder of her predecessor. Samantha had watched the council cart off Marina's squashy sofas and sheepskin rugs with a sense of immense satisfaction that had lasted until Basia had replaced them with vintage iron garden furniture painted a space-age silver and a coffee table made from a life-size elephant head in chicken wire.

Samantha's attempts to expunge Guy's family had met with mixed success in other ways as well. His maddening refusal to break off all diplomatic contact with Marina had been compounded by his insistence that Iseult be allowed to keep her old bedroom in Roland Gardens. Yet it was here that, in Samantha's eyes, Basia had scored her only real designer triumph—the complete removal of all Iseult's hideous posters from the walls, and in particular the one from the Bank of Ganja, signed by the Chief Hashier. The price sticker that remained on one of its peeling bottom corners never failed to remind Samantha that in certain contexts, £3.99 was actually an awful lot of money.

She contemplated Carinthia's bedstead again, noting jealously that it looked even bigger, bouncier, and more glamorous than that traditionally belonging to the pea-troubled Princess in the fairy tale.

Christabel . . . Carinthia. The names were similar. Did her new role, then, mean a whole new place to live? Samantha was not a religious woman, but she believed in destiny. Particularly if that destiny moved Guy out of Marina and Iseult's clutches and into the middle of nowhere.

Meeting Guy in the bank was a perfect example. That it was fate, and not merely being "between films," that had put Samantha behind the switchboard had been obvious the minute her future husband hoved into view across the marble wastes of the mezzanine. Fate had then prompted the subsequent realization on Samantha's part that marrying someone as rich as Guy would remove once and for all the humiliating necessity for her to traipse around to auditions all day long. Fate's final tour de force had been to slip into her head the story about researching the part for the film.

The wonderful thing about fate, Samantha considered, was that not only did it conveniently explain away one's less laudable actions, it also meant that one was rarely wrong. Viewed in this context, the hiring of Basia did not, as Guy insisted, amount to giving her license to vandalize while being paid hundreds of thousands of pounds for the privilege, but was, in fact, a logical progression along destiny's path. Fate had *of course* inflicted Basia on the house in order for her to create an environment so impossible to live in that Samantha would be forced to move. *To the country.*

Samantha gazed dreamily at the kitchen's shiny aluminum ceiling, reflecting both in it and on the fact that the wonderful thing about acting was its unexpectedness. One's life could change in an instant. From millennium minimalism to medieval manor house in the blink of an eye . . .

It is here, she thought excitedly, *in the rustic dream that is her thick-walled, fifteenth-century manor house, where brilliant sunshine floods the stone flags of the hall, that celebrated actress Samantha Villiers takes a well-deserved break from the set of her latest blockbuster film. A lavender-scented silence pervades the ancient dwelling. . . .*

She'd have to talk Guy round, of course. Samantha's lion heart sank slightly at this. Even one such as she, who, alongside generosity, placed optimism as her most marked characteristic, knew that convincing Guy to uproot himself from his clubs, his gym, and most of all the City office where he spent practically all his time would not be easy. She had no idea what he thought about the countryside; perhaps, like herself, he'd never even been there. Which meant there might at least be the possibility of an overnight conversion like her own. But Basia's conversion would be his first concern. The first problem he would raise, Samantha knew, was having one very large and expensive house on their hands already. Roland Gardens was fast taking on the aspect of a very ugly and very uncomfortable albatross. Persuading Guy to leave London would take every trick in what was becoming a very well-thumbed book. She looked at her slim sliver of a watch. She had two hours to think of something before he came home.

As far as convincing Guy to do things was concerned, Samantha had learned that crotchless lace was more persuasive than any amount of cold logic. Her argument for leaving Basia's urban sanctum for something significantly more Carinthia D'Arblay Sidebottom therefore rested principally on a number of points, including a plunging black lace bra with feather trim and nipple holes, a pair of split-crotch knickers, stockings, suspenders, stilettos, and a satin wrap trimmed with marabou feathers. Given this abundance of plumage, Samantha felt like a raunchy half-plucked chicken as she arranged herself on the daybed in the upstairs sitting room, stared at the wire-wool goat, and thought of lavender-scented silence and waited for Guy's return. And waited.

"I'm home, darling." There was a thud as his Louis Vuitton gym bag hit the kitchen floor. The lavender-scented silence dispersed as a waft of aftershave the olfactory equivalent of a twenty-one-gun salute drifted up the stairs. "Everything all right?" he called.

Damn him, why didn't he come up? She heard him rummage in the cupboard for a glass, then rattle it under the ice dispenser of Basia's wardrobe-size refrigerator. He had already dubbed the blasted-steel edifice A Fridge Too Far.

"Wonderful," trilled Samantha, immediately switching the charm on to full. "How was the gym?" Considering Guy was down a staircase and round a corner, striking a balance between irresistible and audible was not easy.

"Resting heart rate of sixty-five," Guy called back. "Fittest fifty-something on the block, I am. Been busy, darling?"

A scuffling sound as he picked up one of the country homes magazines from the kitchen table. Samantha rolled her eyes impatiently. "Come upstairs, darling," she called.

But Guy seemed absorbed in whatever he was reading. An incredulous snort reached her from the basement kitchen. "To shift hard-water deposits from the bases of bathroom taps, scrub with an old toothbrush dipped in vinegar . . ." Guy yelled up the stairs in astonishment. "What's all this about?"

"Christabel," shouted Samantha, as sexily as she could. They were at least getting on to the subject.

"*Christabel?*" echoed Guy disbelievingly. "Who the hell's that? New cleaner or something? Must say it would be nice to have something slightly foxier to look at than Consuela."

Samantha's lips tightened. Not now, not ever was the time to point out that Consuela's lack of foxiness was the whole point of her.

At last Guy jogged up the steps and appeared in the sitting room. "Bloody hell," he said as his gaze descended from the curls tumbling seductively round her face, past her exposed nipples to her fishnetted thighs. As Samantha, running her tongue round her lips, lifted her legs and slowly placed a stiletto-heeled foot on either side of the daybed, he registered the knickers as well.

"Shall we go into the bedroom?" she purred.

"No," gasped Guy, tearing himself out of his clothes. "Stay right where you are."

Like hell, thought Samantha, sitting up so quickly on the daybed that it felt as if she had left half her back behind.

Five minutes later she was slipping her bra straps off her shoulders and admiring herself in the unframed mirror that stood propped against the wall at the bottom of the futon. Beneath the sheer fabric, her breasts rose full, ripe, and brown—the breasts, Samantha thought smugly, of someone ten years younger. Which they could well be—who knew what or who the plastic surgeon had stuck in there.

In her best Mrs. Robinson fashion, she peeled off the fishnet stockings and, pushing a hand through her rumpled auburn hair, smoldered at her husband in the mirror. She had sneaked this into the house in blatant contravention of Basia's rules; its life-or-death necessity was the one thing on which she had stood firm.

Guy, reflected behind her on the futon, was standing pretty firm himself. His stiffly erect penis protruded beneath the swollen roundness of his stomach.

Samantha turned and gave him a burning look from beneath her eyelashes. "I'm a lioness," she informed him in a sibilant hiss. "Hunting for my prey." Her bracelets and watch rattled loudly together as, snarling, she pretended to slash at the air with a paw. Guy grinned appreciatively and grunted in reply. Lion Hunter, Samantha knew, was his favorite game. If this didn't persuade him, nothing would.

But even *here* Basia had managed to bugger things up. The slow, threatening big-cat lope toward Guy, in which the sight of her thigh muscles flexing was central to building up his excitement, was perfectly possible on the thick-piled carpet of old. Even if Marina had put it there. Post-Basia, emulating the Queen of the Jungle was less about growling, more trying not to squeal as the bare beech boards, chosen for their knotted qualities, pressed agonizingly into Samantha's bony knees. Guy, however, noticed nothing of this; his attention was fixed unwaveringly on her breasts as, swaying and spilling generously out of the feathered bra, they approached him over the futon.

Breathing in short, excited bursts, Guy squealed in excitement as his wife cuffed him with a heavily beringed hand. Springing forward, he clamped both hands on Samantha's breasts; she, in turn, locked both legs round his waist so he fell back onto the mattress. A sharp crack beneath announced that Basia's futon base had possibly been the first fatality of the jungle attack. Samantha slid her hips along Guy's thighs until she was sitting on his stomach and bent over to push her nipples in his face. His eyes bulged with mingled terror and excitement.

"Before I kill you, there's something I have to ask you," she growled.

Guy groaned in disappointment. "But I've just got myself all psyched up for a hideous and painful death."

"I have to talk to you about Christabel." Having discussed the significance of the part, it would be easy to move on to moving to the country.

Guy, however, had other significant parts in mind. "Oh, *Christ*. Not her again. Do we have to?" As he wriggled in frustration beneath her, she clenched her thigh muscles tighter. "OK," Guy groaned, half anguished, half ecstatic. "Talk to me about her. Who is she?"

"A temptress. A schemer. A marriage wrecker."

"Bloody hell." Guy looked impressed. "Well, she'll certainly make a change from all those healthcare program breast-checking videos."

Samantha looked stony. For reasons utterly unconnected with the ailing National Health Service, being reminded of her lapse into private health care was not something she appreciated.

"When did you audition for this one?"

"Last week."

"You auditioned for a marriage-wrecking temptress last week?" In Guy's bright blue eyes, the faint light of recognition shone. "But you only had one audition last week."

Samantha nodded.

"The one for the TV drama?"

"That's it."

"But you always said TV drama was the lowest form of thespian life apart from tampon ads."

"Well, even the most experienced actress needs to extend her range from time to time," purred Samantha. "Besides, you never know who might be watching."

"Like Steven Spielberg, for example?" Guy snorted.

"Very possibly." What exactly was he finding so funny? Her clenched thighs, she was uncomfortably aware, were beginning to develop a cramp.

"And you say the part is a femme fatale and a schemer? Helen of Troy and all that?"

Samantha jerked her chin up and down, noticing that, for some reason, the corners of Guy's mouth were quivering.

"So you're not talking about that part as a pub landlady in *Peak Practice*?"

"It's not *Peak Practice*. It's *Country Clinic*."

"The same, isn't it? Doctors shagging each other in hayfields?"

Samantha blasted her husband with a glare somewhere off the bottom of the Kelvin scale. "Why do you have to be so bloody *reductive*? It's a jewel of a role. The possibilities are *endless*. And every part is open to interpretation." Samantha stopped and sighed theatrically. "That's one great thing I learned from Hughie . . ."

"From what I recall about Hughie," Guy sniggered, seeing the undefended goal posts before him, "his parts were open to more than bloody interpretation."

Samantha's nostrils flared. Yet she was determined not to lose her temper.

"So where does the lust come in?" Guy persisted.

"My character, Christabel, *the barmaid,*" Samantha sniffed with dignity, "has an adulterous fling with one of the doctors. He's an alcoholic."

"But why are the consequences far-reaching?"

"Because *Country Clinic* is on a major network, isn't it?" Samantha raged. "It has *millions* of viewers. It's my big break, for Christ's sake." She raised one thigh and clambered stiffly off him. The countryside conversation would clearly have to be postponed, as, by the looks of it, would the jungle massacre. Judging from the flaccid organ flopped over Guy's right thigh, the victim had fled in any case.

CHaPTER 5

"So." Nigel from Kane, Birch & Spankie, Estate Agents, beamed encouragingly. "What do you think?"

Rosie smiled uncertainly. "Um . . ." Phrases existed, she knew, that would precisely encapsulate the hesitation she felt at the large damp stains spreading over the greasy beige walls, not to mention the faintly rancid smell. On the other hand, Mark's point that, as a former fish and chip shop, it suited her nonmeat-eating sensibilities better than the erstwhile butcher's could not be disagreed with.

"Plenty of potential, as I'm sure you'd agree." The agent rattled a vast quantity of loose change in his pocket.

"But it's only got an outside loo," Rosie muttered.

"Yes, but have you *seen* it?" enthused Nigel in a nasal voice uncertainly poised between gruff and squeaky. He wore a badly fitting double-breasted suit, had extravagantly oiled hair combed forward in short spikes, and seemed all of sixteen. "It's an original Crapper. Beautifully enameled and would probably fetch a fortune on *The Antiques Roadshow.* A work of art." He rattled his coins again.

Rosie's heart sank. Within seconds of seeing the board displaying available properties at the estate agents', it had been obvious that, as impossible dreams went, her vision of a period cottage with beams, large fireplaces, a garden, and an abundance of character ranked somewhere above asking for the moon. In their price range, at least. Yet there must be somewhere better than the property they were currently inspecting. Not only was it on a main road, but enormous lorries that shook the place to its foundations seemed to be passing every five minutes. "It doesn't seem to be a particularly safe place to live," she ventured.

"The house is perfectly safe, madam!" Nigel shouted as, right on cue, a huge juggernaut thundered past inches from the windows. Mark, who had been staring absently out of them, leaped back in alarm. "There is," the agent continued, "an entire pavement between the property and the road."

"Which is almost entirely taken up with a vast crash bar," returned Rosie, as gently as she could. There was something rather heroic about the optimism with which Nigel approached his profession.

"We can't be too picky," Mark warned her as they drove off in their spluttering old Peugeot. "Beggars can't be choosers, you know."

"I do know. But it's got to be the right cottage. Or, at least, not something that's so obviously *wrong*."

"Well, you heard what Nigel said."

Rosie nodded. That the overenthusiastic agent was not accompanying them on the next visit, having been suddenly called back to the office, was a relief. His parting shot had, however, been a little alarming.

"Ooh, it's all hands on deck back at KBS," Nigel had announced, shoving a vast and chunky mobile back into his pocket. "Someone's just rung up wanting instant details on all our premier properties. This area's getting very popular, you know. Best to buy while you can." In a gesture pregnant with meaning, he had then handed Mark the large envelope containing the keys and details for the remaining properties on the day's agenda.

"Actually, the next one looks great," Mark said, waving under Rosie's nose the photograph of a cheerful-looking, low-slung building framed by mature trees. "Limestone Cottage. Amazingly low-priced as well."

Rosie crossed her fingers as Mark swung suddenly round a sharp bend of the single-track road. The narrow lanes seemed under constant threat from the burly hedgerows that, running along either side of them, were apparently intent on muscling into the middle.

It was now the end of January, and the sky was a high, pale blue, overlaid with clouds shirred like thinly sliced smoked salmon. A brilliant, low winter sun irradiated fields ridged like green corduroy trousers and stretching to distant heights of blond moor. As Rosie wound down her window to get a view uninterrupted by bird poo, a flood of air as clear, sharp, and cold as a bucketful of water dashed into her face. She smiled, her eyes streaming with the chill and a sudden leaping joy.

Entering the village where Limestone Cottage was located, they lurched up a steep and rocky drive that rose at an awkward angle straight from the road. The cheerful little cottage was set, just as the picture showed, in a frame of mature beech trees.

"Oh, God. Is *this* Limestone Cottage?" Rosie's heart was plummeting faster than those blocks of frozen effluent from plane lavatories that so often seemed to crash through Croydon conservatories and end up in Mark's paper.

What the photograph had failed to even hint at was the expanse of raw, white hillside, ugly boxlike buildings, and piles of sacks on pallets stretching around the cottage on all sides. "It's in the middle of a quarry," snapped Mark.

Rosie felt terribly sorry for the pretty little building, its lawn choked with dust, its mellow stone powdered with limestone aggregate, and its roof slumped in defeat. And yet, even so, it seemed the only graceful spot amid so much ugliness.

"Bloody estate agents," Mark snarled, twisting the key with its brown label agitatedly between his fingers. "Now I see why it's so bloody cheap."

Overwhelmingly in the cottage's favor, on the other hand, was the fact that they could afford it; a rare thing, given what Nigel kept tactfully referring to as their "restrictive financial situation." A situation that certainly restricted all possibilities of sublime properties such as the one currently commandeering virtually the whole of the agency's front window. Rosie, arriving with Mark to meet Nigel that morning, had spotted it straightaway. A beautiful Jacobean manor house set in an old-fashioned garden, the only nonexquisite thing about it had been its name. The Bottoms.

"A perfect country house in miniature," the description had run. *An exceptional Grade I listed country house of great historical interest set in superbly maintained gardens and grounds with far-reaching views. An example of secular Jacobean building at its finest, The Bottoms boasts a number of historical features including a priest hole, molded plasterwork ceilings, heraldic fireplaces, and stone-flagged floors throughout. Five large bedrooms, three south-facing reception rooms, attics, vaulted cellars with capacity for conversion into a gymnasium . . .*

"Horrid idea. I'd never do that," Rosie had said, looking at the sunlit stone front with its carved lions and standing sentinel, age-blackened chimneys, and finialed gables and trying to imagine someone underneath it all sweating away on a running machine.

"I wouldn't worry," Mark had drawled. "We can barely afford the running machine, let alone the house."

As the day went on, the yawning chasm between the estate agents' descriptions and the bricks-and-mortar reality became increasingly evident. Agents' details, they realized, contained a whole code of euphemisms to crack—"lots of potential" almost invariably seemed to translate as "lots of work," while "garden in transitional state" usually turned out to refer to an area entirely paved over in concrete through whose unsightly cracks grass and weeds were steadily gaining ground. As for "mature" gardens, most of the ones Mark and Rosie saw were not only old but positively dribbling with infirmity. One or two definitely had Alzheimer's. So much for the Property Misdescriptions Act. Similarly, details such as "door, Suffolk latch, painted white" were usually a ruse to distract attention from the shortcomings in the bigger picture, such as it not being wired for electricity.

Although, much to Rosie's relief, there were no abattoirs on Mark's list (she had, however, overheard him asking Nigel about them), they did view a converted tripe shop next to a pub that, plastered with signs for Saturday-night karaoke, forthcoming real ale festivals, and caravan rallies, not to mention the dread sign COACH PARTIES WELCOME, had even Mark clearing his throat and muttering about it not being quite suitable. Then came the creepy corner house with the pearlized diagonal fifties' plastic door handles, boxlike rooms, and air of something inexpressibly hideous having happened in the attic. Next up was the cottage whose apparently limitless garden, clearly and gratifyingly visible on the particulars, turned out to be that of the old people's home next door. Last—and probably least—there had been the only tenanted dwelling on their list, a squat building coated with gray concrete rendering and a drive festooned with broken lavatory bowls and piles of crumbling breeze-block. It was the property of a pinch-faced man of few words, and its low price, Rosie and Mark subsequently discovered, reflected a desire to get out quick. "'E's goin'," a shuffling figure passing the end of the drive informed them as they emerged, "because 'e shot 'is neighbor's dog on Christmas Day."

"How *awful*," said Rosie, whose desire to make a speedy exit from the property had been equally strong. "But at least he has the decency to move out fast."

The shuffling figure looked at her with eyes as flat as buttons. "Not that fast. 'E shot it five years ago. But folk don't forget that sort of thing round 'ere."

"I'll tell you what we need," Mark said as they scrambled back into the Peugeot and sped off as if demons were at their heels.

"A seventeenth-century cottage with beams, open fireplaces, a cared-for garden, and a sound roof at about half the price the agents are usually asking?"

"No. Alcohol."

Rosie nodded, picturing a quaint inn with ivy and badges of culinary excellence without and vast beams heavy with brassware within. "Sounds great."

"And here's a pub," Mark announced, slowing down as they entered a village. A long, low building of indeterminate age opposite the village church, the pub was almost romantic. Apart, that was, from its sign, which, creaking alarmingly in the wind, depicted a sixteenth-century woman resplendent in ruff and farthingale but conspicuously lacking a head. Below her was painted the pub's name: The Silent Lady.

"Ha ha ha," said Mark. "Local humor, I suppose."

"Very droll," said Rosie sarcastically.

Inside, it was completely empty apart from a small dog with a very protuberant bottom who sat in front of a roaring fire. As a dolorous landlord eventually shuffled into view, Mark strode jovially up to the bar. "Two pints of your best beer, please."

Rosie shuddered. As a rule, she wasn't keen on beer. Yet she sensed that to ask for city affectations such as a gin and tonic or a spritzer could be asking for trouble.

"'Airy 'Elmet, Belter, or Knickersplitter."

"Um, er, one Hairy Helmet. Oh, and one Knickersplitter. I'll live a little." Mark grinned at the landlord, whose hangdog expression remained resolutely hung. "Erm, could I see the, erm, bar menu?"

"There isn't one," muttered the landlord. "These is t'menu." From her seat by the infernally hot fire, Rosie saw him wave a dismissive hand at two thick plastic covers on the counter.

"Oh, I see. The pork pies look wonderful. Are they homemade?"

Pork pies. At this, even Rosie's vegetarian stomach rumbled. But she couldn't. She couldn't.

"We keep us own pigs round t'back."

"Erm, a *large* pie, yes. And could you possibly cut it in half?"

"Here's t'knife and t'plate. Cut it in 'alf yoursel'."

"Oh. *Right.* Thanks. And this is the mustard, is it—yes, I see, there *is* a scrape or two left. Thanks very much indeed." Mark, grinning, came back to the fireside and sawed the pie in half to reveal close-packed meat of a near-neon pinkness.

"Go on, Rosie," he urged her. "There's nothing else to eat. No one will know."

Rosie shook her head resolutely, keeping her eyes trained on the dog's bottom. As an appetite suppressant, it was very effective.

"They do rooms here," Mark said, returning from the bar with two more pints of beer foaming over his hands and down his arms. Rosie tried to work out whether that was good news. She glanced at the window and decided that, on balance, it was. It was now dark and they needed somewhere to stay, even if this pub's sign bore a picture of a beheaded woman and creaked ominously in the wind. Rosie briefly wondered what the Silent Lady's connection with the pub named in her honor was, then decided she didn't want to know.

Her faint hopes of encountering heartwarming local characters were dashed when the only other person to beard the portals during the en-

tire course of the evening was a wizened walker from Lancashire eager
to share ripping yarns from the fells. As Mark sank gradually into a fire-
and-Knickersplitter-soothed stupor, Rosie listened with resigned politeness to near misses on Bastard Gap and being caught short on Dead
Cow Ridge.

It took some time for the landlord to show them their room, not
least because the door handle was of a variety requiring not just the one
knack but five or six to open it. The gloomy room it eventually dis-
closed had clearly not been occupied for some time.

"And where's the nearest, um, loo?" Rosie asked shyly.

"Darnstairs and artside."

"Think of it as romantic," advised Mark as the landlord shuffled
off.

Rosie looked out of the black square of window to where a full
moon hung in the sky like a huge white balloon. As Mark came up behind her and slid his arms about her, she closed her eyes. It *was* romantic, she supposed, in a misogynistic-pub-sign, outside-loo sort of
way.

"Don't worry," he murmured into her neck. Shivers ran down her
spine at his touch. "We will find our dream cottage somewhere."

"Yes," Rosie said, taking the hands round her waist and squeezing
them, grateful that, even after the disappointments of the afternoon,
their dream of a rural idyll remained intact.

"We have to." There was an urgent note in Mark's voice.

"I know." It was wonderful, Rosie thought, glowing, how the project had united them.

"Otherwise the column gets it."

Rosie woke up in the early hours desperate for the loo and profoundly regretting having taken so much Knickersplitter on board. It
was called that, she realized, her bladder pulsating, for a reason. But
their room, she knew, lacked even a sink to pee in, and the loo, of
course, was outside. There was nothing for it but to brave the great,
dark, cold outdoors.

She groped her way to the door and down the silent corridor. Here
at least she could see; the moon poured through the window like a

spotlight, showing the way down stairs whose treads stuck gummily to her soles. Pushing open the back door, she gasped to feel the cold, although it hadn't felt all that warm inside.

But, oh, the stars. The pain in her pelvis was almost forgotten as she stared, entranced, at the Big Dipper, Orion, Cassiopeia, the smudge of the Pleiades, the dusty sweep of the Milky Way. Then the eerie creak of the pub sign reminded her of her mission—and the wisdom of getting back inside as soon as possible. Groping to the left, she found a crude wooden latch, no more than a stick loosely nailed in the center. She twisted it and pushed the door open to encounter an eye-watering stench, glad it was too dark to view what were obviously medieval toilet facilities. Her fears were confirmed when her feet encountered soft mud. Or worse? Shuddering, Rosie lifted her nightdress and crouched.

With terrifying suddenness, an indignant, high-pitched screech shattered the quiet into a thousand fragments. Rosie's heart shot into her mouth. Did the landlord have a wife and was she having a midnight pee, too? Or—her veins froze—was the headless woman on the rampage? Petrified, Rosie flailed in the darkness, desperate not to fall into whoever—*whatever*—it was. She screamed with fear as something huge, smelly, and hairy knocked her violently aside and charged, snorting, past her through the open door and out into the night.

It had taken a week of hard negotiation, but finally Samantha had done it. Her most subtle diplomatic tactics—violent tantrums, withdrawal of all sexual favors—had combined with a difficult week for Guy at work and secured his eventual capitulation. He had, albeit reluctantly, agreed to spend a weekend in the country. Samantha, although jubilant, had sensed the need to proceed with caution. She had not yet mentioned househunting, much less moving, as Guy's dislike of all things rural had turned out to be rather stronger than expected.

"What do you mean I don't know what it's like because I've never been there?" he demanded. "I grew *up* there, for Christ's sake. It's the most godawful place in the world. Nothing to do, no one to see. During the school holidays I had a job delivering the post. I walked miles, got attacked by everyone's dogs, and none of the bloody houses or farms had a sodding number on them, much less a name. What the hell do you want to go *there* for?"

Yet going there they were, on this brilliant Saturday morning, strapped in amid the luxury of Guy's XK9 with its computer-adjustable super-baby-soft seats made of the unblemished skins of Scandinavian calves. In the plaited ostrich-skin Bottega Veneta document wallet on Samantha's knee was a fat wad of estate agents' details. Details that must, for the moment, remain a secret, and, should Guy inquire, were officially notes for Christabel. Which they were in a way, even if it was unlikely any barmaid would ever have been able to afford the types of property Samantha had in mind. Unless she married the president of the pub company, of course. Samantha raised an eyebrow and smiled to herself. She'd done pretty well, all things considered. Life was good, even if the digital satellite-led trip planner feature on the dashboard currently showed the M1 like a blocked artery and them only just past Junction 3. As Guy gnashed his teeth and swore, Samantha looked serenely out of the tinted window at the (vastly inferior) cars grid-locked on either side of them.

Closing her eyes in satisfaction, Samantha thought, phase one had now been accomplished. Guy had been successfully lured out of the capital. Phase two would be breaking his resistance down and showing him the delicious portfolio of houses she had built up. Forcing him to buy one and get rid of Roland Gardens was phase three: the biggest challenge of all. How this was to be achieved, Samantha had absolutely no idea. The re-granting of sexual favors, perhaps? Even though her entire career was based on the premise that where there's a willy, there's a way, she was aware that this strategy might be required for the success-ful completion of phase two. Destiny, she was sure, would come up with something, although it had better start trying. Hard.

The signs, Samantha had to admit, were not good. The hope she had initially felt, on seeing Guy enthusiastically perusing *Country Life,* faded at the realization that it was the "Girls in Pearls" he was looking at, not the house ads. As the car purred on, Samantha's thoughts flitted to more pleasant subjects, such as the manor house in a mellow stone currently top of her wish list. The fact that it had a stable block was of particular appeal; Samantha had always fancied herself as a horsewoman. Despite never having gotten closer to a horse than watching the Grand National on television, Samantha had no problems picturing herself in skintight breeches, Titian curls tumbling out of a riding hat, looking exactly like those pictures of Stefanie Powers at the polo grounds she had always so admired in the back of *Harpers & Queen*.

Mounted on the sweeping lawns, Samantha Villiers shows off her magnificent frontage . . .

No, that didn't sound quite right.

On the sweeping lawns before the frontage of her magnificent house, the acclaimed actress Samantha Villiers, mounted on a superb hunter, tosses her Titian curls and smiles dazzlingly. Her long thighs lean in Savile Row riding breeches, Samantha oversees the distribution of stirrup cups (chilled Krugz) to the assembled hunt.

"I've always adored hunting," the Punkawallah *star explains, "and we have so much room here it seemed silly not to have the meet on our lawns, which," she adds, completely unaffectedly, "it takes ten full-time gardeners to keep looking pristine." Villagers unite in praise of their celebrity lady of the manor, who, despite her fame and the endless demands of the world's best-known directors clamoring for her services, still finds time to open their carnival, crown its queen, and even set aside the time and effort to judge the Best Decorated House competition (from which Miss Villiers's own residence sportingly exempts itself) . . .*

Soothed by this pleasant vision and the smooth rhythm of the car, Samantha dozed off.

"You look gorgeous when you're asleep," Guy greeted her as she woke with a jolt to find she had dribbled on her shirt. Briefly forgetting she was supposed to be charming the pants and then the objections off him, Samantha scowled viciously at her husband.

"Where are we?" she snapped.

"At the hotel."

Samantha flipped down the mirror and squinted at her makeup. Apart from the dribble cutting a swathe through her foundation, she had survived the journey tolerably well. Guy, on the other hand, looked almost blue with exhaustion as he opened the trunk. "What on earth are you doing?" Samantha demanded.

"Getting the bags."

"But they'll come out and get them. We don't carry our *own* luggage."

"It's only two bags, for God's sake. You're not at the bloody Chateau Marmont now, you know—if you ever were."

Samantha comforted herself by patronizing Reception. "Well," she said pointedly, looking around the hallway, "it's not Chatsworth, is it?"

"No, madam," the receptionist replied smartly. "Chatsworth's a forty-minute drive away."

Samantha cast a furious look at the sniggering Guy.

On their return from dinner in the hotel restaurant (which, loudly supposing it to be the handiwork of untutored locals, Samantha had barely touched, not noticing the wealth of culinary awards on display around the entrance), Samantha saw that her bag remained on the bed where she had left it. She snatched up the telephone immediately. "Excuse me," she inquired haughtily of Reception. "My case hasn't been touched."

There was a brief, surprised silence. "I must say this is very unusual, madam. Most people only complain if there has been interference with their belongings."

"You misunderstand me," said Samantha, biting off each word. "It is not, ahem, how shall I put this, *unpacked*."

Another amazed silence from the receptionist. Mingled with what sounded suspiciously like a suppressed snort. "Guests generally unpack their own cases here, madam. As you so accurately observed yourself, this is not Chatsworth."

Samantha forced out a high-pitched giggle. "How quaint. I haven't unpacked my own case for years."

Meanwhile, Guy, having finally located the piece of fake linenfold paneling concealing the television, was sitting in front of it with a huge glass of whiskey, trying to ignore the drama unfolding beside him. He couldn't cope with a prima donna performance, not now. Please God they weren't heading for a repeat of the weekend in Paris when Samantha had refused to sleep in the bed because the thread count in the sheets was below 250. Normally he could stand up to her, but not after the week he'd had. Not to mention the sleepless nights—very unusual, but it had been hard to sleep with that funny, piercing, burning feeling somewhere in his stomach. Guy's heart sank as Samantha threw down the phone.

It sank further when, suddenly, it rang again. Don't let it be the *bloody* office, he prayed, feeling exhausted at the mere thought of it. The burning feeling intensified as, no doubt anticipating another spat with the hotel staff, Samantha snatched up the receiver. Guy watched as her eyes widened and her face drained of all natural color. You had, he reflected, to look very hard to see that. One hand flew to her throat as she took a step backward. Guy's hand clamped round his whiskey glass like a vise. Bad news, obviously. That crucial deal he'd been handling, without a doubt. He began to struggle to his feet.

"*How* many millions?" he heard her gasp. Inside Guy's head, everything went black. Christ. It *was* that deal. Had to be. Whole bank had sunk by the sound of it. But why the hell were they talking about it to Samantha?

As Guy heaved himself upright, the pain ripped across his chest like a bullet. With a bubbling croak, he slumped back into the armchair. His head slammed forward on his chest the very moment Samantha banged down the receiver.

"Darling! *Darling!* You'll never guess," she squealed excitedly. "Oh, darling, do wake up. I can't bloody *believe* you've gone to sleep now of all times. For Christ's sake, someone—some *film star*—saw our house in *Insider* at the weekend and thinks it's a work of design genius. Wants to buy it. For *millions*." She tugged agitatedly at Guy's arm. "We can't afford *not* to," she urged. "We'll never get an offer like this again. Bloody hell, Guy, *wake up,* you idle bastard."

CHaPTER 6

"I don't know why you're being so touchy about it," Mark said. "It's fantastic material for 'Green-er Pastures.' Absolutely hilarious. Why can't I put it in?"

"Because I'd rather you didn't," pleaded Rosie. "I don't really want the entire nation to read over their breakfast tables that I was knocked over by a pig while peeing in a field at midnight."

"But it's so funny."

Blushing, Rosie looked crossly out of the car window. "Well, it wasn't all that amusing last night." Nor this morning, come to that. If the landlord of the Silent Lady had been far from pleased to find his prize porker running amok in the village, the local shop owner on whose premises the pig had been eventually, messily run to ground had been even less so. They had left the village under clouds both metaphorical and literal and were now working through the list of the morning's properties. Which was comprised of exactly one. Nigel, understandably enough, had not thought it worth coming from the office, and as an indicator of the house's worth and condition, his instructions about finding the key under a planter by the front door had not been encouraging.

"Can't believe you thought it was a ghost," Mark snorted as they drew up outside the house in question. Rosie reddened further, ashamed that she had thought this and not entirely for the reasons Mark assumed. Viewed in the (very) cold light of day, the lady on the sign had a dignity that suggested any kind of grunting and shoving would have been out of the question, even if her head had still been attached to her body.

Mark's mobile shrilled into life as he searched under the planter. The previous viewers, it emerged, had offered £20,000 more than the asking price for the ramshackle dwelling in front of which they now stood. "You could always up their offer," Nigel suggested helpfully.

"Yes, if I win the sodding lottery in the meantime," snapped Mark.

As they walked slowly back to the car to make the return journey to London, Rosie was so disappointed that she could hardly speak. Not finding anywhere at all had been the least expected of all outcomes. Hoping against hope to spot a suitable For Sale sign that had somehow been overlooked, she cast her eyes desperately about the villages as they passed through them.

"Eight Mile Bottom," snorted Mark as they drove into the next one. "What sort of a name is that?"

Eight Mile Bottom was a village Rosie now recognized to be typical of the area, a huddle of gray stone cottages arranged around a central green. The cottages were small and square with thick-linteled windows and solid little doors. Although tiny, plain, and functional, they had a strongly individual appearance; not more than two together, Rosie noticed, seemed the same age or design as the others. Some were set back from the road, some built on it, some boasted pansied window boxes or had pots arranged along the front. Not Bella-style pristine Islington topiary and terracotta these; rather, stained with brilliant green lichen and showing a few skinny, early daffodils. They looked ridiculously cozy, Rosie thought with a pang, especially the ones with gray plumes of smoke rising cheerfully out of the chimneys. None of them, however, was for sale.

The only building that was, was the mullioned manor on the main street, half hidden by sheltering trees. With a twinge of envy, Rosie recognized the same perfection of pearl-gray stone she had gazed at so longingly on the estate agents' display board. The nameplate on the lichened Jacobean gatepost confirmed that this was indeed The Bottoms, the house so far out of their price range it might as well have been Longleat.

"It's beautiful," breathed Rosie. "And the village is so peaceful."

Despite giveaway signs of life such as a village store–cum–post office, a small, school-like village hall, and even a tiny, net-curtained teashop called Penny Farthing, the only local in sight was a fat and lounging cat that plainly considered the entire winding main street its own. Above the roofs, on a brow overlooking the village, a church with a sharp steeple set amid towering ancient birch trees caught the evening sunshine full on its pink stone tower.

"Not bad, is it?" Mark muttered as they drove slowly past the pub. "Let's stop for a drink."

Although the last time she had heard those words they had presaged an evening of Gothic gloom, a headless woman, and a large pig, this time Rosie had no such fears. The Barley Mow's white-painted, sunlit front terrace was crowded with cheerful locals tipping back the last dregs of the day along with the beer.

Inside, lamps burned cheerfully but not too brightly in the deep-silled mullioned windows. Brass glowed against the stone of the fireplace and shining tankards dangled from thick ceiling beams. Completing the friendly picture was a vigorous-looking landlord presiding over a polished brass bar and wearing a T-shirt with a picture of a chicken and the legend HENVIRONMENTALIST. This evidence of a landlord with a sense of humor, however questionable, finally banished the dread possibility that all country pubs were like the Silent Lady. Far from gesturing sullenly at a pile of pork pies, this landlord seemed intensely involved in helping his customers—a pair of weatherbeaten old men with extremely skeptical expressions—make their selection from the menu chalked on the blackboard above the bar.

"Scampi and chips or shepherd's pie?" spat one, who had clearly neglected to put his teeth in.

"Both highly recommended." The landlord smiled.

The toothless man fixed him with a suspicious stare. "Aye, Alan, but which one d'you get t'most of?"

"Why can't they make their sodding minds up?" Mark muttered. "I'm gagging for a drink."

A host of printed notices were pinned down on either side of the bar. Rosie drank them in delightedly. " 'Eight Mile Bottom Horticultural Show,' " she read out to Mark. " 'The Percy Ollerenshaw Trophy for onions goes to Mr. F. Womersley for a specimen weighing three pounds and four ounces.' Three pounds and four ounces," Rosie repeated incredulously. "It must have been the size of a football. How can anyone grow an onion that big?"

On the other side of the bar, Alan raised an eyebrow. "Aye, well, they say it's a trade secret. But the real secret is that all these folks have obviously found a shop trading in massive onions somewhere and they're not telling any of the rest of us where it is."

"Are you saying," Rosie said, smiling, "that some of these vegetable growers are less than honest about their achievements?" She dug Mark hard in the ribs; this, surely, was perfect "Green-er Pastures" material. The sort of thing one couldn't make up.

Alan sucked his teeth and pulled a face. "Far be it from me to cast nasturtiums on whether folks grow their own stuff or not. But put it this way, the tomato stocks in the nearest Somerfield go down noticeably when there's a show on. Noticeably. And some o' them supposedly home-grown bunches o' dahlias are definitely making guest appearances from the Canary Islands. As for them huge carrots—size of submachine guns, some of 'em are—if you subjected 'em to them Olympic tests for growth 'ormones or whatever, there's not one of 'em would pass. Them carrots are on steroids, no doubt about it."

Another notice had caught Rosie's eye. "What on earth is hen racing?" She giggled.

"You've never been to a hen race?" Alan looked at her in cheery mock amazement. "Have them here every year, we do, in the pub car park."

"You race hens in the car park?" It was on the tip of Rosie's tongue to ask if that was cruel, but she swallowed it back determinedly. In any case, it certainly gave a whole new meaning to "free range."

"That's right. Big village tradition, it is. Everyone who's got hens enters them. Mine's called Napoleon and he's heavily fancied this year."

"What makes them run, though?" asked Rosie.

"A trail of corn. Unfortunately, though, Napoleon didn't run fast enough last year. A rogue hen from Milton Keynes won. It was rumored," Alan added darkly, "that it'd had its corn soaked in Southern Comfort."

"Two pints of Knickersplitter, please," Mark interrupted testily.

"Is that cheating?" asked Rosie.

The landlord put the streaming pint glasses on the bar and shrugged. "Not strictly speaking. And if I were honest, there were mitigating circumstances. Napoleon is a three-minute hen and not a four-minute hen and he only runs in fine weather. It was pissing down last year. The Milton Keynes entrant," Alan concluded impressively, "had clearly had wet-weather training."

Rosie turned in delight to Mark. But Mark wasn't listening. He was concentrating on his pint and smacking his lips. "Orange peel, aniseed, honey, nutmeg, touch of, um, yes, *cardamom* even," he rhapsodized, taking large drafts and frothing the liquid about his mouth like a wine taster. Suddenly, he whipped out a pen and began making copious notes on one of the house details.

"Oh, 'eck," said Alan, winking at Rosie. "I'd best have a word with the kitchen. The curry's obviously getting into the beer pipes."

Rosie flushed, her downcast eyes dwelling on the house details. They were of the one where the dog had been shot. "You don't know of anything for sale round here, do you?" she asked suddenly, ridiculously hopeful.

Alan shook his head. "Houses, you mean? There's lists of folks miles long at the estate agents wanting places in villages like this, so I'm told. Property market's gone mad."

"Tell us about it," said Mark heavily, draining his pint.

"Amazing about the hen races," Rosie ventured as they drove back toward the M1.

Mark shot her an incredulous look from the driving seat. "Didn't believe that, did you? For Christ's sake, Rosie, you can't race hens."

Rosie lapsed into silence. Mark's snappy mood, she knew, had its root in panic. For him, there was a direct and increasingly urgent link between getting a cottage and getting a column. Which wasn't to say that she didn't want one desperately as well. It had, after all, been her idea in the first place. As they shot at inadvisable speed down the motorway, she dwelt on the bright pictures in her mind. Fields edged with drystone walls spread like green sheets beneath a pale blue sky. A church steeple standing sentinel over the green. Peaceful rows of cottages, huddled behind pots of daffodils. Window boxes rioting with pansies. As, finally, they turned into Craster Road, Rosie's heart felt as if it were dragging along behind the car like cans after newlyweds.

Just like Guy to steal her thunder by dropping dead, had been Samantha's first thought as her husband slid, blue-lipped, to the floor in front of her.

To her surprise, however, he was not dead, but had merely suffered a massive heart attack. "Well, at least I suppose it shows he has one," Samantha drawled to the paramedic.

From the local emergency medical treatment center, she had transferred Guy to a hospital in London as soon as possible, more for her convenience than his. It had been the work of seconds for Samantha to realize that she—in Guy's unavoidable absence—must now handle negotiations for the sale of the urban sanctum. What was more, she could now take charge of finding them somewhere new to live. By the time he recovered, it would all be over. Against all the odds, destiny had found a way, Samantha thought with glee. Things couldn't have worked out more spectacularly if dear Ridley Scott had done the storyboards.

Yet in the oyster that was her world, there remained some grit; the utter boringness of not being allowed to reveal to anyone the identity of the American megastar who had bought Roland Gardens. The only compensation was being summoned from intensive care to The Afterlife, the megastar's international media and production company, to sign the confidentiality clause. A sequence of vast rooms vibrating to long, atonal chords of sound, The Afterlife offices immediately struck Samantha as familiar. The unmistakable whiff of sage smoke, for instance. The wire-wool goat, too, rang a bell, and wasn't that a Maserati connecting rod like her own over there? Amazing how these ancient tribal artifacts got everywhere, although Guy had laughed uproariously and said "Knightsbridge" when Samantha had once wondered aloud in what part of the bush the Maserati people lived.

"And of course I'm used to *these*," Samantha purred to the froglike Afterlife lawyer as she put pen to dotted line on the papier-mâché desk in his office.

"Really?" snapped the frog, looking at her with bulging, suspicious eyes.

"Being an *actress,* you see," Samantha added hurriedly. "We sign a lot of these in my profession. Agreeing not to look Tom Cruise in the eye and all that sort of thing, ha ha . . . um, where exactly do you want me to sign?"

Roxy, the megastar's long-haired, hamster-faced PA, was slightly more forthcoming. Over what was, again, a strangely familiar white china cup of Japanese green tea, she re-created for a rapt Samantha the precise moment when the megastar, flicking through *Insider* on board her Gulfstream, happened upon Basia's handiwork. "She just, like, *saw* it and she just, like, totally, *had* to have it," Roxy confided in toothy wonderment. "It was just, like, *instant.* Like *totally.*"

"Yes, well, I think that's the way Basia Briggs affects most people," stammered Samantha, who had by now practically lost control of her bowels with excitement. "You either love it or you . . ." she paused, "*ahem,* love it *even more.*"

Samantha was, in truth, almost fond of Basia's work herself now. Particularly given that She Whose Name Could Not Be Revealed had, via the froglike lawyer, practically asked Samantha to name her price. Once she had recovered from the shock and dealt with the tedious incidentals of getting Guy into the hospital, Samantha had driven the most hard and audacious of bargains, although never in a million years had she expected the megastar to agree to the price she was asking.

That the froglike lawyer hadn't either was evident in his tone when he called back to report that they had a deal. Samantha was jubilant, despite wondering whether she could have asked for even more. But what the hell. In one fell swoop she'd gotten rid of Roland Gardens and piled up enough to become lady of whatever manor she fancied. She'd gotten her heart's desire and, gratifyingly, with every appearance of helping Guy recover from his heart attack. He could hardly object now.

Guy's doctor had not only been quick to agree that he needed a period of absolute rest but also that the countryside would be the perfect place to recuperate in. The surgeon had been touched, moved even, by the fact that Samantha was willing to give up what she assured him was a glittering London-based career to move to the back of beyond for the sake of her husband. "I believe in standing by my man, Dr. Carmichael." Samantha had smiled dazzlingly at the doctor, serene in the knowledge that the papers clinching the sale were sitting waiting for her signature in her Fendi Baguette.

Samantha had tackled Guy's bank next, making sure that Bud Hufflestein, Guy's boss and the bank's president, understood that a move from the capital for health reasons would not in any way affect Guy's ability to keep in touch with the office, modern telecommunications being what they were.

Wearing the smallest, tightest skirt in her wardrobe, Samantha had worked hard to persuade Hufflestein that, even though his deputy's twenty-hour working days were over, this was no reason why negotiations for a lucrative nonexecutive directorship should not begin. Several intimate dinners with Hufflestein later, Samantha's cup of joy was running over almost as much as those of her push-up bra.

The only other bit of grit in her shell was Iseult.

One of the more boring consequences of Guy's otherwise frankly rather well-timed illness was that his ex-wife and daughter had reappeared on the scene. Iseult, in particular. Despite Samantha's efforts to maintain a near-ubiquitous presence at her husband's bedside, there were times when she was forced to be absent—using mobile phones in intensive care wards being, for some ludicrous reason, not allowed. And it was through these windows in her bedside schedule that Iseult climbed in. Samantha would never have admitted, even to herself, how twitchy the sight of Guy's daughter in the ward made her. There was something in Iseult's big, cornflower-blue eyes that implied she knew that, contrary to what Dr. Carmichael believed, the only reason Samantha was standing by her man was in order to take the wallet out of his pocket.

In self-defense, Samantha had pruned her call-answering viciously. Those from The Afterlife's lawyer or Bud Hufflestein were accepted, but previously vital personnel such as her aromatherapist, dietician, personal trainer, and even theatrical agent found themselves speaking into the void of Samantha's message box. Unlike the others, however, her agent did not give up after the first three unanswered calls.

"What the hell is it, Russ?" Samantha, shouting into her mobile outside the hospital entrance, watched in fury as Iseult, all long limbs and flowing hair, loped past into the foyer. "Quick, quick, I haven't got all day. Visiting hours, you know," she added, just to lay it on thick.

"Darling, it's the director."

"The director? Steven, you mean?" Had Spielberg called at last?

"The *Country Clinic* director. Christabel, remember? The part you were so excited about?"

Samantha's heart resumed its normal sluggish rate. "Oh. *That* director." Funny how, after all the recent house excitement, Christabel seemed to have lost a little of her luster. The prospect of playing a provincial barmaid no longer seemed particularly glamorous compared to the tantalizing task of selecting the manor of which she would most like to be lady.

"He's a little nervous because he thinks you may have lost interest."

"What on earth makes him think that?" snapped Samantha, playing for time as she racked her brain for excuses.

"Can't imagine, angel," said Russ. "Possibly—and this is just a hunch—it might have something to do with the fact that you haven't turned up for rehearsals yet."

"For God's sake, Russ," Samantha exploded. "Doesn't he realize what I'm *going through* at the moment? Can't he imagine what it's *like*? How it feels to be on the brink? To know that suddenly it could all go wrong and I could lose absolutely *everything*?"

"Darling, I know. I *know*," Russ soothed. "Believe me. We all realize what you're going through. We can all imagine how you feel. And, believe me, we can sympathize."

"So I should bloody hope. For Christ's sake, *I'm trying to sell a bloody house down here.*"

There was a surprised silence. "And *Guy*?" Russ asked pointedly.

"*God*, I mean, *Christ*," screeched Samantha, pacing furiously about the pavement and tearing at her hair. "What am I supposed to *do*? I'm not used to working like this."

"Darling, let's face it, you're not used to *working*," drawled Russ.

"Just get your butt over to the studio for rehearsals. Today. Otherwise, from what I gather, the barmaid gets it."

Samantha stormed back into the hospital. Her fury intensified when, returning to the ward, she found Iseult, as expected, on the chair at Guy's bedside clutching her father's hand. Hunched on the bedside chair, her black top, apparently manufactured from cobwebs, straining across her budding and braless breasts, she was moving her head mournfully to whatever was playing on the state-of-the-art silver CD player balanced on her crotch. A present from doting Daddy, no doubt, thought Samantha viciously, her eye catching the CD cover—*What Did Your Last One Die Of?* by someone called Matt Locke. Her lips twisted as she noticed the grapes she had bought from Harrods that morning had almost halved in number. Despite her only-come-out-at-night appearance, Iseult evidently had a healthy appetite. Trust Guy, Samantha thought savagely, to father the sole member of her generation who wasn't an anorexic, yet was still a waif. Iseult's frail neck, skinny arms, and elegantly gangly legs were, Samantha recognized jealously, gifts that had been missing from her own particular genetic stocking and had been achieved only by practically starving herself.

Ditto Iseult's perfect oval face with its lips so full they were less rosebud, more rose, fashionably thin arched eyebrows, and center-parted hair of a blackness that was almost blue. It was amazing how unlike her father she was, large blue eyes excepted. There was little of the Latin about Guy's florid, Anglo-Saxon appearance, apart, that was, from the eye-watering blasts of aftershave. Iseult was obviously her mother's daughter. If only, Samantha thought, she wasn't her father's.

"I think your father's tired," said Samantha bossily. "Perhaps you should go."

A look of intense dislike slid across Iseult's face. She detached her earphones "Oh, *yeah?*"

"*Yeah.* Er, I mean *yes.* I'll arrange a cab for you."

"Don't bother." Iseult looked at her steadily. "Anyway, I wanted to talk to you."

"What about?" Samantha was determined not to show how surprised she was. If Iseult thought she could get around her with a bit of stepdaughterly bonding, she had another think coming.

"About *what the fuck* you've done to my bedroom."

Samantha boggled. "*Your* bedroom?"

"You've taken down all my posters and painted it shit color. I've just been to see it."

Bugger, cursed Samantha. I should have made Basia change the locks as well. "Your—I mean *that* bedroom," she explained haughtily, "is, along with the rest of the house, the work of the foremost interior designer *de nos jours.*"

"De where? Never heard of her."

"Denosjowers," Samantha repeated. "*Of our times.* Don't they teach you French at your fancy school?"

"Oh, I see." Iseult looked incredulous. Then amused. "*De nos jours,*" she said slowly in a perfect accent. "*Wow,*" she added.

"Anyway," blustered Samantha, "I'm afraid it's not your bedroom anymore. The house is being sold and your father and I are moving to the country." She watched with satisfaction as absolute shock rippled across Iseult's irritatingly symmetrical features.

"The *country?* So where the hell am *I* supposed to go?"

"Wherever you usually go," Samantha drawled. "Your mother's house, I imagine."

"But I've left Mum's." Jolted on to the defensive, Iseult looked panicked. "Her new boyfriend's a drag. I was going to move in with Dad." The blue eyes focused on Samantha with a look that was almost pleading.

Conscious that, for once, she had all the cards in her hands, Samantha gave Iseult the benefit of her best stage smile. "Well, I'm afraid we're not going to be here for much longer. So you'll just have to find somewhere else to live. Won't you?"

For a second, Iseult looked as if she were about to burst into tears. She glanced desperately at her prone and unconscious father, lying, oblivious, beside them. Then, flashing Samantha a look of killer loathing, Iseult stood up and flounced out of the ward as best she could on rubber soles at least five inches in height. Samantha looked after her with satisfaction. Guy snored on.

CHAPTER 7

Bent over her worktable in the corner of the flat on Craster Road, Rosie was daydreaming of Eight Mile Bottom. Nothing that any estate agent had sent through since had come close to the village, although Mark had tried hard to interest her in a barn conversion near Cirencester. The problem with this was that the conversion was yet to be done. By them.

The future was looking bleak. Mark, too, was looking bleak. And looked bleaker every day he went into the office with no cottage to speak of and an increasingly impatient editor.

Rosie welcomed the interruption of the telephone.

"Hello," said a nasal voice with a north-country accent that Rosie did not immediately recognize.

"Hello?"

"Nigel here. From Kane, Birch, and Spankie. You're in luck. Something's come up. Don't know whether you're still interested, but . . ."

"Yes. Yes. Yes!" shrieked Rosie, like Meg Ryan in the restaurant scene from *When Harry Met Sally*. Her heart filled with love for the oily-haired estate agent. "Nigel, you're *fantastic*."

"Thank you, madam." Nigel sounded gratified. "The owners are in a hurry to move, so your not being in a chain helps. It's only just come on the market. We've not put it in the window yet—"

"Oh, *please* don't," said Rosie, giving him Mark's work fax number. Mark rang up immediately, yelping with excitement. Not only was the price extraordinarily reasonable—almost within their range, in fact—but the details Kane, Birch & Spankie had sent through included magic words like "heavy oak beams" and "period open fireplaces."

As soon as Rosie put the telephone down, it rang again.

"Amazing, isn't it?" exclaimed Bella.

"Fantastic." Rosie wondered how she knew. Had Mark been so excited he had called her himself?

"Going for billions, apparently," Bella added.

Rosie gasped. She'd thought the cottage was reasonably priced. Had Nigel been whiting out some of the zeros?

"I hear Nicole Kidman's after it," added Bella. "But of course she's too late."

"*What?* But that's *impossible!*" said Rosie. The pictures of the cottage had not been clear, but even Nigel's most optimistic euphemisms had been unable to disguise that it was not only small but needed rather a lot of work.

"Why would Nicole Kidman be interested in Eight Mile Bottom?" she asked Bella.

"What's Eight Mile Bottom, darling?" asked Bella. "Sounds like a ghastly disease."

"Where Mark and I are buying our dream cottage, we hope. Isn't that what you're talking about?"

"No, darling, I'm talking about the *Insider* piece on that Basia Briggs house. You know, darling, the one you helped me style. It's been spotted by a mystery megastar—rumor Nicole—who's buying it post-Tom for gazillions, apparently." She paused triumphantly. "Unbelievable, *n'est-ce pas?*"

"It *is* unbelievable," Rosie said, appalled. "That house was absolutely disgusting." As were its owners, she added silently as the memory of Samantha Villiers's mean little eyes and purple lips pressed tightly together loomed suddenly and unpleasantly before her. Rosie shuddered. Still, if all went according to plan, she need never clap eyes on her again.

"Well, it needn't bother *you* anymore darling," said Bella, reading her thoughts. "Not now you've found your dream cottage. I must say, I really rather envy you. In *some* ways," she added immediately.

"You *do?*"

"Well, quite frankly, darling, Islington's going awfully downhill. Simon was in bed last night and heard our car being broken into. He shot out of bed, completely starkers, to give whoever it was a piece of his mind."

"How terrible," said Rosie, trying not to smile as she imagined the car thief peaceably going about his business and then being confronted by a very angry, very red-faced, and very naked Simon. "What happened?"

"Well, they ended up having the most dreadful fight. I looked out of the window and saw them rolling down the pavement together. Had to take Si to the hospital this morning to have all the windshield glass picked out of his bottom."

As an image of a nurse patiently attending to Simon's large red rump floated irresistibly to mind, Rosie tried again not to smile. "Oh, dear."

"Well, Simon insists he gave the thief a left hook," said Bella, sighing. "Says that all the time he was in the hospital he knew the thief was also in one. But I'm not so sure. Anyway, darling, I was thinking we might have to move somewhere a bit, well, greener."

"Come with us," said Rosie immediately. "There's the most wonderful manor house for sale in the village."

"Oh, no, darling," said Bella, sounding horrified. "I was thinking more of Regent's Park."

According to Kane, Birch & Spankie Ltd, Number 2 Cinder Lane was "an atmospheric former coal-miner's cottage situated in the oldest part of the historic village of Eight Mile Bottom, near the church." Rosie registered, but chose not to dwell on, the fact that, in her experience, "atmospheric" generally heralded a pervading smell of damp and "near the church" probably meant distantly glimpsed if you stood on a chair in the attic.

Number 2 proved to be the second in a terrace of small cottages running up a lane. "Sixteen forty-nine!" Mark pointed at the date stone above the door. "Three hundred and fifty years old!"

Rosie thrilled to the romance of the wonkily carved numbers, their edges smoothed and blackened with age. How many people had passed under that very lintel since 1649? People, in general, seemed scarce; the row of cottages going up the lane was as silent as the graves in the churchyard at the bottom of it.

For, much to Rosie's amazement, Number 2 Cinder Lane was, in fact, *very* near the church. The tower of pink-tinged stone stood peacefully amid its trees mere feet from the cottage door. She looked admiringly at the timeless scene.

Except that it wasn't completely timeless—an old, gold-figured clock face was mounted on the side of the church tower. As they closed the car doors, it struck.

"Twelve o'clock," said Mark, looking at his watch.

"Sixteen o'clock." Rosie grinned, listening to the bells ringing on inside the pink tower.

"Crunch time," said Mark, swinging the keys.

They started, slowly, to move toward the cottage. Rosie slid her hand into Mark's, suddenly fearful that it would not be suitable. This was, she realized, their last chance. Please, God, Rosie prayed, glancing at the stone tower still reverberating from the seemingly unstoppable bells. Thirty-two o'clock now. Please, God, let this be our dream home.

As they hesitated outside the white-painted stable door, a sudden screech of tires made them freeze in their tracks. Mark leaped round indignantly, fists clenched, face taut with aggression, and fear in his eyes. Fear, Rosie knew, that a richer, rival bidder had come to snatch the cottage and therefore his column away from him. And her dream from her. She, too, whirled suspiciously around.

"'Ow do." The young man leaping out of the shiny red van didn't look the gazumping sort. For a start, the legend ROYAL MAIL was emblazoned across the doors of his van and, besides a wide grin, he wore a postman's pale blue shirt and navy trousers. His very bright black eyes followed over them with intense interest. "You buying this place then?"

Rosie and Mark looked at each other. Direct questions from strangers—apart from "Any spare change, please?"—were not something London life had prepared them for.

"Perhaps," Mark said curtly, clearly determined to release as little information as possible.

"I'm Duffy the postman," the man said, clearly determined to do the opposite. "Where you from then?"

"London." Mark's tone carried with it the expectation that not only would the postman be profoundly impressed by this, but that he would never have met anyone from the capital before.

"Oh, aye? There's a woman from London coming to look at a house up the High Street as well, as it 'appens. Loaded, she is. Rolling in it."

"Lucky her," said Mark heavily, realizing too late that he had revealed more than he intended to of their financial status. Rosie felt the urge to giggle. The postman's newsgathering skills were undeniable.

"Barristers or something, are you?" probed the postman.

"No," said Rosie, resisting the temptation to explain that neither of them could as much as understand the small print on insurance forms. "I'm an illustrator and Mark's a journalist."

The postman looked interested. "Journalist, eh?" he echoed. "Once thought of doing that meself, funnily enough. Investigative, like. Not that it ever came to anything."

"A great pity. I'm sure you would have been very good at it," Mark said. "Now, if you'll excuse us . . ."

Far from looking reproved, the postman grinned more widely. "Aye. I'd best be getting on meself. I'm still doing t'first round o' post—it's all them cups o' tea slowing me down."

"Cups of tea?" repeated Rosie, unable to make sense of this remark.

"Oh, everyone asks me in for a cuppa. To find out what t'rest o' t'village is up to. Right," said the postman briskly, looking through the envelopes in his hands. "Nowt for you—I mean Number Two—so I hope that means they paid that red gas bill they'had before they left. Mind you, that last bank statement of theirs makes you wonder how they could."

The postman picked out a postcard and shoved it through the shiny brass letterbox of the cottage next door. "From your daughter, Mrs. W.," he shouted at someone apparently on the other side of the window. "She's having a lovely time in France, but the weather's not all it could be. Well, ta-ra, then," he added to Rosie and Mark, leaping into his van and driving away with a screech of tires.

"Nosy bastard," said Mark, staring after him. Rosie suppressed a smile, wondering if professional jealousy was an issue; Mark may have been the national newspaper journalist, but there was no doubting the village postman's ability to extract information.

As they moved once again toward the cottage, Rosie had the sudden sensation of eyes upon her. Eyes that came from behind next door's impenetrable net curtains. Was the mysterious Mrs. W., whose daughter's weather wasn't up to scratch, lurking? Quickly, she scuttled after Mark through the stable door of Number 2.

It opened directly on to a tiny sitting room whose timbered ceiling featured heavy central beams the thickness of a man. This led to a tiny dining room and, beyond, a cool and gloomy kitchen.

"Just look at *that*," Mark said in awe, slapping one of the massive pieces of wood and studiously ignoring the small shower of plaster dislodged from the ceiling by the movement. Rosie was too lost in admiration of the vast sitting-room fireplace to notice. Cut from thick shortbread fingers of stone, it contained a wood-burning stove of black iron. Imagining romantic nights before flickering flames, Rosie gazed around, enraptured even by the bare concrete floor, which immediately suggested golden swathes of sisal and individually fired Tuscan peasant tiles. Excitedly, she went outside to explore the back.

The estate agents' claim of the garden's being "in a transitional state" was accurate enough; although "in a state" would have been yet more so. Judging from the expanse of scattered Coke cans, plastic bags, and a vast coil of ribbed plastic tubing, the owners of the cottage had never set foot in it. Yet there was definitely potential there. Rosie, who had long dreamed of a garden of her own, looked around speculatively, imagining herbaceous borders where the plastic bags were strewn, a glossy lawn where the tubing now lay. It was possible. She was certain of it.

Even if it was doubtful she would ever come up to the standards of Mrs. W. The cottage below boasted a neat little strip of a garden with a healthy, thick-grassed lawn bordered with clumps of jaunty daffodils and splashes of red tulips. There were also several hanging baskets, a tidy greenhouse, and a water butt. Rosie smiled to see the plastic cream pots used as bird scarers and the wooden Popsicle sticks—from some grandchild, perhaps—marked with the names of flowers. Mrs. W. was clearly a keen proponent of waste not want not.

Rosie closed her eyes in the luxurious silence. For entire minutes on end, all was peaceful apart from the throaty call of a woodpigeon and the distant sound of a tractor. Quietness in London, Rosie recalled, was as rare and fragile as a lark's egg; one always knew it could—and would—be shattered in seconds. Indeed, one almost wanted it to be, to get it over with. But here it was strong and abundant, with gentle eddies of breeze rippling through it like muscles; a silence so absolute it echoed, ringing, within itself.

A small ledge set into the crumbling wall at the back of the garden looked out over a sloping hillside, on which cattle were grazing. Beautiful beasts, too, Rosie saw, admiring their level backs, sturdy legs, and tufty coats colored, not the normal black and white, but shades of ginger, auburn, black, blond and cream. Rosie tipped her head back in the silence and gazed happily up at the copper-tinted clouds as she returned to the cottage and Mark.

She found him busily exploring the upper floor. There was really only one bedroom, the other room being a tiny, rather damp-looking spare that Mark had already commandeered as a writing room. Rosie was enchanted by the bedroom's glorious deep-silled window ledges, the most ideal size and shape on which to rest her drawing board. And which enjoyed, thanks to the square windows with their pretty, old-fashioned wrought-iron latches, better light to paint in than anything Craster Road had ever had to offer.

"It's perfect, isn't it?" Mark urged, clasping both her hands in his. As he drew her into his arms, Rosie was unable to contradict him—even if she had wanted to. His tongue was gradually exploring her mouth, while, against her hip, she could feel the familiar hardness pressing against her.

"Mark! We can't!" she gasped excitedly. "Not here. What if Nigel comes?"

"May the best man come first, in that case," muttered Mark, fumbling with his trousers.

Before going home, they stopped off once again at the Barley Mow, where, Rosie was delighted to observe, a new sign had joined the results of the local horticultural show. FERRETS, it announced. FREE TO GOOD HOMES.

"Hello again," boomed Alan, the landlord. Today's T-shirt, Rosie noticed, maintained the hen theme already established. POULTRY IN MOTION, it proclaimed in large letters, continuing underneath with BARLEY MOW WORLD CHAMPIONSHIP HEN RACES, AUGUST 1998; GREEN WITH HENVY. For a fictional event, she thought, Alan certainly seemed to spend a lot of time promoting it. She shot a sly glance at Mark, who had apparently not noticed it.

The landlord drummed his palms expectantly on the polished copper bar. "Becoming regulars, aren't you?"

At a nearby table, a man with a neat white beard and twinkling eyes sniggered. "Regular? You don't get to be regular in this village until you've been here at least five generations. And even then you can forget it if you've been away at any time."

"You've got to remember," said Alan, grinning, "that people round here think of the Plague as a fairly recent event. Some would say"—he scrabbled behind the bar and produced a newspaper—"that it's still going on. This is the obituaries page of the *Slapton Sentinel.*"

Rosie and Mark stared at the double-page spread almost solid with photographs and names of the recently deceased. It was an impressive and faintly disturbing sight. "Looks like t'Black Death, doesn't it?" said Alan.

"Local newspapers are of course famous for their obituary coverage," Mark said pompously. "Two pints of Knickersplitter, please."

"Knickersplitter's off. There's Hairy Helmet, though."

"You may joke," said the bearded man, addressing Alan as he pulled the pints, "but my grandfather shook hands with a man who had fought in the Battle of Trafalgar. And if you think about it, it's not that far back to the Anglo-Saxons. Not that far back to Jesus, come to that."

Alan nodded. "You're right there, Bill," he said. "Especially now that the vicar's started a chat room on the church website. We've got God in cyberspace now."

"Gerrawaywithyer," said the bearded man, grinning and raising his pint glass.

Rosie giggled. She liked Alan. She also liked the look of the smiling woman with the shining cap of blond hair who had appeared behind him at the bar. His wife, she presumed. "I'm right, aren't I, Ann?" Alan appealed to her now. "About the vicar's chat room?"

Ann smiled and rolled her eyes. "When are you ever not right? Like it round here, do you?" she asked Rosie and Mark as she came to collect their glasses.

"We're thinking of buying a place," Mark told her. "We found somewhere, as it happens. Things weren't quite as bad as you made out," he added, a hint of triumph in his voice, as Alan came past the table.

"Things never are," said Ann ruefully.

As, reluctantly, they left the Barley Mow, Rosie asked, "Are we still thinking of buying? Or are we actually *buying*?"

"What do you think?" asked Mark. As always, her heart lurched when he smiled at her. It had been quite a while since he had smiled at her in that special way.

CHaPTER
8

Carinthia D'Arblay Sidebottom and her enviable environs had died hard. Samantha's heart was set on a village, as in Carinthia's own Chewton Mewsley, where *the main street meanders casually yet purposefully between buildings that are an architectural potpourri of different periods—here Jacobean mullions, there a graceful neoclassical Georgian portico—and past a splendid, lovingly cared for village church set amid the shade of ancient beech trees. In front of the church spreads the village green with its blue jewel of a duck pond; opposite it the cheerful bustle of the shop–cum–post office, which, together with the little teashop and the beamed and thatched pub, forms the commercial heart of this most uncommercial of villages. . . .*

Chewton Mewsley, therefore, was the gold standard Samantha had set for herself. As she drove off this morning to meet her relocation adviser, the slightly battered copy of *Cottage Beautiful* magazine in which Carinthia had first come to her attention was, as usual, tucked away in her silver folder.

Coming, as he did, from a long line of lionhearted soldiers, Sir Hadley Bonsanquet, Bt., was not the sort of person a country lifestyle magazine would normally fill with dread. Yet his dealings with them so far had not been encouraging. A down-at-heels aristocrat whom circumstances had forced into the theoretically lucrative relocation mar-

ket, he was currently cursing the persuasive young advertisement salesman through whose auspices he had taken an eighth of a page in *Country Life*. An eighth of a page, more to the point, that Samantha had
spotted.

Until this happened, Sir Hadley had always imagined the worst that
could befall a man was what had recently happened to him—being
forced through Lloyd's losses to sell his ancestral estate to, of all people,
a pop star called Matt Locke. Ladymead, a rambling, romantic, tow-
ered, and turreted pile, surrounded by a green sweep of parkland, had
been in the Bonsanquet family since the fourteenth century. To flog it
to some gangly youth in oversize sunglasses had caused Sir Hadley to
suffer more acutely than his distant ancestors had against Joan of Arc
or his more recent ones had against Napoleon and Hitler (the derring-
do of all concerned being commemorated in plaques and tombs in the
Eight Mile Bottom parish church). Yet where the might of foreign
armies had failed, Lloyd's—coupled with disastrous financial advice—
had succeeded.

Since meeting Samantha, however, Sir Hadley could no longer see
what the big problem with selling Ladymead had been. Giving up the
historic family estate was nothing compared to finding an estate for
this preposterously demanding actress. Small wonder that the sight of
Cottage Beautiful struck a worse fear in Sir Hadley's heart than anything
his forefathers had felt facing the arrows of the French. The problem
was not merely that of pinpointing the perfect village. It was also that
Samantha had an additional and constantly changing set of requirements besides the basic components of Chewton Mewsley. During the
weeks he had been working for her, these had included a flagpole, a
ballroom, and a swimming pool. Now, suddenly, Samantha decided
she required a station.

"A station?" quavered Sir Hadley. His watery eyes watered further.
Samantha sniffed the air ostentatiously—on this occasion, as on several
previous ones, she suspected Sir Hadley had been waiting for her not
outside the branch of Barclays that served as their usual rendezvous
(and a cruel reminder to Sir Hadley that the days of deposit accounts
were behind him) but at the pub next door.

"A train station, Sir Hadley." As they got into Guy's Jaguar and

drove off, Samantha shot the relocation agent a beady glare and wondered if, given the fact that she was his undisputed master, she
shouldn't just call him Hadley.

The origins of the station idea, Sir Hadley gathered as they drove
along, came from a newspaper article describing how David Niven, an
actor with whom Samantha had once shared a stage (albeit with almost
a year between their respective roles), would greet his weekend guests
on the village station platform bearing a tray of Bloody Marys. Samantha, Sir Hadley learned, planned to improve it with a few touches of
her own. Champagne cocktails instead of Bloody Marys, for a start. As
an unusually diplomatic director had once told her, even perfection
could be improved on.

As they pulled up outside the first house on that day's agenda, a
house conspicuously lacking so much as a signal box, Sir Hadley sighed
deeply.

An hour later his spirits had not risen perceptibly. Although Samantha had appeared more impressed with the house than he had ever
dared hope, he braced himself for the inevitable post-show-round
abuse as they came outside onto the lawn. Yet, miraculous as it seemed,
his impressions were correct. Lack of station notwithstanding, Samantha was satisfied the property fulfilled most of her criteria.

"Just look at the daffodils," she cooed, pointing at a yellow patch of
crocuses on the lawn.

The owner, Lady St. Felix, looked at Samantha in amazement. Sir
Hadley, meanwhile, shifted from one battered brogue to another.

"Wonderful, aren't they?" Samantha continued in apparent ecstasy.
"I *so adore* wildflowers, Lady St. Felix. Don't you?"

Any reply Lady St. Felix could possibly have made was drowned out
by Samantha's mobile suddenly shrilling "New York, New York."

Sir Hadley gave Lady St. Felix a liquid and apologetic look. "May I
just say again how sorry I am about the floorboards, Catherine," he
quavered. "I'm afraid Miss Villiers simply didn't appreciate what the
appalling consequences of wearing . . ."—he flicked a glance at Samantha's footwear—"um, steel-heeled stilettos would be on four-hundred-
year-old oak. However, I'm sure you can sort something out with each

other's, um"—the thought of Lloyd's never far from his mind, he stumbled over the dreaded word—". . . insurance."

Lady St. Felix flared her nostrils in a strikingly similar manner to the lions rampant guarding her ancient front door. Her eyelids, permanently half closed as if to shield her from the appalling vulgarity of the world, drooped still further. They closed finally as the sound of Samantha shrieking into her mobile rent the air.

"Is that you, Russ? What do you mean what the hell's going on?"

Although Sir Hadley and Lady St. Felix were edging ever farther away from Samantha, Russ's response was still audible.

"I mean what the hell's going on?" exploded the agent, a distance of two hundred and fifty miles and a crackling mobile line not diminishing his fury in the least. "I tell the *Country Clinic* producer you'll turn up to rehearsals, beg him not to write Christabel out of the script, and what happens? *You fuck up.* There's *no bloody sign* of you at the studios."

"Excuse me," Samantha interjected haughtily. "I've had another rather *major* creative project taking up all my available time recently, *actually.*"

Sir Hadley shuddered and wondered if it was too early for a drink. He jumped as the digitally remastered force of Russ's fury squawked from Samantha's end of the telephone.

"Good," snarled Russ. "Because you sure as hell don't have *this* one anymore. The *Country Clinic* director's sacked you. And I'm sacking you as well. I'm sick of your attitude. Who the *fuck* do you think you are? Vanessa bloody Redgrave?"

"Certainly not," snapped Samantha. "I specialize in a different type of character altogether. Nor am I a revolutionary communist."

Lady St. Felix's liver-spotted hand flew to her brooched and collared throat.

There was a strangled yowl, a crash, and then the line went dead. Samantha shoved her mobile back into her bag. "Fuck you as well," she muttered.

"Is something wrong?" Lady St. Felix asked icily.

"Everything's fine." Samantha beamed stagily. "More than fine, in fact. I don't mind telling you this, Lady St. Felix—may I call you Catherine?"

Lady St. Felix's violet-veined eyelids flicked up a little.

"I'm very impressed with your house, Catherine," continued Samantha.

Lady St. Felix's mouth remained a quivering line. For her, as for Sir Hadley, Lloyd's cast a long and expensive shadow. Her stockbroker's recent advice to invest heavily in the dot-com revolution had also proved overoptimistic. Even lighting and heating were optional extras now, and having to sit in the dark every night with only a wind-up radio and two pairs of thermals for company was rapidly succeeding in breaking the proud St. Felix spirit that, in centuries gone by, Cromwell's army had ignominiously failed to do. Even so . . .

Lady St. Felix looked in anguish at Sir Hadley, who shrugged helplessly. She could expect no comfort there, of course, Hadley having recently sold Ladymead lock, stock, and Elizabethan cannon barrel to some scruffy-haired yowler who had apparently grown up on a council estate. To think that between them they had inherited the entire surrounding area. If only they had inherited a grain of financial common sense with it.

"There's just one thing, Catherine." As Samantha, musingly, stretched out her nails and examined them, the sun caught the vast, uncut diamond ring Guy had given her last Christmas.

"And what, *Miss Villiers,* is that?"

"Well, Catherine, it's not that *big,* is it?"

Lady St. Felix flinched. How *dare* the woman? Must she really endure this insolence? Had family pride sunk so low? She raised her withered chin to reveal two slack ropes of wattle running down into her collar and concluded that it probably had.

"It seems a perfectly respectable size to me, Miss Villiers," she faltered. "Generations of St. Felixes, including my ancestor, Wee Gervase, who was over seven feet tall, have grown up here without complaint. Indeed, the house has been admired for centuries as the epitome of small country-house perfection. 'An exquisite jewel,' is how Sir Nikolaus Pevsner referred to it. . . ." The proud St. Felix spirit quailed and the last of the line suddenly found herself unable to go on.

"You only have to read the agency details." Sir Hadley stepped in, waving a handful of papers at Samantha. Having scented closure, he was anxious for some very useful—not to say essential—commission not to slip through his fingers at the last minute. The Bottoms seemed to fulfill most of the appalling woman's requirements, after all. As did the village it was in, now that she'd finally and thankfully dropped the station clause. Sir Hadley crossed his fingers and hoped she would not start inquiring about airfields.

"Bloody stupid address, though, isn't it?" Samantha rapped out suddenly. "The Bottoms, Eight Mile Bottom? Imagine that on my Smythson's notepaper. Writing paper, I mean."

Lady St. Felix, whose own Smythson days had long been succeeded by Basildon Bond ones, swallowed. "I can't say the address has ever troubled the family once in several hundred years. The family crest even makes a virtue of it." She waved an arm toward the carved motto over the doorway. *In Fundi Nostri Fidemus*—Devoted Are We to Our Bottoms.

Sir Hadley, desperate for Samantha not to lose interest and all too aware of that mounting on his own debts, shook the estate agent's details again.

" 'An exceptional Grade I listed country house of great historical interest set in superbly maintained gardens and grounds with far-reaching views,' " he intoned. " 'An example of secular Jacobean building at its finest, The Bottoms boasts a number of historical features including a priest hole, molded plasterwork ceilings, heraldic fireplaces, and stone-flagged floors throughout. Five large bedrooms, three fine reception rooms, attics, vaulted cellars—' "

"Mmmm," said Samantha.

"The historical features really *are* tremendous," pressed the impecunious baronet, finding an unexpected and possibly atavistic determination and tenacity in adversity. (Perhaps his father had been wrong. Perhaps he would have cut it at the Battle of Crécy after all.) " 'The priest hole, for example . . .' " He stuttered and stopped. Surging into his memory came the tricky few minutes that had followed his client's suggestion that a power shower be installed in the hallowed place of the St. Felix family padre's civil war concealment.

"And the decor could do with some work," Samantha had added, looking scornfully around at the white-plastered, flag-stoned surroundings of the Great Hall. "I mean, there's no wallpaper or anything—half the place isn't even bloody decorated, for Christ's sake. Bit of a cheek considering the price you're asking. And look at this!" Samantha slapped her palm with contemptuous force against a crumbling section of fourteenth-century wall. "All these bits of wood showing through. You can see all the foundations."

At this, there was a sharp, quivering intake of breath from Lady St. Felix. For the seconds before the proud family spirit reasserted itself, she looked as if she was about to faint. "That," she had said with steely dignity, "is wattle and daub. Original and of great historical value."

Shuddering at the recollection, Sir Hadley tuned back to the conversation. "But, anyway, The Bottoms isn't the largest house in the area, is it?" Samantha was demanding.

Lady St. Felix flared her medieval nostrils. "Well, of course Ladymead is considerably larger in size . . ."

Samantha put her hands on her hips and raised an interested eyebrow. "That's the massive place outside the village, isn't it? With towers and flagpoles and everything?"

"Ladymead is no longer on the market," Sir Hadley pointed out bitterly. "The Bottoms, on the other hand—"

"Who's bought Ladymead?" Samantha cut in.

"A very, ahem, successful composer of, ahem, popular music," said Sir Hadley, desperate not to dwell on the subject. "Goes by the name of Matt Locke. Something of a recluse, I believe. Very rarely seen in the village. Now, to return to the subject of The Bottoms . . ."

Samantha sighed extravagantly, plunged a stiletto heel into the immaculate lawn, and started to wheel around on it.

". . . although, admittedly, not the largest in the area, The Bottoms is by far the largest house in the *village*." Sir Hadley blinked in astonishment as inspiration most unexpectedly struck. "The grounds, in fact, are so large that the local amateur dramatic society used them for their outdoor production of *Half a Sixpence* only last summer."

"What did you say?" Samantha's head whipped around.

"The manor is, ahem, the largest house in the, um, *village* . . ." Sir Hadley tried hard to remember the magic formula.

"Not *that*." Samantha's eyes shone with a hard sparkle. "About the amateur dramatic society."

"Oh, it's quite all right," Lady St. Felix interjected. "They're not the sort one reads about in the papers—having affairs and murdering one another and all that sort of thing. They're frightfully civilized. Run by Dame Nancy—she's terribly respectable."

"How *fascinating*," said Samantha thoughtfully. Had destiny struck again, providing her with both the perfect country house and the perfect opportunity to exercise her God-given thespian talent? It would seem so. Not only was The Bottoms the largest house in Eight Mile Bottom, the village also boasted a sheeplike bunch of rustics all ready to rally under the banner of her own dramatic vision. When compared to an opportunity like this, even her doubts about the decor paled into significance.

Samantha beamed at Sir Hadley and Lady St. Felix. "Catherine," she declared in ringing tones, "I think we have a deal."

Emerging from the hospital a fortnight later, Guy knew that he was incredibly lucky to have survived a serious heart attack almost un-scathed. Except for overwhelming exhaustion (which the doctors claimed would lessen eventually), the only legacy of what had happened was the occasional struggle to find the right word. Yet words had often failed him when he had been perfectly fit, especially where Samantha was concerned. Rarely had they failed him so utterly as when he was taken from the hospital by Samantha and bundled into the Jaguar to find that life as he had known it had come to an abrupt end.

Discovering that he was jobless was bad enough (although Huf-flestein was apparently working on something). But the news that, thanks to Samantha's having sold the house in Roland Gardens to some film star, he was homeless in the bargain had added insult to injury. The final straw was discovering, halfway up the motorway, that she had moved them to some creepy old village in the middle of nowhere. Not just any creepy old village, either, but one called, risibly, Eight Mile Bottom.

As for the house itself, The Bottoms, words failed Guy again. Apart, that was, from the single-syllable *why*? Or, more to the point, why *not* some nice old Lutyens-designed pile, why *not* some comfortable twen-ties' bungalow? Somewhere the decorating had actually been *done*.

Samantha, he discovered, was obsessed with slapping Designers Guild wallpaper up everywhere—not personally, naturally, but through the offices of an entire army of decorators and designers. Was he to spend the rest of his life walking into stepladders, tripping over dust sheets, and encountering wild-eyed young men rushing about with fabric swatches?

There were magazines everywhere he sat down. Copies of *Perfect Gazebo, Estate Beautiful,* and the blasted *Insider* magazine that had caused all the trouble in the first place lay open at worrying advertisements displaying kitchens with chandeliers and Palladian friezes, stained-glass-surrounded showers with candle brackets, and bathrooms featuring free-standing rolltop tubs festooned with fleurs-de-lis. Amid the swags, stuffing, gilding, and carving, one thing alone was plain. Samantha's refurbishment was designed to do to The Bottoms the absolute converse of everything Basia Briggs had inflicted on Roland Gardens. Where she had been minimal, Samantha would be maximal. No inch of wall, no centimeter of sofa would go undecorated, uncushioned, unstuffed, or, preferably all three. All that the two projects had in common was the cost. Renovating The Bottoms would, Guy recognized, be eye-wateringly, ball-squeezingly, *agonizingly* expensive.

After arriving at The Bottoms, Guy elected to spend most of each day in bed. His doctors had advised this, but it was also handy to avoid the battle zone downstairs. Even the soft drone of the radio, however, could not quite drown out the fact that Samantha had rowed over the refurbishment with three different designers during the last two days alone. One had actually been fired yesterday for refusing point-blank to install halogen downlighters in the vast and ancient central beam of the dining-room ceiling. Lying with both pillows pressed to his head, Guy had still been able to hear the finer points of the discussion.

"But, Miss Villiers, you *can't* just slap modern conveniences up everywhere. Things have to be carefully restored and concealed. This is a historic house. It was in the St. Felix family for five or six hundred years, after all."

"Yes, and it *looks* it," snapped Samantha, gesturing at the plain walls, stone fireplaces, and Jacobean plaster ceilings with contempt. "The place is hopelessly out of date. Look at the painting on that wall over there. It's practically peeling off. The sooner it gets a coat of Umbrian Sun, the better."

The designer swayed backward on his heels before stalking off over the stone-flagged floor.

Such dramas notwithstanding, the days dragged interminably. Today was his second Saturday entombed in the country. Sitting now in the oppressive silence of the garden, Guy felt heavy with boredom. Without the unending hum of London traffic, it was as if the plug connecting him to some vital life force had been yanked out. Samantha, sitting opposite, was loudly professing to be loving the peace. She'd even gotten twitchy a couple of times when a bird sang at too emphatic a volume.

"Isn't it just fabulous?" Samantha exulted. "Sitting here on the lawn before lunch, reading the papers?" Noticing that she was flicking eagerly through the *Financial Times* magazine *How to Spend It,* Guy's convalescent heart sank. Surely she needed no further tips on that.

He took an unenthusiastic sip of Evian. Despite the perfect early-spring day, his sap was far from rising. The precautions he had taken to sit far enough away from Samantha to render her inaudible had been thwarted; she had merely decided to indulge in a virtuoso display of thespian voice-throwing.

"Isn't The Bottoms just *to die for*?" she bellowed.

Guy did not reply. He almost had, after all.

"That sodding postman!" Samantha jerked her head up at a sudden screech of tires on The Bottoms' gravel drive.

Guy glanced up wearily as the postman, eyes rolling, came grinning over the lawn toward them.

"Not much this morning," he reported to Samantha. "A bank statement—my goodness, you've been spending, haven't you—and some telly producer saying he's returning your contract unsigned and that he's never worked with anyone so unprofessional—"

"Give me that." Samantha snatched the letters out of his hands. "How dare you. This correspondence is private. I'll report you to the post office."

Duffy shrugged. "Well, the letters *were* half open, Miss Villiers. . . ."

"Mrs. Grabster," corrected Samantha irritably. "I use my married name in the country. For reasons of privacy, you understand." She narrowed her eyes at the postman.

"So I had to take them out to get them back in properly, if you see what I mean," Duffy continued, not batting an eyelid.

Samantha examined the envelopes. They showed every sign of having been securely sealed previously.

"Some people like me to read their letters for them, anyway," the postman elaborated. "The old ladies especially. Easier than them scrabbling all morning to find their magnifying glasses and then spending all afternoon trying to understand somebody's handwriting."

Talk of infirm old ladies sent Samantha's thoughts flying to the president of the Eight Mile Bottom Amateur Dramatic Society, the eccentric-sounding Dame Nancy, whom she planned to visit that very afternoon. As luck—and the phone book—had it, the leader she planned to oust lived in the very next house on the High Street, a residence with the decidedly bizarre name of Illyria. Samantha allowed a small smile to curve her lips. As coups went, it should be bloodless. Ancient, senile, and very possibly incontinent in the bargain, she was almost certainly one of the postman's old ladies.

"Consuela's rushing across the lawn," Guy remarked in a bored drawl before Samantha could have her suspicion confirmed. "She looks very flustered."

The postman immediately dropped his bag on the grass and began to rummage through it. "Just checking there's nothing else," he muttered.

"I still can't *believe* you managed to persuade Consuela to come to The Bottoms," Guy said as the Filipina neared them. "You were absolutely ghastly to her in London. Paid her peanuts, made her slave all hours. Why on *earth* should she want to work for you again?"

The postman's search became more frantic. He had tipped practically the entire contents of his bag on the lawn and was listening intently.

"I don't know what you mean," Samantha gave Guy an innocent, blinking stare. "How was I ghastly to Consuela? I always let her put whatever she wanted on the CD player when she was cleaning."

Yet Samantha was unable to suppress a smile. For the way she had lured Consuela had been a triumph, even though she said it herself. Samantha had known the cash-strapped maid would be unable to resist the bait of a free holiday at The Bottoms; known, too, that she would find it impossible to go back. Indeed, the Filipina had found staying was the only option once her former mistress had pointed out to her that, her illegal immigrant status being what it was, she would feel duty bound to report her to the authorities should Consuela return to London.

"Madam. Madam."

"What is it, Consuela? Burned the soufflé again, have we?" It had, Guy recalled, been over a year since the incident occurred. But Samantha had never allowed her to forget it.

"No, madam. Ees the Lady Avon. He is in the hall stairs. For seeing you, madam."

Forgetting even to be irritated at Consuela's uncertain grasp of English, Samantha shot a triumphant glance at the gawking postman. Suddenly, she was gratified to have an audience. Her first visit from a local aristocrat was something she was proud—nay, needed—to have made public. "The Lady Avon?" she repeated, caressing the precious syllables with her tongue. "Her ladyship is in the hall stairs? In the hall, I mean?"

Consuela nodded. "He says ees not a rush."

"Why the hell didn't you tell me before?" But Samantha was ranting for form's sake, too jubilant to be really angry. "Surely she telephoned to make an appointment?"

Consuela shook her head vigorously. "No, madam. Ees only just arrived, madam. Weeth suitcase."

"With *suitcase*?" Samantha's head whirled. Was this what happened once you moved into a manor house? Did all manner of aristocracy suddenly descend on you without warning? After all, she thought with mounting excitement, the titled spent weekends in one another's country piles, didn't they? This was her chance to join the musical Chippendale chairs. "Her ladyship must have come to stay," she declared, thrilled.

"Stay?" echoed Guy in dismay. "But where the hell will she sleep? The place is a building site."

"In *our bedroom,* of course," snapped Samantha. Guy's face plummeted. "Get it ready, will you, Consuela? Make sure the wastepaper bin is empty and lined with a clear plastic bag. Oh, and polish the bath. There mustn't be a single drop of water in it." She recalled reading something to this effect about the state bedrooms at Blenheim. "Oh, and put some notepaper out on the dressing table. *Writing* paper, I mean."

"What the hell for?" asked Guy.

"Letters," muttered the postman, his eyes bulging with hope.

Samantha rose to her feet and dusted down the front of her suit. Thank goodness she looked smart. In Dame Nancy's honor, she'd opted for the white waffle Dior this morning.

"Coming, darling? To meet her ladyship?"

Still pawing through his bag, the postman looked up expectantly. *"Coming?"* she repeated, directing the question forcefully at Guy.

Guy shook his head and watched as Samantha trotted proudly across the lawn and through the French windows. Picking up his bag at last, the postman eagerly followed.

CHaPTER
9

With the cottage now the property of Rosie and Mark, "Green-er Pastures" had finally been unleashed on the Sunday-paper reading public. Much to Rosie's annoyance, the first column had included the vetoed pig incident.

"Come on, Rosie, the editor loved it," Mark assured her. "Said it was just the sort of color he was after. And you have to admit, you were a pretty amazing color after you fell over in all that shit."

Shit was right, thought Rosie, glaring at him. "And another thing. Do you have to call me Significant Other? Couldn't I just be Rosie?"

"There you are," said Mark triumphantly. "One minute you don't want to be in the column at all, and the next you're demanding a name check. Make your mind up, will you?"

As he ruffled her hair and kissed her, Rosie, despite herself, melted. She was an idiot to do so, she knew, but life was too short for sulking and, anyway, Mark was irresistible when he was being charming. Besides, there was so much to be happy about at the moment. The owners of Number 2 Cinder Lane, a pair of hesitant teachers, had been positively eager to complete the sale as soon as possible, the reason being new jobs in another county and some relative willing to put them up indefinitely while they searched for a suitable property. Another enormous stroke of luck was both the building society and the estate agents moving with amazing speed to secure the deal. Rosie and Mark moved with even more amazing speed out of Craster Road.

They had almost no furniture of their own. A beanbag chair, a couple of folding chairs, a portable TV, and some sleeping bags comprised the extent of their possessions. Even so, it was amazing how much room they took up. There was almost no space for clothes—much to her embarrassment, Rosie's underwear had been stuffed unceremoniously against the back window, her collection of graying bras and holey knickers providing entertainment for all passing traffic.

As they arrived at Cinder Lane, Rosie glanced up at the clock tower. The dull gold hands were about to move into the two o'clock position; as she watched, the hammer hit the bell. "One. Two. Three," counted Rosie. "Four."

"Bloody hell," said Mark.

Five. Six. Seven.

"Oh, it just needs fixing."

The rest of the lane was silent and deserted as before, yet Rosie was sure that, behind Mrs. W.'s net curtains, someone was watching. Still, she decided as they began to unload the car, carrying in their few possessions under the concealed eyes of one neighbor was better than doing so under the collective gaze of an entire street. The screech of tires interrupted her as she struggled with the beanbag chair.

"Duffy to the rescue. Here, let me help you with that."

Rosie willingly relinquished the beanbag and, amused, watched Duffy try to keep it under control the few steps from the car to the cottage.

"Nothing for you in the post today," he told her as he returned to the open hatchback. "But Mrs. Sidebottom's vet's bill is enormous, which is funny when you think she's only got a goldfish. And Jack up at Spitewinter Farm's having a lot of trouble finding the right mail-order bull semen."

"Fascinating." Rosie grinned. *Spitewinter.* What a strange and sinister name. Suddenly worried she may have sounded sarcastic, she added, "I'm afraid I haven't met Jack."

"Farms cattle and sheep, and some dairy, he does, at the top of the lane. Mrs. W. next door's his auntie." Duffy paused and shook his head. "Them's his cattle at the back of your garden."

Rosie looked at him with mock exasperation. "Honestly. Is there anything around here you don't know about?"

"Not much, to be honest." The postman's eyes creased with amusement. "No, I tell a lie. Matt Locke. I know bugger all about him."

Rosie looked blank. Matt Locke? The name sounded familiar.

"Is he an actor?" she hedged.

Duffy looked almost scornful. "He's that pop star. Lives round here, he does. You never see him around, though. *Very* reclusive."

"Oh, of course." Rosie suddenly remembered, weeks ago, Mark poring over the pictures of Matt Locke in the *Daily Mail*. Pictures of Matt Locke in his country manor, she recalled. "He lives round *here?*"

"No need to sound like that," Duffy chided. "There's plenty of famous people living round here, let me tell you. And some who just seem to think they're famous," he added darkly as Mark appeared at the door, threw a scowl in his direction, and vanished back inside again.

"Have you met him?" In Mark's absence, Rosie felt obliged to dig for column material. The more she could find for Mark to put in about other people, the less he might write about her. He was, she knew, planning to mention the prominent glass-fronted display of her underwear for almost the entire length of the M1 in the next column.

"I haven't met him exactly," Duffy admitted. "But I'm working on it."

"I'm afraid I don't know much about him."

"*Posh Totty* was his first number one album," Duffy told her, casting a disparaging glance at the box of Mark's records he was unloading, on top of which Rick Astley featured with criminal prominence. "It went double platinum, and so did his second album. Then he went AWOL. Disappeared. Cracked under the pressure to repeat his success, they say."

"So he came here?"

Duffy nodded. "Lives at Ladymead, that big house out on the moor. You must have seen it."

Rosie shrugged. "I haven't, actually."

"Oh, well, it's behind a lot of trees. And as I say, no one ever sees him. But I see his post. Fan mail, mostly—you wouldn't believe what some people send. Knickers and . . . *things*." The postman's eyes widened. "Some of them aren't even *washed*."

Embarrassed, the postman suddenly cleared his throat. "Well, I'd best be off. See you later." With the regulation squeal of tires, he tore off in his van. Rosie waved. It was only then that she realized Mark hadn't lifted a finger to help with the unloading.

"Well, can you blame me with that bloody nosy postman about?" he grumbled when Rosie eventually located him on the loo seat reading a magazine. This, she was unsurprised to see, was the Sunday supplement containing the first "Green-er Pastures."

"He's got lots of local color though," said Rosie, recalling that this was what Mark's editor was keen on.

"You're telling me. Looks as if he rubs his face with bloody sandpaper."

"He can't help being red-faced," said Rosie. "What I mean is that he's full of gossip. He might be useful to you. He told me that there's a pop star—"

"Bound to be rubbish." Mark waved a dismissive hand. "Probably someone who supported the Kinks in about A.D. twenty-four. The countryside's full of old hippies like that. Seriously, I don't know why you encourage him."

You can lead a columnist to water . . . thought Rosie. But perhaps it was boring, after all. What did she know about newspapers? She slapped the two ancient, twisted beams running parallel across the bathroom's roomy ceiling, rejoicing in the smooth and ancient wood beneath her hand. Theirs. All theirs. At last. She bent and peered through the tiny window next to the bath. "You can see the church clock from here! You can lie in the bath and see what the time is. Or isn't," she added, giggling.

"Um, not quite yet you can't," Mark said, gesturing at the large crack in the tub and a damp patch the shape and almost the size of the USA on the bathroom wall above it.

Looking up, Rosie saw that, since their last visit, a whole new network of cracks had appeared in the ceiling. "Oh, well," she said, leaving Mark to complete his ablutions. "Nothing that a bit of plaster won't sort out, I imagine." She decided not to dwell on the fact that the only sort of plaster she and Mark had previously applied was the type one put on a blister. They'd got their dream cottage, hadn't they? Nothing—least of all a few cracks—was going to be allowed to spoil it.

She went back downstairs to find that a folded piece of paper, printed on both sides, had been pushed through the letterbox. The village newsletter, Rosie realized with delight as she opened it. She leaned against the window ledge, lost in the romantic detail of church cleaning rotas ("Would the person who failed to return the Lemon Jif kindly do so?") and the need to select a carnival queen for the next summer fête ("The persistent rumor that last year's queen is currently up on a drug charge is unsubstantiated and should discourage no one."). As Mark thundered downstairs, Rosie was buried in the continuing controversy surrounding the village recreation ground, where trouble had sprung up due to the cricket net's position too near the basketball court. Balls, it seemed, were flying indiscriminately in all directions.

"Look," she said, holding out the newsletter. "There's stacks of material here. It's so funny and sweet."

As before, Mark frowned. "I wouldn't put anything as obvious as *that* in 'Green-er Pastures.' Credit me with a little originality, *please*."

"But the cricket net story's hilarious. It's carnage on that recreation ground by the sound of it."

"What's for dinner?" asked Mark, emphatically changing the subject.

"The bath is fine if we stick one of those rubber shower things on the taps and keep the water away from the cracked bit," Mark announced the next morning after they had both washed in the bathroom sink. "We can't afford a new one anyway."

Rosie rubbed her aching back. One night in a sleeping bag on the gritty floor had made her begin to wonder whether their almost complete lack of furniture was the romantic adventure Mark insisted it was. Starting from scratch was all very well—Rosie dug with her nail at the small red bump on her ankle—but not if things were biting you as a result of it. She added Jungle Formula insect repellent to the mental shopping list she had spent much of the sleepless night compiling.

"We really should go shopping," she said gently. "We need a sofabed and maybe a kitchen table. Perhaps there's somewhere we can get them cheap. We only need to ask someone."

"But who?" asked Mark. "Not that bloody postman. Don't want him getting into our business any more than he is already."

Rosie remembered the cream pots and Popsicle sticks being put to use in Mrs. W.'s back garden. Their thrifty neighbor would certainly know where cheap furniture was to be had.

"Yes, she might." At the suggestion, Mark opened his hazel eyes innocently and flashed Rosie a devastating smile. "Why don't you go and ask her?"

"Why me? Why don't you go?"

"You're better at it."

"No, I'm not. You go. You might get something for the column out of it."

Mark snorted scornfully. "Doubt it. No, seriously, you go. I've got work to do. Got to start thinking about the third column."

The knickers and bras were obviously staying. With a sinking heart, Rosie went outside and knocked on the door of the cottage below. A thrill of fear slithered through her stomach. She was about to discover who, or what, lurked behind the mysterious net curtains.

Fully expecting a crabbed and bent crone, Rosie was confounded to find the door opened by a bright-eyed old lady with a flowered apron tied over a polka-dot dress. "Come in, do," she said to Rosie. "I've been meaning to pop round and say hello. But I've been that busy!" She let out a girlish giggle and stretched out a hand. "Dora Womersley. How do you do?"

The first thing about the dark and low-ceilinged interior that struck Rosie was that the air smelled thickly of gravy. Lunch was clearly well on its way. The second was an old man in a burgundy sweater and carpet slippers beside the fire. Despite what sounded like the local sports program turned up to a window-shattering volume, and the radio's position on the mantelpiece on a level with his ear, he seemed to have just woken up. "Hello, duck," he shouted, catching sight of Rosie. "Thought I heard someone come in." He was clearly very deaf.

"Hello," Rosie bawled back. "I'm Rosie. I've just moved in next door."

"That's right," shouted Mr. Womersley. "Come and stand over here by t'fire and get warm." The glowing coals beside him packed the punch of a smelting furnace, Rosie realized as she took up his suggestion. After less than a minute she had some insight into how chicken tikka must feel in a tandoori oven.

Roasting, Rosie noticed several pairs of old-lady's bloomers strung up to dry on the chimney breast.

"Yon's her Harvest Festivals," bellowed Mr. Womersley.

Rosie stared. What on earth was the old man talking—or rather yelling—about?

To her embarrassment, Mr. Womersley pointed straight at the bloomers. "Them knickers you're looking at. Harvest Festivals, I call 'em. Because all is safely gathered in."

"He's awful, he really is," Mrs. Womersley grumbled affectionately. Rosie smiled. Married several hundred years and still making jokes with each other. Would she and Mark be so comfortable together fifty years from now?

She watched as Mr. Womersley was handed a large glass of something pale.

"Sour milk," explained his wife proudly. "He drinks a pint of it every day with castor oil and sugar in. Best recipe for a long life, according to my mother. She lived till she was ninety. I'm eighty and he's seventy-eight."

"She was obviously right," Rosie yelled politely over the radio, hoping not to be offered some. Glancing at the odd-colored liquid that was exuding an unpleasant smell, it struck her that there were some circumstances in which a short life could be a merciful option.

"I don't know if you take sugar," Mrs. Womersley said, offering Rosie a cup of tea and a saucer, "but I always put a spoon in anyway. Stops you spilling it, then."

"Oh, she's full of them tricks," shouted Mr. Womersley. "Potatoes on t'carpet, tights in t'fridge . . ."

"Shut up, you." Mrs. Womersley laughed as the radio roared on. "But it's true," she told the puzzled-looking Rose. "If you put packages of new tights in the freezer for an hour or two, you'll get a lot more wear out of them. And there's nothing like a slice of raw potato to treat a burn mark on a carpet. Fancy a scone with that tea?" The old lady rattled a tin out of a cupboard and wrenched off the lid.

Rosie eagerly put her hand in the tin and picked out one of the oddest scones she had ever seen.

"Funny, aren't they?" boomed Mr. Womersley with delight. "Square."

He was, Rosie thought, just like a naughty, if somewhat deaf and ancient, little boy.

"Yes, because it saves you dough," bellowed his wife. "Think of all that waste if you cut 'em into rounds."

"They're delicious," Rosie said truthfully as the buttery scone melted in her mouth. It had been years since she had savored anything as authentically homemade-tasting as this. Outside the clock struck fifteen. Rosie was reminded that she had not yet broached the subject of furniture.

"Erm . . ." Her voice was starting to crack. Sensory overload was the last thing she had expected from the cottage next door, but the combined heat, volume, and taste were proving overwhelming. "I just wanted to ask you—"

"Are you liking Eight Mile Bottom?" Mrs. Womersley interjected, her eyes bright and questioning above the rim of her teacup.

Rosie nodded. "Yes, but I need—"

"You'll need to meet some people, definitely." Mrs. Womersley nodded understandingly. "Well, I'd *love* you to meet my nephew Jack. He'd be a nice friend for you."

"Jack up at the farm? Spitesomething?" Rosie could not quite remember the name.

Mrs. Womersley flew to the radio and turned it down. She smiled and nodded vigorously. "Winter. Spitewinter. So you've met him?" She looked delighted. "He never said. Nice boy, Jack. Works very hard."

"No, the postman told me." In the sudden silence, Rosie's ears were ringing almost as loudly as the radio had been. "Said he'd been having a few problems with his, um, cattle feed."

Mrs. Womersley frowned. "That postman. Sickening nuisance, he is. Poking his nose in where he's no business, left, right, and center."

"Anyway, about furniture," Rosie said, making a final desperate lunge at the subject.

"Slapton," said the old lady immediately. "You need to go to Slapton."

Rosie nodded. Slapton, as she well knew from driving through it from the motorway, was the local small town whose setting at the bot-

tom of a basin surrounded by high hills gave it an aspect of unremit-
ting gloom.

"Bought our settee there when we got married, we did." Mrs.
Womersley waved a wrinkled hand at an ancient piece of furniture almost entirely covered with assorted hand-knitted rugs. "Mind you,
that were fifty year ago. Fifty year and not worn out yet," she said,
glancing fondly at the exhausted-looking sofa.

"Well, I've had you fifty bloody year and haven't worn *you* out yet,"
boomed her husband from the fireside.

Mrs. Womersley rolled her eyes at Rosie. "Men, eh? Who'd have
'em? You're lucky to live on your own."

Rosie stared. "But I don't. I live with my boyfriend."

Mrs. Womersley looked amazed and disappointed. "Ooh, I didn't
realize. I never saw anyone else beside you and that postman."

"He's a writer," Rosie said, as if that somehow explained Mark's failure to help with the furniture moving. "That's one of the reasons we
moved here, actually," she added eagerly. "For the peace and, um, quiet."

During the past few minutes, Mr. Womersley had stealthily been
turning the radio knob back up. It was now almost as loud as before.
"Peace and quiet?" he interjected, hand cupped behind a very large and
reddened earlobe. "It's like the bloody Somme up here sometimes—all
them kids yelling and banging."

"What kids?" Rosie asked, alarmed. "I haven't seen anyone else."

Kids, however, explained how so many bizarre items had arrived in
her grass. A bent tin tray, a doll's head, a deflated football, among others. Not the sort of things a couple of childless teachers would be expected to have.

"Them kids that live next door to you. All away at one of them
New Age hippie festivals at the moment, they are," Mrs. Womersley
supplied. Rosie's mouth dropped open in shock. "But we don't mind
'em really. They can be a bit noisy, though. Fred's deaf so it doesn't
bother him."

Mark looked up from his laptop as Rosie reentered the kitchen. "It's
so peaceful here," he said happily. "Much better to write in than Craster bloody Road."

Thinking of what Mrs. Womersley had said about the absent, noisy children, a tremor of apprehension shot through Rosie. Perhaps this was not the time to mention them.

"You've been ages," Mark said. "What on earth have you been talking about?"

"Oh, just furniture," Rosie said quickly, slipping out of the back door into the garden.

Outside she surveyed the as yet undisturbed heaps of rubbish and tried not to think of their rumored provenance. Turning her thoughts quickly to flowerbeds, Rosie did not hear the latch lift behind her. Mark's arms suddenly slid round her waist. "Careful," she muttered as he began to nuzzle her neck. "What if Mrs. Womersley sees us from her back bedroom window?"

"Can't say I care if she does." Turning her to face him, he kissed her long and hard, his probing tongue flicking over and under hers. Without detaching his mouth, he pulled her down to one of the few grassy patches. The slow, steady drumbeat of desire struck up within Rosie.

"I'm going to screw you in every single room," he muttered thickly, holding her eyes with his own. He was always so confident she wanted him. But then he was right. Arching her back with pleasure as he pushed up her fleece and buried his face in her braless breasts, Rosie surrendered. Glancing nervously at Mrs. Womersley's upstairs window, she hoped desperately that she wasn't in the vicinity. And that this episode was not going to appear in the third "Green-er Pastures."

CHAPTER 10

Though two days had passed since the Lady Avon's visit, Samantha could swear she still saw Guy's shoulders shaking. She had even cleared her dressing table of makeup because the merest glimpse of a lipstick seemed enough to set him off. She had not known him to laugh so much since the local newspaper interview she had given to trail a pantomime performance. Being reduced to pantomime was bad enough; far worse was the printed plug for the production describing Samantha as "staring at the Theatre Royal, Ilford."

"For Christ's sake," she snapped, spotting her reflected husband giggling to himself as she clamped on her eyelash curlers before the mirror. "Grow up, will you?" Yet her braggadocio hid a secret pain. After the raised social hopes and expectations her advent had occasioned, the reality of the Lady Avon had proved a dire disappointment.

Although Samantha had clacked across The Bottoms' marble-floored hall with her smile undiminished, the first sight of her ladyship had not exactly been as expected. The small, plump figure with the orange-penciled eyebrows had been something of a shock to one like Samantha, who had been anticipating an elegant personage with aristocratic ankles and earls on both sides. There were most certainly *pearls* on both sides, however—vast plastic encumbrances weighing heavily on each of the Lady Avon's ears.

A second surprise was the extent to which her ladyship seemed occupied by the subject of personal grooming. Over drinks in the drawing room, the conversation had roamed widely over the rival advantages of various mascaras, all of which her ladyship seemed to be wearing at once. During lunch, the talk had moved on to men's moisturizers. It was only when the Lady Avon announced to Guy that it didn't matter if he had skin like a Brillo pad, she just happened to have some male facial serum with her, that everything suddenly made sense. As she opened the case beside her chair, Guy's nonplussed expression gave way to barely suppressed hysteria as he realized that they were entertaining not the Lady Avon but the Avon Lady, a native of Eight Mile Bottom called Lorraine Biggs.

Samantha's reception of the news had taken a different, angrier turn, particularly after she had been informed, as part of a "free facial evaluation," that her crows-feet were "irreversible but possibly disguisable." The trauma had been such that, even after Lorraine had beaten a swift, scented retreat down the graveled drive with her case, Samantha had felt too unsettled and upset to contemplate the planned visit to Dame Nancy of the Amateur Dramatic Society.

Today, though, at breakfast on a terrace amid a scenario faithfully copied from a recent front cover of *Gazebo Beautiful,* Samantha felt the trauma of the last two days begin to melt away. Resting against Cath Kidson floral cushions and carefully pressing a crisply ironed tattersall checked napkin to the corners of her lips, Samantha contemplated with something akin to pleasure the antique biscuit tins, jugs of carefully clashing flowers, vintage porcelain, and deliberately mismatched Victorian knives and forks.

Samantha folded her napkin and placed it on the table beside her untouched croissant. Though never more than a birdlike eater, the Lady Avon disaster had been enough to put her off her food altogether. What she needed was a great social triumph. Inspiration struck as she pondered the possibility of making the postponed call upon the president of the Amateur Dramatic Society. A visit to Dame Nancy would be just the thing to lift her spirits. Once she let slip her acting credentials and suitability for directing all future Eight Mile Bottom thespian operations, she'd be running the show before you could say Steven Spielberg.

Minutes later she was crunching down the gravel drive in Guy's Jaguar. Dame Nancy might only live next door, but Samantha had no intention of making anything less than a grand entrance. Feeling the powerful car purr beneath her, she felt restored. Omnipotent, even. She put her foot down, hard.

Her contentment was short-lived. As Samantha shot through the gates and out onto the road, she shrieked and slammed on the brakes, stopping a mere few inches from the back of a large herd of cows swaying up the village street.

Nails dug into her padded steering wheel, Samantha stared furiously at the lurching bottoms blocking her path. Bloody farmers. Cluttering up the road with their sodding livestock at times when important people like herself were trying to make important calls.

Cursing, she threw open the car door and stumped to the side of the herd, loathing the inelegant animals as they lumbered clumsily forward, caked with mud—or worse. Catching sight of the swaying, vast, veined udders, Samantha felt sick. "Shoo! Shoo!" she shrieked at the puzzled beasts, waving her arms and stamping her stilettoed feet.

Panicking, the animals began to turn in all directions, including, to Samantha's horror, up The Bottoms' own drive. Bellowing in confusion and fear, the cattle's hornlike blasts counterpointed Samantha's indignant, high-pitched screams as, banging their bony backsides with her Fendi Baguette, she attempted to chivy the beasts back onto the road. "Move, you disgusting, noisy, horrible, dirty things. Ugh!" she screamed, as a stray mud-plastered tail almost scored a direct hit on her beige Armani.

"What the hell do you think you're doing?" A hulking man in overalls appeared, running up from the front of the herd. "What are you doing?" he repeated.

"And who might you be?" Samantha reverted with professional ease to the freezing, interrogative tones that had launched her career. One of her first roles had been as a barrister in *Crown Court.*

"Jack Meverell. Spitewinter Farm. And this is my dairy herd. Now what the hell are you doing?"

"I am trying to get these *revolting* creatures out of the way," snapped Samantha, feeling, despite her bluster, slightly wrong-footed that the man before her was not one of the stunted, scrofulous, crotch-scratching examples of local manhood she had glimpsed so far. All his features were not only roughly in the right places but were also actually quite reasonable. Handsome, even.

"Must they run amok all over the road?" Samantha demanded.

"You're new to this village, aren't you?"

Samantha fixed the farmer with a beady, mascaraed stare. "As it happens, my husband and I *have* just moved here. From *London*."

"Thought so," said the man.

Samantha dimpled fetchingly, delighted that her air of expensive urban sophistication was evident even to mud-spattered rustics. "How did you work that out?"

"Because otherwise you'd know that my cows cross this road twice a day to the milking parlor," said the farmer flatly. "That's what cows are for. Milk."

Samantha scowled. New to this village or not, she was determined to put her foot down. Lay down some ground rules. Looking at the road beneath the swaying, eye-rolling herd, she saw with disgust that quite a few steaming ones had been laid already.

"But do they have to make such an appalling noise?" she demanded.

"Don't you think it might be normal for cows to be heard in the countryside?"

Samantha's nostrils flared indignantly. "Unfortunate, though, isn't it?" she returned acidly, leaping back in the Jaguar without another word.

As Samantha disappeared down the drive, Guy, though relieved, was conscious once again of the oppressive silence of The Bottoms. Perhaps it was the sheer age of the place that made him uneasy; the thought of all those people who had been born, lived, and, in particular, died here over the last five and a half centuries. It seemed to him that the house had a peculiar atmosphere, although mentioning this to Samantha had achieved nothing. But then Samantha was not particularly sensitive to atmosphere. She was not particularly sensitive to anything.

Besides, thought Guy, she had created a pretty peculiar atmosphere of her own. The centuries-old whitewashed walls, expanses of ancient oak, and exposed stonework were now submerged beneath a tidal wave of bric-à-brac.

"What do you think?" Samantha had asked him, showing him round her finished handiwork.

"It looks," Guy had told her, "as if you bought the entire contents of an antiques shop and just stuck it up everywhere."

Samantha had turned, open-mouthed, from her attempts to light a cigarette off the stove. "How the hell do you know about that? You were in the hospital at the time."

There were toffee hammers in the loo, a mangle on the half-landing, even an antique typewriter case hanging, flanked by several corn dollies and an Edwardian summer hat, from the beam in the center of their bedroom. The tiniest cranny had failed to escape Samantha's attentions; every minuscule recess, every little gap had its own particular arrangement of fans and dried flowers. The result, in Guy's opinion, was the complete smothering of the noble proportions and considerable character of what had been, despite its odd atmosphere, a fine seventeenth-century manor house.

The kitchen, formerly a cool expanse of stone flags, whitewash, and timber, now contained enough pewter tankards to supply an Elizabethan tavern. An antique knife-grinder stood on a table between an utterly purposeless can punctured with holes in a heart shape and a miniature dried tree in a pot. Barely a square inch of wall went unfestooned with chopping boards, clocks, and absurdly small pictures of absurdly large pigs, while in the center of the room, a carved and stenciled butcher's block stood stuffed with wicker baskets, its surface a riot of gingham and empty wine bottles.

Clay pots and bowls lay scattered about everywhere, resembling an astonishingly well-preserved archaeological haul. Hanging from the ceiling were copper pans, dangling so low that Guy, who was well over six feet, smashed his head four times making the return journey from the fridge to the kettle.

His head aching with the intensity of the decorations, Guy wandered, mug of tea in hand, into the sitting room. The traditional restraint of the decoration—plaster cornices and a carved fireplace—had now given way to what looked like an explosion in a toile de Jouy factory. No chair, no surface seemed to have escaped being smothered in what Guy, who had come to hate it, thought of as that bloody awful printed stuff. Even the fender sported the same, hideously familiar groups of lounging swains and shepherdesses.

The room was otherwise dominated by a scattering of chaises longues, small footstools, and occasional tables, so named, Guy supposed, because he occasionally fell over them. Each supported an array of silver baskets, blue and white china vases, and countless painted bowls, filled with nuts, chocolates, or small marble balls of puzzling uselessness.

Amid the Drambuie, Amaretto, and Cointreau on the mock-Georgian drinks cart, two decanters sported silver labels engraved with "His Lordship's Tipple" and "Her Ladyship's Tipple" respectively. While Guy hated the labels with a passion, Samantha loved them. A frequent topic of dinner conversation was whether (Samantha) or not (Guy) they should buy a title. Since the visit of the Lady Avon, however, the subject had thankfully been dropped.

Surrounded by this riot of decoration, Guy found himself longing for somewhere old, dark, and deeply traditional. Somewhere that served beer as well, preferably. He could take advantage of Samantha's absence to nip round the corner to the Barley Mow. Recently, on the pretext of taking healthy walks around the village, Guy had spent an increasing amount of time admiring Alan's beautifully kept Hairy Helmet. Samantha, however, had begun to suspect something.

"You're not drinking anymore?" she had demanded.

"No. I'm not drinking anymore," Guy had replied, crossing his fingers behind his back. Just the same amount as before, he thought.

But far more worrying than her policing his alcohol consumption was Samantha's plan to fit out The Bottoms' vaulted cellar with gym equipment. "I'm putting an exercise bike in," she informed him briskly. "And some machines for your weight training."

Guy was appalled. His weight, he decided, did not need training. It was perfectly well behaved as it was. In any case, had Samantha but known it—and he sincerely hoped she didn't—"going to the gym" was the euphemism he had used when going to see Lalla. And although his mistress's St. John's Wood apartment had borne little resemblance to an exercise studio, visits there certainly had been a workout of sorts.

Sighing wistfully at the memory, Guy shrugged on his overcoat, picked up his mobile, and closed the door behind him. He walked slowly down the drive thinking longingly of Lalla. Another reason why moving miles away to the bloody countryside was a pain in the bloody arse. It wasn't as if Samantha was bad in bed—on the contrary, she was more imaginative than most—even if she had recently taken to wearing frumpy embroidered nightdresses to "blend in more" with the "period atmosphere" of The Bottoms. Although what period it now was, Guy couldn't imagine. The sort that gave Samantha headaches and made her less interested in sex than usual, he supposed. That had never been a problem with Lalla. Nothing was a problem with Lalla—she could even fire ping-pong balls out of her front bottom, something she had apparently picked up while backpacking in the Far East when a student. A student of what, Guy had never asked.

It was, he knew, imperative not to get overexcited, difficult though that was while dwelling on the memory of a Nordic nymph in her early twenties with breasts like globes and a body as brown and smooth as a new chestnut. Guy sighed heavily as he crunched toward the bottom of the drive. Off the top of what seemed to remain of his head, he had no idea what her number was and it was unlikely Lalla would be in directory inquiries.

An idea suddenly struck him with the force of a thunderbolt. *Lalla's number was programmed into his mobile.* He could arrange a reunion. Now that he was getting better all the time, and Hufflestein had actually offered him that nonexecutive directorship of the bank he'd been talking about, there were bound to be a few meetings coming up. Slipping into London should be simple enough. Slipping into Lalla, even simpler.

Before he could start flicking through his mobile's address book, however, its green face lit up and it shrilled into life.

To his amazement, it was Marina, his first wife.

"Hello, darling." Though they were divorced, the relationship between Guy and his ex-wife had, despite Samantha's many attempts to sabotage it, stayed amicable. Only just, though—Marina had not been impressed at Samantha's efforts to whisk the father of her child to the middle of nowhere without leaving a forwarding address.

At her friendliest, however, Marina rarely called for small talk. She hadn't now. Guy listened to his daughter's latest antics with increasing concern.

"Iseult's done what? She *hasn't*!" he exclaimed after a few tense minutes. "Expelled for *what*? What in God's name is *car surfing*? You stand on the roof and someone else drives it around? Whose? The high mistress's Mercedes?"

He listened again. "Let her come up here? Darling, of course she can't come up here. Why not? . . . You know why not," he said through gritted teeth. Marina could be so dense sometimes. Or just plain provocative. "Yes, I know it would be good for her to be somewhere quiet for a while, but, believe me, it wouldn't be quiet if Samantha found out about it . . . well, if you think that's spineless, I'm sorry. Of course I want to see her, too. Perhaps next time I come to London . . ."

Trying to find a utensil in another person's kitchen is notoriously difficult—do you know where your neighbor keeps their lemon squeezer?! Trying to find it in your own, however, should not be beyond the wit of man. Since moving to the cottage, Significant Other has been distributing household essentials in the most illogical places! Teaspoons reside in a jug on the shelf, the coffee in a jar marked "Chutney," and the garlic in a striped yellow and white sugar bowl hidden behind some jars of lentils.

Mark sighed. Hopefully this was more the domestic local color the editor wanted. He no longer felt certain, the first attempt at this week's column having been rejected in the most uncompromising terms. Detailing the Significant Other's hilarious adventures as she overhauled the garden, had, Mark thought, read rather amusingly. Unfortunately, the editor had failed to make the connection between the piece's main subject, Mrs. Womersley's tip to Rosie to dab eucalyptus oil on used tea bags to keep cats off the flowerbeds, and its title "Border Control."

"This isn't bloody Northern Ireland," the editorial E-mail had blazed. "You're writing a funny column about the country, remember?"

Mark stared at his screen and sighed.

"Characters," the E-mail had demanded. "Color, action, characters." But just where, Mark thought, am I supposed to get characters in Eight Mile Bottom? Let alone color and action? The only character he had seen all day was old Mr. Womersley fetching in the morning coal in his underpants, and Mark doubted they were the kind of color, let alone the kind of action, readers of an upmarket Sunday broadsheet would relish with their toasted ciabatta and free-range eggs.

Just then, a slight tremor shook the walls of the kitchen. Mark paused, ears cocked, temper rising. Rosie, back from the garden center already? Bang. There it was again. A sort of crash, like someone throwing a hand grenade at the front of the cottage. *Dammit.* How was he supposed to work in these conditions? The editor was right. It wasn't Northern Ireland. But it sure as hell sounded like it. Throwing his chair back with a strangled yelp, Mark rushed out of the kitchen to the sitting-room window.

He stared out in disbelief. There, a mere foot or so away on the other side of the pane, an enormous and unkempt black and white dog was relieving itself enthusiastically all over the pansies Rosie had only just bought, potted and put outside to brighten up the front.

"Oy!" yelled Mark, flinging open the front stable door and cursing as its top half swung back and crushed his knuckles. "Get off my fucking plants!" As the dog, which seemed rather aged, scampered away with difficulty, Mark realized that he was not alone in the street. Standing outside the cottage immediately above and regarding him with an unblinking stare were two small, skinny, tracksuit-bottomed boys with wing-nut ears and closely shaved hair. Surmising that the large black football rolling languidly from one to the other was the source of the noise he had heard, Mark looked at them with dislike. His suspicions that they had been kicking it hard against the front of the house were corroborated by the fact that those of Rosie's pansies to escape a canine golden shower were looking distinctly bent.

"Are you our new neighbor?" one of them demanded.

Mark looked at them steadily. "Well, if you live there," he said, denoting the cottage above with the jerk of a thumb, "I suppose I am."

A whippetlike man and a cross-looking woman appeared in the doorway of the cottage in question. The man wore leggings and a tie-dye jerkin. Lank, knotted ropes of thin hair dangled down his back. He looked medieval, Mark thought. Like King sodding Arthur. The woman, too, had something of the fourteenth-century gargoyle about her.

"This is my mum and dad," announced the first boy, confirming Mark's worst fears.

"Wesley Muzzle. How ya doing, man?" muttered King Arthur, extending a tattooed arm dangling with various filthy cotton bracelets. Reluctantly, Mark left the sanctuary of his door to shake his hand.

A woman in red dungarees, staggering under the weight of an enormous baby, was mooching down the lane to join them. As she approached, the wealth of ironmongery along her lip became apparent. Behind her came a further scattering of screaming children and a man with wild eyes, baggy cotton violet-striped trousers, a hairy black and red Dennis the Menace sweater and, to crown it all, a blue and yellow velvet jester's hat, sprouting with bell-strung pointed ends. Noting that the woman's untidy blond hair was shot through with neon pink and, underneath the hat, the man's sported a wealth of orange, green, and yellow string, Mark felt his hands go clammy. As local color went, this was even less desirable than Mr. Womersley's underpants.

"Welcome to the liveliest street in Eight Mile Bottom," said Dennis the Menace, grinning, rolling his eyes, and shaking his head so the bells rattled. Like Santa's bloody sleigh, thought Mark, staring with violent loathing at the hat. Just what was it about the mere sight of those hats that made one want to throttle the wearer?

"Liveliest street?" Mark repeated, forcing his lips across his teeth in as much of a smile as he could manage. "Well, I must say it's been as silent as a tomb the whole time we've been here."

"That's because we haven't been around." Dungarees laughed as the children continued to scream and chase one another up and down the lane. "We've been away. Just got back, in fact."

She gestured toward the bottom of the lane, where what looked like the contents of a scrapyard were heaped up along the church wall. Filthy, battered, and with headlights and windows missing, all that was new about these vehicles was the fact that they had just arrived. Despite the "Go Green" and "Save the Planet" stickers plastered liberally over the windshields, they looked as if, collectively, they could destroy the ozone layer in nanoseconds.

Mark's chest felt tight. A movement in his own upstairs window caught his eye. That the children had disappeared he had vaguely registered; what he had failed to notice was that they had disappeared through the door of his cottage.

"Would you mind," Mark asked Dungarees, "removing your children from my house, please?"

The blonde looked him up and down. "Blathnat, Satchel, Indigo, and Tallulah," she yelled. "Get out of there."

"Blathnat?" echoed Mark as the children dragged themselves insolently past him out the door.

"It means Irish queen," Dennis informed him, bells jangling triumphantly.

Mark smiled tightly as he went back inside. He slammed the cottage door violently shut.

Returning, ten minutes later, loaded up with plants and compost, Rosie immediately knew that something was wrong. About twenty screaming children and what looked like a couple of clowns revving up the engine of a filthy Ford Transit parked next to the church wall were clues. As, when she entered the cottage, was the sight of Mark bent over his laptop with half a roll of cotton wool in his ears. "The neighbors are back, then?" Rosie asked with an insouciance she did not feel.

Mark's deranged and violent stare was all the answer she needed. Looking down again, his fingers began to storm over the keyboard.

Heaving her bag of compost on her shoulder, Rosie retired to the safety of the garden. Here, at least, it was relatively silent. The children seemed to prefer running up and down the lane in front to being at the back, but, given the condition their garden was in, this was perfectly understandable. One peep over the wall that divided Number 2 from Number 3 had revealed a landscape of sprung and soggy sofas, abandoned stoves, broken concrete slabs, vast and lurid plastic barrels, and household rubbish of every imaginable description. It had made the garden of Number 2, even in its original condition, look like something by Capability Brown.

Since starting to work on it, however, Rosie had managed to move mountains—of rubbish, at least. In the course of doing this, she had made a number of heartwarming discoveries. A long-buried stone path. An elderly lavender bush, which, once the ribbed plastic tube crushing and strangling it had been removed, had started to recover its strength.

As geraniums seemed to be on permanent special offer at the garden center, Rosie had planted them everywhere, along with alyssum, lobelia, ivies, and marguerites. Under the wall dividing Number 2 from the Womersleys', she had made a tiny herb border, in which hebe, sage, and mint had not, as expected, given up and died immediately, but actually seemed to be flourishing. The mint in particular, inspiring fantasies of mint juleps and Pimms at sunset in the summer. The result of all this for Rosie was not only something firmly resembling a garden, but the discovery that she had far greener fingers than she had ever suspected.

That most of the time they were black with soil was not a problem. What was, was that they were no longer black with ink. It was increasingly hard to ignore the fact that, since arriving at Eight Mile Bottom, illustration work had practically dried up. New commissions were, for some reason, much harder to drum up than Rosie had anticipated, despite the many assurances the magazine art editors had given her before she left London. The suspicion that her lack of work was related to her having moved beyond the magic boundary of the capital was one she tried hard to suppress. Even a particularly promising book illustration project, spawned from a party invitation design and practically in the bag when they had lived on Craster Road, seemed recently to have drifted as well.

Rosie sighed as she pressed the ivies into pots. "Let Me Entertain Ewe" had been a ghastly enough party-invitation-card pun; the design Rosie had come up with to illustrate it, of three sheep doing the cancan, had, if anything, been worse. But the card company had been thrilled with it, and their parent corporation, a big children's publishers, even more so. They had been on the brink of commissioning Rosie to illustrate a whole book based on the characters just before she and Mark had moved to Eight Mile Bottom. Since then, communications had gone dead. "We'll call you back," the previously keen editor would assure her, then conspicuously fail to do so.

Watering her plants, Rosie made a concerted effort not to think either about this or the precarious state of their finances in general. Mark had never been keen to share with her the fiscal arrangements surrounding "Green-er Pastures," and she had tried hard not to press him. But when she finally did, it was a shock to discover that not only was the fee a pittance, but a pittance forming more or less their entire income.

"For Christ's sake, this is a great opportunity for me, Rosie," Mark had exploded defensively. "I can't expect to be paid a fortune as well."

"It certainly is a great opportunity," Rosie returned hotly. "For the paper to set a record low in freelance rates."

That it was Mark's big break, she was less sure. The column was actually showing alarming signs of becoming his big breakdown. It had not escaped her notice that he seemed to be having problems getting material together. Yet none of the subjects she suggested—Duffy, the Womersleys, the Barley Mow, all apparently bursting with rural color and humor—seemed to interest him.

"I'll decide what goes in my column," he would snap. "Anyway, isn't it time you started drumming up some work of your own? You're spending far too much time—let alone money—in that bloody garden."

Rosie, heavyhearted, pulled some weeds from around the base of the lavender. Still, at least the Womersleys appreciated her efforts. Both devoted to their own pristine patch, they were delighted at Rosie's attempts to improve the scruffy plot of land behind Number 2 and had started slipping cuttings from their own garden over the wall to her. "Here," Mrs. Womersley would say, thrusting a plant in a plastic pot at Rosie. "Have one of these."

The key to Mrs. Womersley's gardening success, Rosie had discovered, was relatively simple. "Slug pellets."

"But isn't that a bit cruel? I mean, shouldn't you use beer traps and eggshells and things?"

"Cruel?" The old lady's eyes were steely. "Ever seen what they can do to a garden?"

Mr. Womersley, meanwhile, was a passionate vegetable grower. "These is my prizewinning onions," he yelled at her one day, brandishing a white-skinned bulb of frightening proportions over the fence at her.

Rosie remembered the village show notices pinned up around the bar at the Barley Mow. "Of course. And didn't you win the potato class as well?"

"*Taters?*" Mr. Womersley looked disgusted. "I'd never grow taters, not as long as I live." Rosie, who had not realized she was casting aspersions, racked her brain for a soothing remark. But it was too late. Anxious to distance himself from what he plainly considered the lowest root vegetable of the low, Mr. Womersley had plenty more to say on the matter. "Do y'know," he added contemptuously, "some tater folk have special tater boxes built, so they can carry their prize specimens around with them? Ridiculous, I call it."

"You really should put the Womersleys in the column," Rosie urged Mark, repeated the story over the pasta and pesto that now comprised the evening meal with such alarming frequency that she was seriously beginning to wonder about scurvy.

Her hopes rose when, instead of dismissing her out of hand as usual, Mark looked thoughtful. "I was thinking of something I could do with them," he admitted.

"Really?"

"Yes, they could be in my syndicate."

"What's a syndicate?" Rosie asked. Was Mark considering the national lottery as a way out of their problems? "They don't seem the betting kind," she hazarded.

"Not a betting syndicate, a news syndicate," Mark said impatiently. "You know," he added as Rosie continued to look blank, "where you get together and take it in turns to go to the newsagent's to collect and deliver everyone's papers. Syndicates work really well. There's a flourishing one in the Lake District, apparently."

"But . . ." It was hard to imagine Mrs. Womersley agreeing to go all the way to the nearest newsagent's—as far away as the next village, as Mark had discovered to his disgust—and staggering back, presumably on the infrequent local bus, with the entire pile of nationals that constituted Mark's Sunday reading. Rosie sighed. Would an ever-

rising tower of yellowing broadsheets be as permanent a feature of
their new home as it had been of their old? Apparently not: Rosie tried
to disguise her relief—as well as her amusement—when Mark returned the next morning from making over-the-wall representations
with the news that the old lady got all the information she wanted
from the village newsletter and a good deal that she didn't from the
postman.

As Rosie reluctantly scattered the most merciful slug pellets the garden center could offer sparingly under her newly planted gooseberry
bushes (oh, the pies, crumble, and jam she planned!), the back door
suddenly opened and Mark blinked into the wintry sunlight. Rosie
quailed, expecting just the furious speech about the neighbors she had
come out here to avoid. But he merely said, "Phone for you."

She slowly followed him in, crossing her fingers that it wasn't the
bank manager again. Still worse, the building society.

Five minutes later she bounced ecstatically back into the kitchen.
"Remember that illustrated book those publishers were talking to me
about?"

Mark shook his head. His eyes did not move from his laptop screen.

"Remember that 'Let Me Entertain Ewe' card I did a while ago?
That spinoff book? Well, it's finally come off. They were just waiting to
get a writer, it turns out, and now it's got the go-ahead. They want it
to be about a globe-trotting sheep, called *A Ewe in New York* . . ." Rosie
paused. Mark was not reacting. "They're, um, offering quite a bit of
money as well. We can do the roof."

Even the determinedly optimistic picture the building society sur-
veyor had painted of Number 2 Cinder Lane hadn't quite been able to
ignore the fact that when you poked your head through the loft opening in the bedroom ceiling, it looked like the black night sky scattered
with vast and brilliant stars. Each star being the most enormous hole.
In addition, the wind whistling through the gaps resulted in large
quantities of roof grit being deposited into the room below. Rosie and
Mark were now used to waking to find their hair and pillows full of debris; brushing the bed before they got in was as much of a nighttime
ritual as brushing their teeth.

"The only thing is," Rosie said musingly, "I'll need some more animals to base the characters on. Cows and sheep to sketch and so on.
What I need is a friendly farmer."

"No such thing, is there?" grumbled Mark.

"Let's go to the Barley Mow to celebrate," Rosie suggested. Now
that money was on the horizon, they could afford a variation in diet.
Ann's fish pie, for example. And the pub would be a good place to start
inquiring who might have sketchworthy sheep and cattle.

"Been away, have you?" Alan hailed them as they walked through
the door. Rosie shook her head and smiled, reluctant to admit to the
whole pub that it had been penury and not Portofino that accounted
for their absence.

"Oops. 'Scuse me," Alan said, diving to answer the ringing phone
in the kitchen. "Yes, on today," Rosie heard him assuring someone.

"These two old ladies," he explained, returning to the bar, "ring up
on Wednesdays, regular as clockwork, to check that we've got liver on
the menu. Addicted to the stuff, they are. Me and Ann call 'em the
Liver Birds."

"Hate liver, I do," interrupted the man with the white beard, arriving at the bar with a man with a very long, very red, and very wet-
looking nose. "Vile stuff. Couldn't eat it. Not even with gravy."

"Met someone called Vile once, I did," Alan chipped in. " 'Vile by
name and vile by nature I am,' she told me. She was about twenty stone
and said she hadn't taken her makeup off for two years. Mind you, she
thought she was gorgeous. Said the bloke next door was a Peeping Tom
who'd drilled a hole in the fence so he could look at her legs when she
walked down to the outside toilet."

There was an impressed silence at this. The man with the long nose
sniffed. "Your nose is running," said the man with the white beard.
"You'd best wipe it."

"You wipe it," said Long Nose. "You're nearer."

Shoulders shaking, Rosie nudged Mark. He had missed the whole
bizarre exchange. At least he was very obviously not listening to it.

"Do you know any friendly farmers?" Rosie asked Alan as, some
time later, he deposited a huge and delicious-smelling mound of fish
pie on the table in front of her.

"Now there's a leading question," said Alan, eyes twinkling. "I know some pretty strange ones, that's for sure."

"You bloody would," muttered Mark under his breath.

"There's some who run a farm two villages away," continued Alan in his quick, high voice. "Family of eight brothers and sisters, who no one ever sees. Avoid people, they do. They're very shy."

"How do you mean?" Rosie's eyes were round with curiosity. She spoke emphatically to alert Mark to a possible story. Mark, however, positively radiated indifference.

"Put it this way." Alan pulled up a bar stool. "When the postman tried to deliver a parcel there recently, they wouldn't even open the door."

"Very sensible of them," interjected Mark sourly.

"He looked through the letterbox and saw eight pairs of shoes crouched under the kitchen table," continued Alan, unabashed. "Well, I say shoes, but they were pretty strange shoes. Sort of medieval. They wear what their remote ancestors wore, you see. Sort of medieval jerkins and hats as well."

"Sounds familiar," said Mark bitterly. He was, Rosie knew, thinking of Cinder Lane.

"And they haven't been to bed for sixty years," Alan added, clearly getting into his stride. Mark made a strangled noise of disbelief.

"Impossible," said Rosie.

"Not if you live on Cinder Lane, it bloody isn't," muttered Mark.

"No, they all sleep upright in armchairs, you see," Alan explained. "Keep the same hours as their cattle. And their dogs sleep in a tree. And the last time one of the sisters appeared in public she was walking backward down the village street, strangling a rat in a bucket."

Rosie looked eagerly at Mark. If this wasn't color, she didn't know what was.

"I think," Mark said, seizing his plate of liver and mash and standing up abruptly, "that I'll finish my lunch outside."

They walked back to the cottage in silence. Rosie escaped immediately into the garden and went to admire the cattle over the back wall. Gold, white, and auburn backs swaying together, they presented a timeless picture. Looking at their noble heads bowed contentedly to the hillside grass, Rosie felt soothed.

"Margaret says if you take your trousers down she'll do it," came Mrs. Womersley's voice, high and sudden, from the garden next door. "Says she'll put that new zip in, I mean," Mrs. Womersley added crossly, as if something altogether more exciting had occurred to her spouse.

"Sorry to interrupt you, Mrs. Womersley," Rosie said, jerked out of her bovine contemplation as an idea occurred to her. "But you know you mentioned your nephew the farmer . . . ?"

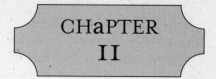

Illyria. Bloody odd name, thought Samantha, pulling up outside Dame Nancy's house. Bloody odd place, too. Her gaze dwelt with great satisfaction on the shabby Georgian building less than half the size and definitely less than a third of the value of The Bottoms. A mud-spattered Peugeot lurked at the side of the house. Samantha lost no time in parking the gleaming Jaguar right next to it.

So far, so satisfactory. Samantha was confident that the air of galloping decay about Dame Nancy's house accurately reflected the dilapidated state of its owner. The only puzzle was the dame bit. Possibly, Samantha thought, the reward for a lifetime's dedication to Meals on Wheels or for embroidering a record number of church kneelers for the diocese. In which case, persuading her to relinquish the reins of thespian power would be like taking candy from a baby. She would probably never have met a proper actress before. Let alone a celebrity.

The days of the Eight Mile Bottom Amateur Dramatic Society were numbered. Standing in the wings and fidgeting with impatience were . . . cue drum roll . . . the Samantha Villiers Players. Forget Gilbert and Sullivan. Forget *Half a* bloody *Sixpence*. She'd have them doing Pinter and Ayckbourn before you could say Tom Stoppard.

Samantha swung her legs elegantly out of the Jaguar and admired her sleek kneecaps with satisfaction. She pointed the key fob at the car.

The reassuring beep was, however, drowned by a disconcerting squawk. Looking down in panic, Samantha saw with horror that a large bird with blue-black feathers was staring at her ankles with mean little eyes. Fear mounted within her as it stabbed the ground near her ankle with its beak. Huge, gleaming, and with intimidating-looking red wobbly bits all over its face, it looked, she thought, like a vicious creature. Like a pheasant crossed with an eagle. Or maybe even a vulture.

"Fuck off!" Samantha flapped furiously at the bird. Squawking indignantly, it retreated to join a number of others pecking about the dusty corners of Illyria's moldering portico. As she stood rooted to the spot, the peeling front door flew open to reveal a woman wearing an apron and holding a cerise feather duster.

"What are you laughing at, you *naughty* things?" she demanded to the birds bobbing and pecking about her feet. As Samantha watched in disgust, she swooped down, grabbed the largest, and held it in her arms. "Oh, so sorry," she said, spotting Samantha. "I do hope they didn't startle you. They are rather curious, I'm afraid."

"Very curious," Samantha said shortly, looking at the feather duster and wondering if this was Dame Nancy's cleaner.

"Adorable, aren't they?" The woman smiled. Samantha couldn't help noticing that she was rather glamorous for a cleaner. As well as possessing an unexpectedly deep and sexy voice—unexpected for a home help, that was—the woman was tall and straight-shouldered, with white-blond hair framing an elegant, high-cheekboned face. "Larry and Judi are Black Orpingtons, but Denholm and Dirk here are Buffs," she was saying. "And in the back we've got Vanessa and Prunella, a couple of Brahmas . . ."

Samantha smiled, eager to get the upper hand. "Orpingtons. Oh, I *thought* so. Knew they weren't hens, at any rate."

The cleaner, who, for some reason, looked vaguely familiar, was now staring in amazement at Samantha. "But they *are* hens. Apart from Larry, who's a cockerel, of course. And they're all very fast—they always do terribly well in the Barley Mow hen races."

Samantha gaped. Hen races? What on earth was the woman talking about? "I've come to see your mistress," she said haughtily.

"Mistress?" A slight frown creased the suspiciously miraculous smoothness of a brow of at least fifty summers. Dame Nancy was paying her cleaner far too much if she could afford Botox injections. Samantha smiled. The old woman was obviously even battier than she had imagined.

"Dame Nancy. Of the Amateur Dramatic Society."

The cleaner laughed huskily. "That's me."

Samantha could not have been more shocked if she had plunged her steel stiletto heel into an electrical socket. Thank God, she thought, that her acting training allowed her to appear glacially composed despite any amount of inner turmoil.

"You look rather surprised," observed an amused Dame Nancy. She made a long-fingered, elegant gesture at her apron. Which, Samantha now noticed, was tied to a splendid, statuesque figure. "Sorry if I look a fright. Been doing a spot of housework. What can I do for you, anyway?"

"I'm your new neighbor, and—"

"Oh!" Dame Nancy clasped her hands rapturously to an exceptionally shapely bosom. "From The Bottoms? How wonderful. We've all been dying to meet you. We've heard all about you."

Samantha's smile tightened. Not from that bloody postman, she hoped. It was hard not to be flattered, however.

Dame Nancy was practically hopping from foot to foot in excitement.

"Do come in, please," she urged. "Larry will lead the way. He really is very proprietorial." She kissed the top of the cockerel's head, put him on the ground, and followed him as he scurried into the house. "Have to carry this everywhere in case he poos," she explained, whisking a cloth out of her apron pocket. "But chicken poo isn't too bad. Dries quite quickly."

Suddenly feeling as if she were about to throw up, Samantha followed her hostess into a shabby but elegant hallway. She looked nervously behind her at the following hens. Would they poo on her Armani? How could this bizarre woman even think about having them in the house? But the place was hardly a palace, Samantha thought with satisfaction, noting an ancient and thin-legged chair covered in extremely tatty fabric. Dame Nancy must really be up against it to have furniture like this.

Noticing her looking closely at the chair, Dame Nancy tapped the back of its delicate frame. "Louis Seize. You can sit on it though."

Samantha looked at her uncomprehendingly. Who was Lewie and why had he said that?

Dame Nancy smiled at her. "This calls for a celebration. Martini? Bit naughty, I know, but it's not too far off lunchtime, after all."

"Perfect," said Samantha, flattered. Obviously, she wouldn't dream of jumping to conclusions, but doubtless Dame Nancy, knowing of her immense fame as an actress, was merely assuming that this was a celebrated film star's drink of choice. Samantha watched the elegant, tanned fingers, apparently complete strangers to tapestry needles, selecting the bottles on an amazingly well-stocked drinks tray. The many large rings clinked against the glass. "Shaken not stirred," Samantha added. It would do no harm to impress Dame Nancy with her scintillating wit.

Gratifyingly, Dame Nancy burst into a husky peal of laughter. "Everyone says that. It really is impossible to live down."

Samantha permitted herself a slight frown. "But why should the Bond films be lived down?" she demanded, slapping on her film hat at the first opportunity. Best give Dame Nancy the cue she obviously craved. Then they could get on and discuss Samantha's achievements in full. "They're the jewel in the British celluloid crown," she continued, "Masterpieces of the genre."

"I agree," came Dame Nancy's deep, smoky voice. "*Agent of Consent* is, of course, considered one of the best Bonds ever made. Its special effects—"

"Quite," barked Samantha, regaining what was, after all, *her* special subject. But she could not prevent a certain sourness of tone. The fact that one special effect *Agent of Consent* had felt it could do without was herself still rankled. Even after so many years it hurt to remember how some upper-class blond model had snatched the starring role of diamond-smuggling Bond villainess Tiffany Blue from under her nose.

"Who, after all, can forget the scene where Tiffany Blue gets tipped into a tank of man-eating tortoises?" continued Dame Nancy.

"Or the scene where Tiffany paints Bond's penis with platinum paint?" returned Samantha smartly, recognizing that *Agent of Consent,* even if it hadn't consented to her, was the perfect vehicle to introduce the crucial subject of her career and celebrity. Indifferent, for once, to her latest spate of orthodontistry, she ground her teeth at the memory of the role-snatching upper-class model. Tiffany had been the cow's first break; Samantha had itched to give the model her second, third, and fourth ones. Preferably with the aid of a large stick.

Dame Nancy sighed. "Yes. I suppose what I mean is that it's odd none of us knew we were making a masterpiece at the time."

We? What did the absurd creature mean? Samantha was suddenly sick of pussyfooting around the subject. Time to make the bloody woman sit up and take notice. "I was offered that part, as it happens," she said. Well, she'd been offered the opportunity to audition. What was the difference? And the reigning Bond at the time had taken an active—very active—interest in her.

To her irritation, Dame Nancy merely stretched languorously back in her chair and lit up a Marlboro Light. "Darling, everyone on the set was offered that particular 007's part," she drawled in a cloud of smoke. "Practically ran his own casting couch, if I recall correctly. Used to get all these no-hope actresses in, virtually promise them the part, then dip his dick in champagne before getting the poor saps to give him a blow job. Heightened the sensation, apparently."

Samantha reddened slightly.

"I said no, though." Dame Nancy held her cigarette hand in the air and examined her diamonds. "My rule of thumb is never to sleep with my costars. Until after you've married them, of course."

Samantha spluttered on her drink. Of course. *This* was the woman who had beaten her hands-down all those years ago. *No bloody wonder* she looked familiar; those very same features had, twenty-one years ago, been reproduced a million times over on the universally displayed *Agent of Consent* poster.

The woman opposite her slugging back a martini and dressed like an alcoholic housewife was, Samantha realized in horror, the Hon. Nancy Brooke-Sullivan, aristo model turned actress whom Bond's opening murmur of "That's a very nice dress you're almost wearing" had catapulted to international stardom in *Agent of Consent*. Her dazzling early fame, followed by a distinguished career in theater, film, and the more lucrative of the divorce courts, had been crowned by a Dame of the British Empire ten years ago.

"You're an actress yourself, did you say?" Dame Nancy turned on Samantha eyes of an extraordinarily keen blueness.

Ignoring the last three words—it was obviously impossible that Dame Nancy didn't know who she was—Samantha prepared to do battle. One *Punkawallah* was, after all, definitely worth a Bond film. Even if the subsequent acclaim had been less of the popular variety and more of the critical. Very critical, some of it, as Guy never missed an opportunity to observe.

"But that's marvelous," Dame Nancy interrupted before Samantha, still in the foothills of her *Crown Court* days, had even gotten to the summit of *Punkawallah*. "You must of course join the Amateur Dramatic Society."

Join it? When she had been intending to take it over? Samantha's hand clenched around the icy glass of martini.

"Quite a number of us are former professionals, you know. Some of the others are really rather well known . . ."

Some of the *others*? Samantha's blood boiled.

"It would be wonderful if you might accept a part. I've got just the thing in mind, as it happens. We're doing *The Dream* next—*A Midsummer Night's Dream,* of course—and . . ."

Draining her glass, Samantha's spirits rose slightly. Even if the prospect of taking over the society in its entirety had receded, a great deal of face could be saved by taking to the stage as Titania.

". . . we were thinking it would be fun to have a female Bottom. Great potential, don't you agree? And the fact that you live at The Bottoms would give it a certain . . . *resonance.*"

Samantha froze with horror. The *humiliation*. Bottom! She couldn't. She really *couldn't*. She racked her brains for a way out.

"Actually, Dame Nancy . . ."

"*Nancy.* Please."

". . . Nancy, um, I'm rather busy with the house at the moment. There's a great deal of work to do. The place was an absolute mess when we bought it."

Dame Nancy's fine eyebrows shot up. "Yes, Catherine St. Felix—a *dear* friend of mine—tells me you've been making quite a lot of changes. We're all *dying* to see what you've done," she added, flashing Samantha a dazzling smile.

At this, hope stirred anew in Samantha. It struck her that one way still remained for her to impress her superiority on the rest of the village. No one in Eight Mile Bottom, after all, owned a house remotely resembling the scale and splendor of The Bottoms.

"The reason I came to see you," Samantha gasped, "was to, um, ask you to an, ahem, *party* I am giving to mark the completion of the renovation works at The Bottoms."

Dame Nancy clapped her hands. "What an absolutely wonderful idea. I adore a good party. And I've been to some pretty good ones in my time, let me tell you. Me and *Larry—Olivier*, of course, not my cockerel, ha ha—"

"Of *course*." Samantha was eager to display the reverence expected of one celebrated thespian for another.

"—once raced round Mayfair at four in the morning passing magnums of champagne to each other from our cars. Then we went back to his flat. *Amazing*. The place was *full* of constables."

"How wonderful," breathed Samantha reverentially. "I imagine his taste must have been exquisite. I didn't realize he was an art collector though."

"He wasn't. I mean it was full of policemen."

Following Mrs. Womersley's directions to her nephew's farm, Rosie walked up Cinder Lane the next morning feeling an intense sense of relief. She was glad to be out of the cottage. The day had not started well, partly because the evening before hadn't. Thanks to their recent purchase of a powerful convector heater, the USA-shaped bathroom wall stain had lately shrunk by a couple of states. A sudden and violent rainstorm just before bedtime had, however, heralded the reappearance of Florida, South Carolina, and Georgia. It had taken Rosie and Mark until midnight to reapply damp seal, during which time they noticed that the fungus they had scrubbed off in the first flush of ownership was starting to grow once again.

But this was far from being her only problem. Mark, apparently permanently immured in his bad mood, had temporarily withdrawn all sexual favors. The passionate nights Rosie had been accustomed to, and which compensated for so much, had given way to Mark lying awake until the small hours racking his brains for possible column subjects. By the time morning had come, he was invariably wound up to such a pitch of fury that even the noise of an engine outside—especially that of Arthur's transit van—had him cursing violently under the pillows. The Muzzle family was a daily thorn in Mark's side. "If only I could bloody muzzle them!" he would curse. Once the screams of the children and the thudding of the ball against the cottage wall had begun, Mark usually lost his temper altogether.

"Those bloody noisy brats," he spat. "We're supposed to be here for the bloody peace and quiet." Then, as Guinevere rushed outside and quadrupled the amount of noise by bawling furiously at her sons to shut up, he raged, "It's like living next door to the world's smallest council estate."

Rosie's knees had trembled beneath the duvet. She lived in fear of Mark demanding they go back to London, column or no column. However imperfect Cinder Lane was—and she could see it had its less than idyllic aspects—it was heaven compared to Craster Road. Even if Mark had undergone a complete and alarming personality change since moving to the country, she would still rather they were here. Unlike in London, there was always the hope things might get better.

"But, darling," she pleaded. "There are bound to be problems to begin with. Teething troubles."

Mark snarled back that Dungarees' baby certainly had those, if the amount of wailing it did was anything to go by. "Although," he added, "it's so bloody old they're probably wisdom teeth. Bloody ridiculous, breastfeeding it at that age." But the sting, Rosie noticed, had gone out of his fury; not for the first time she wondered whether the twice-daily sight of Dungarees' naked breasts passing the front door was, for Mark, one of the few compensations of life in Cinder Lane.

"Just look at it this way," soothed Rosie, hoping to appeal to his better instincts. "Everyone knows that a huge issue in the countryside is that young families with children can't afford to live in villages anymore. People like the Muzzles are being priced out of the market. We should be pleased they're living next door to us—it's more . . ." Rosie struggled to find the right word, "*authentic.*"

Mark cast a sleep-deprived look of disgust at her. "And what about the National Antique Vehicle Collection dumped at the bottom of the road?"

"Well, I don't suppose they have any money. Rural poverty is another big issue, you know. We can hardly expect local young families to be driving round in people carriers and Land Cruisers."

"So it's fine for them to riot in the street all day, is it? When people like me are trying to earn a decent living?"

Rose refrained from pointing out that what Mark's editor was paying could hardly be called decent, much less a living. "Well, they're bound to sound noisy," she said. "It's so quiet round here, if someone drops a pin you can hear it the other side of the village."

Mark stared. "Pin? The only bloody pin the people next door are ever likely to drop is out of a bloody hand grenade."

Rosie sighed. What on earth had gotten into Mark? Having spent the last few years in a flat above a Turkish weightlifter who shook the building with the volume of his television even more than he did with his dumbbells, it seemed absurd to object to the occasional yell. But then Mark hadn't been writing a column on Craster Road. It seemed to Rosie that the beginning of "Green-er Pastures" had coincided with the end of Mark Green's Sense of Humor. Her half-serious suggestion that he write about the Muzzles, for example, had met with unmitigated fury. "What? Give that white trash the oxygen of publicity?" Although Mark had never been known for his liberalism, moving to Cinder Lane seemed to have turned him into Archie Bunker.

"We need to be reasonable," she urged, going into the breach for the final time. "We're newcomers, remember. It's very important that we're not seen as intolerant. We mustn't try to impose ourselves on the existing status quo too much."

At this, Mark had turned on his bare heel and winced as a number of splinters slid into it. "You've missed your vocation, you have, Rosie. Forget the art, you should be a sodding social worker. You've got more woolly ideas than a knitwear factory. This is what being a bloody vegetarian does to you."

No, thought Rosie, as she toiled up the last agonizing stretch of Cinder Lane. It had not been the best of mornings. Please, God, she prayed, glancing up at the sun breaking through a sea of patchy clouds, let Mark find something to write about soon. Or else . . . But Rosie could not frame the thought. Things would get better. They had to.

Pausing to get her breath, Rosie's mood lifted as she looked around her. The agony of effort was instantly obliterated by the view from the top of the hill. She gazed admiringly down on Eight Mile Bottom spread out below.

The village, she saw, was not merely one but three different clumps of civilization, each nestling in the hollows between small hills of brilliant green. Directly behind her was the motley cluster of farms and cottages around the Barley Mow, while away to the left lay the slightly more ordered universe of the green, the duck pond, and the surrounding cottages. Nearby, its gray roof sunlit amid mature trees, was The Bottoms. Squinting into the sunshine, Rosie picked out the High Street as it curved up through the village to the lime-green moorland above. As the road led away between its bordering drystone walls, a tiny lane forked to the right to a collection of buildings that, even from this distance, looked imposing. A flag fluttered amid a cluster of castellated towers. Screwing her eyes up so hard they hurt, Rosie could just about make out that what looked like a small town was in fact a large house. Set, to judge from the cedars of Lebanon and avenue of oaks, in a park of some distinction.

Rosie stared, knowing that this must be Ladymead, home of the reclusive rock star Matt Locke. The music industry's millionaire Sleeping Beauty, the reclusive boy with the Midas touch whose record company was praying would wake up and shoot to the top of the charts again. She paused, intrigued, then shook herself and walked on. She had little sympathy to spare for burned-out stars, having problems enough of her own. Still, it was comforting in a way to know that millionaires didn't have perfect lives either. Then again, there seemed no reason why not. Ladymead was a perfect place, after all; Matt Locke certainly wouldn't have fungal growth to contend with, and his noisiest neighbors were probably ring-collared doves. She scowled at the cheerfully fluttering flag. So what the hell was his problem?

Her gaze returned to the village. There was the pink-towered church, with Cinder Lane behind it. Spotting what looked like part of their roof, she visualized Mark toiling over his laptop inside. Or, worse, not toiling but pacing up and down, frustrated and furious.

Still, at least her own professional star seemed on the rise. The book project was perfect, just the type of thing she'd been desperate to do for ages. And, with luck, she'd even found a friendly farmer to provide her with animal models. "You'll like Jack," Mrs. Womersley had urged, eyes twinkling. "He's a lovely boy. So friendly and kind. Very handsome, too." Rosie had resisted reminding the old lady that she already had a handsome boyfriend. No doubt Mrs. Womersley was joking, and in any case Mark was looking considerably less gorgeous than usual at the moment. His attractive features and smooth skin were invariably screwed up with irritation, his generous sensual mouth constantly pressed into a cross line.

As the old lady had instructed, Rosie climbed onto the stile to the right of the hilltop and jumped down into the field. Bingo, she thought. Scattered over the plump green mounds of grass to either side were great shaggy barrels of just-delivered sheep, their newborn lambs reclining nearby. Rosie, always easily moved where animals were concerned, found it for some reason ridiculously touching that their little black faces were the exact width of each erect ear. Her eyes misted with tears. "Poor little lambkins," she murmured, torturing herself with images of abattoir-bound lorries and racks of chops crowned with white frilly hats.

"Which one of you is Edna the Ewe?" Rosie asked them, scanning the curious, ovine faces. One, she noticed, had a look in its eye like a surly adolescent hanging out at a bus stop, the sort of look that would command respect from the most hardened of soccer fans. Blacker-faced than the rest, it was the only sheep grazing apart from the flock. No lambs lay anywhere near it. "It's up to Ewe, New York, New York," Rosie sang to it. Looking back at her with freezing contempt, the sheep emitted a jeering baa.

"Oy!" A man's sharp shout interrupted her musings. "You there!"

Rosie looked up, heart pounding. A tall, broad figure was striding purposefully toward her through the gate on the opposite side of the field. He did not sound friendly. Nor did his dog, a small, darting sheepdog, that ran straight up to Rosie and yapped at her furiously.

What was it about being barked at by a dog, Rosie wondered, that made one instantly feel like a criminal? She resisted the strong urge to run away.

Trying not to panic, Rosie smiled as pleasantly as she could as the man approached. He was unusually tall. Taller than Mark. So tall, in fact, that he blocked out the low sun. Its rays shone behind him, gilding his thick, wavy, cropped brown hair and surrounding his mud-spattered blue overalls with a halo of light. He looked, Rosie thought, somewhat like an agricultural saint.

His expression, however, had nothing remotely benevolent about it. His mouth was as set and straight as a level; beneath glowering brows, a pair of wide-set blue eyes glinted suspiciously out of a tanned and rough-hewn face. "Shut up, Kate," he muttered at the sheepdog, which, subsiding immediately, rubbed her face against his overalled thigh and scrutinized Rosie with the superior air of an es-tablished favorite. Under the liquid black gaze of the dog, and the hard blue stare of the man, Rosie quaked. Mrs. Womersley's nephew might be a lovely boy, but he had some decidedly unlovely people working for him.

"You're trespassing," the man told Rosie flatly.

"I'm sorry," she gasped. "I thought I was expected."

"*I* wasn't expecting you."

Mrs. Womersley's voice floated into Rosie's head. "So friendly and kind. Very handsome, too."

"Oh, my God. Are *you* Jack?"

The man moved his broad head in a curt nod, proving, Rosie thought, that Mrs. Womersley's eyesight was not all it could have been. At first sight, her nephew conspicuously failed to measure up to any of his prepublicity.

"It's just that your aunt sent me here and—"

"You're a friend of my aunt's?" The ice chips in Jack's eyes melted infinitesimally. The glowering eyebrows relaxed.

"I'm her new next-door neighbor."

Although he was far from her idea of handsome, Rosie could now at least see what Mrs. Womersley had meant. Thanks to her stammered explanation, the creases that ran across his forehead suggested thought rather than fury, and although it lacked the sharp perfection of Mark's face, Jack's had a certain dignity about it.

"Oh. Yes. Now I come to think of it, my aunt did mention something about you." He gave her a long, speculative stare, during which Rosie wished she had paid slightly more attention to her personal grooming that morning. Mark had spent so long sulking in the bathroom that there had been no time for anything beyond a cursory scrub of her teeth and a quick finger-comb of her hair.

"Sorry," Jack said. "Got the wrong end of the stick. Thought you were a right-to-roamer or something. Walker," he added, as Rosie looked blank. "Bloody nightmare, they are," he continued. "Wandering all over the place up to no good. Cutting trees down. Leaving the gates open. Last time they did that, one of my cows escaped, ended up in the river, and damaged its leg on the stones."

"Oh, dear," Rosie said politely.

"But they're never about when you need them, oh, no," the farmer went on, his mouth a straight line of exasperation. "During lambing or when a sick cow needs help, they're nowhere to be bloody seen. But the minute summer arrives, there they bloody are, demanding to know why there isn't a ford or a stile where their maps say there should be."

Rosie twisted her hands. What, after all, was she expected to do about it?

Jack seemed to collect himself. "What can I do for you, anyway?" He sighed.

Rosie rapidly explained she was an illustrator and had been commissioned to do a book on farm animals. She hesitated to say more; Jack may have warmed up slightly, but he still didn't appear the sort of person likely to be impressed with the idea of a sheep shopping at Macy's, still less taking in a production of *Much Adewe About Mutton*. Both these rather questionable plot lines had appeared in the post that morning from the writer. Oh, well, Rosie had thought. It was money, wasn't it?

"No problem," Jack said. "Draw whatever you like."

He had, Rosie now noticed, a crumpled quality, a rather bruised, sad-puppy air reinforced by the sloping, melancholy set of his eyes and brows.

"Thanks," she said, and was rewarded with an unexpectedly warm smile.

"I was just on my way back to the farmhouse. Come and have a cup of tea. You can pick your models on the way. Come on, Kate," he added to the dog.

Rosie had never met anyone who covered ground as quickly as Jack did. To her downturned eyes, ever-watchful for cowpats, the grass was little more than a blur of green as, with Kate galloping alongside, they shot across the fields, through a gate, and up a stony, muddy track. Never, thought Rosie, had painting seemed so exhausting. And she hadn't even picked up a brush yet.

SPITEWINTER FARM proclaimed a sign at the top of the track. Once she plucked up her courage, she might ask him about that odd name.

"Careful," Jack said, looking doubtfully at her trainers as he dragged open the battered gate. "It's a bit muddy."

An understatement, Rosie saw. Any lingering, town-bred, toy-farm idea that farms were romantic places with neatly stacked hay bales, hand-brushed cattle, and sparkling cobblestones evaporated as she saw the ground now beneath her Nike Airs. It was a sea of stony mud, with dank, pewter pools of rainwater here and there reflecting a suddenly cloudy sky. In fact, the yard of Spitewinter Farm bore a strong resemblance to the back garden at Cinder Lane before she had gotten to work on it. Piles of breeze block, lurid plastic barrels, and lengths of tubing lay scattered about between rusting hulks of tractors and other alarming-looking items of farm machinery whose purpose Rosie could only guess at. It was obvious, even to her inexperienced eye, that Spitewinter was a far from wealthy concern. Roughly arranged around the yard was a jumble of buildings of different sizes, the largest of which was a ramshackle barn from whose dark interior came a strong smell of fermented hay and the sounds of bovine mooing, stamping and clanking. It sounded, Rosie thought, like an orchestra tuning up.

"It's a bit scruffy," Jack said, apparently reading her thoughts. "Not much money for hanging baskets, you see. Used to be better, but it's only me running it now."

Rosie looked at him in surprise. What on earth made him think she was expecting hanging baskets? She may be an ex-townie, but even so . . . "The house is lovely," she said diplomatically.

It was true. Opposite the barn was a long and graceful gray-stone farmhouse whose ancient roof swooped down low at the front over a row of deep-set, mullioned windows. Behind it lime-green fields piled one on top of the other to the horizon.

Jack dragged off his wellingtons and bent to enter a low front door that was a good foot less than his own height. Removing her mud-clogged trainers, Rosie put them carefully by Jack's boots, which looked exactly twice their size.

When she entered the deliciously warm farmhouse kitchen, Jack was standing with his back to her at the stove. In the gloaming, Rosie could see him throwing tea bags into mugs.

"Why's the farm called Spitewinter?" she asked.

Jack turned, pushing one sloping eyebrow up into his creased forehead. "Because it spites the winter. Keeps you warm, in other words. The walls are about three feet thick, even if the roof's pretty much a colander."

"I know what you mean." Rosie smiled. "So's ours."

Did Jack have a wife? She looked for signs of a woman but could see none. No flowers, no magazines, no fragrant stew on the stove.

"Milk in your tea?" Jack asked, interrupting her thoughts.

"Yes, please."

Perhaps his wife was out at work? And would she necessarily be a wife, anyway? She could be a cohabitee. Or even a boyfriend, although that seemed unlikely. Rosie had nothing to go on but gut instinct, but she sensed something firmly heterosexual about Jack.

He bent to look in an ancient fridge. "Damn. I've run out."

"Oh, don't bother . . ."

"It's OK. Hang on a minute."

He picked up a jug and strode out of the kitchen. Rosie watched him lope across the muddy yard, swinging it, and took the opportunity to look round without inhibition. The darkness of the room seemed intensified rather than illuminated by the pools of light, dancing with dust motes, that flooded in from the deep-silled windows overlooking the yard.

Spite the winter it may well do, but now, in the spring, the room had an empty air. Of the solid chairs at the thick-cut slice of ancient table, only one was pulled out—disproving, possibly, the theory that anyone else lived there—while, with its back to the table, a single worn armchair sagged before an enormous fireplace practically the height of the ceiling. Set into its cavernous space was a brisk little log-burning stove, yet despite the warmth from this and the kitchen stove, the chill from the stone flags seeped into Rosie's thin-socked soles.

"Milk," Jack announced, stooping into the room with the jug carefully balanced in his hands. As he put it down on the table in front of her, Rosie breathed in the warm, slightly sour smell.

"How wonderful to never run out of milk," she said enviously, sipping her tea from a mug extolling the wonders of a cattle-feed company. "Amazing how different it tastes when it's fresh. Not like normal cow's milk at all."

"That's because it's sheep's," Jack said with a grin. "The cows have been milked once already today and they'll be done again tonight. So I got some off one of the ewes. Needed some for the little fella here, anyway. It's his feeding time." Jack gestured over the top of the table toward the armchair before the fireplace.

Astonished, Rosie leaped to peer over the chair's back. Had someone, then, been sitting in it all this time?

Dozing before the fire, on the worn patchwork cushion lining the armchair, lay a tiny black creature that seemed to be asleep. "A lamb!" she exclaimed in delight. "It's a little lamb!"

Hearing her voice, the tiny creature tried to raise its head. Once again, she felt helpless tears rush to her eyes. "Does he have a name?"

"Oliver. So called because he always wants more. Finishes the bottle in seconds flat, he does." Holding a baby's feeding bottle in a hand as broad as a spade, Jack filled it with milk from the jug as he spoke.

"Why are you feeding him with that? Is he ill?"

"He's lucky he's not dead," Jack said, stepping clumsily round to the front of the armchair. "His mother rejected him a couple of days ago, as soon as he was born. He's been bottle-fed since then."

Rosie remembered the contemptuous-looking sheep with the black face. The only one with no lambs.

"I know which one his mother is," she said excitedly. "I saw her in the field. Blacker face than the rest."

Jack nodded. "That's her." Hunkering down, he gently put the teat to the lamb's mouth. There was, Rosie thought, something infinitely touching about the sight of someone so huge ministering so tenderly to something so tiny. She felt her heart beat slightly faster.

Jack glanced up at her. "Want a go?" Rosie, nodding, was powerfully aware of his strong brown hand as he handed her the bottle. "That's right. Just hold his head and keep the milk flowing. He'll finish it soon." Holding the teat in his mouth as the animal sucked, Rosie felt the surprisingly strong draw of his hunger.

"There's always one lamb that gets into trouble," Jack told her. "Sometimes more. Last spring, there was still snow in the fields when the lambs were born. Some of them nearly froze to death. Had to bring them all into the kitchen and revive them with teaspoons of whiskey."

"Here you are, Olly darling," Rosie rubbed her nose on the lamb's tiny, tufty forehead and kissed it. She looked up at Jack. As they smiled at each other, she felt something warm and unexpected surge within her. Somewhere not a million miles from her lower pelvis.

A sudden squeal of tires, a slammed car door, and the slap of envelopes on the floor broke the spell. Jack glanced irritably toward the open door.

"Post," yelled Duffy, sticking his head through. "Better news on the bull semen today, Jack." Suddenly his eyes, bouncing round the farmhouse like squash balls, spotted Rosie in the gloom holding Oliver. They widened in amazement. "Eh, up," he said, grinning. "Y' all right then?"

"Fine, thanks." Rosie was unable to stop herself from reddening. It dawned on her that there was something very intimate in being in the darkened kitchen of a man she had never met before. Not to mention sticking a teat into the mouth of his pet lamb.

Duffy obviously thought so. He raised his eyebrow, grinned, and left in a squeal of tires.

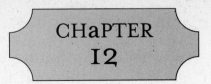

CHaPTER 12

Something had woken Guy. He squinted up into the sylvan sorority of toile de Jouy shepherdesses in the canopy above the bed and groaned when he recognized, in the garden below the window, the hectoring voice of Samantha as she lectured the unfortunate gardener over preparations for her bloody awful-sounding party.

"Tulips down by the gate are looking beautiful, madam," Wilbursdean was saying in an obvious effort to please. He was the latest in a line of four, and a man looking increasingly likely to go the way of his predecessors.

"What color tulips?" Samantha snapped.

"Red, madam. A lovely bright scarlet, they are. Really nice, it is—"

"Red!" Samantha shrieked. "I will not have red tulips in my garden. Red is revoltingly common. Disgustingly vulgar. Go and get rid of them now."

Guy heard the door slam as she stormed back into the house. He recognized the conversation as fatal. From the way Wilbursdean was swearing as he crunched off down the road, the gardener had obviously come to the same conclusion. Torder, the last gardener, had been sacked for allowing some large yellow daffodils to remain in the herbaceous borders. "What was good enough for bloody Lady St. Felix is not good enough for me," Samantha ranted as she appeared before him in the bedroom.

"I've had a terrible night's sleep." Guy groaned.

As a powerful waft of garlic drifted her way, Samantha wrinkled her nose. "You're always saying that," she snapped, thinking she'd have to give Consuela another talking to. Her cooking definitely left something to be desired, and that something wasn't Guy after he had eaten it.

"Well, it's true. I've never had such appalling nightmares in my life as I've had here. Last night I'm pretty sure I saw a strange woman in the bedroom . . ."

Remembering some of the strange women—particularly that one called Lalla—she had deleted from his mobile phone memory while he was in the hospital, Samantha scowled.

"What I'm saying," Guy went on, "is that I think there's something creepy about this bloody place."

Samantha took a long, deep breath. As ploys to move back to London went, they didn't get much more obvious. "Well, I've never noticed anything."

Guy rolled his eyes. That, he thought, could be written on her gravestone. "I know it sounds mad," he continued evenly, "but I'm sure I've heard someone having a swordfight."

"You're right," said Samantha.

Guy looked at her in wild surprise. "You've heard it, too?"

"No. I mean you're right. It does sound mad."

"But I *heard* it. Clashing metal, screams, everything."

"Don't be ridiculous, darling. Consuela sounds exactly like that when she's cleaning the cutlery. And the scream is probably when she drops it on her foot or something. You know what a clumsy cow she is."

"But Consuela's hardly going to be washing knives and forks in the middle of the night, is she?"

"Very possibly," said Samantha. "Consuela has quite a backlog of cleaning to catch up on. As I want everything looking wonderful for the party, I've, ahem, *encouraged* her to work the longest hours she feels she's able."

Guy's heart sank. The party again. Just as he had lulled himself into imagining his worst fears were of the supernatural variety.

"Anyway, darling," Samantha added briskly, "there's something I've been meaning to talk to you about. You know this is the time of year we normally change from our winter to our summer champagne. . . ."

"Is it?" said Guy. The heart attack had been quite useful in some ways. A spring clean, almost. Entire files of useless information seemed to have disappeared in an instant. Including that. His eyelids, despite his efforts to keep them up, pushed heavily down.

"You know perfectly well it is, darling," said Samantha smoothly. "Well, I suggest we change from Pol to Veuve this year. Starting with the party."

"Fine," muttered Guy sleepily.

"And I thought as a party centerpiece we could buy one of those water features from the garden center and get the champagne pumping through it. I'm sure Wilbursdean could manage to fix it, don't you?"

"Depends on how long he's here."

"And we'll have it from six to eight." Ignoring the last remark, Samantha wrinkled her Botoxed brow, trying to remember whether it was smarter to say o'clock after the time or P.M. "Don't you think, darling? Darling?"

She looked contemptuously across at her snoring husband. He could pretend to be asleep all he liked, but she was determined not to shoulder the burden of the party alone. Although she fully intended it to be her night of triumph, Guy, or at least his checkbook, had to be involved. For a start, a number of important catering decisions were yet to be made.

Of course, there was one surefire way of raising his level of interest. As well as everything else. Screw your courage to the sticky place, Samantha urged herself, snaking a hand over Guy's clammy chest and down toward his sleeping penis. Strange how Hamlet stuck in the mind. She was amazed to find him as hard as iron.

Guy, who at that very moment was lowering his mouth onto one of Lalla's nipples, awoke with a start. "What ths . . . ?"

Samantha maneuvered herself on top of him. He'd gotten very fat lately. Like sitting on a bloody waterbed, she thought, stuffing him determinedly inside her and starting to grind slowly back and forth. "Fork supper or finger buffet?" she demanded.

Guy, sleep-fogged and conscious of nothing but the strong clench and release action of Samantha's vaginal muscles, grinned happily up at her. If this was a new game, he liked the sound of it. "Finger buffet definitely," he said, circling her nipples with his perspiring digits.

Samantha was delighted. Decisions at last. Now for the menu. "Miniature Peking duck rolls," she recited at him. "Baby hamburgers and tiny tartes au citron." Guy's eyes widened. Even Lalla had drawn the line at food tricks. At this rate, if he played his cards right, he'd be getting the Ping-Pong balls in the bargain. He nodded hard. "Whatever you say."

"Lavatories," Samantha said suddenly, clenching him hard. Guy goggled. He only got the Chinese clutch on very special occasions as it was, and now she seemed to be suggesting golden showers. "If you're sure," he croaked.

"Well, I'm not," said Samantha. The glossy catalog sent to her by the mobile lavatory-unit specialists, Royal Flush, featured two clear favorites. The Oxford, a gleaming navy-blue van with a marble floor, fresh flowers, gilt-framed mirrors, and prints of medieval herbs on the walls, and the Cambridge, a gleaming ice-blue van with a black-and-white-check floor, concealed cisterns with gold flushing handles, and pictures of stately homes. Both were exquisite. Samantha, remembering the concealed cisterns with particular pleasure, moaned ecstatically. Her hands moved upward with slow rapture over her nipples. "It's a question of how blue we want to go, I suppose," she murmured.

"Very blue," gasped Guy, jiggling up and down beneath her excitedly. "The bluer the better."

The Oxford then, thought Samantha, mentally ticking the Toilets box in her head. Really, this was more efficient than a board meeting. Which reminded her. "Sod it," she spat, leaping off Guy at the precise moment he was about to erupt like Vesuvius. "My meeting with the party organizers was five minutes ago."

For Samantha was taking no chances. Everything about the party was to be as sumptuous and professional as possible. The party would be, Samantha was determined, the most lavish that Dame Nancy, let alone the rest of Eight Mile Bottom, had ever seen. It was her opportunity to fight fire with fire-eaters, not to mention with mime artists, with canapés, and with living statues. To this end—and for the delicate matter of the guest list—Samantha had sought expert and expensive advice from Lady St. Felix and the northern editor of *Tatler*.

They were awaiting her in the sitting room. At first, they were difficult to pick out among the mass of decorations and pictures, but after a few moments of persistent peering Samantha spotted them by the fireplace.

"Fancy dress," she declared, trotting bossily toward them. "It *must* be fancy dress. Marie Antoinette and her court, I thought." She had spent the last few days picturing herself undulating up and down in panniers and a straw hat tied with ribbon. "Now we're living in the country, I simply must do her during her Hameau period," she had declared to Guy.

"Why not do her during her post-revolution period?" had been his uncharitable suggestion.

"Awfully ten minutes ago, Marie Antoinette," sniffed the northern editor of *Tatler*, a girl of twenty-two with no chest whatsoever, the biggest overbite this side of the Natural History Museum dinosaur section, and the name Boudicca Anstruther-Gough-Cleethorpes. She crossed one racehorse leg over another. "Arabian Nights are *much* more fashionable. Zany Hohenzollern-Brigg's brace-removal party was Arabian Nights and it got a double-page spread in the magazine."

Samantha looked thoughtful. It was certainly an idea worth considering. The scene in *Punkawallah* where, as the viceroy's daughter, she had stripped off to a sequined bikini, joined an Indian wedding party, and taught them all the hokey cokey, had, after all, been a sensation. And if it meant a double-page spread in a society glossy . . .

The meeting moved on to the guest list. At the top of Samantha's was the mysterious pop star who lived in what several neck-craning drives past had revealed to be an establishment of truly enormous proportions.

"What's he called again?" she demanded, glittering silver pencil poised over a pad of neon-pink notepaper specially bought for the occasion.

"Matt Locke," drawled Boudicca.

"But he'll never come," Lady St. Felix added. "He's a hermit."

Samantha's eyes sparkled. "What, he was in Herman's Hermits? *Fantastic.* I used to love them." She'd show them she knew a thing or two about pop music.

Boudicca sniggered. "*Who?* They're prehistoric, aren't they? Matt's only twenty-four, bless him."

Samantha went red with fury.

"Hermit as in never seen in Eight Mile Bottom," supplied Lady St. Felix, as Boudicca's bony brown shoulders continued to shake.

Samantha, her discomfiture forgotten, gave her a calculating stare. "So, he's never been to anyone's party in the village before?"

Lady St. Felix pursed her lips. "Wouldn't even open the village fete last year. So I stepped in. Noblesse oblige and all that."

Samantha's heart swelled with excitement. She knew a challenge when she heard one.

"Yah. After both Matt's albums went double platinum, he became a virtual hermit—you know, a sort of recluse," declared Boudicca. "They're saying in the music industry that he's absolutely terrified of his next album being, you know, panned."

Samantha licked her lips, certain she knew better. Of course Matt was a recluse. Bound to be if all the available local company was a load of muddy yokels, tombstone-toothed Sloanes, hen-keeping dipso actresses, and dried-up old toffs. Well, his problems were over now that she was here. There was no doubt he'd leap at the chance to come to a party with miniature Peking duck and smart hired toilets. And what a coup *that* would be. Her star guest, in every sense of the word.

Despite four cups of coffee, half a package of cookies, and five Marlboros, Mark was feeling far from well. The throbbing in his head had intensified. The knowledge that he was a good ten miles from the nearest migraine medicine did not help. Nor did the fact that Rosie had found the whole of last night's episode hilarious.

Why, Mark demanded of himself, was it so amusing that, desperate for inspiration for the column, he had gotten up in the middle of the night and gone walking in the woods at the top of the hill by moonlight? What was so chortlesome about his slipping, smashing forehead first into a tree, and returning home in the early hours with a mild concussion and an egg-shaped lump protruding from his head?

"Thanks for all your sympathy and support," he had snapped at Rosie. "It's not easy, this column business. Try thinking of a few ideas yourself for a change." When Rosie had pointed out indignantly that she was always suggesting things, Mark had lost his temper completely. Information such as her latest offering, that someone had altered the teashop sign and painted out the *h* in Penny Farthing, was hardly going to get the newsroom conga-ing. It had been a relief to see the back of her when she'd left to go to the farm.

Alone in the upstairs box room, Mark stared furiously at his laptop, waiting for inspiration to strike. The banging in his head was almost indistinguishable from the constant thudding on the other side of the wall. Hopefully Guinevere was battering one of the brats to death in the attic. When it came to the slaughter of the firstborn, Mark thought savagely, he was with Herod all the way. After four attempts, the most recent "Green-er Pastures" had struggled past the editor, yet here he was, a week later, facing the tortuous process anew. And with a few special requests from On High to consider. "Get some animals," the editor's last E-mail had read. "Readers like animals. Rumor has it there are quite a lot of them in the countryside." Mark scowled. Sarcastic bastard.

As a series of screams from the road outside rent the air in synchronicity with a staggeringly loud crash from the other side of the wall, Mark sank his head in his hands. Animals seemed about the size of it. Maddeningly, though, Rosie seemed serenely oblivious to the horrors of the rest of the street.

Animals, he thought. Perhaps they *were* the answer. It would be easy enough to keep them—plenty of people round here did, after all. That field at the back was full of cattle that seemed to require no attention of any sort. Cheap to feed as well, just grass. He and Rosie could easily keep, if not a cow, then certainly some smaller-scale herbivore such as a goat or a sheep in the garden. Now that Rosie had gone to all that trouble to sort the lawn out, it seemed ludicrous to leave all that grass unused when it could easily support some livestock. He would get around her by pointing out that not only would it browse back and forth, neatly clipping the grass, but in doing so would also produce eminently useful milk. Not to mention column fodder.

Add a few hens, for the hell of it, not to mention the eggs of it, and you'd be away. Free material as well as free food. Mark slapped his thighs in triumph. What a brilliant idea. Amazing he hadn't thought of it before.

It was surprisingly easy to look the whole subject of animals up on the Internet. Once his modem had battled its personal demons and heaved itself onto the cyber superhighway, Mark was gratified to find a multitude of sites devoted to animal husbandry. There seemed very few animals, in fact, that you could not husband, although he desisted exploring some of the more unsavory-sounding sites suggested by the search engine. Sheep or goats? Pigs or hens? All four? An entire farm, even; you were bound to be able to order one off the Internet, possibly at www.old-macdonald.co.uk. You could, after all, buy practically everything else on it. Mark had even seen a penis for sale once, a wrinkled gray specimen in a jar of formaldehyde, offered on a slightly sinister auction site.

Half an hour later his spirits had sunk again. There was one aspect of animal rearing he had failed to take fully into consideration. The cost.

"You need a minimum of one acre for a sheep," www.mintsauce.co.uk had informed him. Well, that was a downer for a start. Even the optimistic estate agent's details hadn't managed to expand the strip at the back of Number 2 to more than four hundred square feet. An acre would have to be rented. Cost, already, and that was before you'd even got to the animals. "Pedigree lambs cost around £50 for a ewe to £90 for a ram . . ." Mark whistled softly under his breath. "Three sheep is a good minimum. Additional costs include sheep minerals, shearing, vaccinations, plus, when the time comes, £20 to 25 to slaughter and butcher a sheep. Vet's visits cost around £30 a time, or £70 for an emergency call . . ." "Bloody *hell*," muttered Mark. He hadn't realized sheep were a luxury sport.

Chickens, then. Surely they couldn't involve that much outlay, as it were? According to www.cockadoodledoo.co.uk, you'd be looking at £6 to 10 per bird—*that* was more like it. "Costs also include £300 to 400 for a henhouse, food and drink dispensers, fencing against the fox, poultry mash or pellets, shavings . . ."

Next Mark had tried goats. "Goats get lonely so you need a minimum of two," said www.billythekid.co.uk. "Goats need a waterproof, insulated, and partitioned goat shed plus antiterrorist-strength fencing. Cost around £200 to 500 to include hay racks, milking equipment tools, and winter coats. Annual costs £300 to 350 a year for two."

Finally, desperately, he tried bees. Surely they would be cheaper? The discovery that a new hive cost a cool £200 and a nucleus of bees £100 seemed to argue otherwise. Even his next great idea—catching some out of the air—became less than feasible when it emerged that the necessary protective clothing was £80. There was, Mark realized glumly, no such thing as a free bee. Despite what everyone said about journalists getting lots of them.

Costs like these, Mark knew, were out of the question. He and Rosie simply didn't have the money. Yet the editor wanted animals and animals he would have to have. In which case the paper would have to pay for them. Mark sent off an E-mail and girded his loins for the reply.

"You must be bloody joking," shot back the editor. "When I want to blow that much money I'll take up polo."

Mark groaned. The morning was turning out to be a nightmare. The concussion incident had been bad enough, but there had also been the visit from the postman. Duffy had breezed in reciting the contents of two red bills and with the news that some film star in the village was planning a lavish party.

"Film star?" exclaimed Mark, his celebrity sensors out on stalks and outraged at the thought that someone famous lived in the village and hadn't personally come round and introduced themselves.

"Everyone who's anyone in the village is going." Duffy twisted the knife in the wound. "She's even asked Matt Locke."

"Matt Locke?" wailed Mark. The fact that he had tried and failed to find any story whatsoever concerning the reclusive celebrity was a secret source of anguish. A Matt Locke quote or anecdote would have lifted "Green-er Pastures" into the stratosphere. Neither, however, had been forthcoming and Mark dreaded the day the editor discovered a famous pop star lived within a hundred-mile radius of Eight Mile Bottom, let alone eight minutes outside it.

"Not that he's sent his reply card back yet," Duffy added.

"Who *is* this woman giving the party?" Mark demanded.

"She's called Samantha Grabster."

"Never heard of her. Still," Mark said with the air of one who knew all about these things, "I expect she has a different stage name."

Mark sat staring at the door for several minutes after the postman's departure, grinding his teeth with agitation. "If anyone who's bloody anyone is going, why the hell hasn't she asked *me*? Doesn't she realize I work for a sodding newspaper? Doesn't she know *who I am*?"

Rosie, walking slowly up the lane to Spitewinter, was also reflecting on a miserable morning. She was guiltily aware that, much as she needed to get on with the book drawings, the real reason she had left the cottage so early was to get away from Mark again. Any resemblance between the charming, handsome, witty companion she had shared the London flat with and the carping tyrant with whom she now found herself sharing a collapsing cottage seemed purely coincidental. Their sex life, once so satisfying, was history, as were the days when he spoke to her with anything approaching politeness.

"Where's the bloody milk?" he had demanded that morning, violently rearranging the contents of the fridge.

"We don't have any." Rosie sighed, the image of Jack and the feeding bottle springing suddenly to mind. "Honestly, don't you think it *would* be easier if we got it delivered?"

Mark's refusal to have the milk delivered was meant to be an economy measure, but resulted only in rows about whose turn it was to go to the village shop to buy more. Worse than this, though, was his recent ban on visits to the Barley Mow.

"But why?" demanded Rosie.

"Waste of money. Not to mention dull."

"Dull?" Conversation at the Barley Mow had struck Rosie several times as being far more amusing than that at London dinner parties. The story about Mrs. Vile, the legs, the hole in the fence, and the outside toilet still made her smile, as did Alan's rendition, performed on a more recent visit, of his ill-fated attempts to learn watchmending, para-chuting, and ballroom dancing at evening classes. "I'd been paired up with the butcher's wife," Alan had said. "We're both supposed to be doing the quickstep but she starts to rhumba. So she trips me up in a rugby tackle, we both fall over, and I've got me hand trapped under her bust. Her husband runs over and says, 'Oy, what do you think you're bloody doing with me wife?' "

"Dull," Mark had replied conclusively. "Do you think I've got time to sit around in pubs listening to people going on about ferrets, ball-room dancing, and inventing hen-racing competitions? I've got a col-umn to write, in case you've forgotten. I need to think of material."

"Milk deliveries," persisted Rosie, "would save you time and be more convenient." And hopefully put you in a better temper as well, she added silently.

Mark looked at her suspiciously. "What, not getting enough of that sodding farmer even though you're seeing him every afternoon?" he snapped. "Want him round here every morning rattling his bottles as well, do you?"

"Don't exaggerate. It hasn't been every afternoon."

Yet now, as she lifted the gate to the farmyard, Rosie admitted to herself that Mark had a point. Perhaps she was getting fitter, Rosie thought, but the walk to the farm seemed more enjoyable all the time. Furthermore, *A Ewe in New York* was progressing at an astonishing pace. She had made a couple of visits since the first, none of which had revealed any female inhabitant of Spitewinter beyond the dairy cows. Rosie was intrigued by this, and by the fact that Jack, rather than being out in the fields, was always in the farmyard when she arrived. It was almost as if he was waiting, expecting her, although he was careful al-ways to look surprised when she appeared through the gate.

Today, though, there was no sign of him. Confused by how disap-pointed she felt, Rosie started a systematic search of the outbuildings. He must be here somewhere.

"Round the back of the house," called the low, gravelly voice, ac-companied by Kate's familiar bark. Rosie walked quickly down a nar-row, mossy alley along the side of the farmhouse to find Jack in the paved yard, bent before a chicken coop.

As he looked up and smiled at her, her heart lurched unexpectedly. "Come over here and meet Wellington. He's a champion bird."

"Really?" Rosie peered doubtfully through the wire at a large white hen pecking a tomato. It stopped, one scaly ivory leg raised, and blinked at her. "Champion at what?"

"Hen racing, of course."

The hen races at the pub, Rosie thought with a twist of the lips. The ones Mark didn't believe existed.

"Big village tradition, it is," Jack said. "Everyone who's got hens enters them. But Wellington didn't win last year."

"I know." Rosie grinned. "A rogue hen from Milton Keynes did."

Jack looked impressed. "That's right." He stood up, brushing against her in the confined space. Acutely aware of how near he was, Rosie could almost feel the warmth of his skin, the faint peppery scent of his soap. As a blush rose unstoppably to her cheeks, she tried to combat it by summoning images of Mark at his most charming to her mind. Given recent form, it was difficult.

"How's Oliver?" she muttered, looking up at him through the tousled blond strands of her bangs. Hopefully that way he wouldn't be able to see how red her face was.

"Back in the field," said Jack. "Greedy little bugger, he is. Still, the quicker he grows, the quicker he'll be off my hands and on someone's Sunday dinner table."

Rosie, shellshocked, stared at Jack in horror. "But isn't he your pet?"

"*Pet?* Of course he's not a pet. This is a livestock and dairy farm. All the animals here are raised for milk and meat."

"But that's so cruel," Rosie gasped. "How *can* you send Oliver to an abattoir? Or any lamb?"

"You're a vegetarian, I take it." An edge of steel had crept into Jack's tone.

Rosie nodded.

"Have you ever considered that if they weren't reared for slaughter, lambs wouldn't exist at all?" Jack began to stride away from the hen coop in the direction of the sunny farmyard.

"Wrong. What do you mean?" Rosie hurried after him. "They'd exist more, surely. If people like you weren't bent on slaughtering them all."

"The only reason they're here is because there's a market for them. No one would bother breeding them if they couldn't sell them. No more than we'd bother to breed cows if we couldn't slaughter them for meat or sell their milk. Farming's a job. More than that, it's a way of life. What it isn't is a bloody hobby."

"But it's so *wrong*," Rosie flung back, passionately. "Animals have rights. Including to be allowed to live."

"And don't you think I've got a right to make a *living*?" Jack's voice was low and level. "On the land my family has farmed for hundreds of year?"

"Not if you're killing animals for profit."

"Profit!" Jack slapped a hand to his forehead. "Some farmers are dumping their sheep at RSPCA centers these days, that's how profitable animals are."

He turned to look at her, his boot heels grinding stones into the ground, his eyes boring into her like lasers. With a stab of fear, Rosie recalled the hulking, intimidating, suspicious creature she had met on her first day at the farm. As she did so, she wished fervently she had kept her views on animal welfare to herself. A farmer, after all, was hardly likely to sympathize.

But it was too late. "Have you any idea," Jack demanded, "what it's like to run a farm like this? Last year I did the lambing single-handed. There I was afterward, sitting in the bath at four in the morning, knackered and starving, eating baked beans out of a can. I almost gave up on the spot. And do you know why I didn't?"

"No-o," muttered Rosie, unable to tear her eyes from his freezing Prussian-blue glare.

"Because I bloody couldn't, that's why. An hour later I had to go out and milk the dairy herd. And do you know what *that's* like?"

Rosie dumbly shook her head, aware that she was about to find out.

"It's like getting out of bed at five on a freezing morning only to be slapped repeatedly round the face by a shitty tail. It's like being casually stamped on by a South Devon or kicked through the door by a bad-tempered Galloway. If you're lucky. Because after they go back out to grass after a winter eating silage, guess what happens then?"

"No idea," whispered Rosie.

"Well, let me tell you," bellowed Jack. "Their system goes berserk and they shit all over you, that's what. And all for milk that doesn't even realize the cost of producing it. And it's all your bloody fault!" he shouted.

"My fault?" Driven into the ground by the tremendous force of his indignation, she was almost prepared to believe that she, personally, was to blame for his woes.

"Bloody rich yuppies like you. City types, getting everything from supermarkets, giving them the power to drive milk and meat prices to rock bottom. Then you move to the bloody countryside and send the property prices rocketing. Local families can't afford to live here anymore. Let alone bloody farmers."

"I know," Rosie interrupted eagerly, seeing a chink of light at last and wanting to tell him how often she had this argument with Mark about the Muzzles. Tell him, too, that far from being a rich yuppie, she didn't have a bean in the world apart from those she had planted, more in hope than experience, in the garden border. She felt her hands begin to shake.

Jack, however, was far from finished. "Don't you understand that it's livestock farmers like me that keep the countryside looking the way it does?" he hurled at her. "Green and pleasant and all that crap? The reason you bloody newcomers come here in the first place? People like you make me sick. You and that bloody stupid woman the other morning telling me my herd was too noisy. *Too noisy!* Someone else from the bloody city. Someone else who thinks the countryside's just Knightsbridge with sheep."

Rosie was moving steadily backward down the yard.

"Do you know what we call people like you round here?" Jack shouted.

Rosie did not stay to find out.

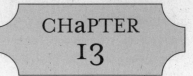

CHaPTER
I3

Really, Samantha thought serenely, life was so perfect it was almost worrying. Even the maddening row the birds made, particularly those ridiculous bloody ducks on the pond, seemed less irritating than usual this morning. As the locks of the Jaguar slid back with their reassuringly expensive clunk, it half occurred to her to wonder about the proximity of good therapists. Just in case she came down with a nasty case of Paradise Syndrome.

The refurbishment complete and all the major decisions having been made about the party, all that remained was to find something dazzling to wear. Samantha considered her wardrobe less than satisfactory, not least because the Harrods furniture deliveryman had smashed it hard against the low ceiling of The Bottoms' front door and had gone on to demolish two light fittings and a mirror as he carried it up the stairs. The theme of the party was now firmly settled on Arabian Nights, but something a little more imaginative than Lurex knickers and old velvet curtains was required. Best leave that, Samantha thought pityingly, to Dame Nancy and her troupe. Samantha sighed. If only her own unique dramatic vision had been allowed to prevail. But then a prophet was never recognized in her own country. Let alone the countryside.

There was, however, one small errand to run before she was free to indulge in retail therapy. Although Samantha had posted most of the party invitations, she planned to deliver Matt Locke's by hand. If she dropped in at Ladymead on the way to town, she might not only meet him but also get a peek at the house as well. No doubt he'd invite her in for coffee; no celebrity ever refused refreshment to another.

Reaching the turn for Ladymead, Samantha, intending to impress the leopardskin pants off any watching rock god, put her foot down and shot as far and as fast up the Ladymead drive as she could. Just round the second bend Samantha screeched to a halt, the nose of the car mere inches from one of many revolving video cameras and complex-looking security gadgets. The gates were, Samantha noted jealously, light-years ahead of the ones at The Bottoms; so high-tech, in fact, that it was impossible to figure out how to alert anyone to her presence.

After several fruitless minutes gesticulating wildly into the cameras, Samantha settled for making a long, passionate, and, she liked to think, professional speech to CCTV. She informed camera one that she was just popping by to introduce herself, had recently moved into the village, was actually *quite* well known as well, *ha ha,* and would simply *adore* it if Matt saw fit to grace her little party with his presence. Samantha gave the performance her all and was disappointed when, despite having a distinct feeling of being watched, no chart-topping celebrity was forthcoming at the end of it. Gathering up the remains of her dignity, Samantha slipped the invitation card marked "Mr. Matthew Locke Esq." into the letterbox and drove away.

Twenty minutes later she entered Cobchester and piloted the car toward a space in the cathedral car park with PROVOST ONLY written across it in large white letters. Do the crusty old provost good if people think he drives a car like this, anyway, Samantha thought, tottering off toward the shopping center.

It did not take long for Samantha to establish that Cobchester's fancy-dress outfits were not numerous. A short trawl round the party-wear section of the one department store revealed rack after rack of collarless suits in matronly sizes or shapeless chiffon tents in beige. Yet Samantha persevered; it wasn't until after she had barked "Where's the Dior?" at an assistant in the smartest boutique she could find and been pointed toward the shop's front entrance that she finally admitted defeat.

As she pushed open the door in question and allowed it to smash unceremoniously into a mother and an all-terrain stroller exiting the store behind her, Samantha's eye chanced to fall on the window of a bookshop opposite. Books. Now there was something she could do with.

The oak shelves in the large paneled *bibliothèque* of The Bottoms remained gapingly empty, following Lady St. Felix's speedy and irritating removal of the set of twenty-five original Waverly novels and other historical literary gems Samantha had imagined were thrown in with the house. Offering her a fiver per yard to leave them had failed to have the desired effect; the result was that she needed old books and she needed them now. And not necessarily by the yard. Pushing open the door with a ping, Samantha wondered if they were available by the mile.

The bookshop was of the old-fashioned variety—undulating skyscrapers of volumes piled in every available space and dusty shelves marked Folklore and Occult Psychology stretching up to the damp-swollen ceiling. It was, Samantha thought delightedly, just like *Notting Hill,* except that the corpselike assistant slumped behind the sales desk bore no resemblance whatsoever to *darling* Hughie. Still, Samantha thought, fanning her Titian waves out over her shoulders, at least she looked enough like Julie Roberts to make up for it. As well as being a film star into the bargain.

And a better actress. Samantha ran her fingers repeatedly along a row of gold-stamped cloth spines marked "First Editions" until she'd got the gesture exactly right. If she lived to be a hundred she'd never understand why darling Hughie hadn't insisted she play the role of Anna Scott. Roberts, after all, couldn't act her way out of a bus ticket, or however the saying went.

"Can I help you?" The dusty assistant had risen from the grave. As his cadaverous face appeared round the corner, Samantha emitted a squeal that was more squashed cat than Hollywood's highest-paid female actress. If this were really *Notting Hill,* she thought, this would be the point at which *dear* Hughie spilled orange juice all over Julia's T-shirt and fell in love with her. The corpse, she noticed with horror, held a Styrofoam cup of coffee in its bony hand.

"No, thank you," she stammered, snatching an experienced-looking volume off the shelf behind her and pretending to thumb through it. As the corpse nodded and disappeared, Samantha glanced down at the book in her hand. Some old claptrap called *Ghosts of the Area.* "A Vision of Doom" read the chapter heading on the first page. "Concerning the Phenomenon of a Mysterious Apparition with Protruding Eyes and Ashen Lips." *Iseult!* Samantha snorted and read on.

It really was too hilarious. According to this volume, the entire surrounding county was riddled with headless horsemen, black dogs, ladies ranging from green through gray to white, and other supernatural phenomena. Doubtless all with completely sensible explanations—"Loud Footsteps and Heavy Breathing," for example, sounded exactly like Guy coming to bed.

One would, Samantha considered, have to be insane to actually *believe* in any of it. Take this, for example: "One of the most Haunted Houses in the Area," promised the chapter heading.

Over the centuries, this charming building has been remarkable for the sheer volume of supernatural activity concentrated on the spot . . . read the opening paragraph. *A ghostly cat, a black dog, screams, the clash of swords and a green lady said to be the spirit of a murdered previous owner of the house are but a few of the supernatural dramatis personae reported. One guest in the 1920s woke up in the middle of the night to see what he described as a "terrifying black ball of hate" flying toward him out of the gloom, while another witnessed a white lady reclining on a chaise longue and smiling at him . . .* Tutting with disbelief, Samantha turned the page. *Less friendly is the oft-reported sighting of a screaming woman with a large knife stuck in her back . . .*

For Christ's sake, thought Samantha impatiently. Black ball of hate, indeed. The place had obviously been occupied by a succession of alcoholics, drug addicts, and others prone to wild fantasies. She glanced at the picture of the house accompanying the text. Pity, though. Nice place. Rather like The Bottoms.

Amazingly like The Bottoms, in fact. Samantha's heart started to race as she peered more closely at the dark black-and-white reproduction of a three-story building in gray stone with gables, mullions, curved bays, and stone lions on either side of the front door. "The Bottoms, Eight Mile Bottom," read the caption. "Home to the St. Felix family for over 500 years."

The blood drained from Samantha's face. She snapped the book shut, shoved it back onto the shelf, and rushed out of the shop as fast as her stilettos would allow her.

Notting Hill had just turned into *The Amityville Horror.*

Rosie sat at the top of the stile, looking apprehensively at the field in front of her. The sheep had gone, as had the lambs, and in their place were several large cows. She would have to walk through the cows to reach the farmhouse. Would they rush past her and knock her off her feet like the pig at the Silent Lady pub?

Could cows, like horses, smell fear? Making reassuring noises in her throat, Rosie locked her eyeballs on rolling bovine pupils and, her workbag with its sketchpads, paints, and paintbrushes banging clumsily against her thigh, climbed carefully down off the stile onto the grass. Amazingly, and most obligingly, the cows started to dance backward, mooing and parting like the Red Sea at her approach. Rosie felt weak-kneed with relief. All much easier than expected. Now for the truly terrifying prospect: Jack.

Mrs. Womersley had been apology itself. Her wrinkled face was puce with embarrassment the afternoon, a few days ago, she had explained over the garden wall that Jack hadn't really meant it.

"You mustn't mind him," the old lady had said pleadingly, her hands wringing her apron in anguish. "He doesn't mean it. He's just had one or two bad experiences. Anyway," she added, before Rosie had time to inquire exactly what she meant, "he sends his apologies. Says he's sorry he overreacted and that he hopes you might consider coming back to the farm to finish your drawings." The old woman's eyes were anxious. "Do you think you might?"

Why did she care so much? "I'll think about it," Rosie promised.

"Have a plant," said the old lady, ripping one up from the border beneath her and thrusting it over the wall.

It hadn't taken much thinking about, in fact. Just the few days she had spent exclusively in Mark's company. Days that only served

to reinforce how impossible he had become to live with. He had insisted on working downstairs in the kitchen, with the result that
everything Rosie did in there excited his irritation. It was, she had
discovered, no longer possible even to wash up, unless one moved
crockery silently about under the water like submarines, ever fearful
of it clanking together and disturbing his fragile-as-blown-glass
process of column composition. As if this weren't enough, snatches
of her last, furious exchange with Jack ambushed her at unexpected
moments. "I've got a right to make a living . . . rich yuppies . . .
Knightsbridge with sheep." He'd made it pretty obvious what he
thought of her. And who could blame him? With the banging and
shouting of the Muzzles an uneasy backdrop to her thoughts, she
had stared out of the grimy window at the mackerel sky and reflected that she'd better start looking elsewhere for animals to draw.
Her stomach had twisted in regret, especially when she remembered
the calm before the storm. That look of surprised welcome, that wry
twist of smile, that peppery nearness . . .

As Rosie crossed the field, she wished Bella was there to talk this
over with and not at Val D'Isère. Still, it was probably just as well.
She would put a decent face on it, but there would be no disguising her delight that Rosie's relationship with Mark had hit the
rocks. Rosie breathed sharply in. Is that what had happened? It was
the first time, even in thought, that she had admitted it. Could
things be that bad?

As Rosie came into the farmyard, a sudden breeze whipped past her
nose, carrying with it the now-familiar beer-sour smell of silage. It
clung, not unpleasantly, to her nostrils. The yard was deserted, as was
the barn. Checking behind the farmhouse revealed Wellington unat-
tended in his coop. Jack was obviously out in the fields somewhere. Or
in the house? The door was closed, but Rosie peered in through the
low-slung mullioned farmhouse windows. All was dark and still.

"Rosie?" The voice came from the yard behind her.

She pressed her forehead briefly against the glass. Naturally he
would have to wait for her to be doing something embarrassing before
coming on the scene. Gawking through his windows, for instance.

"Oh. Jack. Hi." As Kate came yapping up, beating muddied paws liberally all over her, Rosie tried to sound as casual as she could. She glanced fearfully at him. Would he still be angry?

He was coming through the gate, wellingtons squelching in the mud. His tan had intensified—there had been a few days of fine spring sunshine since she had last seen him. A flash of blue eyes, that quick, twisted smile, and Rosie felt unsteady with relief. "I was just, um, seeing if you were in," she mumbled.

Jack gave a short laugh. "In? I've not been in the house since four o'clock this morning. Since I got up to sort out the stock."

"Oh, of course. Sorry." Jack, she had pondered many times over the past few days, had more in common with city yuppies than he realized. The only other person Rosie knew who got up at five to sort out stock was Bella, who had once done it to make a soup base for a dinner party. She sensed, though, that this was not the time to share this information. Not ever, perhaps.

Jack cleared his throat. "Well, help yourself to the animals." He jerked out a hand in a general, expansive gesture.

"Right-o." Rosie nodded emphatically.

"I've told them all to suck their cheeks in." His features, screwed up against the sun, attempted to straighten themselves out into a smile.

"Thanks."

"You'll find the sheep in the far field today." He pointed in a direction on the other side of the farmhouse.

"Thanks."

Silence.

"Listen," Jack said awkwardly. "I went a bit over the top the other day, I know. Not your fault. I was still angry about that bloody stupid woman telling me off about the cows making noises. Not that that was the last of it, either." His eyes hardened.

"She's complained about them again?"

"Threatened to have them monitored for the noise they make. Now she's opposing my application to add a free-range poultry unit to the farm. Anyone would think I was trying to put up a nuclear reprocessing plant or something. BANANAS. That's what she is."

Rosie raised her eyebrows slightly. As expletives went it seemed amazingly mild. Considering the depths of invective Jack was capable of.

"BANANAS," Jack repeated. "As in Building Anything Near Anyone Is Not Allowed."

Rosie giggled. "I'll be off, then," she said. "And don't worry, I'll keep out of your way."

"You don't have to do that." With apparent spontaneity, Jack moved a step closer. "I think I owe you an apology. You have your principles. I should have treated them with more respect."

His nearness fizzing in the air between them, Rosie suddenly felt she had no principles at all. Unable, suddenly, to look into his eyes, she stared at his upper lip.

"I've been thinking about it," the lip said. "And it struck me that, after all I'd said, you must wonder what the hell I'm working on a farm at all for."

"I've been thinking, too," Rosie gasped, eager to grasp the opportunity to apologize. "Just because I don't eat steak doesn't mean you're not allowed to make a living. On the land your family has farmed for generations." The lip was, she noticed, broad. Clumsily cut, but curiously soft-looking.

"I suppose it's because it's a way of life," Jack continued, so near now she could almost feel his breath. "Meverells—that's my family name—have always farmed here. It was their life and now it's mine. Such as it is. Seven days a week, one day off a year if I'm lucky. Doesn't make much sense, does it?" The lip stretched in a grin. "Must be off my bloody rocker." His face turned, looking toward the fields spreading behind and beyond. "But I suppose I like my own space." He was looking at her, his expression urgent. "Do you understand what I mean?"

Rosie looked over his shoulder to the flank of hill and nodded. "If it was my space, I'd like it, too." She lowered her eyes to his hands. Rough, broken-nailed, they hung heavily by his sides, the solid fingers curved inward.

"I've missed you, you know," he said softly.

"Have you?" Rosie meant to sound assured, but it came out as a squeak. Hearing it, she suppressed the near-overwhelming urge to laugh.

"Got used to having you around, I suppose. Even though you haven't been coming long. You seemed to fit in here somehow." She could feel his eyes searching her face but kept her own trained on the hand moving almost undetectably toward hers. As he brushed a thick digit against her forefinger excitement juddered up and down her arm almost painfully, as if she had touched an electric fence.

"It's nice to have you back," Jack murmured. Rosie had no doubt that he was glad to see her. Unless that was a cattle prod in his pocket.

Half an hour later Rosie came back down the lane, passing rapidly through the tangle of screaming children kicking the inevitable football against the inevitable cottage. The pebbledash rendering of Number 2 was now bald in several places. But Rosie noticed nothing of this. She was full of Jack, her insides alternately leaping with excitement and trembling with dread at the powerful attraction she had felt. Her lips burned and her hand tingled where he had touched it. Her heart was spinning, her stomach a rollercoaster and her head chaotic, like a messy bedroom. She had no idea what to do. If only Bella were around.

Rosie tried determinedly not to catch the eye of Mrs. Womersley, bent busily over her flower trough outside the front door of Number 1. She did not succeed.

"Been up to Spitewinter?" The old lady's eyes were bright with question.

Rosie nodded, feeling the leap of delight and an accompanying crimson tide of blush rising up her neck. There was a satisfied look in Mrs. Womersley's eyes as she turned back to her borders.

Mark was still bent over his laptop as she came in. He did not look up. If anything, he looked more down than he had when she had left him. A riptide of guilt overwhelmed Rosie.

Yet what had she done? Nothing—in deed. In her head, however . . .

"How's it going?" she asked Mark in her brightest voice, filling a glass of water at the kitchen sink to hide her guilty face.

Mark jerked his head up savagely. "Great," he said sarcastically. "The editor's rejected two attempts at 'Green-er Pastures' in the space of the past few hours. The kids have been rioting ever since you went and the bedroom door's fallen off its hinges."

"Oh, dear," murmured Rosie.

"Quite. And there's another thing."

"*What?*" Rosie looked at him sharply, terror hammering in her heart. Had someone seen her and Jack? The postman . . . ?

"Bella called about an hour ago. She's back from Val d'Isère and wants to come up and stay. *This week.*"

In theory, Rosie could not—barring the lottery jackpot—have asked for more welcome news. But talking to her on the telephone was one thing. Actually having her to stay was quite another. "Bella? *Here?*" Rosie looked round the kitchen. What on earth would Bella think? The small, shabby room with the chipped paint floor could not have been further removed from Bella's pristine Islington cucina. Which, besides being half operating theater, half gastro-temple, was also the size of the entire ground floor of the cottage. Rosie gazed in despair at the galloping damp on the wall and the piles of dirty crockery.

"Yes. Here," Mark confirmed flatly. "Wants to come up and have some serious girl time with you or something," he added in disgust.

"Oh, so she's coming on her own?" That at least was something.

"No. She's bringing the Antichrist."

Bella's dreaded son, Ptolemy. Rosie's stomach gave a sudden lurch for reasons utterly unconnected with Jack.

That night, through the curtainless windows—another thing they'd never gotten round to remedying—Rosie watched the light from the almost full moon silver Mark's profile. He seemed, for once, to be sleeping, but there was none of the regular breathing that usually signaled unconsciousness. Rosie lay drinking in for the millionth time that long, straight nose, bony swell of cheekbone, jutting lip, and sweeping jawline. His arrogant, delicately cut beauty could not have been further removed from Jack's crumpled charms, although there was a resemblance. If Jack was the rough-hewn block, thought Rosie, Mark was the stone after a skilled sculptor had worked it with a chisel.

She was not accustomed to initiating sex—not very millennium woman of me, Rosie thought miserably. But then she had never had to; Mark seemed to prefer to be in control and she had grown used to the fact that, two or three times a week, he would slide under the duvet, roll over, and begin the rhythmic stroking and nuzzling that set Rosie off on the pathway of delight. Not a pathway she had trodden recently.

Sliding her hand tentatively through the hole in his boxer shorts, Rosie's fingers touched the flaccid warmth of Mark's penis. She moved her fingers up and down it, applying pressure where she knew he preferred it. There was no welcoming stir. Asleep or not, Mark grunted and rolled over with his back to her.

Rosie stared miserably up at the moonlit ceiling and thought it was just as well they weren't bouncing off it, as no doubt that would have resulted in yet more cracks. They were numerous enough as it was. She sighed. "Green-er Pastures" seemed to have as much of a struggle appearing in the flesh these days as it did in the newspaper.

Steering the Jaguar with the top of one fingernail, Samantha slashed frantically at the carphone as she swept along.

"Prestige Property Services? Get me Sir Hadley Bonsanquet. *Now.*" The stuck-up old poof had some serious explaining to do. Such as why she had to find out from *Ghosts of the Area* that he'd sold her a turkey, not to mention a white lady, a haunted cat, and the three bloody musketeers battling it out on the staircase. Oh, and a black ball of hate into the bargain.

"What do you *mean* he's not fucking in?" Samantha yelled at the speaker. "*When* will he be back? *Tomorrow?*" Pause. "September, you *hope?* . . . In *six months' fucking time?* Lengthy period of rest following *complete nervous breakdown?*" Samantha's eyeballs rolled with fury. "I'll give him nervous bloody breakdown," she yelled. So loudly was the blood pounding in her ears that she couldn't quite catch what the receptionist said, but it sounded suspiciously like "You already have done." Samantha stabbed the end of call button with such force it broke her nail.

Black ball of hate . . . Samantha's face twisted with loathing. What she wouldn't give to take that black ball of hate and stick it straight between Sir Hadley's beef curtains. And as for Lady bloody St. Felix, who had not answered her phone all day, Samantha itched to plunge an entire block of Sabatiers between those erect and rigid shoulder blades.

Rounding a vicious bend, she ground the gears and her teeth simultaneously. By no means the least of her difficulties was deciding what she was angriest about. The fact that she was about to have the shit haunted out of her? The fact that ghosts probably spirited away thousands from the value of the house? The fact that Guy might find out? Samantha shuddered at the prospect. He'd be thrilled, no doubt about it. He'd been banging on about the house giving him the creeps for weeks, and the news that the place was riddled with spooks would be just the excuse he needed for insisting that they abandon Eight Mile Bottom and go straight back to South Kensington. Which was, of course, completely out of the question now that the party, and with it her social domination of the village, looked set for glittering success.

The party. A shocking thought suddenly struck Samantha. The *guests*. How many of *them* knew the house was riddled with the undead? Lots of invitees had not yet replied—was this because The Bottoms had roughly the reputation of the Bates Motel? Terror pounded in her temples as she imagined the black ball of hate bouncing in the big silver bowl and spattering everyone with champagne cocktail mixture. Or, worse, emerging unheralded from the depths of one of the Oxford's pristine oak-topped lavatory pans. Samantha clutched the soft leather of the wheel in despair and, heedless of the fact that she was speeding into a blind bend, wailed aloud in horror.

"Shit. Fucking *shit*." As the figure of a girl shot into the center of her windshield, Samantha slammed her foot on the brakes. The car skidded on the loose scree and hurled itself across the road into the hedgerow while the girl and what looked like hundreds of sheets of paper flew through the air in the other direction. The Jaguar scythed through the muddy verge and a mass of pebbles clattered against its side, battering the flawless bodywork.

Samantha staggered out and stared at the filthy wheels in disgust. *"You bloody idiot!"* she shrieked. "Look what you've done to my fucking hubcaps."

The further expletives she was planning dried in her throat. Wasn't there something familiar about the girl a few yards away? Samantha squinted. Perhaps she *should* wear her glasses when driving; Sophia Loren managed to get away with them, after all. Young, thin, dressed in something baggy . . . Blond, yes, but Iseult could have dyed her hair. Peering in the girl's direction, Samantha's much-put-upon heart skipped a beat. Ever since that last encounter in the hospital she'd been expecting trouble.

"Look at my *drawings*," howled the girl. "My *work*."

Samantha almost fainted in relief. Not, after all, her hated stepdaughter. Not her voice anyway, and she'd mentioned work, for God's sake, a word Iseult had no comprehension of. As for drawings, the only ones Iseult was capable of were out of her father's bank account. Samantha scowled as she remembered a conversation on the subject during one of the girl's few visits to Roland Gardens. They had been alone together in the kitchen at the time.

"I need some bread," Iseult had said in the Haight-Ashbury drawl that amused her father but infuriated her stepmother.

Samantha had exploded. "Bread!" she had repeated in mocking triumph. "I might have bloody known. You're not here because you want to see your sodding father. You're here because you want his sodding money."

"No," Iseult had said. "I want bread. Like, *wholemeal* or something."

Samantha's wandering thoughts returned to the matter in hand. The almost-crashed Jaguar and the girl in front of her who so gloriously was not Iseult. Yet Samantha was sure they had met before.

"Don't I know you?" Samantha purred. "Didn't you used to wait outside the stage door of . . . ?"

"No," snapped Rosie, whose life, already complicated, had suddenly taken a turn for the worse. Not only had she been practically squashed flat by a maniac, but the maniac had turned out to be, of all people, the ghastly Samantha Villiers.

"I know I've seen you somewhere." Samantha tapped her forefinger on her chin. "*Got it.* You were third assistant wardrobe on that Krispi cheese voiceover I did."

"We met at your house. I was helping on a magazine shoot."

"Of *course. Such* exciting news about the sale."

Rosie suddenly recalled Bella saying something about this. "Oh, yes," she said without interest. "Nicole Kidman."

Samantha wriggled coyly. "Well, of course I can't say. The buyer begged me *personally* not to reveal *anything*. And how could I refuse, as they've allowed us to buy our dream house." With any luck, there would be another *Insider* feature in this for her. Another megastar to take The Bottoms off her hands would come in very useful just now.

Dream home. That explained it, Rosie thought. No doubt Samantha was in Eight Mile Bottom handpicking Elizabethan oaks for her garden decking. She shuddered, imagining another handsome London house defaced and destroyed.

"You really must come round some time," trilled Samantha, climbing back into her Jaguar. "With the rest of the *Insider* team, of course," she added, skidding off and spraying both Rosie and her drawings liberally with mud.

But as she drove back into the village, her demons, quite literally, returned. Proceeding up The Bottoms' drive, she looked sourly at the gracious building glowing in the sunlight. The gray stone no longer looked friendly with age and use. It looked forbidding. The tiny leaden panes between the mullions no longer winked in the sunlight but leered. Even the lichened stone lions flanking the door seemed to snarl in warning. Samantha's trepidation increased when, after opening the front door and calling loudly into the hall, she remembered that Guy had gone to a meeting in London. With *Ghosts of the Area* never far from her mind, she was suddenly reluctant to be in The Bottoms alone.

She twiddled the car keys for a second, then decided to drive round the village. Nothing, after all, cheered one up as much as seeing how much smaller and cheaper everyone else's houses were besides one's own. Even if one's own *was* the Spook Sheraton. These cottages here, round the green, for example. *Tiny*. One bedroom at the most. Slums, really. Samantha was beginning to feel better already.

She braked in horror to avoid a black and white cat lounging in the middle of the road. Was it the haunted cat? Well, if not, it almost bloody was, Samantha thought, missing its front paws by millimeters as she swerved to the right at the top of the village street. Finding herself in a previously unexplored part of Eight Mile Bottom, Samantha felt fear claw at her heart. Her nerves were more shredded than a steak tartare. That she and the supernatural did not mix had been illustrated several times in her professional career, most recently at her audition for the stage version of *The Witches of Eastwick.* Or *The Bitches of Chiswick,* as she had dubbed it after having been put through her thespian paces by two female directors who subsequently decided to pass on her talents. "But why?" Samantha had stormed at Russ. "I thought I was definitely slated for the part."

"You were slated, definitely," Russ assured her, which had seemed a weird sort of explanation. And his pre-audition good-luck message, "Break everything," had not, in retrospect, been particularly encouraging. She was, Samantha thought crossly, pressing her foot on the accelerator, better off without him.

Suddenly, and most unexpectedly, a large, heavily decorated sign of the cross appeared in the center of her windshield. Samantha let out a prolonged shriek of terror. How much more of this could she stand? *The Amityville Horror* had become *The Omen;* expecting unscheduled decapitation any minute, Samantha's hand flew to her neck. A second later she realized the cross was actually the top of a spire and she was driving up to the church.

Enlightenment dawned. Who better to rid a house of ghosts than a man of the cloth? Double-parking the car with a screech, Samantha dashed out and headed through the church door.

"But *something* must have happened," Mark insisted desperately. "Gothic multiple murders, that sort of thing?"

"Not really, sir," said the duty sergeant at Slapton Police Station. "We don't get that sort of thing round here. Most trouble in this area is usually down to the Four Ds."

"The Four Dees?" Mark frowned. And who the hell might they be?

"Drugs, Drink, DIY, and Domestics," intoned the constable. "Oh, and the occasional bit of knicker-sniffing."

Slamming the receiver down in disgust, Mark returned to his laptop. His stomach ran cold with dread at the thought of E-mailing the editor to report that his column's investigations into rural crime had proved even more fruitless than Rosie's snail-ravaged gooseberry bushes. He dragged his fingers hard through his hair and reached for an unopened package of chocolate chip cookies.

Still, hopefully the editor would be merciful. Crashing and grinding the cookies in his teeth was a relief of sorts. Reaching for another, Mark heard the now-familiar screech of wheels followed by the slither of envelopes across the sitting-room floor.

"Better get that red bill paid," shouted Duffy. "They'll be cutting you off if you're not careful. Takes ages to get reconnected as well. Mrs. Sidebottom hasn't had it for months—mind you, that's no surprise to anyone." As the postman leaped back into his van, Mark returned to the silent kitchen and the empty screen of his laptop. Was the problem that he had promised the editor too much? Too late he had realized the genius of Househusband had been to keep editorial expectations as low as possible. Genius and Househusband—two words he had never imagined it possible to use in the same sentence. An indication of how low he had fallen.

Pacing back into the sitting room, Mark was shaken out of brooding by the sight of a pair of naked and shapely breasts walking past the open front door. Dungarees was taking the lunchtime air, or as much of it as she could given the cigarette plugged into her mouth and the large baby clamped to her left nipple. Even to Mark's inexpert eye it was definitely too old to be breastfed; this, as well as other darker thoughts, were obviously going through the mind of Mrs. Womersley as she looked up from weeding her daffodils to give Dungarees a disgusted stare. Her expression didn't change much when it switched to Mark, now hanging out of the front door. Swiftly, he went back inside to his laptop. There was something sinister about that old bag next door.

Mark had typed no more than two words before the familiar thudding sound began on the cottage's front wall. Walking over to the window, Mark saw the Muzzles' cheeky-faced eldest boy Satchel kicking his large black soccer ball hard against the front of Number 2, aided and abetted by Blathnat. Mark glared murderously at them through the grubby old glass, then he raced across the sitting-room floor and almost ripped the front stable door off its hinges.

"Just shut up, will you, *aaarrgggh*," he yelled, as the top half swung back, as usual, and crushed his fingers. "I'm trying to bloody work in there. If you two don't stop making all that bloody noise," Mark snarled, shaking his hand to relieve the pain, "I'll tear off both your arms and beat you with the soggy ends." One of his masters at school, he remembered, had used this threat to great effect.

"Hey, hey, *hey*. Hang on *right there* just *one* minute. *Whoo!*" Dennis the Menace was loping toward him down the street, shaking his head and waving his arms. "Hey, hey, *hey*. Don't ruin the vibes, man. We don't shout at the kids round here."

"Well, that's pretty bloody obvious," snapped Mark, catching the insolent eye of Satchel. *Satchel.* That was a laugh. Bloody kid obviously never went *near* a classroom. Making "calm down" gestures with his hands, Dennis retreated back up the lane, the wind billowing through his rainbow-colored tie-dye trousers whose crotch was on a level with his knees.

As the hated children began kicking the hated ball noisily about the street again, Mark resisted the overwhelming urge to run away and never come back. Hands rammed violently into his pockets, he walked slowly back into the cottage, glancing at the bottom of Cinder Lane as he did so. He was amazed to notice a gleaming Jaguar XK9 double-parked alongside the Muzzles' rusting vehicles. Surely not the vicar's? The vicar was a sight better off than the usual pastoral padre if that car was anything to go by.

A thought struck Mark with the force of a thunderclap. Hell, the vicar might even make a story. He rushed into the church and started clearing his throat exaggeratedly to announce his presence. It had instant results. A figure came hurtling out of the gloom of one of the side chapels. As it passed a stained-glass window, Mark saw with surprise that it was a woman. It was a lady vicar then. With long red hair, a very short skirt, high heels, and what, even from this distance, looked like a definite case of TT. Terrific Tits. Mark's heart soared. The editor was going to love this. A sexy woman vicar with a Jag. No doubt about it, this *was* definitely a story.

"I'm so glad to see you," Samantha exclaimed dramatically. "I need your help *desperately.*"

"You do?" Mark asked, gratified.

"Yes," Samantha gasped huskily. "I need someone who knows about black balls of hate."

Mark's mind flew immediately to Satchel's football, which, at this very moment, was being slammed against the cottage wall with destructive regularity. "I'm your man," he said.

"They're called Jennifer and Britney?" Rosie echoed as Jack introduced her to his two favorite cows.

"That's right. After Jennifer Lopez and Britney Spears," Jack admitted, not without a certain reddening of the ears. Rosie was also embarrassed—to think that someone who had spent half his life in a cowshed seemed better versed in popular culture than she was. Yet Jack, it turned out, liked nothing better than plowing late at night with the radio on full-blast in his tractor. Just like his uncle, Rosie thought, remembering the first time she had encountered the Womersleys.

"Both naughty girls. Jennifer likes to snatch my hat off in the winter, and Britney always gives me a shove when she passes."

Yet after this promising start to the day, Rosie was disappointed when Jack kept out of her way all morning. Was he regretting their charged encounter of the day before? Perhaps he was, after all, embroiled in a relationship somewhere. Although where and with whom he was embroiled Rosie couldn't imagine. There was no sign of any embroiling on the farm.

In his absence, however, she made some of her best animal sketches ever of the cows in the upper field. Jennifer and Britney in particular turned out to be natural models. Coquettish, self-conscious, they pranced obligingly around for her, turning with a skittish flick of their tails. Samantha's wholesale destruction of all her early sketches became increasingly insignificant as Rosie, her pencil flying across the pad, improved on what had gone before. By the end of the morning, the character of Camilla the theater-producing cow, complete with a necklace of fat golden dandelions, had sprung exuberantly if improbably to life.

The smooth and lichened rock on which Rosie sat was at the summit of the highest hill on Jack's farm, commanding a view not only of Eight Mile Bottom but of the receding hills and valleys beyond it. Rib after rib of rolling green stretched away to the sharply defined horizon, their vibrancy of color almost audible in the still air. Two hills in particular caught her attention. They looked, she thought, like sharks' fins jutting from a grassy sea. Or like two crumpled dragons that had collapsed in combat centuries ago.

It was a sparkling blue and green spring day. From within a square foot of where she sat, Rosie could count nine different types of leaves, in colors ranging from emerald to brilliant lime. Flowers, too—daisies led away in paths over the sheep-cropped turf, while the trails of brilliant yellow blazed by the dandelions were visible for miles. The sky seemed filled with competing birdsong—one a clear, glassy plink, another a piercing soprano fizz, rising, falling, and rising again.

Her back to the field, Rosie did not see the tall figure approaching. But she felt the something cold and wet that suddenly thrust itself into her hand.

"Kate! Bloody hell." As her hammering heart subsided, Rosie patted the dog gingerly.

"Sorry," said Jack. "Didn't mean to make you jump. But Kate and I wondered if you might like to join us for lunch. It's past two o'clock, and we don't do starving artists on this farm." He set down a battered rucksack on the grass, while Kate sniffed and nudged Rosie's paintboxes and brushes.

"Thought you might enjoy trying a few of the local delicacies." Jack produced two brown bottles of beer, a round loaf of crusty bread, and a couple of wax-paper-wrapped parcels.

"Ooh, yes." Thinking of her unvarying diet of pasta and pesto, Rosie looked at the parcels with longing. Then fear flexed its icy fingers and snatched at her heart. What was in those parcels?

"It's not . . . is it?" she stammered, unable to frame the dreaded word.

"Meat?" Jack looked at her. Rosie gazed pleadingly back and nodded.

His teeth flashed in a grin. " 'Course it isn't. Matter of fact, it's cheese. Made in a local dairy with the milk from these very artist's models here." He waved his broad hand at the cows tearing at the grass, their tufty coats shining in the sun. His tone was light. He did not seem to be about to add any depressing statistics about the milk fetching eight pence a pint while the cheese cost £4 a pound.

Rosie brightened. Her stomach rumbled as she realized how hungry she was. Mark had eaten the last of the Weetabix that morning, using up all the milk in the process.

"The Bottom Blue is particularly good." Jack cut open the packets with a wood-handled knife.

Rosie imagined the explosion of salty curds on her tongue. "I adore blue cheese. It's always delicious."

"Isn't it? Particularly when it's been maturing for a while, like this one."

Rosie swallowed.

"Because then it's really special," Jack continued airily.

"Is it?" Rosie's salivary glands were working overtime.

"Yes. It's then that you get the maggotty bit at the bottom. We locals like to dip our bread in it."

Rosie, feeling as if she were about to be sick, tried to stop her face from contorting in a rictus of disgust. Then she noticed the corners of Jack's mouth quivering and realized he was joking.

Jack finally liberated the cheese, opened the two bottles of beer, and passed her one. The ale was deliciously cool and nutty. As he drank, Rosie watched the muscles in his strong throat work the liquid down.

Rosie demolished a hunk of bread and cheese and sighed happily. "This is wonderful," she said, beaming at him. "Thank you so much."

Jack did not reply. His eyes had flicked upward.

"Listen." Jack spoke suddenly. "The lark. Can you hear it?"

It was the high, sweet sound she had heard earlier. "I've never heard one before," she confessed, entranced by the rising and descending notes.

"Don't hear them that often these days. It's just up there, look. Tiny black dot, over to the left."

As Jack pointed into the sky, Rosie squinted desperately, scanning the blue without result. Suddenly, her eyes seemed full of dots: floating contact lens debris, transparent worms, and hazy blotches drifting past like plankton. None of them seemed much like larks.

"Can you see it?"

With a surge of relief Rosie finally spotted the tiny creature pulsing upward into the sun. They watched until it finally disappeared and the distant hum of a plane replaced the fizzing song.

"I never get tired of this view," Jack said after a pause. "Even though I've seen it every day for the last thirty years."

"It's magical." Rosie raised herself on her elbow. "I've been looking at those hills over there," she added quickly. "Very odd shapes." She stopped short of telling him she had compared them to sharks' fins and collapsed dragons. No doubt he would think that just the kind of absurd romantic fantasy typical of a city dweller. Did she not realize these hills were working hills?

Jack nodded. "Strange, aren't they? Amazing knobbly spines. I know it sounds mad"—he shot her a shy look—"but I've always thought they looked like dragons or something. Sort of collapsed. As if they'd been fighting each other."

Their eyes locked in a smile.

As he leaned over to kiss her, Rosie's pelvis melted into liquid fire. Liquid everything, as Jack, sliding a pleasingly confident hand between her legs, eventually attested. Pushing up her shirt, he brushed his glistening forefinger over her hardening nipple and covered it with his lips.

It felt like wrenching herself from quicksand.

"I've got a boyfriend," Rosie muttered, turning her head away and addressing a clump of cowslips that nodded understandingly in a sudden breeze. Surely Jack must know about Mark? Even if Mrs. Womersley hadn't filled him in, it was impossible that Duffy had passed on the opportunity to do so.

Jack sat up abruptly, his arms hanging over his knees, and tore at the head of a dandelion.

"I can't leave Mark," Rosie said gently. "We gave up everything we had in London to come here . . . been together for years . . . he couldn't afford the cottage by himself . . ." Even to her own ears, her voice rang hollow. Who, after all, was she trying to convince? And yet . . .

Jack nodded, his mouth a set line. "Well, I have to respect that, I suppose." He paused, as if struggling with what to say next. "At least you're not one of those women who ride roughshod over relationships. Stringing two blokes along at the same time and all that."

"No." Rosie twisted a blade of grass nervously around her fingers. "I've never been very good at that femme fatale thing."

"I'm glad to hear it." Though he was muttering to his knees, he seemed to be doing so with feeling. Was he speaking from experience?

"But we can still be friends, can't we?" Rosie ventured. "I mean, I can still come up here? I'd like to . . ."

Jack nodded slowly. "Of course. Besides . . ."

"Yes?" she looked at him apprehensively.

"You might change your mind."

Rosie reddened, his wry smile tugging at her heart.

"I'll be here if you do," Jack said.

The evening sun was gilding the fields in a filter of yellow light as Rosie walked slowly home. Her brain ground like a pestle against the mortar of her skull. She had regretted spurning Jack's advances the second the Spitewinter gate had closed behind her. For what, after all, had she spurned them? Spiteful, carping, explosively bad-tempered Mark . . . Well, she'd had enough of that, Rosie decided as she approached the cottage. The worm had turned. From now on, she would fight fire with fire. Any displays of bad temper would be more than matched. Then, at least, she would not have turned down Jack for nothing. To her amazement, however, she arrived at the cottage to find Mark positively skipping round the sitting room.

"Amazing church," he said.

"You were *in church?*" Rosie's feeling of guilt intensified. Unprecedented though it was, Mark had spent the afternoon in the house of the Lord, while she, harlot that she was, had spent the afternoon on the verge of contravening the Ten Commandments. Nevertheless, she looked at him with concern. Had things gotten so bad that he had sought divine help with "Green-er Pastures"?

Mark nodded. "The vicar was showing me round. Pretty bloody old, some of it. There's a tomb of some medieval bloke who fought against Joan of Arc . . . What's that bloody awful burning smell?" Rosie fled to the kitchen, where the toast Mark was making sat incinerated in its racks, the smell drifting in a dense cloud round the room.

"So you were looking around out of interest?" Rosie asked. Odd that the tomb of a fourteenth-century knight could form the centerpiece of the column when all other aspects of the village had failed.

"Yes, sort of," said Mark quickly. Telling Rosie that he had spent the afternoon in semidarkness with a film star suddenly struck him as too much information. He *had* been talking to the vicar, anyway. When, that was, the real vicar had turned up, saying he had been telephoned by a parishioner claiming to have seen some funny-looking people entering the church.

Hilarious, Mark thought, how he and Samantha had imagined each other to be the vicar at first. Anything less like a person of the cloth was impossible to imagine. The miniskirt out of which those gazellelike legs had spilled had been short of material in general, being the approximate width of a hairband. Rosie never wore miniskirts, despite having legs that were more than reasonable. These days, she rarely seemed to be out of the ancient jeans and shapeless fleece she wore for her visits to the farm. By contrast, Samantha had been all woman. All older woman, too. He'd always had a slight Mrs. Robinson complex, all the more so after Samantha told him that *The Graduate* role had gone to Anne Bancroft only after she'd turned it down herself to do some film about punks. Funny, but he hadn't realized punks were around in the sixties. Funny, too, that he recognized none of the titles of her films. But then he hadn't been listening all that closely. Not after he had worked out that here—right here in front of him, asking for his help— was the woman the postman had mentioned, the woman about to give the biggest and grandest party Eight Mile Bottom had ever seen. The party that after days' festering about the fact he had not been invited, Mark now felt ready to kill to go to.

"What's the vicar like?" asked Rosie.

Mark rolled his eyes. "Happy clappy. Full of jokes about having once been a rep for an industrial bulb company until he saw the light. Had a road-to-Damascus conversion on the road to Scunthorpe or something."

"He sounds great for the column."

Mark flared his nostrils and pursed his lips. "*I'll* decide what is or isn't good material, thank you. Actually, what *was* really interesting was that he was helping someone exorcise."

"Exercise?"

"*Orcise.* Ex*orcise.* This, um, woman thinks her house is haunted and wants the vicar to get rid of the evil spirits."

"And will he?"

Mark shook his head. The vicar had pissed on Samantha's parade well and truly by saying he wouldn't get rid of her ghosts and that the party would have to go ahead with them on the guest list, or was that the ghost list, ha ha. Samantha had not appreciated this joke. As sticky moments went, Mark considered, that one was a full-scale toffee pudding.

Until he himself had brilliantly come to the rescue. "Why don't you have a marquee *outside*?" he had suggested to Samantha. "No need for anyone to go in the house then. It would fit in better with the Arabian Nights theme as well."

Samantha had practically had an orgasm on the spot. She'd kissed him, hugged him, called him a genius, and promised to send him an invitation to what she made sound a more celebrity-packed event than the Oscars. At this point, Mark, eager to acquit himself of obscurity, had mentioned—just dropped into the conversation—the fact that *he,* as it happened, was *quite* well known himself, thanks to having his own column in a national newspaper. In which, yes, well, it wasn't impossible—he might well see his way to mentioning her party. Samantha had almost gone into orbit. It was a pleasant memory.

"Why won't the vicar exorcise the ghosts?" repeated Rosie loudly, wondering why she had had to ask three times. And why Mark had that soppy grin on his face.

Mark tuned back in with a shock. "Doesn't believe in it. Thinks that ghosts have got every right to be there and that she should get used to them. Said it wasn't up to newcomers to start calling the shots with people who've lived there before them. Even if they happen to be dead."

"Yes," said Rosie. Satchel's football began thudding against the outside wall once more. "Just what I've always said about the Muzzles."

Mark threw her an irritated look and dived to the door. His expected howl of rage did not come, however. He stood apparently paralyzed, looking out into the lane.

"What's going on?" Rosie asked. Everything had gone suspiciously quiet.

Mark looked tragically over his shoulder at her. "Bella's here. With the Antichrist."

Rosie hurried to the door to see Bella, resplendent in brand-new jeans and virgin trainers emerging from a BMW as dark and shiny as her hair. As she swung up the lane with Ptolemy in one hand and a bottle of champagne in the other, the church clock chimed thirteen.

"Beware of parents bearing champagne," Mark snarled, beating a hasty retreat to the neglected box room. "It means they know their kids are a nightmare."

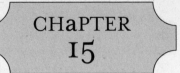

CHaPTER 15

Rosie, although desperate to discuss the matter, was unable to tell Bella about Jack until Mark had gone upstairs.

"A farmer fatale!" Bella's eyes lit up. "I must say, I'm dying to see him, darling."

"We-ell . . ." Rosie said doubtfully. Jack had said she could go back to the farm, but whether he would welcome half of Islington as well was another matter.

Bella, however, had made up her mind. "It would be *marvelous* for Tolly to see a real farm," she pressed. "As you know, darling, part of the *entire* reason I've brought him up here is so he learns not to be afraid of the countryside."

Rosie avoided saying she had never met a child less afraid of anything than Ptolemy. Bella's fears that, as a delicate London infant, her precious son would not mix well with tough country children had proved unfounded as, within minutes of his arrival, Ptolemy had leaped on Satchel and started pounding him into the road. This marked the first-ever occasion on which Mark had smiled at Bella's son. His smile soon vanished when, told to calm down and do something peaceful, darling, by his mother, Ptolemy proceeded to color in the seagrass mat before the fireplace with felt-tip pens. Told to stop this, darling, by his mother, he then began to explore the different ways of entering the room through the windows. Told to stop *this,* darling, by his mother, he began jumping on the sofa with his shoes on and kicking the cushions in the air.

Bedtime, when it finally, thankfully, came was shattered by a terrifying tantrum once Ptolemy realized he had forgotten his bath toys. The resulting deafening flamenco of tiny feet (Ptolemy did not seem to have been taught to pitter-patter) on the wooden floor of the bathroom seemed certain to result in the complete capitulation of the woodworm-weakened planks. "Little sod," Mark snarled through clenched teeth. Rosie sensed it was beginning to dawn on him that there were children in the world who were if not worse than the Muzzles, then just as bad. Children, puzzlingly, vastly better educated and privileged into the bargain.

But the effort required to deal with Ptolemy had one beneficial effect, which was to distract Bella's attention from her sleeping quarters. Their sleeping quarters to be precise—Rosie and Mark had given up their room and faced the daunting prospect of the sofabed downstairs. Rosie was aware that their damp-speckled, grit-flecked bedroom might not coincide with Bella's idea of luxury. Despite the fact that she had put a vase of flowers on the window sill.

Yet Bella had, so far, been exceedingly polite about what Rosie remembered Nigel describing as the "transitional" nature of the cottage interior. She seemed less alarmed, in fact, by the bathroom door being off its hinges and the wind whistling all night through the gaps surrounding the bedroom window frame than she was by Rosie looking "really rather rustic, darling."

"Don't you think you're letting things slip a little?" she asked when Rosie confessed after Bella's morning bath that no, she didn't have a hair dryer.

Rosie countered with what she felt was the ingenuous explanation that the less makeup she put on, the fewer mistakes she would make with it. "You know how you used to despair over my clumpy mascara," she said.

Bella considered this. "It's all very well looking *natural,* darling, but you actually have to put a lot of makeup on to make that just-scrubbed look work."

But at least the garden, if not Rosie or the cottage, showed signs of someone having worked on it, and it was out here that Rosie dragged Bella and her son after breakfast. Much to Rosie's delight, the scented narcissi planted by the previous occupants had recently started to nod from the borders among the pansies and flowering herbs she had put in herself. It was into these, the first flowers in Rosie's first garden, that Ptolemy now started drop-kicking a large and familiar-looking football.

"He's *ruining* my pansies," Rosie wailed.

"Darling," Bella soothed. "You mustn't mind too much. Blue's a *dreadfully* common color for a pansy."

Rosie eyed Ptolemy with dislike. How odd that Bella, so acute on every other front, was utterly blind to the faults of her adored son. Just as Bella had always imagined that she, Rosie, was oblivious to the glaring faults of Mark. That, at least, had changed.

"Let's have lunch at the pub," Rosie suggested. Bella's visit may have meant Ptolemy, but it also meant the opportunity to break Mark's embargo on the Barley Mow. If it got Ptolemy out of the house, he was unlikely to object.

"Couldn't keep away from the beer forever, then?" Alan called out to Rosie from behind the bar. "The call of the mild?"

Rosie grinned and introduced Bella. "My friend from London."

"London, eh?" mused Alan. "Heard the one about the farmer from Eight Mile Bottom who went to London? He found it easy enough to get there—just followed all the signs—but couldn't understand it when he wanted to come home and there were no signs back to Eight Mile Bottom!"

Bella looked nonplussed at this. Her eyes dwelt on Alan's Green with Henvy T-shirt, and she read the accompanying details about the World Championship Hen Racing.

"Look, darling," she urged Ptolemy, who was busily inserting his fingers into Alan's sound system. "This gentleman holds a sort of Olympics for hens."

"Poultry in motion, it is," Alan told him, leaning over the bar and prizing Ptolemy's digits away from the recording buttons. "You should see my champion hens. Fastest birds in the world, they are. Some go at over a hundred miles an hour."

"That's impossible," snapped Ptolemy. Then, as the landlord shrugged and turned away, he demanded, "Show me."

Alan sighed theatrically. "I'd love to, believe me," he said, placing both hands on the bar. "But I can't. Wrong time of year for hens."

"What do you mean?" asked Bella.

"Bit early for them. They'll be back in the next couple of weeks."

Ptolemy's red bottom lip was sticking out like the drawer of a cash register. "Where are they?"

"Africa somewhere," said Alan matter-of-factly. "Didn't you know hens go south for the winter?"

Bella looked uncertain. Rosie pushed a hand firmly over her mouth but could not prevent her shoulders from shaking.

"Oh, yes," continued the landlord, catching Rosie's eye. "Great flocks of 'em. You should see 'em when they set off. Millions of 'em, all sitting on the telegraph wires. Amazing sight, it is. And what's even more amazing is that they all come back. Homing hens, you see."

"I didn't realize hens migrated," Bella said doubtfully as Rosie attempted to convert a snigger into a sneeze.

"They don't everywhere, but they do this far north. Too cold for 'em here in the winter."

Bella's eyes widened. "How far north are we?"

"Put it this way," Alan said, busily polishing a glass. "Go out the door, turn right and up the hill, and it's the North Pole. Now," he added as Bella's eyebrows shot into her hairline in mixed amazement and suspicion, "what can I get you ladies to drink?"

Rosie, trying to avoid making eye contact with Alan, looked up at the signs above the bar. Mr. Womersley's onion supremacy, she saw, remained intact, although the ferret sign had disappeared. "Gone to good homes, have they?" she asked. "The ferrets?"

"Dame Nancy Brooke-Sullivan took some," Alan told her, "and the rest went somewhere up your way. Some family up Cinder Lane."

Rosie swallowed. A few escaping ferrets were all Mark needed to tip him over the edge from hysteria to homicide.

Bella, meanwhile, was staring in amazement at the beer labels. "Hairy Helmet . . . Old Knickersplitter . . ." she read in amazement.

Meanwhile, Ptolemy, having spotted the potential of the red plush banquette running round the barroom, was now throwing himself up and down on it.

"Careful, darling," murmured Bella. "Those shoes were awfully expensive."

The second crisis was when Ann's chips met with Ptolemy's furious disapproval. "They're too thick," he wailed.

"He's used to McDonald's," whispered Bella apologetically.

"And what's *this*?" Ptolemy demanded disgustedly, pulling out large bits of ham from his sandwich.

"It's very nice ham, carved from a proper joint." Stung by Ann's proximity into defending a meat product, Rosie tried hard not to feel guilty about it.

"This isn't *ham*," spat Tolly, his face contorted with revulsion as he examined the thick pink pieces edged with fat.

"It's just that he's used to that wafer-thin stuff from Sainsbury's, that's all." Bella shrugged at Ann. "Go outside and play, darling," she instructed her son, while Rosie hoped fervently that the Barley Mow had full building insurance.

Nonetheless, she seized the opportunity offered by his absence.

"So when can we go and see this farmer?" Bella demanded.

Rosie hesitated. Desperate though she was for her friend to approve of Jack, she was reluctant to inflict Ptolemy on him. Yet how else were they to meet? It seemed unlikely Mark would baby-sit.

Just then Tolly came hurtling back in floods of furious, screaming tears. It took some time for Bella, who had immediately imagined a pedophile attempting to abduct him, to discover the cause of her son's distress. "He's been trying to turn himself into Superman in the phone booth," she explained, "but there's some woman in there making a very long phone call, apparently."

Out of the corner of her eye, Rosie saw Alan listening avidly at the bar.

Once Ptolemy had been calmed down with promises of exotic holidays and expensive video games, he was unexpectedly keen to go along with his mother's suggestion that he sit in the BMW and be quiet. This surprised Rosie until she heard the sound of a car horn blasting repeatedly from the car park. Something cold and heavy, and in no way related to the cheese roll she had recently eaten, slithered through her stomach. The visit to the farm could be put off no longer.

The trouble started before they'd even gotten to the gate.

"Look, darling," Bella pointed out to Tolly. "Look at those wonderful sheep."

Ptolemy immediately clapped his hands to his eyes and marched past the field. "Missed them," he declared triumphantly.

"Don't you like animals?" Rosie was surprised. Then again Ptolemy confounded most ideas of what was normal in children.

"Oh, he loves them, don't you, darling?" Bella rushed in. "Adores his dog, don't you, sweetheart? Although," she added in an undertone to Rosie, "we had to get rid of the last nanny after I caught her putting Berengaria in the microwave. She actually believed Tolly when he told her it was the quickest way to dry her. That's the trouble, you see. He's much too clever for his nannies—*don't miss the horse, darling,*" she suddenly urged her son. "Just look at him there in that bottom field."

Ptolemy looked with contempt at the big, glossy chestnut. "Hate horses," he snarled. "They're so slow at racing."

"Slow?" echoed Rosie. The horse, she knew, belonged to the well-to-do wife of one of the local businessmen who rented the field from Jack. Rosie had often seen her belting up Cinder Lane to the farm at a velocity anything but leisurely.

"He means as opposed to Formula One, darling. He's been trying to persuade Simon to buy him a mini–racing car for ages."

As she lifted the Spitewinter gate, Rosie tried not to think about Jack's likely reaction to the child. Running him over with the combine harvester, most likely.

"At least Ptolemy's got confidence," Bella said proudly. "That's the most important thing you can give your children, apparently."

Rosie privately thought that the most important thing Bella could give Ptolemy was a good smack. It was, she had found, one of the few matters on which she and Mark agreed.

"And he's *so imaginative.* The other day we were in Sainsbury's and he spotted a woman in a yashmak. 'Look, Mum,' he yelled at the top of his voice. 'It's Darth Vader.' *Can you imagine?*"

"Yes," said Rosie truthfully, before she could stop herself.

"And he's awfully competitive," Bella continued as they came into the farmyard. "Simon keeps telling him, 'Remember, son, it's not the taking part that counts. It's the winning.' Hilarious, isn't he?"

"Rib cracking," said Rosie, thinking that, much as she loved Bella, her friend definitely had hidden shallows. As for Simon, his sense of humor had clearly not improved of late. Even when the relationship had been in its heady early days, Bella had confessed that her fiancé was hardly a laugh a minute. Personally, Rosie had always wondered whether he managed a laugh a year.

Rather to Rosie's relief, Jack was nowhere to be seen. Almost immediately, neither was Ptolemy, who shot off into one of the barns. Rosie's fear that he might fall in the silage clamp or suffer a hideous, mangled death in some machinery or other—fear in which a certain amount of hope was mingled—proved unfounded when Ptolemy was found safe and sound poking a sharp stick at Wellington in his chicken coop. Dragged forcibly away by Rosie, Ptolemy then attempted to climb inside the large rusty tube with the conical top that stood in a corner of the farmyard. Only when Rosie explained that it was Jack's grain silo and not the Spitewinter Farm Independent Space Project did he desist.

"Jack must be out and about somewhere," Rosie suggested.

Walking them to the fields, she moved as fast as she could in the hope that, by the time they found Jack, Ptolemy would be too exhausted to do anything other than behave himself. But Ptolemy, unfortunately, was as energetic as he was evil. It was, of course, just when, oblivious to Rosie's and Bella's screamed instructions to stop, he was rushing at wailing herds of sheep and pretending to bark like a dog that Jack appeared on the horizon, silhouetted against the sky like an avenging god.

"What the bloody hell's going on?" he howled, catching up with Ptolemy in a couple of huge strides and grabbing his arm. "You little bastard. How dare you . . . Rosie!" He stared at the women in astonishment.

Rosie felt she might explode with shame. Conscious of Bella's amused eye upon her, she clumsily performed the introductions. "Ptolemy has never seen a real-live farm before," she gasped, as if that in some way explained why he was being forcibly restrained by a real-life farmer.

"Yes," chimed in Bella, flicking her smile on to dazzle. "I was hoping he might learn something about the countryside. Perhaps you could talk him through some of the trees and flowers or something." She batted her eyelids furiously, thrust a hip forward, and shook a glossy black lock wantonly in front of her eye.

To Rosie's amazement, instead of erupting with fury Jack merely shrugged. She had forgotten the power of Bella's charm. Or was it the power of Bella's tight little white T-shirt and designer jeans that showed off every curve?

"Well, you can come with me to the top field if you like," Jack offered. "There's a lot of hedgerow along the lane."

"Look at the hedges, darling," Bella urged Ptolemy as all three traipsed behind Jack. "The nice man's going to tell you what all the flowers are."

For a second Ptolemy looked as if he was going to cover his eyes again. Catching Jack's steely glare, however, he thought better of it and stared resentfully at some buttercups.

Jack pulled at the lacy, green-white blossom leaning out into the road. "Know what this is?"

Ptolemy shook his head violently.

"Cow parsley?" guessed Rosie after a few minutes' silence from the others.

"Very good." She felt ridiculously proud of his approval.

"And those are forget-me-nots," Bella said immediately, pointing at the bright blue flowers.

"Excellent," said Jack, flashing her one of the wry smiles Rosie had grown to regard as her personal property. She felt a stir of jealousy. "And that blossom at the very top is . . . ?"

"Don't-give-a-toss," spat Ptolemy.

"Darling!" Bella flashed an apologetic glance at Jack.

"Nearly," said Jack neutrally. "Love-in-a-mist." He briefly flicked Rosie's eyes with his own. She blushed, and her stomach turned over.

Jack was now shaking a long, lolling, dusty-red bloom at Ptolemy, who glanced at it with loathing and pressed his hands to his eyes.

"Valerian," said Jack. "Came over with the Romans. You must be interested in the Romans, surely, Ptolemy?"

"Yes, darling," urged Bella. "You love the Romans, don't you? All those Christians being mauled by lions and gladiators murdering each other and everything?" Ptolemy brightened.

"And this is wild garlic," Jack interrupted, looking disgusted. He ran his fingers through the patches of white bell-heads and shiny leaves. The plant's savory tang rose up into the air, mixing with the heady sweetness of the neighboring bluebells. "And these," Jack added, touching with the tip of his finger some tiny white flowers. "Know what these are?"

Rosie looked at the miniature petals, rising proudly on pink stems out of the clutches of fleshy leaves. She shook her head.

"London Pride," said Jack with emphasis. Rosie wondered miserably at which of them the barb was aimed. All, probably.

The botanical master class apparently over, they walked in silence back to the farmyard.

"Are you organic?" Bella asked Jack conversationally. Rosie clenched her fists apprehensively, silently urging Bella not to go on. Talking to Jack about his farming methods led to nothing but disaster in her experience.

Jack's brows had drawn together. "No," he said.

"Well, surely you should be," Bella pronounced decisively, blundering, as Rosie had feared she would, straight into the lion's den. "All farmers should be aiming at sustainable farming systems that maintain the long-term fertility of the soil."

"That's arable," said Jack shortly.

"What's so horrible about it?" demanded Bella. "The fact of the matter is that intensive methods, while they produce heavier yields, are also destroying our wildflowers and wildlife. As well as endangering our children's health by allowing all that poison to enter their systems." She looked fondly at Ptolemy, who was busy slashing viciously at the hedgerow flowers with a stick. "That's what horrible."

"Been reading all that off the leaflet that comes with your organic delivery box, have you?" Jack's tone held an unmistakable note of contempt.

Bella blinked. "Well, yes, actually."

"Thought so. Otherwise you'd know that when I say arable, I mean that Spitewinter isn't. I don't grow crops here. I've a mixed cattle and dairy farm. I don't need to put chemical fertilizers on the land. In fact, the worst danger to plant life in the entire place at the moment is your son."

"Stop that, darling," Bella snapped at Ptolemy, who, busy beheading a clump of bluebells, ignored her completely.

They had now reached the top of the hill overlooking the village. Bella paused and peered intently at something. "What's that?" she asked, pointing into the distance. "That group of buildings over there?"

"Ladymead," Jack said without emotion.

"Who lives there? It looks *enormous*."

"Some pop star," the farmer said dismissively—for all the world, thought Rosie with amusement, as if he didn't own a couple of cows called Jennifer Lopez and Britney Spears.

Bella clapped her slender, beringed, and red-nailed hands. "*Wonderful*. So Eight Mile Bottom's got its requisite wrinkly rocker, has it?" She looked laughingly at Jack, the organic clash apparently forgotten. "Is he one of the Rolling Stones?"

Jack, however, did not forget so easily. At least, Rosie assumed this was why his face had darkened. "No. He's a bit younger. Well, quite a lot younger."

"Who? Is it Robbie Williams?"

"Matt Locke, he's called."

Bella breathed in so sharply she coughed. "*Matt Locke!*" she choked. "Not *really*! The one who disappeared into the middle of nowhere? So *this* is where he disappeared to?" Bella, eyes streaming, whirled round on Rosie. "Darling, you never told me you lived near *Matt Locke*! I'd have been up *much* sooner . . ."

Thanks a lot, thought Rosie. "Forget to mention it," she muttered.

"*Forgot!*" Bella's look clearly implied that, as far as Rosie was concerned, all hope was lost. She turned back to Jack. "How much land does he own?" she demanded, her eye drinking in the sweep of green between where they stood and the cluster of towers in the distance.

Jack shrugged. "Quite a bit. Most of these big fields here in front. Used to be mine, but there was no point keeping them once the herd had to be reduced."

Rosie stiffened. Oh no, she thought. Here we go.

"Matt has a thing about fields," Bella cut in. "He's wandering across vast prairies looking mean and moody in almost all of his videos."

Rosie stole a glance at Jack. Cut off in his prime, he was looking pretty mean and moody himself.

"Did you sell it to him?" Bella asked Jack.

"Had no choice." Jack effortlessly picked up the thread of gloom again. "Need every penny I can get. All us farmers do these days. It's madness, what's happening to us. People pay a pound for a tiny bottle of water and I get paid eight pence a pint from the dairy for my cows' milk. And guess how much it costs when it gets to the shops in a carton? Twenty-nine pence, that's what. Is it any wonder we've got our backs against the wall—"

"I didn't mean *that*," interrupted Bella impatiently. "I mean, did you meet *him*?"

Jack looked amazed, then furious. "As a matter of fact, I didn't. Some lackey of his dealt with the sale—"

"Er." Rosie was thankful for the excuse to interrupt. "Isn't that a bull in that field Tolly's walking through?" She did not add that her concern was mostly for the bull.

Over warm gin and flat tonic at Cinder Lane that evening, Bella regaled Mark and Rosie with recent events in the capital, including the news that she and Simon had recently gone to a wedding where a tennis ball machine costing £1,399 had been on the gift list. Also that Florian—"who, of course, you'll remember from the dinner party"—had recently picked up an award for a fly-on-the-wall documentary following a number of minor Royals as they did a home swap with a family on a council estate.

Her voice was quite unable to block out the fact that, of the children running and screaming up and down the lane outside, Ptolemy was screaming the loudest of all. He and Satchel seemed to have hit upon a modus vivendi instead of merely hitting each other. Rosie tried not to wince as Ptolemy smashed the black football hard against the glass of the window. Only with the greatest of efforts, she noticed, was Mark restraining himself from going outside and tearing him limb from limb.

"It must be wonderful to be out of the rat race." Bella sighed. "To live at a leisurely pace in the peace and quiet. Not have someone putting the pressure on all the time."

Thinking immediately of the dreaded editor, Rosie deliberately did not look at Mark.

"London's *soooo* exhausting," Bella went on. "Everyone desperate for their children to do everything first, as long as it's not drugs and sex and shoplifting. And social climbing like you wouldn't believe. I know one mother who's got Prince Harry lined up for her daughter. At least you never get anything like that round here . . ."

Rosie's mind leaped to the party invitation Mark was so desperate to get his hands on. He hadn't mentioned it lately, though. Perhaps he had forgotten about it.

"So, enjoying it here, are you, darling?" Bella turned brightly to Mark. "Must be very quiet after London."

As he opened his mouth to reply, Rosie tensed. "Not at all. Positively packed with thrills," Mark drawled sarcastically. "Such as a new flower coming out on one of Rosie's bushes, for instance."

Rosie hoped Bella would drop this line of questioning. Still, as long as she didn't mention the column . . .

"Column going well, is it?" Bella inquired next.

"Fine." Mark's tones sounded dangerous.

"Have you seen Champagne D'Vyne's column?" Bella trilled. "Rather good, I think."

"Who's she?" Rosie was desperate to get the subject off columns. Even if it exposed yet another yawning gap in her knowledge of the rich and famous.

"You *know*," Bella urged. "That gorgeous blond model-cum-whatever with legs up to her armpits. Huge tits, very posh, writes this column called 'Champagne Moments' every week about all the parties she's been to?"

"Oh . . . *yes*." Rosie was amazed to find she actually did know. The column ran in a rival Sunday to Mark's. When they lived on Craster Road, he had regularly hurled it violently across the room in disgust, saying it was the only thing worse than "Driving Miss Daisy." More recently, however, Rosie had discovered him on several occasions studying it quite hard.

Bella went on blithely. "She's famous for being famous, of course. And for having famous boyfriends. Used to go out with Matt Locke, in fact. Supposed to have been the whole reason he became a recluse. He never got over being dumped by her, apparently." Bella paused and grinned. "Probably the whole reason he came to Eight Mile Bottom, if you think about it."

As Ptolemy, outside, let rip an ear-splitting scream, Rosie looked pleadingly at Bella. "Do you think supper will be ready yet?"

It was, Rosie thought, leading the way out of the sitting room, almost worth putting up with the horrors of Ptolemy for the joys of his mother's cooking. For Bella was a proper cook. She could chop onions in that professional way where the knife scythed rapidly into the onion and not, as when Rosie tried to emulate it, into the fingers.

And there were other reasons for getting her into the kitchen. Surely, following her recent exchange with him, Bella must have realized Mark's behavior was worse than ever. There was also the fact that Rosie had spent the entire journey back from Spitewinter waiting for Bella to pronounce on Jack. So far, however, she had said nothing about either of them.

"Dreadful shame," Bella observed as she tore up a lettuce.

"What is?" Rosie asked eagerly. That she was sticking with a sulky prima donna when she should be going for a hunky farmer?

"About no organic vegetables," Bella continued disappointingly. "I was rather counting on piles of home-grown carrots, potatoes with the earth still on them, broad beans, and all that kind of thing."

Kind of like Bella's organic delivery box in Islington in other words, thought Rosie. Not to mention the Arcimboldo bowl. It had been hard to explain to Bella that, for some reason, it seemed far more difficult to get your hands on organic vegetables in the country than it did in the city. Vegetables of any sort, come to that. The village shop stocked mostly white bread, tins of beans, and Indian sauces.

"But can't you grow your own?" Bella had asked, amazed.

"Yes, but they take ages. And we haven't been here all that long."

In any case, Rosie's research into what was, for her, the brave new world of horticulture had taught her that much of it was touch and go anyway. A whole host of assassins, she now realized, lurked in the soil waiting to demolish anything trying to grow there. According to the Womersleys, beans in particular needed what practically amounted to a twenty-four-hour suicide watch to protect them from snails, slugs, and greenfly. One look at what snails had done to her herb border gave a whole new meaning to the ravages of thyme.

"Can't your neighbor give you any?" Bella had peered longingly over the wall into the Womersleys' garden, where serried ranks of different vegetables poked neatly up from the soil. "Theirs look wonderful." Rosie forbore to mention that the Womersleys, like herself, threw slug pellets about like confetti. Bella would almost certainly not approve, although Rosie was increasingly amazed that anyone ever grew anything without them. How, she wondered, had the Elizabethans managed?

"Surely they could spare you a few onions," Bella said longingly. "I could make a wonderful salsa."

Rosie felt mildly shocked. Asking the old couple for vegetables had never occurred to her; nor had the offer ever been made. The thought of Mr. Womersley's prize vegetables meeting so ignominious an end as being eaten was unthinkable. As the Womersleys themselves seemed to exist on Fray Bentos meat pies with canned peas, served with thick gravy, it seemed the vegetables were grown for show alone. And certainly not for salsa.

"I can't believe you can't get any in the village shop, even." Bella sighed as she scrubbed some extremely orange carrots. "Look at them," she muttered. "*Stuffed* with water and *crawling* with poisons. Tolly's simply not used to anything that isn't organic. Everything he eats at home has Soil Association Approved practically stamped all the way through it. He starts the day with organic cereal served with freshly squeezed organic oranges from Spain, then organic pasta with organic cheese for lunch, and then multigrain eggs fried in organic butter for tea . . ." She was arranging what looked to be, despite everything, a wonderfully fresh vegetable salad on four plates. A delicious-smelling spaghetti sauce bubbled on the stove. "Oh, well. Supper's ready. Could you tell Tolly to come in, darling?"

"He says he's had his dinner," Rosie reported after making unsuccessful representations in the lane.

"He can't have." Bella put down her wooden spoon and strode out.

A few minutes later she returned, Ptolemy's arm clamped firmly in hers, her face as angry as Rosie had ever seen it.

"Yes, and it was *all* GM," Ptolemy was shouting. "I had chicken nuggets. Fried. And onion rings. *Fried.* And a whole king-size Mars bar for pudding. Dipped in tea to make it go all melted. Wow. Satchel's mum's a great cook. Much better than *you*, Mum."

"*That's it,*" Bella said through clenched teeth. "I'm awfully sorry, darling, but I'm afraid we'll simply have to go back to London in the morning."

"*That's fine,*" said Rosie and Ptolemy in perfect unison.

Dinner passed with Ptolemy pressing lengths of spaghetti into the grooves in the table and refusing to eat anything. Mark, who stared at the child with ill-concealed hatred throughout the meal, disappeared into the box-room as soon as it was over.

"Sit quietly now," Bella warned Ptolemy, putting on a *George of the Jungle* video in the sitting room while she and Rosie returned to the kitchen to finish their wine. Finally, Rosie thought, her friend's verdict on Jack.

"I'm awfully sorry about the neighbors," she began, although she had actually thought it extremely hospitable of Mrs. Muzzle to share the family dinner with Ptolemy. But then Ptolemy's see-want-have mechanism being what it was, she probably hadn't had much choice in the matter.

"Oh, God, darling, don't worry." Bella sucked on a cigarette. "The chicken nuggets are only an excuse. I'm dying to get back to London and hand him over to the nanny. This mother-son-bonding business is awfully hard work. Next time I come I'll do it differently."

"You'll come on your own?"

"No, I'll bring the bloody nanny as well." Bella blew out two plumes of smoke from her nostrils.

There was a silence.

"Erm, Bel?"

"Mmm?" Bella was now scrutinizing the parish newsletter that lay crumpled among the debris on the table. "Hilarious, this, isn't it?" She recited gleefully. *"The Barley Mow Talent Night was won by local builder Barry Foreshaw, who sang 'Norwegian Wood.' The Eight Mile Bottom Ferret Olympics will be held at Park Bottom on Saturday. All entrants to register with Dame Nancy Brooke-Sullivan."* She paused, turning over the page. *"The Annual Fruit Cake Bake-Off was won by Mrs. Gilman, whose edges were the most even, whose cherries were the best distributed, and who was judged to have sunk the least . . .* Lucky Mrs. Gilman, I say. This is priceless," Bella gasped, waving the newsletter. "No wonder Mark says the column's fine. This must practically write it for him."

"Er, actually he doesn't write an awful lot about the village in the column," said Rosie. At last, the opening she'd been hoping for. They could discuss Mark's behavior first. Then get on to Jack.

"Why ever not? I would have thought it was obvious."

"That's what he says—it's obvious. He says it would be too easy, too boring to write about all the eccentric characters and village life and everything."

"But that's mad," said Bella.

Encouraged, Rosie warmed to her theme. "He thinks the village newsletter's beneath him. Even though it's put together by the local headmistress, who you'd imagine would be a good source of stories. But Mark says all that's just dull. He thinks everything's dull. Even village cricket. We got a thing through the door the other day asking if he wanted to join the team—"

"Perfect!" said Bella. "Long shadows across the grass and all that."

"But Mark says he was never any good at sport and doesn't fancy tongue sandwiches in the pavilion."

"Sounds like good fun to me, darling."

Rosie smiled wanly. "He's having a dreadful time with the column, but he goes mad if I suggest anything. Says the ideas aren't the problem, he's got plenty of them flying round in his head—"

"Just having a tough time getting them to land, eh?" finished Bella, her eyebrow raised.

"Something like that." Rosie sighed. "He isn't interested in any of the wildlife either. The one time I dragged him out to listen to a lark he said it sounded like a modem."

"Which is why you were tempted by young MacDonald up there, I suppose," Bella said lightly, jerking her head in the vague direction of Spitewinter.

Rosie nodded, feeling her stomach lurch at the long-awaited moment of truth. "What did you think of him?" Bella *must* have been impressed by the pains Jack had taken to amuse Ptolemy. And his hulking physique. Bella liked big men—very big men if Simon's straining waistline was anything to go by. Rosie watched her friend's face anxiously.

The verdict was as short as it was devastating. "Not a lot, to be honest."

Rosie felt the earth shift slightly beneath her. She groped, desperately, for a logical explanation. "Because of Mark, you mean? You don't think I should have a fling with anyone else?"

It was Bella's turn to look amazed. "Hell, no. The way Mark treats you, it would serve him right if you ran off with the old bloke next door. No, there's something funny about that farmer. Sort of bad-tempered. Dark horse–ish."

"Well, that's hardly fair," Rosie said hotly. "Just because he lost his temper about organic vegetables when Tolly was traumatizing practically every animal on his farm. You can't expect him to be thrilled about it."

"Well, I may be wrong, of course." Bella's lofty tone implied the exact opposite was the case. "Just thought I detected something a little, um, *irritable*. I mean, he's hardly sweetness and light, is he, darling? Talk about the moans of production being in the hands of the workers."

"Farming's a hard life," said Rosie loyally.

"You're telling me, darling. The way he tells it makes Stalin's gulag sound like a holiday camp. To be honest, I think he's a tad bitter about something. Any idea what his romantic history is?"

"No," said Rosie, wondering what was coming.

"Troubled, at the very least," said Bella decisively. "Lots of turmoil and confusion there."

"But you can't blame him for being upset about selling his land to Ladymead. Or the fact that he only gets eight pence a pint for his cows' milk. His family has run Spitewinter for generations."

"So I gathered." Bella rolled her large eyes. "Farm here to eternity."

Bella closed her eyes and swallowed. "If you must have a fling with someone—and I absolutely agree that you must—you're wasting your time on a *farmer.*"

"So who do you suggest?" Rosie demanded crossly, her teeth clashing on the glass of wine she raised abruptly to her lips. "The postman? The pub landlord?"

Bella looked at her, wide-eyed. "Of course not, darling. Someone eligible, rich, handsome, and famous, obviously."

Rosie looked at her blankly. She had gathered from Duffy that there were a number of elderly actors in the village, although they hardly sounded her type.

"Matt Locke, of course," urged Bella.

As Rosie exploded on her Merlot, Bella realized that the sitting room had gone very quiet. She rushed into it, Rosie close behind her, to find Ptolemy stuffing handfuls of cold spaghetti from his pocket into the mouth of the video.

CHaPTER 16

As Bella's shining BMW turned and disappeared around the corner the next morning, Rosie felt relieved. She was not best pleased with her friend. If pouring cold water over her new friendship while her brat of a son poured everything everywhere was Bella's idea of serious girl time, then she could forget it. As for the Matt Locke idea, that was about as useful as a chocolate kettle.

As she was returning to the cottage, the postman's red van came hurtling up the road. It shuddered to a halt in front of her.

"You're very honored," Duffy yelled as he leaped out and slammed the door.

"Am I?" asked Rosie doubtfully.

"Most certainly you are." Duffy preceded her into the house, settled himself at the kitchen table, and placed a large, thick cream envelope amid the toast crumbs. Addressed in neat italics in thick blank ink, it looked very imposing. The postman was looking at her expectantly; whatever it was, there was a price for handing it over. Resignedly, Rosie reached for the tea bags.

"You're looking very nice today," Duffy said conversationally. "Off to Spitewinter, are you?"

Rosie's face reddened. As a matter of fact, she *had* half planned a visit to the farm. There were a few sketches to tweak and, of course, she needed to apologize for Ptolemy's appalling behavior. Most of all, though, she needed to satisfy herself that Bella was wrong—*completely* wrong—about Jack.

"Must be nice for Jack, having a pretty young thing like you about the place. Be just like old times for him."

Rosie, dunking Duffy's tea bag in his mug, twisted around so fast the muscles in her neck crunched almost audibly. "Old times?"

"His wife, of course. Pretty young thing. A bit like you, now I come to think of it. Except dark, not blond. Bit more makeup as well."

Rosie's mind reeled under this vast, heavy new piece of information. "His *wife*?" Jack was *married*?

Duffy nodded, delighted at her consternation. "Ex-wife, I should say."

Rosie blinked. Jack was *divorced*? "What happened to her?"

Duffy paused and looked expectantly at the package of chocolate chip cookies. Obediently, Rosie pushed them in his direction.

"City type, she was," continued Duffy, pulling out a cookie. "Didn't like farm life, she didn't. Brokenhearted, he was," he finished chirpily.

So Bella had been partly right. Troubled romantic history . . . emotional turmoil . . .

A crash as the front door swung back and the inevitable curse as Mark caught his fingers announced both his arrival—he had finally, ungraciously, gone out to get the milk—and the end of the opportunity to find out more. Duffy leaped up from the table.

"Your post," he said, thrusting the cream envelope into Mark's hand as he stomped into the kitchen. "You're very honored."

"Honored?" Mark slammed down two pints of milk and tore at the cream envelope. Had some literary agent spotted "Green-er Pastures" and written to offer him a book deal merely on the strength of it? About bloody time, too.

"What is it?" Rosie watched Mark's narrowed eyes eagerly scrutinize the card. With even more ill grace than that with which he had gone for the milk, he shoved the long-awaited party invitation unceremoniously into her hand.

Guy was desperate for the party to be over. What had started out as drinks had now assumed the proportions, the expense, and practically the status of a coronation. Not that this was inappropriate given that Samantha was clearly building up to be crowned queen of Eight Mile Bottom.

Sholto, on the other hand, was very much present and correct. Present and Correct also being the name of his wretched party design company that Samantha had suddenly and inexplicably—at least, she hadn't explained to Guy—hired at vast expense to turn the lawns of The Bottoms into the Casbah. Despite the house being easily big enough for a party even on the scale Samantha was now planning, she was determined not to hold it inside for some reason.

Sholto infuriated Guy. There was no escaping him. Since his arrival two days ago, he had assumed All Access at The Bottoms. No room was free from the risk of his mincing in with his shiny tan, spiky blond hair, black linen Nehru jacket, and mobile permanently glued to his ear. It seemed to Guy that the very air was filled with his high-pitched and uniquely irritating voice, shrieking about what he habitually referred to as his "erection" at the builders. Camp as a row of sodding tents, thought Guy savagely. And a row of tents, as it happened, was pretty much what was planned—a vast central marquee to be flanked by ancillary "annexes," all draped inside with pink and purple silk, festooned with lanterns, dotted about with cushions, and peopled with what Sholto referred to as "mixed exotica." This, though sounding to Guy exactly like those vile hanging baskets Samantha brought back from the garden center, apparently meant belly dancers and waiters with jewels in their navels.

"Belly dancers always go down very well," Sholto assured him with a series of lewd winks that made Guy feel sick. "Everyone likes a bit of wobble."

Except me when I see the bloody bill, Guy thought. "Sounds like a sodding Turkish Delight ad," he muttered, and was horrified when Sholto turned, beamed delightedly, and informed him that yes, how clever of him, that was exactly the effect he was going for. The retro advertisement theme was wildly fashionable at the moment, and after this he was doing a party themed around the seventies' Martini ads starring Leonard Rossiter and Joan Collins.

But if Sholto was a bad dream, Samantha was a nightmare. Watching her stamping about the lawns barking commands at the army of helpers Sholto had assembled with amazing speed—as well he might at the prices he was charging—Guy decided that the party had finally turned Samantha into the monster she was always going to become. Although "selfless" and "considerate" were words not even Samantha's own mother could use with regard to her daughter (partly because Samantha's mother hadn't spoken to her daughter for over ten years), Guy had stuck with his second wife in the face of all criticism. Even that of his daughter—difficult though it was to withstand her bitter railings and the passionate letters from school that, stained with tears and smeared with ink, begged him not to leave her mother. Letters that, Guy suddenly realized, he had not seen since moving to The Bottoms.

There were a lot of things he hadn't seen since coming to The Bottoms come to think of it. Samantha in her full split-crotch raunch regalia, for one thing, Lalla's phone number in his mobile address book, for another. The whole point of marrying Samantha, after all, was that her bedroom technique had been second only to his mistress's. Marina's lack of enthusiasm for sex had been one of the main reasons for their split. That and Marina's discovery that Samantha was making up the deficit.

Yet Guy, whose sex drive seemed only to increase with the years, had been more than happy to sacrifice the peace of the domestic hearth if it meant hitting the ceiling in the bedroom. The problem was that since Samantha had buried them in the country, the ceiling had remained unassaulted for quite some time. It infuriated and frustrated Guy that the only ceiling hitting authorized by Samantha was by the various minions putting chandeliers up in the Casbah, while the only permitted erection was Sholto's. Guy stiffened as he heard the hated voice shrieking instructions about curtains. "I like them very well hung."

Guy struggled up from the bench where he sat brooding. He needed to go for a walk as well as make a phone call. Marina's last call about Iseult had concerned him. It was more than time to ring and find out the latest news. He mooched down the drive and dug out the mobile.

A man answered at Marina's. Guy's hackles rose, knowing it to be Jez, the Royal Opera House ice cream hawker his ex-wife had recently taken up with. "I'll get Rina," he drawled in a mid-Atlantic accent that made Guy boil. *Rina!* "Who's calling?"

"Her *husband*," Guy said emphatically. "Ex-husband, I mean," he muttered.

Marina came to the phone. "What do you want?" She was, Guy knew, suspicious about his new interest in their daughter. He had no explanation for it himself apart from suddenly feeling bitterly ashamed of his past neglect. Neglect that, although he could not blame her entirely, Samantha had enthusiastically encouraged. Nevertheless, he persevered and succeeded in extracting the information that, following her expulsion from school, Iseult had left home "to stay with some friends."

"What friends?" Guy demanded.

"School ones, I think," Marina said vaguely. "You know. People from that band she's in."

"Band?" Guy had not realized his daughter was in a band. She had never struck him as the sousaphone-playing sort. Marina did not enlighten him further.

"Look, I really have to go," she said. "I'm doing *La Traviata* set in a commune and it takes ages to get my flares on. I have to lie down on the floor and zip them up."

Commune? *La Traviata*? "You mean the Paris Commune?"

"No, well, *yes,* it is a commune in Paris, I suppose. Viletta and Alfredo get it together during a love-in. It was Jez's idea."

"Ah, yes. Jez," said Guy. "Ice cream seller or something, isn't he?"

"Director, thank you very much," snapped Marina. "Don't you start on him as well. He had enough to put up with from Iseult."

A wave of approval for his daughter coursed through Guy. "Don't they get on?"

"Not brilliantly," Marina admitted. Mr. Whippy, as Guy was determined to think of him, was obviously still in the room. "But she's at that difficult age. She says I'm a drag and I wig out on her too much."

"What?" A vision of Marina in a vast rainbow-colored Afro hairpiece flashed up in Guy's mind.

"You know, get cross," said Marina impatiently. "She talks in this weird seventies' Californian slang, for some reason. I suppose all the girls at the school must do it. By the way, she said she was trying to ring you. Have you spoken to her?"

"No." Guy's suspicions were aroused. Had Samantha been intercepting the calls? Did bears piss in the woods? Was the pope a Catholic?

"I must go," Marina said urgently. "She'll be back, don't worry. She's just being a bit rebellious at the moment. You can't blame her—it was you, after all, who made her take her GSCEs at fourteen."

"Did I? Christ, what a bastard I was."

"Competitive, you called it. But she'll be fine. She'll ring me when she's ready. She always does."

"You seem very sure about it," Guy snapped. He felt furious. The thought of Samantha taking Iseult's calls was more than he could bear.

"If by that you mean I'm a bad mother, you can sod off." Marina's tone was sharp. "Who's been bringing her up all this time while you've been swanning around with *that slapper*? Or else buried in your bloody bank."

"Yes, well, I know I haven't been . . . I mean, I was hoping things could be sorted out a bit now. You know, I'd really like to see her. You, too. We need to try to work as a family a bit more . . ."

An amazed silence ensued from Marina's end. Then, to Guy's horror, she laughed.

Guy was indignant. "What's so funny?"

"Jez is just showing me the rest of the Violetta costume. There's a huge rainbow-colored Afro wig."

It was odd, Guy thought, putting the mobile away, but since the heart attack, work had become less important than it had been. Having been reminded of his mortality in so dramatic a fashion, thoughts unprecedented in their paternalism had begun to occur to him. Now that Samantha, always opposed to children, was also opposed to all activities that usually led to children, Iseult looked to be the only person to carry the Grabster seed into future generations. Being on nonspeaking terms with her just to please his wife seemed to Guy to be an increasingly stupid idea. Not least because Samantha was making no efforts whatsoever to please him.

Iseult had been trying to ring him and he hadn't known. He'd kill Samantha for this.

When she rang again, Guy promised himself, he would try to persuade his daughter to stay at The Bottoms for a while. And *bugger* whatever Samantha thought about it. He smiled. If she rang again. His smile faded.

Suddenly, Samantha appeared at the top of the drive. His courage evaporating, Guy shoved the phone back into his pocket. "Going out, are you?" she yelled after him in a voice implying he should be spending the afternoon ironing rose petals or whatever other absurd tasks Sholto had been going through with her with the clipboard this morning. "Remember that we're one belly dancer short. She needs to double up as a cocktail waitress as well. One of them's not coming. Mother's dying of cancer or some such crap."

Guy nodded curtly and shuffled out through the gate. Just where was he supposed to find a cocktail waitress in Eight Mile Bottom? Most of its female natives looked as if the nearest they came to a Rusty Nail was the one in the outside loo on which they hung their torn-up strips of newspaper.

His thoughts returning to his daughter, Guy's mood plunged as he heaved up the hill past the pub. He considered going in but decided against it, not being in the mood for Alan's banter. The fact that Sholto had taken to dropping in "for the atmosphere" posed an additional risk. Guy did not want his cover blown by Sholto. He didn't want anything blown by Sholto.

By the time he stomped up the road to the church, his spirits had plummeted still further. He stopped and leaned against the churchyard wall, looking without interest up the small lane of scruffy cottages in front of him. Cinder Lane, he read on the sign attached to the crumbling wall. It looked like a godforsaken bloody place to him. Even if the church was practically on top of it.

Exhausted, Guy closed his eyes for a few minutes and opened them again. And opened them wider. A smile spread itself slowly across his face. For walking down the lane directly toward him was one of his favorite sights. A pair of really nice big breasts, albeit with a rather large baby plugged into one of them. Those nipples, he thought, were just *made* to have big silver tassels attached to them. Against all the odds—and some of the women in this village looked pretty bloody odd—he'd found a belly dancer. A cocktail waitress as well. Someone, he knew insintcitvely as he caught the woman's bold gaze, who knew exactly what went into a Slow Comfortable Screw. Not to mention a Screaming Orgasm.

"It's the party tomorrow and I haven't a clue what I'm going to wear." Although dreading the event itself, Rosie had seized on it as a subject with which to break any ice that had formed on Jack since Ptolemy's visit. She was also at pains to conceal from the farmer that she knew about his ex-wife. Jack would no doubt be furious that Duffy was peddling his troubled romantic history for chocolate chip cookies. Even if he was unlikely to be all that surprised.

Except, Rosie thought, that she didn't know all about it, Mark's arrival having stopped the postman's revelations about what had happened. But it had clearly been seismic. Perhaps his wife had died, left him a young widower with a farm to run. She considered Jack's habitual crushed look, his hurt expression, his bouts of temper as if railing against his own unhappy experience. It would explain them all.

"It says Arabian Nights . . ." She flashed a glance at Jack. His face was set and preoccupied.

"Aren't you listening?" she asked him playfully. "I've got a crisis on my hands." Mark, certainly, had been determined to view it as such. "So what's bloody new?" he had demanded when she had admitted party-outfit failure, having rummaged through every item in the washing basket, which, increasingly these days, served as a wardrobe. Her panic-stricken scouring of Cobchester had similarly failed to address the situation. Yellow jackets with padded shoulders and rail after rail of beige tents hardly seemed to fit the bill, let alone herself.

Jack shook himself and looked at her. "Sorry," he said. "I was thinking about a crisis of my own, to be honest."

Rosie's stomach looped the loop. Was he thinking about his wife and what had happened? Did he want to talk to her about it?

She felt panicky. How could she possibly introduce the subject? She didn't want Jack thinking her nosy as well as stupid and possessed of ghastly friends with ghastlier children. On the other hand, it seemed rude not to demonstrate a degree of concern.

"Is one of the animals ill?" she hedged.

"The animals are right enough." Jack flashed her a white, mirthless smile. "It's the whole farming business that's sick."

Several minutes later, after Jack had lectured her about Environmentally Sensitive Areas and the chaos that listing fields and hills had brought to Spitewinter, Rosie felt sick as well.

"Oh, God, I'm sorry," she muttered, feeling an overwhelming rush of guilt at having thought for one minute that not having anything to wear for the party counted as a problem of any sort.

With an effort, Jack retrieved his features from the doomed creases into which they had sunk. "It'll get better. I'm thinking of converting to organic with the cows. It'll add a bit of value and let me keep more of the milk profit. Such as it bloody is," he added savagely. "It'll cost me, though. Conversion means a big investment and there'll be a dip in production by at least twenty percent. And even after that I need to think of other ways to diversify if I'm to keep the place going." He paused. "But why the hell I just don't sell up, I don't know. Hand over the whole lot to some developer and let the whole of Spitewinter get covered in executive homes with brick drives and built-on conservatories covered in plastic bloody squirrels."

Rosie gasped in horror. "Because Spitewinter's beautiful and your family has had it for centuries," she declared passionately. "Besides, you probably can't develop it. It's an Environmentally Sensitive Area." An oversensitive area, even, she thought, knowing this was what Bella would say and feeling immediately guilty.

"Yes, of course. I'd forgotten." Jack spoke with heavy sarcasm. "Because farmers aren't allowed to think of easy ways out, are they?" His voice was rising; Rosie's heart sank. Here he went again. "We're the custodians of the landscape even if we work our fingers to the bone and get nothing but grief for it. You're right. My family has had Spitewinter for centuries. But there's no family now, apart from me. Or likely to be," he added bitterly.

"You were married, weren't you," Rosie said gently. She had to know. This seemed as good a time as any to find out.

Jack leaned against the wall of the farmhouse and crossed his arms defensively. "For about a year, yes."

"Tell me what happened."

Jack paused before proceeding, as Mark would have put it, to give her the headlines. "Her name was Catherine, she was beautiful, she was from London, I met her in the Barley Mow when she was up for the weekend visiting a friend who lived nearby."

"She was from London?" This was unbelievable. If Jack had fallen in love with a London girl, why was he so set against city people?

He nodded. "Yes. We were very happy. For a while. Until a year after we got married, when she . . ."

"*What?*" Rosie's heart banged loudly against her rib cage. What had happened? Oh, Christ, she *had* died after all.

". . . screwed the sheepnut salesman in the cow shed," Jack said flatly. He raked a hand roughly through his hair. "I came back one lunchtime and caught her at it."

"Oh, my God," breathed Rosie. Her legs felt suddenly weak with sympathy and shock.

Jack's eyes hardened. "She thought she'd like the countryside, but she found that actually she hated it. London type, you see. Hated not being able to ever lie in, hated having to get up and do the milking. Always staying in, always mucking out, she used to say. She said it was no fun. Too quiet . . ." His voice trailed off. "Well, she was having plenty of fun when I found them. Not being all that quiet about it, either."

Rosie's heart contracted with pity. Poor Jack, carrying the burden of Catherine's betrayal around like a snail with its shell on its back. No wonder he looked so crushed.

"One good thing came out of it though," Jack added heavily. "Bloody animal-feed firm had always been unreliable, but Catherine insisted we buy from them. Once I knew why, I sacked the bastards." He gave Rosie a rueful smile.

"No wonder you're wary of Londoners." It all made sense now.

"Well, after that I was pretty wary of women in general," Jack said shortly. "Never thought I'd trust a city lass again, that's for sure." He gave her a piercing glance. "Until now, that is." There was a charged silence before he added, "But you might change your mind. And I can wait."

Doubt tore savagely at Rosie. It would be so easy now to say she had had second thoughts. As his sad blue eyes under their sloping brows met hers, she opened her mouth to do so. Unlike Mark, he had been hurt. Unlike Mark, he needed her. She could heal him. Make him happy again . . .

A sudden screech of tires interrupted them. "Cricket club's in uproar," shouted Duffy cheerily. "They've lost that cup they won last season—rumor has it the vice captain's sold it. *Oh,*" he added as Jack came down the side of the cow shed with Rosie. "Been out for a walk, have you?" He grinned.

"Walk?" Jack snorted. "Joking, aren't you? Farmers don't have time for walks. Or anything else, come to that. Been checking the sheep in the upper field."

"Been showing you the ways of the wild, has he?" Duffy turned delightedly to Rosie, who blushed violently. But Jack seemed utterly unruffled. He took the post, turned on his heel, and disappeared into the farmhouse.

"Looking forward to the party, are we?" Duffy yelled at her as he climbed back into his red van. The party. She'd forgotten about that, and that, as yet, she had precisely nothing to wear. Mark would go spare if she let him down. But perhaps she should let him go spare—on his own, in other words. It seemed the easiest way out.

"That postman missed his vocation," observed Jack as Rosie ventured into the warm gloom of the Spitewinter kitchen. "Should have been a spy."

"He talks too much," said Rosie. "And he's not quite got the James Bond looks, let's face it." As Jack handed her a mug of tea, Rosie tried to ignore the animal-feed company logo on its cracked side.

"Think I might be able to solve your crisis, by the way," he remarked.

Crisis? What crisis? After all Jack had suffered through his marriage, and was continuing to suffer through his farm, Rosie had temporarily forgotten she had any problems at all. "My party clothes, you mean?" Was he about to offer her some of his blue overalls? Did he have a pair of gold lamé ones he saved for best?

"My aunt was a dressmaker in her young days. Got loads of old dresses."

"*Mrs. Womersley?*" Rosie's mouth fell open. Sharon Stone may have turned up in a Gap polo neck to the Oscars once, but was Jack seriously suggesting that she should wear one of Mrs. Womersley's castoffs to the Party of the Century? Mark would go ballistic.

"I'll ring her up later and ask her if you like," Jack offered. "She copied designer clothes for herself and local women who couldn't afford Dior and such-like. Did them all. Pucci, Balenciaga, Chanel, Yves St. Laurent. Still has a lot of them. Won't throw them away for some reason." He looked at Rosie, his mouth turning up again slightly. "Excuse me, but I thought vintage couture was very fashionable. Am I wrong?"

Rosie nodded. The last *Vogue* she had done a food illustration for had been practically devoted to the subject.

"Catherine used to get *Vogue*, you see."

Another silence. Bella had been right about his romantic history, Rosie reflected—but she was wrong about him being bitter and twisted. Was he not trying to help her with her party costume, in the full knowledge that she would be going with Mark? Given the circumstances, such generosity seemed positively heroic. Was Jack, Rosie wondered, now trying to change her mind through actions rather than words? As he drained his mug of tea, silhouetted against the window, Rosie couldn't help remembering the feel of his hot, thick fingers, and she tried to divert her thoughts from what was beneath the blue overalls.

CHaPTER 17

Bang, bang, bang. The noise was coming from the back this time. That was the last straw. He'd officially had enough.

Mark leaped up from his laptop and ran down the stairs so hard his thighs hurt. *"Just shut the fuck up, will you?"* he yelled as he shot out of the kitchen door into the back garden. The first thing he saw was Mr. Womersley, staring indignantly at him from the other side of the wall.

"Well!" said Mr. Womersley.

The old bastard might be as deaf as a post, but he'd heard that all right. "Not *you,*" snapped Mark.

Bang bangety bang bangety bang bangety band. As he knew it would be, the noise was coming from the Muzzles' garden.

"Them!" he shrieked, pointing violently at the wall dividing Number 2's now orderly garden from the Muzzles' rubbish-strewn patch.

Trampling all over Rosie's flowerbeds, her pansies and narcissi irrelevant in the face of his all-consuming fury, Mark stuck his head through the tattered remains of what had once been a small fence on top of the wall but which the combined and irresistible forces of children and weather had succeeded in destroying almost utterly. Nothing was visible in the next-door garden apart from a sea of rubbish, from the middle of which rose a rickety-looking stick and sheet construction vaguely reminiscent of a teepee. It was from here that the banging noise was coming.

"Oy!" Mark screamed.

The banging stopped as if a plug had been pulled out. "What's up, man?" came Arthur's uncertain, reedy voice.

"What the *fuck's* going on?"

The twigs swayed and the sheets surrounding the construction bulged and parted. It seemed to take a full minute for Arthur's lanky body to unfold.

"Hello, man," he said, blinking in the sunlight. With the parting of the curtains, a powerful blast of marijuana smoke turned on the breeze and hit Mark full in the face. He coughed savagely and his eyes began to stream.

Once the smoke had cleared, Mark noticed that Arthur's white and skinny arm held a large and battered-looking pair of bongos, their metal surrounds glinting in the dull sun. He looked at them with loathing.

"Any particular reason why you can't play those inside the *house?"* he demanded, biting each word viciously as it came out. As a loud crash from Arthur's kitchen was followed by the bull-like bellow of Guinevere and the screams of his children, Arthur's slitlike eyes briefly met his.

"Well, *that,* man," he muttered. "Does my head in sometimes."

A red mist flickered behind Mark's retinas. He was conscious of his heart having picked up speed. The feeling that if he didn't leave the scene at once he might vault over the fence and do Arthur's head in once and for all threatened to overwhelm him.

Turning on his heel—and Rosie's narcissi—he stomped back over the lawn. As he wrenched open the back door, he noticed Mr. Womersley still standing there watching him. "And you can sod off as well," he snarled.

Mr. Womersley cupped his hand to his ear. "Pardon?"

When Mark returned to his laptop, the envelope icon was flashing in the corner. He'd got mail. The editor would have read this morning's attempt at "Green-er Pastures" by now. It was, Mark thought, calming down slightly, rather a good one.

After much thought, he had deftly sidestepped the problem of not having his own animals by going to the local children's zoo to write about theirs.

He had begun, *Have you ever noticed the way animals at the zoo stop doing anything interesting the moment you reach their cage? The elephants turn their bottoms to you, the gorilla leaves his climbing frame and goes into a trance . . .* Mark opened the editor's E-mail. *Have you ever noticed the way columnists stop writing anything interesting when you send them to the country? You're fired.*

Mark stared at the screen in disbelief. *Fired?* He was *sacked?* This was *impossible.* The editor couldn't just get rid of him. The column represented his sole income. Especially given the fact that, for some odd reason, the paper had been utterly unable to syndicate it. There must be some mistake. Perhaps the editor had meant to send the E-mail to someone else?

Panicking, Mark looked at his watch. Half-past two; there'd be time, if he moved quickly enough, to get down to the newspaper offices and sort things out before the editor swept off in his chauffeur-driven Mercedes for the evening. It was, after all, easy to sack someone when you couldn't see them. Even the editor might think twice about it in the flesh. In the unlikely event that he had meant it.

It wasn't until he was on the train that he remembered he hadn't left a note for Rosie. Still, it would do her good to wonder where he was for a change. She was definitely taking him for granted these days.

Rosie did not miss him immediately. Party clothes were her most pressing agenda. On her return from the farm she went straight to Mrs. Womersley's to see if what Jack had promised in any way translated into reality.

Jack had phoned ahead, and Mrs. Womersley seemed not just eager but determined to help. Wondering what she had let herself in for, Rosie followed the old lady up her gloomy staircase, followed by the riotous noise of Mr. Womersley's radio.

As Mrs. Womersley pulled back the sliding door of her teak wardrobe with a veined and liver-spotted hand, even the poor light of a seventeenth-century cottage bedroom as the afternoon drew to a close could not quite dim the glory of what lay within.

"Incredible." Rosie was entranced. It looked, she thought, like the fashion cupboard of a glossy magazine before a haute sixties' shoot.

From beneath sheaths of clear plastic peeped pastel pinks, bright blues, and shimmering silvers. Jewel-colored sweeps of crushed velvet were suspended over serried ranks of high-heeled shoes. Hats, boas, and bags of all descriptions were piled on the shelves.

"Haven't got anything Arabian Nighty, mind," Mrs. Womersley said. "Not much call for it in Eight Mile Bottom. It's more flannelette nighties round here."

"I'm sure it doesn't matter. Anything partyish will do." Rosie's eyes were glued to the glittering and intensely partyish row of dresses.

"This would suit you." Mrs. Womersley pulled out a soft tweed two-piece so utterly Jackie Kennedy that Rosie longed to try it on and feel the beautifully lined fabric brush coolly over her back and encase her in vintage First Lady elegance.

"But it's an evening do, isn't it?" Mrs. Womersley whisked the suit back out of her reach. Sliding her papery arm into the wardrobe again, she brought out a plastic sleeve encasing a slim black dress.

Rosie looked at it doubtfully. An LBD. Elegant, undoubtedly. But unforgiving. You needed a body as hard as Barbie's to get away with that sort of thing.

Mrs. Womersley was back in the wardrobe, shoving aside shoes, boxes, and bags in her quest.

"How about this then?" She removed the clear plastic sarcophagus surrounding something tailored and white.

Rosie's eyes shone as Mrs. Womersley held up a beautiful white suit with wide lapels. "Fantastic. Pure Bianca Jagger."

Mrs. Womersley looked surprised. "You're right there," she said. "Made this for Marilyn, the butcher's daughter after she married Mick Jagger. After Bianca Jagger did, that is," she added hastily. "Marilyn married a chimney liner from Cobchester. Never wore this, though. Couldn't fit into it. Too many pork pies, I told her. Should fit you, though, easily. You don't look like you eat many pork pies."

"No, I don't."

"Nice, though, a pie is. With mushy peas or a bit of mustard."

Rosie shuddered, recalling the violent vermilion of the pies at the Silent Lady. Not actually wanting to remember anything more about the Silent Lady, she looked longingly at the St. Tropez wedding outfit suspended from the padded hanger.

"Go on, try it," urged Mrs. Womersley. Rosie hesitated, then shrugged off her fleece. Remembering too late her graying bra, she comforted herself with the thought of Mrs. Womersley's Harvest Festivals stretched out above the chimney breast. Besides, in this light, everything looked gray.

Except the suit. Rosie shuddered as the cold silk lining made contact with her back and gasped as it pressed against her front. Climbing into the skirt, she sent up a silent prayer of relief as the zip whizzed unhindered to the waistband to enclose her hips in a perfect fit. She buttoned the jacket, straightened her shoulders, and grinned at Mrs. Womersley. "How does it look? Shame I haven't got dark hair."

"It's not a shame at all," said Mrs. Womersley. "You look very nice, you do. A sight better than Marilyn Sidebottom ever would have done in it, pork pies or no pork pies."

Rosie padded across in bare feet to the long mirror that gleamed darkly in the corner. Even given the stone in weight that a narrow mirror shaves off one's reflection, she had to admit she looked good. The fitted curves of the jacket drew in gently to the waist; the skirt fell in a generous column to what seemed impossibly tiny ankles. Suddenly, she looked as if she'd stepped straight from a glossy magazine shoot rather than, as Mark said she usually did, the set of *This Old House*.

Even her hair, uncut for many months and mulched down into an unmanageable mass of blond curls, looked right. Shining intensely in the limited light, it framed what had become her small and delicate face before spilling wildly and glamorously over the suit's razor-sharp shoulders as if she had spent five minutes curling each strand. Even her breasts looked good; studying the long V-shaped slash of flesh diving uninterrupted from her clavicle to her navel, Rosie felt a rare gratitude for their tininess. It wasn't the sort of suit you wore a bra with. Perhaps that was where Marilyn Sidebottom had gone wrong.

"Can I really borrow it?"

"Course you can, dear." Mrs. Womersley beamed. "I'm glad to help. It's a treat having you next door. You've done wonders with that garden."

Eyes sparkling, Rosie stared back at her reflection. "It looks so incredibly modern. I could probably go into Gucci this minute and buy something exactly the same."

Mrs. Womersley's smile faded slightly. "Is that what you think?" she said, shoving both hands in her apron pockets. "I must say, I quite liked the early Gucci designs, but I'm not at all sure I approve of the way that Tom Ford's taking it these days."

"Must have caught on something in the delivery van," Duffy said, handing over the battered cardboard box to Samantha. Through its jagged apertures, a quantity of chiffoned sequin was clearly visible.

"There's some fancy stuff in there and no mistake," the postman added as Samantha slammed the front door of The Bottoms in his face. "I'd be careful of those glittery knickers though," he added through the letterbox. "Look a bit scratchy, they do."

Samantha turned her back and began to rip the box open—farther open, that is, than Duffy already had done.

She was seething. The range of requested *Arabian Nights* outfits had arrived from the Covent Garden theatrical hire firm only just in time. The party was a mere twenty-four hours away.

"*Sheherezade*," spat Samantha, reading the label attached to the costume on top, a white silk bikini glittering with sequins and accompanied by swathes of white chiffon. "Why the *hell* have they sent me something called that?" she demanded of an empty hall. "What *is* Scheherezade? Is it like lemon*ade* or something? *Bugger*," she added, panic-stricken. "Should I have gotten Sholto to put it on the menu?"

Guy, who had been snatching a few minutes' rest on the daybed in the sitting room, wandered reluctantly through. It was impossible to sleep in any case, the chaise longue's floral print being louder than a crowd of football supporters.

"Scheherezade," he explained wearily, "was the woman who told one thousand and one stories in the *Arabian Nights*. I think her husband was going to kill her otherwise." He resisted the temptation to add that he knew exactly how her husband felt. The party was driving him close to the edge. Or, to be more specific, Samantha was. Her behavior was becoming worse by the day—by the minute, in fact. As long as he lived, which given his current levels of stress would not be long, he would never forget the Trainer incident.

Guy winced at the memory. After another disturbed night in which he could have sworn some vast black soccer ball had bounced repeatedly round the inside of the canopy, he had come leaden-eyed into the morning sunshine to find Samantha attacking one of the workmen about, of all things, his footwear.

"Just *look* at them. They're a *disgrace*," she had been yelling, pointing at the ragged piece of dirty leather flapping over the gaping hole along the inside of her victim's right foot. "Can't you buy some new ones?"

The workman shook his head. "Can't afford it," he had mumbled. "I've got four kids and the work's not regular."

Poor sod, Guy had thought. Sholto clearly kept his staff on a rein as tight as his own trousers. An idea had occurred to him and he had shuffled back inside the house.

"Here," he had said, reemerging and shoving the wad of notes from the bottom drawer of his study at his wife. "I'm sure this will be useful," he added to the workman, whose face lit up with delight.

"Brilliant idea, darling," Samantha had cried, taking the wad and snapping the elastic band off the notes. "*There*," she had said, extending her hand to the workman.

He had looked at it bemused.

"Go on," Samantha had urged, waggling the elastic band between her fingers. "Take it. Put it round your shoe. It'll hold it together for the rest of the day at least."

Guy, slipping the workman another wad once Samantha had stormed off, had felt guilty at not having taken her on immediately. He had wanted to but feared his heart would not survive the encounter. If only Iseult were here to give her a piece of her mind. Guy longed more than ever for the company of his daughter. He had still not found her letters. Possibly, however, that was a good thing; given that their general thrust had been "Don't marry Samantha, Daddy, she's a bitch and she'll make you unhappy," they would be salt in his wounds. He had been keeping a close ear on the phone, but Iseult seemed not to have called again. Did she think that he didn't want to speak to her and had stopped trying?

"What about this?" Samantha's voice dragged him back into the present and the party. Abandoning Sheherezade on the grounds that not only was it unpronounceable but also the gold rivets in the knickers looked as if they might chafe, she had scooped up a pale pink nylon and gold ensemble so overwhelming in its decoration that, Guy thought, it could have practically gone to the party by itself. "It's got some initials in it," she said excitedly. "J.S. Who's J.S.?" She paused before exclaiming, "*Jean Simmons.* Of course. She must have worn this in, um, er . . ."

"*Spartacus?*" suggested Guy.

"*Spartacus!*" Samantha pressed the costume to her bosom in rapture. "I've got Jean Simmons's costume from *Spartacus.*"

"Or Joan Sims's from *Carry On up the Khyber,*" said Guy nastily.

Samantha came out of her trance immediately. The proportions of the costume were, admitted, more matronly than one might have thought necessary to cover the lissome form of Kirk Douglas's love interest. She scowled ferociously and tossed the costume on the floor. "That leaves *Cleopatra.*" Samantha grabbed a glittering magenta silk two-piece complete with gold turban out of the box.

"Didn't realize Cleopatra went in for turbans," said Guy.

"Course she did," snapped Samantha. "She was the Joan Collins of her day, wasn't she? Now, what are *you* going to wear?"

Guy conveniently remembered his reservations about the festive food and disappeared. Samantha looked furiously after him as he fled, muttering something about checking with Consuela that the waitresses would have plenty of sausage. In particular, that one he'd picked up in Cinder Lane.

The following afternoon, anyone driving from Eight Mile Bottom along the Slapton road would have noticed a sharply handsome but bleary-looking man with tousled blond hair walking shakily after the bus that was heading to the village from the railway station. The bus driver had swerved violently, brakes screeching, into every bend between Cobchester and Eight Mile Bottom, and Mark, his stomach finally unable to bear any more, had gotten off to walk the last stretch.

His trip to the capital had not been a success. Unless, that was, you were coming from the point of view of one of the landlords in whose establishments Mark had blown the rest of his month's money. The rest of his money period.

His head pounded and from time to time his legs buckled beneath him. But if going out drinking with former newspaper colleagues the night before had not been a good idea, crashing out on the production editor's sofa had been less advisable still. His back ached agonizingly and someone seemed to have been standing on his neck all night. Worst of all, nothing whatsoever had been achieved. The editor had refused even to see him, let alone reinstate him.

Mark now recognized that giving up his job to write a damned countryside column had been a disaster. But was it his fault there was nothing to bloody write about in the sticks? Was it his idea, even? No. The inspiration for the whole bloody shooting match had been Rosie. No wonder he'd never been able to get it to work. Whatever the editor might have said—quite forcibly—to the contrary, Mark knew that it was distance from the paper rather than inadequate copy from himself that had been to blame for his downfall. It would never have happened had he remained in the capital and not disappeared to the middle of nowhere on some stupid whim of Rosie's. Because, make no mistake about it, moving to the countryside in the first place had been *her* great idea.

With Herculean effort, Mark managed to prevent himself from throwing up on the grass verge. This small success cheered him. He raised his drooping head. Hell, he was still a writer, wasn't he? They couldn't take that away from him. His thoughts flew to Samantha, the first woman he'd met in ages who had appreciated him. She was in films, wasn't she? Maybe they could collaborate. Do a screenplay or something. He'd always fancied a screenwriting Oscar. The British Matt Damon. He could write, she could star. She was supposed to be famous—she was bound to have connections. As another sweep of nausea threatened to overwhelm him, Mark closed his eyes and saw Academy Awards loom out of the rushing red. He should get over there now and start the ball rolling. Not to mention the cameras.

"*Hey*, there. Excuse me."

Mark turned. A thin, dark-haired girl was standing behind him. He

registered her lank, uncombed hair, long tie-dye skirt, and an arrangement on her upper torso consisting of about three separate thin-
strapped black vests and a cardigan apparently made of cobwebs. There
was a stud through her nose, a ring through her mouth, and another in
her navel. Remembering Dungarees' collection of facial metalware,
Mark felt the tension rising. No doubt she was in search of the Cinder
Lane commune.

"*What?*" he snapped.

The girl smoothed back her hair and grinned at him. "I'm looking
for some joint called—"

"Over there." Mark jabbed a finger in the direction of the church.
Even from this distance he could see the rotting row of clapped-out vehicles collapsed against the church yard wall.

"Cool." The girl raised a pencil-thin eyebrow. Her bruised-looking
mouth turned slightly upward. "You psychic or something? How did
you know what I was going to ask you?"

Psychic. Sodding hippies, Mark fulminated silently. Full of spiritual
crap, all of them. She'd be asking him if he fancied a bloody Indian
head-massage next. He continued gesturing at the Muzzles's cottage.

The girl took a step nearer and peered in the direction of the
church. "So The Bottoms is over there, is it?"

"The Bottoms?" Mark looked at her in amazement. "Are you *sure*
that's where you're going?" The pits, surely, was nearer the mark.

"Sure, I'm sure." She had, he noticed, eyes of an exceptionally clear
blue. Her voice, too, for all the California drawl, had a firm undertone
of Chelsea, and not the Stamford Bridge terraces at that. If she was a
hippie, Mark realized, she was a smart one. It wasn't impossible she was
a friend of Samantha's. *Samantha.* Oh, God. *The party.* He'd almost
forgotten, what with the trip to London, the film plans, and the rest of
it. He'd better get over there now. They'd have an hour to discuss Op-
eration Oscar, as he had already christened the project, if he went
straightaway.

"So you're here for the party, are you?" he asked the girl as casually
as he was capable.

"Party?" She looked blank for a minute. Then light seemed to
dawn. "Oh . . . yeah. Sure. I'm here for the party."

"Know Samantha, do you?" One of her thespian friends perhaps. That would explain the scatty bit. She looked like one of those alternative actress types, the sort that banged on about kabbalah and drank their own pee.

"Yeah, I know her."

"She's a great friend of mine," enthused Mark. "Wonderful woman. Amazing."

"*Completely* amazing. Like, far-out amazing," agreed the girl. Mark wasn't entirely sure what to make of her tone.

CHAPTER 18

The evening of the party had finally arrived. In the master suite of The Bottoms, Samantha was squeezing Cleopatra's satin magenta skirt over her hips and reflecting furiously on Guy's absolute refusal to try Faisal, Aladdin, or any other of the costumes she had, at great effort and expense, called in for him. To make matters worse, the familiar front doorbell chime of "Greensleeves" had just resounded through the hall. A glance at the ormolu clock, whose face was so heavily decorated that it took several minutes to make out what the actual time was, confirmed Samantha's suspicions that if this was a party guest, they were *hours* early. Still, what could be expected from yokels?

But she was almost ready. The gilt body polish having been thoroughly applied by Consuela earlier—"For Christ's sake, be careful. I'm Cleopatra, not bloody Tutankhamen"—all that remained was to dust brown eyeshadow down the sides of her nose, a trick picked up from the early days to make it look thinner. Legions of makeup artists may have described her nose as Grecian, but even Samantha knew it needed work to make it Helen of Troy and not Zorba.

No doubt the premature arrival was the vicar. He'd telephoned earlier explaining that he had a couple of dying parishioners to attend to and would she mind if he popped in before things got going. Although whether he meant the parishioners or the party, Samantha was not sure. People died at the most bloody inconvenient times, she thought crossly, cursing as one gilded toenail snagged in the strap of her gold stiletto sandal.

But she had to keep on the right side of the vicar. The ghost situation was getting ridiculous. Even Consuela had heard something shrieking in the gazebo, although that could well have been Sholto, whose stress levels had gone off the meter as the day of the party approached. The straw that broke the camel's back had, appropriately enough, been the nondelivery of a much-anticipated pair of stuffed dromedaries intended to create a desert atmosphere at the marquee entrance. Having to substitute them with a couple of stuffed sheep from a design shop in Cobchester had, Sholto had declared, driven him almost to his wits' end. "Not very far, then," Guy had observed, prompting Sholto to resign and then, possibly mindful of his fee, retract. Given the speed with which The Party had been put together, Sholto had demanded and been granted an enormous premium.

After the party, Samantha vowed, she'd have a go at the vicar about the spooks again. Get the bloody local bishop involved, if necessary. The pope himself, if she had to.

Spraying almost an entire bottle of Shalimar into the air before her, Samantha swept through the perfumed cloud and proceeded magnificently downstairs.

Her guest was not the vicar, however. It was that rather handsome journalist—Martin or something—she had met in the church a couple of days ago. Acutely aware of the need to balance her turban, Samantha inclined her head in gracious welcome. Unfashionably early he may be, but Martin had been an inspiration. Had it not been during their conversation that she'd had the brilliant idea of erecting a marquee on The Bottoms' lawn thus sidestepping the whole issue of undesirable apparitions—apart from Guy, that was—spoiling the occasion. "How wonderful to see you," Samantha said in queenly fashion, stretching a hand out for him to kiss.

"You look wonderful," muttered Mark, feeling suddenly shy as his lips slid about the back of Samantha's greasy gold hand. Draped in the brilliantly colored, clinging silk, she looked, he thought, spectacular. She'd descended the staircase like a head-spinning hybrid of Mata Hari and Scarlett O'Hara. A diamond the size of a quail's egg nestled in her navel, while her breasts, thanks to Cleopatra's cantilevering, stood out like two golden rockets ready for launch.

Such was the weight of her false lashes, Samantha's eyes were almost completely closed. The effect was to give her an air of freezing hauteur, and Mark quailed as her contemptuous glance lingered on his jeans and crumpled gingham shirt. "This is supposed to be an Arabian Nights party," she said crisply. "You don't look remotely Eastern. Unless we're talking Norwich."

Mark felt that if he'd had a hat in his hands, he would be twisting it.

"Come upstairs," purred Samantha, who had just had a very good idea. Half terrified, half excited, Mark was unable to believe his luck. He had not expected their collaboration to start so immediately. Let alone so physically. For this seemed undoubtedly what she had in mind.

"This way," Samantha breathed, looking deeply into his eyes with a laughing, kohl-ringed gaze as they reached the top of the stairs. "This is my bedroom."

Mark swallowed. Were his Mrs. Robinson fantasies about to be fulfilled? As he followed her through an arched doorway into a room dominated by a vast, canopied bed and blazing with floral wallpaper, the sound of "Greensleeves" boomed out once more in the hall.

"*Quick*," urged Samantha, pulling him inside the room and closing the door. "There isn't much time. Get your clothes off."

"Ees the vicar, madam," Consuela screeched up the staircase. On the other side of the closed door, Mark smiled slowly at Samantha. The sense of her closeness—at least the scent of her Shalimar—was overwhelming him. The idea of a man of the cloth waiting downstairs, albeit only the happy-clappy vicar, gave the already charged situation an extra frisson of excitement. Mark closed his eyes, opened his mouth, and leaned forward, expecting to feel the touch of Samantha's brassy lips, the glistening tip of her tongue.

Instead he felt something scratchy in his arms. Mark snapped open his eyes to discover not Samantha but a pile of gold and silver material, pinned to the top of which was a label marked "Aladdin." He looked up in horror.

But Samantha had already swept from the room.

*   *   *

"Well, good luck, darling." Bella's voice floated airily down the line. "From what you've been saying, you'll be the belle of the ball. Your outfit sounds divine."

Rosie stared at herself worriedly in the smeared mirror of the compact she held in her other hand. Doubts about her appearance had begun to creep in. Was her hair glamorously tousled or did it look like a nest occupied by a problem family of birds? Then there was the suit. The fact that Mrs. Womersley thought she looked wonderful suddenly seemed neither here nor there. It was, after all, the opinion of someone who frequently appeared in public in curlers and carpet slippers.

"What does Mark think of it?" Bella asked, hitting, as usual, the bull's-eye on Rosie's worry target.

"He hasn't seen it yet," she confessed. "He wasn't here last night."

"Where was he?" Bella sounded indignant.

"No idea. He didn't leave a note."

"Didn't leave . . . ?" Bella gasped. "What the hell are you supposed to think?"

Think? thought Rosie dully. She was too exhuasted for that. Having sat in the suit for hours in order to surprise him when he got home, Rosie's hopeful anticipation had turned to anguished panic when, by midnight, Mark had still failed to appear. His recent behavior faded into insignificance as Rosie, frantically dialing every police station and hospital within a twenty-mile radius, imagined him lying in an intensive care ward or, much worse and more probable, bleeding to death in the emergency room. Her search proving fruitless, she had gone to bed but had not slept, in the faint hope that he would come home in the early hours. Her eyes now felt as hard, dry, and heavy as golf balls and ached with exhaustion.

"Do you think he's in London?" Bella asked.

"I don't know. Why?"

"No reason," Bella said. "Except I hear on the grapevine that he's been sacked from the newspaper."

"Sacked?" A small, weak ray of relief penetrated the dark turbulence of Rosie's mind. *Sacked.* The weekly agony would at last be over. "Oh,

God. He'll be devastated. That must be what's happened. He must
have gone away to . . . think about things."

"Bloody cheek," snapped Bella. "I can't believe he never even told
you. Well, actually, I can. But aren't you furious?"

"Well, yes, I am," Rosie said hesitantly. The hope was growing in
her heart that now the column had gone, the old Mark might return.
It was not too late, after all.

"Apparently they're planning to replace him with 'Champagne Moments.' You know, that party column by—"

"Champagne D'Vyne. Matt Locke's ex-girlfriend. The one who
broke his heart and all that," Rosie interrupted, feeling real fear once
again. If Mark knew *that,* he'd be at the bottom of the Thames. No
doubt about it.

"Well, you needn't be so dismissive. Matt'll be at this social event of
the rustic year, I take it? This party?"

"Possibly." She felt irritated with Bella. Not least because the hours
she had recently spent pacing about the cottage had unearthed yet
more evidence of Ptolemy's brief but devastating visit. Bits of chocolate
trodden down into the spaces between the floorboards, chewing gum
under the kitchen table, and sticky sweets under the cushions, to mention but a few.

"So you're going to the party? On your own?" Bella sounded
astonished.

"Yes."

By the time morning had arrived, the one decision Rosie had made
was to go to Samantha's party. Perverse though that seemed in the circumstances—Bella, for one, clearly thought so—there was method in
Rosie's madness.

Given the fuss he had made about being invited, there was no
doubt that if Mark was alive and on the planet, he would be there.

"That weird farmer's not going as well, is he?" Hoping it would ex-
cite her sympathy, Rosie had told Bella about Catherine, the cow shed,
and the sheepnut salesman, but it seemed to have had the opposite effect. "Confirms everything I said," Bella had said grimly. "He's got an
ax to grind. I told you."

"No, he's not invited," Rosie said sadly.

"Good."

"Glad you think so."

"Look, darling," Bella said. "I know things aren't exactly going your way at the moment, but you're not the only one with problems. My boiler burst last night."

"Oh, dear." The boiler was one of the few appliances in the cottage yet to self-destruct, but Rosie supposed it was only a matter of time. Whenever it rained, there were so many leaks that the water dripping into the various buckets sounded at times like Concerto on a Theme by Severn-Trent Water.

"It was dreadful. Simon was away and Tolly was spending the night in the science museum, so there was really only one thing for me to do."

"Fix it?"

"No. I went to stay at the Berkeley."

Going to a party on her own was embarrassing enough. But walking through Eight Mile Bottom looking like something from *Boogie Nights* set new levels in Rosie's experience of personal discomfort. Pressed into a wall with embarrassment, Rosie heard the roar of a tractor behind her. Jerking the bulky machine up onto the pavement as effortlessly as if it were a pony, Jack stopped the engine.

It seemed to Rosie that Jack looked at her for a long time, his eyes moving steadily from where the suit clung to where it flared. She tossed back her hair from her shoulders and wished the jacket didn't reveal so much cleavage. Even if, in her case, there wasn't that much to cleave. "That one of my aunt's?" The usual wry smile was wider, more appreciative.

She nodded. "Thanks for the tip."

"You look great." He paused. "You on your own?"

"No, well, not really. I'm meeting Mark there," Rosie awkwardly assured him, wondering, through her fog of tiredness, whether she still wanted this to be the case. She was, she knew, as purple as the lobelia on the nearby wall.

"Have a good time." Jack started up the engine again and lumbered off the pavement just as a Mercedes stuffed with pashas obviously bound for the party came up the High Street behind him and hooted.

Rosie waved after him, her stomach heaving with a mixture of guilt and regret, then started up The Bottoms' infinitely long and relentlessly winding gravel drive.

Although the front of the house was in darkness, shrieks of laughter and the clink of glasses indicated a party under way in the garden at the back. The smell of smoke and spices hung heavily in the gathering dusk. Rosie swallowed. Her palms were suddenly clammy with fear. She would know no one apart from Mark. If, indeed, he was there.

The heavy oak door of The Bottoms was so crowded with an array of objects in decorative brass that Rosie had difficulty locating the doorbell at first. Then she spotted it above the engraved letterbox, to the left of the door knocker shaped like Shakespeare's head. A crosshatched center of a brass Tudor rose.

Rosie raised her hand to the bell. *Christ,* she suddenly thought, glancing at the back of her fingers. The fake tan she had hurriedly slapped on her face, chest, and hands was now fully developed, and the full extent of how badly she had applied it was becoming horribly apparent. The back of her hand looked like a sunset in sepia. Her front probably looked more camouflage than cleavage. The chill evening air ruffled her nipples as, panicking, Rosie pulled back the lapels of the jacket to peer at her breasts.

"Still there, are they?"

Rosie gasped and whipped her hands back together so swiftly that her knuckles collided painfully. A wary-looking man with a pinched face was picking his way toward her with the loping stride of a dog.

"Sorry," he said, looking penitent. "That was a bit rude of me."

"Doesn't matter," muttered Rosie.

"What are you waiting for?" asked the man, gesturing at Samantha's brass-festooned door. "Don't you want to go in?"

Rosie clenched and unclenched her fists. "Not really. I don't like parties very much," she muttered.

"Me neither." The stranger gave her a strained smile. "Particularly fancy-dress ones. Which is why I didn't bother." Looking at his crumpled jeans, ancient baseball boots, and experienced-looking hooded top, Rosie—possibly for the first time in her life—felt ridiculously overdressed.

"Do you know the woman giving this bash?"

"Mrs. Guy Grabster?" Rosie fished the invitation out of her pocket. The fact that Mark had failed to take it hadn't worried her. No doubt he had memorized every detail. "No. I've never met her."

"Me neither. She sounds pretty scary. Some sort of film star, isn't she?"

Rosie shrugged. "I don't really know. I'm no good on famous people, I'm afraid."

"That makes two of us." He seemed, Rosie noticed, to speak with feeling. He also had very good teeth. As he revealed them further in a hesitant smile, she felt slightly better. With luck, everything would be all right. With more luck, Mark would be inside. And, luckiest of all, he would not have found out about Champagne D'Vyne.

"Oh, well," he added, looking at the doorbell. "I suppose we'd better go through with it."

Rosie stabbed the Tudor rose, then leaped back, startled, as "Greensleeves" bonged loudly out of a concealed speaker in the ivy surrounding the lintels. A closed-circuit camera swung simultaneously out from behind one of the mullions. Black and white and intensely decorated, it was unlike any Rosie had ever seen before.

"Bloody hell," said the scruffy stranger. "Original Elizabethan closed-circuit. Half-timbered, no less."

The door flew open to reveal an Amazonian figure whose impressive and gleaming gold breasts were barely restrained by a bra of magenta silk sparkling with gold sequins. Her face was almost entirely obscured by a gold turban heaped with jewels, as well as an astonishing amount of makeup.

Nevertheless, Rosie recognized her. She realized that, subconsciously, she'd been expecting all along to see her again. At least, since an incident involving a Jaguar a couple of weeks ago. The identity of the woman persecuting Jack about his herd and his free-range henhouse suddenly struck her as well. Of course. Who else?

"Hello, Samantha," she said.

Damn it, Samantha seethed as she beckoned them in ungraciously. She really *had* thought it would be him this time. With the help of the ever-resourceful Sholto, who happened to be a Matt Locke fan, she'd been studying every permutation of his famously flamboyant stage persona, every outfit he had ever worn, to be sure not to miss him when he arrived. But so far *nada*. Instead, it was some woman with scruffy hair who seemed to think she knew her and some bloody builder's laborer. The one she'd lent the elastic band to, by the looks of it. Still, she'd best let them in. Country gentry often looked like cleaners, in her experience. At least they had invitations, even if the laborer's was crumpled and covered in coffee rings.

"I thought you said you didn't know her," Rosie's companion hissed as they were borne down the hall on a tide of revelers in turbans.

"I didn't realize I did," she confessed. A procession of waiters carrying platters piled with food suddenly forced their way between them. As the scruffy stranger, looking terrified, was swept away on a tide of falafels, it occurred to Rosie that she had never found out what his name was. Oh, well. Taking a deep breath, she prepared to wade into the crowd to look for Mark.

Snatches of conversation ebbed and flowed in her ears.

"Yes," a large old pasha was observing to a woman dressed as Lawrence of Arabia. "She's appallingly rude about him. Going around mocking him for buying his own furniture. Bloody cheek, I'd say, coming from someone who's had to buy her own *castle*."

"Absolutely," agreed Lawrence of Arabia.

"If you can call it a castle," added the pasha witheringly.

Were they, Rosie wondered, talking about Samantha?

"My name's Florence," a well-built lady in a turban with the bone structure of a shire horse was informing a thin, bearded man dressed as a vicar. "I've lived here for what seems like hundreds of years. They should call me Renaissance Florence, really."

"Any idea where the drinks are?" a deep female voice suddenly rasped behind Rosie. An inquiring squawk followed her words. Looking round, Rosie saw she was being addressed by a tall blond woman in a sequined yashmak holding a cockerel.

"That way," shouted a couple of portly ancient Egyptians, pointing down the corridor.

"Shocking," said the lady with the cock, her green silk pants swishing indignantly as she followed Rosie past a display of flat irons

mounted on the wall, some antique forks in frames, and a mangle festooned with rustic hats. "Catherine St. Felix told me it was like a
bloody Harvester in here and she's right. Though it could have been
much worse, apparently—this Grabster woman wanted to put a horizon pool in the ha-ha until the planning authorities got involved.
Nancy Brooke-Sullivan by the way," she added, sticking out a hand.
"And you are . . . ?"

"Rosie."

"Love the suit, darling. Used to have a similar one myself. Hell's
bells, look at this." They were passing through the French windows
at the end of the hall and entering Samantha's Arabian Nights marquee. "Must have cost a bloody fortune. Talk about sheikhing it all
about."

Rose looked round in amazement. Against the billowing purple and
magenta silk walls, palm fronds and flaming torches abounded; across
the floor, a foot deep in sand, lay artfully arranged piles of tasseled and
embroidered cushions. A noisy throng of people dressed as everything
from Tudors to Chewbacca shouted and waved at one another, grabbing handfuls of food from the numerous waitresses. One particularly
lascivious Roman, Rosie noticed, was grabbing handfuls of waitress as
well. Mark, however, was nowhere to be seen.

Suddenly, Nancy's cockerel erupted in a flurry of feathers and
squawks. It was, it seemed, fighting desperately to avoid the proximity
of a passing python wound around Sholto, who also sported a sequined
fez and the inevitable mobile clamped to his ear.

"Do you always go around wearing snakes?" asked Nancy witheringly. "Rather off-putting, don't you think?"

"It's tame," Sholto shot back. "Which is more than can be said for
that thing," he added rudely, gesturing at the still-struggling bird. "Do
you always go around wearing hens?"

Nancy bared her teeth in a dazzling smile. "Oh, I always bring my
own cock to parties," she rasped smokily. "Far safer than ending up
with some stranger's. Don't you think?"

Rosie giggled.

Sholto sighed theatrically and ran a hand dramatically across his
forehead. "What are *those* doing out?" he shrieked suddenly as a wait-

ress passed with a large bowl of cocktail sausages. "It's supposed to be
the Arabian Nights, not a PTA barbecue."

Sholto stormed off, colliding with one of the belly dancers. As the
girl swore violently at him, Rosie noticed that her tasseled bra seemed
several sizes too big for her and she had a ring through her navel.

"Nancy, *darling*." Three excited men had rushed up to them. They
all, Rosie noticed, wore beards, glasses, and tight cotton jellabas topped
off with scarves and hats with large floppy brims. "Where on earth
have you been?" they clamored.

Nancy turned to Rosie. "Meet Johnny, Jimmy, and Larry. The back-
bone of the Eight Mile Bottom Amateur Dramatic Society—even
though they're all professionals, of course. As you can probably tell
from those luvvie scarves and hats. Darlings, this is supposed to be
fancy dress."

"Nancy!" chorused Johnny, Jimmy, and Larry chidingly.

"How can you *say* that," added Larry, rolling his eyes in mock horror. "You know we were all given our scarves and hats with our RADA
leaving certificates. We can't *possibly* not wear them."

Nancy swept up a passing glass of champagne the size of a vase from
a waiter with a ruby glistening in his muscular navel.

"Have that boy washed and brought to my tent," muttered Larry,
eyeing the impressive bulge in the waiter's white trousers.

"Hands off," commanded Nancy, taking a step closer to the waiter
and giving him a look that even through a yashmak would never have
gotten past the film censor. As the bulge in the waiter's trousers increased
in size, she threw her head back and laughed throatily, revealing a row of
teeth of which someone in their twenties would have been proud.

As the waiter stumbled off, reddening, with his tray, Rosie looked
on with admiration. Nancy, though undeniably glamorous, was also
undeniably heading toward fifty.

"I don't think he speaks English." Nancy grinned, turning back to
the group. "Never mind. You can do what I'm interested in, in any lan-
guage."

"There ain't nothing like a dame," chorused the three actors in admiration. "Nancy's a dame, you know," Johnny told Rosie. "We're all
very jealous. We want to be dames, too."

"I didn't realize Eight Mile Bottom was so full of superstars." Rosie giggled, halfway down a vase of champagne and feeling considerably more at ease. This is what she had been missing, spending her entire time at Spitewinter. She had never met these merry sybarites in the village shop even. But then, they hardly looked like Mrs. Oakerthorpe's target customers. No doubt they bought everything by mail order from Fortnum's.

The three actors were looking delighted.

"Well, I *was* once in a film with Tom Cruise," said Johnny as the others groaned. "It's *true*." Johnny turned indignantly to Rosie. "I was a transvestite alcoholic and tried to pick him up in a bar."

"In the film, you understand," boomed Jimmy.

Johnny ignored the gibe. "Oh, yes," he continued to Rosie, "money was no object, of course. The bottom of the bar was in Dublin and the top in Rome. I *adore* Rome, of course. The Eternal City is one of my very favorite places. I love nothing better than standing around admiring old ruins."

"Yes." Larry smirked. "You did rather a lot of that at one time, I seem to remember. At that pub in Shoreditch called Brief Encounter."

Johnny glowered at him and slammed his empty champagne glass on a passing tray with such emphasis that the waiter buckled.

"Well, *I* once had a scene with Judi Dench," Jimmy announced impressively, amid assorted cries of "Oooh" and "Get him!" "We were supposed to be having prawn cocktail at lunch," he added, "and my line was"—he straightened his back and raised his chin before booming— " 'This is the best entrée of marine origin I have eaten in nineteen years.' "

"Coincidentally," boomed Larry, immediately stealing what thunder there was, "my own favorite theatrical anecdote also concerns a crustacean. When I was doing *Hamlet* at Stratford . . ." He paused dramatically. "*When I was doing* Hamlet *at Stratford*," he repeated, "we tried every night to make the gravedigger laugh by putting something silly in the grave. Got him eventually with an inflatable lobster."

"Anyway, enough about us," interrupted Nancy, turning to Rosie, her bejeweled hands clasped elegantly around the stem of her champagne glass. "Tell us about yourself, sweetheart."

"Yes. *Tell us. Tell us*," the actors beseeched her.

"I'm an illustrator," Rosie said. "I draw and paint pictures. Very dull, I'm afraid."

"How absolutely marvelous," declared Jimmy. "I must say I love a bit of a dabble myself. Do you use very thin brushes or quite big ones?"

"Thin ones usually," Rosie said. "But very thick stiff ones are useful from time to time."

"Hear, hear," said a voice behind her. Rosie whipped around to find herself staring into the red and shiny face of what was clearly a very inebriated man. His drunken eyes rolled lasciviously over her. "Very well put. I have to say I agree." He stuck out a clammy hand. "Guy Grabster. How do you do. You've got the most enormous grease mark on the back of your jacket, by the way."

"Oh, no!" Rosie thought with horror of Mrs. Womersley. "Someone must have pressed up against me with a cocktail sausage."

"Lucky you." Guy sniggered, gazing straight into Rosie's cleavage. "This is obviously a better party than I thought."

Rosie looked around in panic. The Eight Mile Bottom Amateur Dramatic Society had melted away to watch a muscular young man swallowing fire. "Haven't had anything *that* hot in my mouth for years," Nancy could be heard observing to Johnny.

She was stuck with this ghastly man, Rosie realized. As Guy clapped a hot, sweaty hand on her back, she groaned. Despite the splendor of the tent surrounding her, the rest of the party was clearly going to be torture. The Marquee de Sade, no less. Where was Mark when she needed him? Where was he at all, come to that?

"Excuse me." Someone suddenly threw his arms around Rosie and planted a kiss full on her lips. Her relief gave way to confusion as she realized it was not Mark who was snogging her but the scruffy stranger she had met at the door.

"Friend of yours?" asked Guy.

"That's right," said the stranger.

Guy shrugged. Just then, his favorite big-breasted waitress, sporting tassels on each nipple, strode boldly up to him offering to refill his cocktail glass from the receptacles she carried in each hand. "I say." Guy hiccuped. "That really is a magnificent pair of jugs you've got there." He put his arm around her shoulders and led her away.

The stranger flashed an apologetic grin at Rosie. "Sorry about that. But you looked as if you needed some help."

Rosie nodded. "I did." She was, she realized, blushing. His unorthodox way of rescuing her from her plight had not been unpleasant. It was a long time since Mark had given her a spontaneous kiss. "Thanks."

Her rescuer grabbed a bottle of champagne from the tray of a passing waiter. "Come and sit down." He gestured at a shadowy corner flickering with candles and piled high with embroidered cushions.

Rosie hesitated. "I have to find my boyfriend."

The stranger grinned. "All the more reason to sit down then. He's bound to come past at some stage."

He gestured with the champagne bottle toward the glittering masses eddying around the richly draped and dramatically lantern-lit marquee interior. Watching sultan collide with snake charmer and Bedouin bang into belly dancer, Rosie could see she would never find Mark in a crowd that resembled rush hour at Pantomime Central. This man was right. If Mark was here—and he *was,* she *knew* it, he *had* to be— her best chance of a reunion was to sit tight. Increasingly tight, she thought, as the stranger refilled her glass.

"Know that type," he observed conversationally. "Bit of an arsehole. What my girlfriend used to call MTF. Must Touch Flesh."

Rosie spluttered on her champagne. "What do you mean? You haven't even met him yet."

"Calm down. I don't mean your *boyfriend.* That guy you were talking to. Bit of a lech."

"Oh. Yes." Rosie suddenly felt exhausted. Her nerves were raw with lack of sleep as well as everything else. If only Mark would make an appearance. Then she could go home to bed, safe in the knowledge that he still walked the earth. She stared hard at the crowd.

"We never introduced ourselves," the stranger said, smoothing out a cushion and gesturing for her to sit down. "I'm, um, Kevin."

"Rosie."

"What do you do?"

"I'm an illustrator. How about you?"

He ignored the question. "An illustrator?" he repeated eagerly. "Can you paint? Portraits, I mean."

"Sort of." The one of her mother's golden retriever painted last Christmas had been very sort of, Rosie recalled. Then there was the birthday one of Mark that, on the grounds of being insufficiently flattering, had never made it to the wall. Come to think of it, Rosie wasn't sure it had made it to the cottage.

"Could you . . ." Kevin started to say, but he never finished his sentence as at that precise moment, all hell broke loose.

CHaPTER 19

The guests were arriving in earnest by the time Mark descended the stairs in as dignified a manner as he could, given the weight of his jewel-festooned turban and the difficulties of walking in tight brocade slippers with turned-up toes. He felt utterly ridiculous. The thought of anyone seeing him like this was horrendous, but he did not dare disobey Samantha. There was the screenplay to consider, for one thing. And there might still be a chance of some Eastern promise later if he did her bidding.

The film project, *Charlotte in Love,* had now attained full-blown blockbuster status. In Mark's imagination, at least. Following the huge success of *Shakespeare in Love,* the time was surely right for an exploration of the romantic life of another great English literary figure, the creator of *Jane Eyre.* He already had a cast in mind. Joseph Fiennes, after all, was born to wear a stovepipe hat, while Samantha had whalebone corsets written all over her. Which would come in handy if, as he planned, *Charlotte in Love* spawned a whole series of Authors in Love, next up, the similarly underpinned Jane Austen.

As Sholto passed the bottom of the stairs and directed a look of frank appreciation toward his crotch, Mark felt sick. And not only with embarrassment. The pair of ludicrously tight gold trousers had forced the realization, as he struggled to button the waistband, that his previously flat stomach, thanks to all the chocolate chip cookies, was now more cheese board than washboard. The trousers were also agony to wear and possibly ruled out fatherhood on a permanent basis. Having slowly but successfully reached the bottom of the stairs, Mark snatched at a passing champagne glass to drown his sorrows and, he hoped, anesthetize the pain in his abdomen. He launched himself on the variously costumed and screeching crowd.

"Hello," said someone dressed, rather unconvincingly, as a vicar.

Recognizing, through the whorls and refractions of the champagne glass, that it actually *was* the vicar, Mark lowered his drinking vessel.

"Didn't recognize you. Was looking through a glass darkly," he added, sniggering.

The vicar looked pained.

"How's business?" Mark snatched another brimming glass from one of the constantly passing trays.

"Brisk," the vicar said bullishly. "I've got to go in a minute to attend to a couple of deaths, and there's a marriage to sort out."

"Sort out?"

"Young couple getting wed in a month or so. They want to have 'The Owl and the Pussycat' read out during the service, but I've found out it's only because the groom wants to hear the word 'pussy' in church."

As the vicar disappeared toward the front door, Mark staggered through the entrance to the marquee, narrowly missing a pair of ridiculous stuffed sheep.

"Hi," drawled someone to the side of him. It was the thin girl he had met on the hillside earlier in the afternoon. All traces of tie dye and cobwebs had gone; a silver-sequined yashmak, a glittering silver bra, and a matching skirt split to the thigh were their somewhat spectacular replacements. The bra, Mark noticed, was several sizes too large.

"I know," said the girl, following his gaze. "Made for someone breastfeeding, I guess."

"Breastfeeding who?" Mark gawked at the capacious cups. "The five thousand?"

The girl shrugged. "Dunno. I just sneaked in, grabbed it, and shoved it on."

Somewhere in the foggy depths of Mark's brain suspicion stirred. An unaccustomed flash of illumination struck him.

"You're not really supposed to be here, are you?" he asked her.

The girl regarded him narrowly. "Why you giving me the third degree, man? You a cop or something?"

Mark stuck his chest out and drew himself up. "Actually, I'm a journalist." At the unwelcome remembrance that he wasn't one anymore, he grabbed at another passing champagne vase.

The girl looked unimpressed. "A couple of my friends from school want to be journalists. They're all doing crap media studies courses now. One of them," she snorted, "is writing a thesis on 'The Significance of the Invisible Questioner on *The Naked Chef*.'"

"Whatsh that?"

"You know. That woman on the program that you never see who asks the Naked Chef all those stupid questions all the time."

Mark nodded slowly, despite having no idea what she was talking about. What woman? Personally, he made a point of never watching the chirpy TV cook in action; along with every other male of his acquaintance, he loathed the Naked Chef with messianic passion and prayed for the day he suffered a fatal accident on his scooter or burst into flames with the friction of sliding down that nauseating banister. Mark hated to think of how rich he must be. And the fact that a mere bloody cook was taking up space in *The Times* that could be filled by a trained journalist. Like himself, for example. *Bastard.* He forced his thoughts off the vile subject.

"You at school?" he asked her. She was quite pretty, really, if you didn't look too closely at the ironmongery.

The girl shook her head. "I split. It was a turnoff."

"Why?"

"The drug scene, for one thing. So dumb."

Mark nodded. "Very stupid. I've seen so many careers go down the tube because of too much charlie." He hadn't—not least because salaries at the paper were barely enough to keep the staff in aspirin, much less Class A narcotics. But he wished to appear worldly-wise.

The girl looked witheringly at him. "Hey, don't get me wrong. What was dumb was that most people were so goddamn stupid they couldn't tell whether they'd been sold an eighth of grass or an eighth of dried lawn."

Mark stared. No doubt about it now. That degree of denseness confirmed all his suspicions about her accent. Public school, definitely.

He slugged back the rest of his champagne. "You know," he slurred, "you remind me of myshelf at your age."

The girl looked considerably less flattered than he had expected. Yet it was true; the memory of his eighteen-year-old self looking at eighteen-year-old girls and wondering what it would be like to screw them was flooding back strongly.

"No, really," Mark continued, "you do. What *are* you doing here, anyway?" he pressed.

"Meeting someone."

"Who?" Shuffling unsteadily closer, Mark slapped a clammy hand on her back. "Boyfriend?"

"No, not boyfriend. Someone I haven't seen for a while." She paused. "Thing is, they don't know I'm coming. *Hey, look,*" the girl suddenly exclaimed, "isn't that Matt Locke over there? Down in the corner?" She pointed excitedly. "Oh, God, I think it is. I *love* him." Her laconic manner having completely evaporated, she was staring ecstatically into the distance as if she had spotted Leonardo DiCaprio and Prince William rolled into one.

"Matt Locke?" Mark echoed unsteadily. "What, you mean *Matt Locke*? The livesh on the moor and never comes out of his houshe Matt Locke?"

The girl, thrilled, was bouncing up and down beside him. "*God,* how fab. I mean groovy," she added hurriedly, reining in excited schoolgirl and replacing it with laconic L.A.

Mark peered hard in the direction in which her finger was pointing. This was difficult, considering there suddenly seemed to be two of everything. Could she really mean those . . . that thin, scruffy youth sitting in the corner of the tent? The candle flame illuminating his features revealed nothing at first, but then he smiled at his companion and Mark recognized the famous face. "Christ. Looksh in a bit of a bloody shtate, doeshn't he?"

The girl looked at Mark in disgust. "Haven't you heard of casual chic, man? Matt's far too cool to go in for this fancy-dress crap, *obviously.*" Her eyes ran contemptuously up and down Mark's costume. "It's a good idea, anyway. Everyone knows he's supposed to be reclusive. He probably doesn't want to be recognized, and no one apart from us seems to have worked out who he is. He's practically on his own." She threw a scornful look round the inebriated crowd. "Anyway, this gang wouldn't notice if the queen came and mooned them."

Mark cleared his throat and tried to look sober. "At least his girlfriends look good." He screwed up his eyes again. They *were* very glamorous, those two girls sitting next to the alleged star. They wore suits—surprisingly similar suits; perhaps they were twins—that showed a lot—*a lot*—of cleavage. The type of thing Rosie would look good in. *If,* Mark's lips twisted, she could ever be bothered.

"Whaddya mean, girlfriends? There's only one of them."

Mark tried hard to focus. The two women gradually fused into one. One who looked, for some reason, familiar. It was difficult to see her face, what with her hair dangling everywhere and the flickering candlelight, but something about that mass of blond hair and the line of her cheek reminded him of . . . *Rosie?* Hang on a minute . . .

"Thatsh not *hish* bloody glamorosh girlfriend. Thatsh *mine.*"

The girl looked at him with respect for the first time.

This breakthrough went unnoticed by Mark, the inside of whose head was tossing with an explosive mixture of champagne and jealousy. *"Oy!"* he yelled, lumbering over like an angry bull whose motor skills and sense of direction weren't everything they could be. *"You lot."* There seemed to be four people now. Two sets of identical twins.

Hearing something loud coming her way, Rosie looked up sharply. Relief shuddered through her when she saw Mark, albeit in a costume from the further side of fancy-dress common sense. "My boyfriend," she said to Kevin, and scrambled to her feet. "Mark!" she gasped. "Darling! I've been so worried about you, disappearing like that. I was frantic. Where have you been?"

Mark reeled as the blood came to a boil in his head. She had the bloody cheek to ask him where he'd been? When here she was, practically *in flagrante* with a bloody pop star? A man whose riches and success were beyond Mark's wildest dreams? Even if said superstar did look like a builder's laborer, Mark knew he looked nowhere near as ridiculous as he did himself.

The loss of the column had had a worse effect on Mark than Rosie had feared. He looked more than agitated. Ferocious, even. And drunk, quite possibly. "I'm so sorry about 'Green-er Pastures,' " she whispered, touching Mark's arm and, in doing so, setting light to the blue match tip of his fury.

Vicious with drink and jealousy, he exploded. "Shorry?" he bellowed. "You don't look like you're bloody shorry."

Definitely drunk, Rosie thought. Drunker than she had ever seen him, in fact. This was no time to row about why he hadn't left a note. Aware of Kevin watching closely, she took both Mark's hands, hoping the gesture would bring him to his senses. "To be honest, I'm not all that sorry," she said, intending to launch into a speech about there being more important things in life than by-lines. "I'm glad—"

At this, Mark erupted spectacularly for the second time. *"Glad?"* he screamed, ripping his hands out of her grasp. "Glad, are you? Glad! Yes, you look pretty bloody happy. Sitting there with your tongue down his bloody throat"—he stabbed a finger angrily in Kevin's direction— "while I sweat down to London and grovel to save my bloody job."

Rosie felt as if a bucket of icy water had been flung into her face. "What?" *Tongue?* Was Mark joking? She looked incredulously into his red-veined and furious stare and concluded swiftly that he wasn't.

"We were just talking—"

"Talking?" yelled Mark. "Ugandan bloody dish cushions, more like. All that shtuff about never knowing who anybody bloody famoush is when you can shpot a shelebrity in dishguise at fifty paces. Even if"— Mark looked contemptuously at Kevin—"he looksh like a fucking tramp."

"Thanks a lot," muttered Kevin.

Rosie reeled backward. Had Mark gone mad? Had he lost his mind as well as his column?

"Shelebrity—I mean, celebrity?" She looked down at Kevin and then incredulously back at Mark. "But he's not anyone famous. He's *Kevin.*"

Kevin? Mark felt as if his head was about to blow off with fury.

"Kevin?" he roared. "Just how shtupid do you think I am? Thatsh Matt Locke there. And you know bloody well it ish."

Rosie's face went white with shock. Or *guilt,* thought Mark savagely. She looked in horror at Kevin, who gave her a strained and apologetic smile.

"Guilty as charged," he muttered.

"But I didn't know, I mean, I had no idea . . ." Rosie looked desperately at Mark. "And in any case, I wasn't—"

"Oh, no. Thatsh why you've got your bloody titsh out." Mark stabbed his finger violently into Rosie's sternum.

At this, Kevin/Matt got swiftly to his feet.

Despite the fact that a red mist consumed his peripheral vision, Mark was aware that a small crowd had gathered behind him. Boiling with violence, he itched to hit something; glaring at Rosie, he started to raise his hand.

"Nice boyfriend," he heard Matt Locke drawl a nanosecond before a hard and accurately aimed punch landed with devastating force on his nose. As Mark crashed to the ground, Rosie screamed and buried her face in her hands. "One, two, three," yelled the crowd, cheering as if they were at a boxing match.

Rosie peered through her fingers at where Mark lay out cold in the sand among the cigarette butts. One of his feet twitched. He was alive, at least, unless that was rigor mortis.

"*You hit him!*" she shrieked at Matt.

"Yes."

"How could you?"

"He'll come round in a minute," Matt said lightly. "More's the pity."

A few seconds later the crowd had dispersed. A rival attraction had appeared at the other side of the tent. Samantha, eyes blazing like fireworks, was chasing a dripping and terrified-looking Guy through the party.

"Heavens," Johnny murmured to Larry as they headed toward the action. "I thought I'd seen all the violence I wanted in *The Godfather.* But it's got nothing on this."

"Didn't realize *you* were in *The Godfather,*" said Larry jealously.

"I wasn't," confessed Johnny. "But I've *seen* it."

As she pursued her husband round the marquee, Samantha pushed all obstacles out of her way, heedless of the fact that they were Sholto's cherished handiwork and had cost a fortune. Petal-strewn mosaic miniature fountains, decorative tables, ornate vases, tasseled cushions, and inlaid mirrors all crashed, broke, or scattered in her wake. When, shrieking in fury, Samantha demolished a lantern-draped bower in its entirety, the crowd whooped.

"Mare's going very well," Johnny said to Larry. "Gaining on the stallion all the time. Oops, nearly fell at the water jump there," he added as Guy narrowly missed stumbling over the rose-petal-strewn fountain now strewn all over the floor. "I must say, I don't fancy his chances much."

"Don't fancy his anything much," Larry said, smirking, as Guy charged past, his red face purple with strain, drops of water flying from his dripping suit. "Someone else clearly does, however. Apparently our divine hostess just caught him in the bathroom shagging one of the waitresses. Tried to drown him in the bidet, I hear, but he got away."

As the flames from the lanterns crashing in Samantha's wake began to lick at the marquee's silken edges, Sholto sank his head into his hands.

"Escaped, did he?" said Johnny approvingly. "Good for him. What's that burning smell, by the way?"

The next moment there was a universal wail as Guy, glancing fatally back over his shoulder at Samantha, failed to see the stuffed sheep lurking at knee level and tripped violently over it. Seconds later Samantha had grabbed Guy triumphantly by the collar and dragged him to his knees. Now firmly in Colosseum mood, the crowd cheered hysterically. "Jugular, jugular," yelped Johnny.

"I hope," Larry said heavily, "that you aren't going to try to convince me you were in *Gladiator*."

Yet, even as Samantha stood over him like Russell Crowe about to strike the death blow, Guy's attention seemed to be elsewhere. There was a gasp from the ring of spectators as, with what sounded like a howl of delight, he struggled to his feet and hurled himself at a young girl in a yashmak and a sequined bra several sizes too big for her.

"Heavens," murmured Larry. "Some people never learn, do they?"
"Daddy!" gasped Iseult.
"Darling!" croaked Guy.
"Bastard," hissed Samantha.
"Christ," said Matt Locke.

She had drunk far too much, Rosie realized the next day as she cautiously opened one eye. The light poured through the window with agonizing brilliance, albeit from a sky as gray as old underwear.

As Rosie yawned, the air stuck like Velcro to the furry insides of her mouth. Her brain felt tight and a migraine was skewering her right pupil. Everything seemed unusually blurred and out of focus; Rosie remembered her contact lenses were currently stuck to a saucer by the bed under a skin of soaking solution. By the time she'd finally gotten home, snapping them carefully into their container had seemed as out of the question as brushing her teeth.

The lumps in the mattress pressed into her back. She turned over and buried her face in the pillow, knowing, even as she did so, that it was a bad move. The churning sickness in her stomach instantly doubled in intensity; the ache in her throat got steadily worse. It seemed impossible; she felt too sick to be sick, but by the time the saliva had started to ache in the back of her throat it was clear that the game was up. Realizing she'd passed the point of no return, Rosie threw back the duvet and made a dash for the bathroom.

"Oh, my God," she groaned. Facedown on the bathroom floor, she stared fixedly at the flotsam and jetsam—hairpins, shreds of loo paper, dust, earplugs—gathered beneath the lavatory pipe. The fragile networks of dirt balanced on fine frameworks of hair, disturbingly in colors belonging neither to her nor to Mark, loomed at her with the dread hyperreality of a truly vile hangover.

It was the earplug that brought what she was trying to avoid thinking about crashing into her consciousness. As the situation with the column had gotten increasingly worse, Mark had taken to shoving earplugs in his ears so that nothing—not even the Muzzles—could come between him and his muse. *Mark. Uggghh.*

Finally, Rosie retched.

Last night. The party. Matt. She placed her arms around the lavatory bowl and heaved again. There had been little else to do in the end but leave Mark lying in the marquee. He looked comfortable enough, once she had pressed the Eight Mile Bottom Amateur Dramatic Society into helping her move him onto a pile of cushions.

"Reminds me of *Spartacus*," one of them had remarked, looking down admiringly as Mark slumped, bare-chested, over the cushions in the candlelight.

"You definitely weren't in *Spartacus*," snapped another.

"I'm not saying I was. But it does remind me of it."

Mark had not, Rosie now realized, come home. The cottage was utterly silent; she had slept in their bed alone. Feeling nausea rise up again, Rosie resisted thinking about any of the previous night's events. She felt too ill to make sense of it, if sense there was to be made. Yet, like a rearing horse fighting the bridle, her thoughts pulled violently in the direction she did not want to go.

Mark had been more drunk last night than she had ever seen him, but even if it had been the champagne talking, the champagne had made some unforgivable remarks. The relationship was over. He had blown his last chance. She had put up with enough. More than enough.

Funny how flat she felt, having finally accepted what had probably long been inevitable. Shaky, yes, but that was mostly the hangover. Resigned, really. Calm, almost. As dull and leaden as the skies outside the window. The pain seemed more in her head than her heart. But perhaps it had not sunk in yet.

As a riptide of agony hit the front of her cranium, she groaned faintly. It was now so obvious what a fool she had been. Occasionally irritated, yes, but essentially blind to Mark's flaws, she had been crushed into submission by his powerful personal PR machine—the one that assured her she was living with a genius who must be deferred to in all things. Until last night, that was. Even Mark's good looks—always, if she were honest, the most attractive thing about him—had lost their power. He had looked less than godlike, snarling and spitting at her with drunken fury. He'd looked fatter, too. Florid, bloodshot, puffy with alcohol and hate. Ironic how coming to live in the country had made him look far more like a hack than he ever had in the city.

She might at present be blundering in a myopic blur, but the scales had well and truly fallen from her eyes. What a waste of time he had been. And to think she had turned down Jack in order to endure last night's humiliation . . .

At the sound of the telephone ringing downstairs Rosie raised herself off the bathroom floor slightly, then slumped back down, head swimming. It was hardly likely to be Jack. Even at the height, such as it had been, of his wooing her, he had never called for fear Mark might answer. It was Bella, more probably. Wanting the lowdown on last night's party. Well, she felt low and Mark had been knocked down. That was all there was to it. End of story. As well as everything else.

But was it? One thought flashed repeatedly at the front of her brain like the beam of a lighthouse. Could she go up to Spitewinter and ask Jack if he still wanted her? Dare she? From the longing way he had looked at her on her way to the party, there seemed no doubt as to what the answer would be. Not yet, though. If ever. Rosie forced the thought, along with her feelings of nausea, determinedly down and went to make a cup of tea.

Among the clanging and seething in her brain, she discerned the familiar screech of tires.

"*Well,*" said Duffy, striding into the kitchen. "You *survived,* then." As he drew out a chair, the noise of the legs on the concrete floor scraped down Rosie's brain. Still not tiled, she thought, looking down at it. To think of the plans she and Mark had once had for the cottage.

She swallowed hard, her head bent over the sink as she filled the kettle to disguise the sudden tears.

"Sounds like the blooming First World War to me, that party does," chirped Duffy. "Fancy Matt Locke smacking your chap on the nose like that."

Matt Locke. There had been all that business as well. Yet the additional embarrassment of having not recognized an internationally famous pop star, despite having spent much of the evening talking to him, hardly seemed to matter now. *A mere* detail, compared to last night's wholesale destruction of the rest of her life. Even so, Rosie's fists clenched slightly at the thought of Matt Locke. If it hadn't been for him, none of it would have happened. She would have found someone else to talk to, he wouldn't have hit Mark . . .

"Gone to the hospital, has he?" Duffy asked, darting a swift glance around the kitchen.

"I don't know where he is," snapped Rosie, still trying to work out how far Matt Locke could be blamed for the evening's incidents. He had lied to her, hadn't he? Called himself Kevin. Lured her into a corner so that Mark had leaped to conclusions. Well, pole-vaulted to them, really.

"And then Mrs. Grabster attacked her husband."

Rosie tuned back into the present to find that Duffy was midway through a dramatic account of the events of the night before. "Attacked her husband?" she echoed. She vaguely remembered seeing the gold turban racing around the marquee like a fake hare at a dog race but had not understood why.

"Yep," confirmed the postman. "Caught him in the bathroom with old Yo-Yo Knickers from up the lane there." Duffy jerked his thumb in the direction of Dungarees' cottage. "Tried to drown him in the toilet, they say."

Rosie blinked. "The toilet?" She remembered seeing, dripping wet, the drunken, red-faced man who had been leering at her before Kevin—Matt, rather—had rescued her. She twisted her lips. Some rescue that had turned out to be.

"Then Mrs. Grabster went berserk because Mr. Grabster's daughter was at the party." Duffy's eyes rounded in wonder. "Didn't know she was coming, apparently. Shows you've got to RSVP, doesn't it? I always tell people they have to. But you'd be amazed at how many don't."

"His daughter? What do you mean, his daughter?"

Duffy looked at her slyly. "A biscuit wouldn't come amiss, I must say. I've just been to Dame Nancy's and she's clean out of custard creams."

Rosie recognized the deal. The cookie package rustled deafeningly as she passed it over. The postman, she thought resignedly, truly took the cake.

"Insults his daughter from his first marriage," Duffy told her, pulling one out.

"Insult? She's called Insult?"

"Something like that," said Duffy, with what, had Rosie been less incapacitated, exhausted, distracted, and ill, would have struck her as a revealing lack of interest in accurate detail. "Lived with her mother until recently, didn't see much of her father. Mostly, it turns out, because Mrs. Grabster couldn't stand her and wouldn't have her in the house."

"How absolutely awful." Rosie felt an unexpected twinge of sympathy for Guy and his daughter. Samantha was obviously even worse than she appeared.

"*Very* embarrassing for Mrs. G., making scenes like that in public. People don't forget that sort of thing round here, they don't."

Not with *you* around to remind them, thought Rosie.

"And the fire can't have helped things."

"*Fire?*" exclaimed Rosie, as another wave of pain crashed against the inside of her forehead.

Duffy reached for another cookie. "You've not heard, then? Big fire, there was. Mrs. G. knocked over a lamp or something. Sheet of flame in seconds, the side of the tent was. Went up in smoke, the whole thing did. Surprised you didn't see it."

"I must have left by then," Rosie murmured, something starting to work at the back of her brain. Funny, given the perfect recall she had of the Mark episode, including the explosive row with Matt Locke at the end of it, she could remember so little about getting home. She had a very vague memory of stumbling out and walking barefoot down the High Street with the vintage high-heeled white sandals Mrs. Womersley had lent her dangling from her wrist. Someone had been with her. . . .

"*Must* have," said Duffy, his voice pregnant with meaning.

Who had it been? Rosie tried to rack her brains, but they were fully engaged in undergoing some other form of torture. Someone, she was sure, had accompanied her to the very door of Number 2. . . .

"How bad was the fire?" Rosie demanded. An unnameable fear, which had nothing to do with her mystery escort, started to build inside her.

"*Very* bad. Fire brigade managed to stop it before it reached the house, but there's nothing left of the tent. Or anything inside it," Duffy added with relish. "Burned to a cinder, the stuffed sheep were, they say. Like a furnace, it must have been in there."

Rosie felt her heart begin to bang like a drum.

"Did they get everyone out of the tent?" she whispered. Mark had been unconscious when she left. During a fire, with the air thick with smoke and everyone panicking, it would have been easy not to notice a body slumped underfoot in the stampede. . . . "He'll be all right," Matt's unconcerned drawl echoed in her memory. "He'll come round in a minute, more's the pity." But what, Rosie thought, panic clutching her throat, if he *hadn't*?

Duffy shrugged. "Who knows. Why?"

Rosie shoved her trembling hands under the table as images of body bags, courtrooms, and jail scrolled hideously through her mind. "If you'll excuse me," she declared in as steady a voice as she could manage, "I'm just going over to The Bottoms."

Duffy looked surprised. "Left something there, did you?"

Even the joyous reunion with his daughter could not dispel the dread Guy felt about facing Samantha over the lunch table the day after the party. A vicious row was more than he could bear, even if he hadn't happened to have the mother of all hangovers. But to his amazement, Samantha arrived not, as anticipated, in the most vitriolic of tempers but calm, cheerful, and wreathed in smiles.

Of all possible outcomes, this was the least expected. The disaster had, after all, been infinite in its variety. The fire—started, as far as anyone could make out, by Samantha herself knocking over some lanterns—had been the worst aspect. But ancillary incidents such as the collapse of the main buffet table, thanks to some old slapper shagging one of the waiters under it while her cockerel screeched at the top of its voice, had hardly helped matters. Nor had Sholto's subsequent screeching at the guilty lovers, for which he had been rewarded by a stream of insults and falafels from a bunch of camp actors. And it had, Guy admitted to himself, been regrettable in the extreme that Samantha should come violently into the bathroom just as he and the waitress were doing exactly the same.

Yet Samantha, toying delicately with her lunch, did not so much as mention the events of the night before. She had apparently not even noticed the succession of workmen walking past the window bearing the cremated remains of the marquee. It was, Guy thought, her finest acting performance ever.

Pushing his fork lugubriously through his couscous, he wondered whether they would be eating the caterers' leftovers for the rest of their lives. Yet even this strong hint that something of an Eastern persuasion had recently taken place failed to elicit an acknowledgment from Samantha. He winced as he bit on a preserved lemon.

Was there, Guy wondered, a clue to Samantha's carry-on-regardless attitude in Iseult's presence at the lunch table, albeit late, sulky, and lurking behind a cloud of cigarette smoke? It was just possible that Samantha was determined not to give her stepdaughter the satisfaction of seeing her admit that anything untoward had happened. Attack, she seemed to have decided, was the best form of defense.

"Tell me," Samantha's voice was all concerned brightness, "do you have a *boyfriend,* Iseult?"

Iseult looked coolly at Samantha. "Sort of."

"How fascinating. Do tell me about him. We're all ears, aren't we, darling?" Samantha bared her gums at Guy, who looked fixedly at his plate. "Where does he live?"

"On an estate," Iseult muttered.

"An estate?" Samantha was on red alert. Guy could see the possibilities rippling through her brain like destinations on the Waterloo noticeboard. Badminton, Woburn, Alnwick . . . "What, with land and farms?" she gasped.

"Sort of a farm, yeah."

"What's it called?"

"Broadwater Farm. It's a council estate in North London." It took all of Guy's effort not to snort at Samantha's confounded expression. "Actually, I was thinking of asking him up here if that's all right with you," continued Iseult, the picture of blue-eyed innocence.

There was a silence.

Guy waited for the fireworks, but they did not come. Instead, Samantha rose to her feet, bundled up her napkin, and dropped it on the table. "Excuse me," she said with exaggerated politeness. "I have some business to attend to."

"Oh, really, darling?" said Guy, expecting any moment to feel the hot, molten lava of her fury.

"Acting business, as a matter of fact. Something very big and exciting has just come up."

Iseult sniggered, pretending to stir her tea despite there being no milk in it. Milk, suspected by Samantha of harboring calories, was banned from the table.

As Samantha left the room, Guy sighed. "Bit close to the edge, that, darling. Samantha doesn't like being laughed at. Even when she's in a good mood."

"Could have fooled me. The woman's a comic genius. That outfit last night. Last night in general—"

"We're not talking about last night. We will *never* talk about last night. Last night is out of bounds. More than that—it never happened."

"Good at blocking out the past, aren't you." Iseult tossed her hair back over her narrow shoulders. "Like me, for example. For about eighteen years."

Guy pulled a face. "God, I'm sorry. I was a terrible father," he admitted, abandoning the pretense.

"You bet you were." Iseult fixed him with her candid blue stare. "What about that time my tooth came out, but I lost it and put a note to the tooth fairy under my pillow explaining what had happened. I got a note back the next morning saying 'No tooth, no money.' In *your* handwriting. How generous was that?"

"An early lesson about disappointment, darling," Guy said lightly, hoping to disguise a sharp pang of guilt.

Iseult fiddled in the sagging black-beaded bag apparently welded to her shoulder and dragged out a new pack of Marlboro Lights. "Well, I suppose I was hardly the ideal daughter," she said easily. "I was spoiled rotten. Remember when Mummy tried to make me take piano lessons and I stuck peppercorns down the keys to block them?"

Guy, nodding, felt slightly prickly about the eyes. Thank God she didn't seem to think it was too late for him to make amends. Because he would. And enjoy himself in the process. Now firmly persuaded that the heart attack had forced him to take stock, he was almost grateful that it had happened, even if it had meant entombment in The Bottoms. Still, he was working on that. And now that Iseult was here, she could work on it with him. It seemed incredible that he had actually preferred amassing piles of money for Samantha to spend rather than spending time with his daughter. She might be oddly dressed—his eye ran resignedly over a long tie-dyed skirt and a T-shirt obviously pulled out from under the bed—but without a doubt she was a beauty in the making. His proud glance lingered on Iseult's brilliant blue eyes, so like his own, the full lips, so like her mother's and so unlike the thin ones that Samantha had to double in size with the judicious application of her lipstick pencil.

"Well, you weren't very interested in music. A shame, because you always had a lovely voice."

"But I am interested *now,* Dad," Iseult said earnestly.

"Well, you can always join the choir of whatever university you decide to go to."

"I don't want to go to university. I want to be a singer."

"Yes, well, you've definitely got your mother's voice," said Guy, wondering where all this was leading. "What," he asked with elaborate casualness, "is her new boyfriend like?"

Iseult rolled her eyes. "A creep. He's persuaded Mum to be Violetta in this version of *La Traviata* set in seventies' Islington. Mum has to fall in love with Alfredo over the melon and ginger. Her death from TB is supposed to be some sort of allegory about Watergate, which is itself an allegory about spin doctors and corruption in contemporary politics."

Guy winced. "I've heard about it. I always thought your mother hated things like that."

"Oh, Jez'll have screwed her into it," Iseult said matter-of-factly. "They're at it all the time at home."

Guy's eyes bulged. He stirred his tea thoughtfully.

"Anyway," said Iseult, "I don't want to be an *opera* singer. I'm in this band called Thrilled Skinny and everyone thinks I'm really good . . ." She fumbled in her bag. "Here's our demo tape. Will you listen to it?"

Guy wasn't listening to anything. Remembering Marina's soft and curvy body, he was busy comparing it to Samantha's bony frame. Beside Marina, screwing Samantha was like screwing a ladder, though without the warmth and responsiveness of the average ladder.

Just then Consuela appeared at the door. "Ees someone . . ." she announced haltingly, seconds before Rosie, wild-eyed and hysterical, burst into the room.

"My boyfriend . . ." she gasped, her eyes a vicious blur of redness and tears. "Been searching . . ." (hiccup) ". . . the garden . . ." (gulp) ". . . no sign of him . . ." (hiccup) ". . . knocked out at the party . . ." (sob) ". . . probably dead . . ." (hiccup) ". . . don't know what to do . . ." (sob). Turning to the wall, Rosie threw herself against it and wailed in hopeless anguish into William Morris's *Strawberry Thief.*

Calmly filling a glass of water from the jug on the table, Iseult took it over to Rosie. Guy, meanwhile, grabbed at the bottle of Macallan's lurking under His Lordship's Tipple on the Georgian drinks cart. Unwelcome and alarming though the news was, he was unable to stop himself hoping the fatality was Sholto.

"Dead?" he said. "Who's dead?"

"My boyfriend," gulped Rosie, about to add "ex-boyfriend" and realizing with horror that he was now ex in every sense of the word.

"The one Matt Locke hit?" asked Iseult. "The one in the, um, gold trousers?"

"I'm not at all surprised, in that case." Guy was swigging vigorously from his tumbler. "Those trousers were tight enough to kill anyone."

At this, Rosie's anguished, jerking sobs began once more. "I'll probably end up in prison," she wailed.

"Of course you won't," said Guy, upon whom the whiskey was beginning to have an unfortunately jocular effect. "If anything, the costume company will. You'll get millions in compensation."

"Shut up, Dad," snapped Iseult. "Can't you see she's upset?"

"The last I saw of him he was lying unconscious," Rosie said, sobbing, terrified. However much Mark had upset her, she had certainly never wished such a grisly fate upon him. "He died in the fire. Everyone must have stampeded over him and left him there. I should have taken him home with me. . . ."

"Well, I hate to say this . . ." said Iseult.

Rosie's heart froze. Confirmation then. All hope gone.

". . . but he seemed to have a great time after you'd gone."

"Great time?" Rosie frowned. "You mean, he was . . . *conscious*? Alive? Well?"

"Not sure about well. When everyone who was left went into the house after the fire, he talked to my stepmother practically all night. Hardly behavior of the sane."

There was no doubt in Samantha's mind that the party had been a triumph. It had, however, taken her some time to reach this conclusion. After the ghastly business of Guy and the waitress, followed by the horror of realizing her wretched stepdaughter had infiltrated the guests, it had seemed to Samantha that things could get no worse. Until, that was, she stood watching the flames from the marquee roaring into the sky and resisting the strong temptation to fling herself on the pyre of her destroyed social ambitions.

Her pride as devastated as her party tent, Samantha had been at her lowest ebb when Dame Nancy came to stand supportively beside her. She felt pathetically grateful for the company. It became quickly apparent, however, that Dame Nancy was there less to offer thespian solidarity than to get a bird's-eye view—as well as a cock's-eye one, the bird being still clamped to her bosom—of the firemen training jets of water on the blaze.

"They've got marvelous hoses, haven't they?" Dame Nancy murmured admiringly. "So big and thick. And powerful." She turned to Samantha. "Splendid party," she said. "I enjoyed myself enormously."

Even through her misery, Samantha registered the "enormously" and recalled something about Dame Nancy, a collapsed buffet table, and a well-endowed wine waiter. She noticed, too, that for some reason Dame Nancy had bits of falafel stuck all over her hair.

"Never mind about the fire, dear," the actress added. "Bound to happen at some stage. We were all expecting something of the kind."

"What do you mean?" Samantha demanded hysterically. How could she possibly be expected *not to mind*? This was, after all, her darkest hour even if—her eye caught the flames illuminating the night sky for miles around—it was, in a sense, her lightest as well.

"Well," Dame Nancy said mildly, "anything could happen in a house as haunted as this."

Shocked to the core, Samantha went gray beneath her gilding, which was itself dissolving in the heat from the conflagration. Was there no closely guarded secret that tonight was not going to lay bare? Her hands trembled. Not content with the other devastating blows she had had to endure over the space of the past few hours, fate had seen fit to deal her the lowest one of all. People other than herself and Guy—who only suspected, anyway—knew about the haunted Bottoms. Or was Dame Nancy trying to catch her out? Samantha steeled herself to brazen it out and looked back blankly at her interrogator.

"You do know what I mean, don't you?" pressed the president of the Eight Mile Bottom Amateur Dramatic Society. Whose crown Samantha had once aspired to. How long ago that seemed, she thought bitterly. "The ghosts. Surely you've seen them?"

Samantha shook her head in vigorous denial.

"Oh." Dame Nancy looked disappointed. "Pity. I do hope they've not gone. The Bottoms always had such *splendid* ghosts. By far the best in the area, we always thought."

Samantha's head was whirling with panic, but these words managed nonetheless to penetrate it. "The *best* in the area?" she repeated. Surely Dame Nancy meant the *worst*?

"Absolutely. Splendid spooks. We like our ghosts round here, you know. Love them, in fact. Most of us only have one or two and we're all wildly jealous of The Bottoms because it's got about ten. Funny *you've* never seen any of them though."

"Well, there might have been something in the passage . . ." Samantha hedged.

"The white lady probably," said Dame Nancy excitedly. "Was she on a chaise longue?"

"Not sure," Samantha said cagily.

"Oh, bound to be. Poor thing, jumped off the roof with her lover at the age of fourteen."

"An appalling death," intoned Samantha, trying to sound simultaneously sympathetic and proprietorial.

"Oh, she didn't *die,* dear. Broke both her legs though, which is why she's on the chaise. But a fine ghost, a very fine ghost, indeed. Larry de Lisle's always saying he'd trade his black dog and his gray cat and throw in his poltergeist as well just for one night with the white lady of The Bottoms."

"So there's a pecking order?" Samantha tried to sound casual. Dame Nancy's cockerel looked at her with interest.

"Of course there is, dear. Taking it from the bottom, a gray, white, or black cat is just about passable, but a black dog is better, particularly if it howls at a full moon. A headless horse is good, but twice as good with a headless horseman *on* it."

Samantha goggled. "So people—dead ones, obviously—are the best?"

Dame Nancy nodded emphatically. "But there's a top ten there as well. Take the white lady, since we're talking about her. One white lady equals two green ladies. Or one and a half gray ladies."

"What about sword fights?" ventured Samantha, on whose brain the offending paragraph from *Ghosts of the Area* had been branded in letters of fire.

"Interaction is good, so The Bottoms' sword fights score very highly."

Samantha swallowed. Now for the big one. "Black ball of hate?"

Dame Nancy pursed her lips. "Average-ish. Johnny's got a red ball of hate, although he says it could be gout. Or an ingrown hair."

Samantha felt offended on the ball's behalf. It sounded well above average to her. According to Guy, it had been terrifying. Disappointed with the way her stock had suddenly fallen, she almost decided to leave it at that and just rest on her laurels. On the other hand, there would never be a better opportunity to find out more. Samantha decided to risk it. "What about," she asked, "the screaming woman with the knife sticking out of her back?"

Dame Nancy drew impassioned breath. An expression of pure reverence radiated from what could be seen of her face under the yashmak. "Now that really *is* something. Only a few houses in the country have a ghost even *remotely* resembling that one. Ghosts with knives in their backs are exceedingly rare, because only in very, *very* haunted houses— such as The Bottoms—do you see them at all."

"Remind me of why that is?" Samantha wrinkled her brow as best she could in an apparent effort to recollect. Her heart started to thump.

"Because," said Dame Nancy in tremendous tones, "ghosts are *fantastically* cutthroat and competitive. Even more than we actors are, dear. As well as being *extremely* territorial. If there are too many, or simply not enough corridors, bedrooms, cellars, and so on to go around, from a haunting point of view, one *always* gets stabbed in the back by the others." She paused, admiringly. "You really are *terribly* fortunate to have one, dear. The whole county is green with envy."

"Yes, I *am* very lucky." Samantha simpered, looking at her home through new, wondering eyes.

"So you see," Dame Nancy concluded, "the fire was bound to happen. With all that psychic energy around and everything, the risk of spontaneous combustion must have been enormous."

The biggest risk of spontaneous combustion, Samantha recalled with a twist of the lips, had probably been when she discovered Guy in the bathroom with the waitress. But that was behind her now. She beamed at Dame Nancy, thrilled to the very core of her being. As owner of what was officially Eight Mile Bottom's most intriguing house, her social future now looked assured. As did, incidentally, the likely outcome of her insurance claim. Very satisfactory, thought Samantha.

Nor was this all. The fire had worked as a crucible for her talent as well. Was it not in its afterglow (quite literally) that she had dreamt up the idea of the *Charlotte in Love* film project with that wonderfully helpful young journalist? Martin, was it? The stinking remains of the marquee no longer represented the crematorium of all her ambitions but the glorious scene of her phoenixlike rise from the social and thespian ashes.

Rosie decided to leave it a few days before seeing Mark. A few years even. She didn't care if she never saw him again. It was over now; what was there to see him for? That he was not coming back to the cottage was a huge relief; she had gathered from Duffy that he was staying at The Bottoms, although doing what was unclear. "Having a treatment," the postman had reported. Rosie had visions of Samantha wrapping Mark in seaweed, until Duffy, exercising his usual right to the free interpretation of events, said it was something to do with a film.

Still, who cared what it was. It kept Mark out of her way. Eventually, of course, they would have to get together to divide up the folding chairs, the knife and fork drawer, the videos, and the books that formed the depressing limit of their worldly possessions. The beanbag he could have. Neither would she sue for custody of the Rick Astley album, which Mark always claimed he'd been sent by a publicist trying to get the singer in the paper's "Chillin" slot.

Besides, she had other fish to fry.

"You might change your mind," Jack had said. "I'll be here if you do." So far, she had not dared take him up on his offer. In the week immediately following the party, blanking her mind of everything but the task in hand, Rosie had thrown herself into finishing *A Ewe in New York*. It was art therapy, she thought. Heart therapy, even more so.

It was ironic how closely these post-apocalypse days resembled the kind of country life of which she had originally dreamed, full of peace—the Muzzles seemed to be away—and a soothing rhythm of work. Getting up with the dawn and going to bed with the dusk was reassuring, as well as necessary, given the now near-terminal state of the electricity wiring. Yet this monastic existence appealed to Rosie, who wished to see no one—the postman least of all—still less talk on the telephone until she had had time to think about things. The constantly ringing phone went unanswered. Duffy's knocks on the door unheeded, Mrs. Womersley unchatted to in the garden—Rosie hid behind the wall—and her suit unreturned. There was only one person she wanted to see, and she did not yet feel ready. One day, however, Rosie woke up and felt, finally, that she did.

The walk to Spitewinter would do her good. As would talking to Jack. She wasn't, after all, intending to fling herself on him or anything. Just to tell him what had happened. She needed to let him know; after all, what he didn't hear from her now, he would hear from Duffy later. If he hadn't—dreaded thought—heard already.

Rosie walked tremulously up the lane. She had noticed before that greenness could soothe, and the bright emerald of the fields spreading around her exuded a sense of peace. Her heart lifted. There was, she thought, something aislelike about the hedgerows, their full, frilled borders of cow parsley like exceptionally lavish pew decorations. Spring had truly sprung, not, as in London, like the inside of an old sofa, but with the exuberant color and force of a jack-in-the-box. A Jack even.

Whatever had happened, she was now free. She could make her own choices.

Joy swelled in Rosie as she saw the forget-me-nots nodding out of the crumbling walls, noticed the purple flames of clover in the fields, heard the hum and twitter of birds and insects.

"Never thought I'd trust a city lass again."

What a fool she had been to turn Jack down for Mark. An act of insanity no less. From the minute she had met him, it had been obvious who the better man was. In Jack's care, she would flourish the way she never had with Mark; everything about Spitewinter, after all, reflected its owner's noble qualities. Jack's countryside was not as other countryside. The trees were prouder. The grass seemed glossier. The cows in the field looked straight out of the Elgin Marbles, wrinkled of neck, sleek of back, and proud of feature. Rosie paused, admiring their pale, shining, pearly flanks and the elegant curve of their horns.

After the recent past, the here and now was the best place to be. Mark may have pushed her from the high wire, but she had an emotional safety net to catch her. She smiled as she unhooked the cord holding the farm gate. She had Jack.

As Rosie entered the farmyard, Jack was sitting on an upturned bucket in his overalls, scraping mud from the sides of his boots with a knife. He seemed utterly absorbed in the task. At least, he did not look up.

Rosie felt light-headed with relief at the sight of him. Yet Kate, stretched out in the sun by the farmyard door, had hardly seemed to notice her, let alone bounce to her paws with the usual rattle of chain and chorus of barking.

"Jack?"

He gave her a swift glance, followed by an unfathomable grunt. Rosie hesitated, feeling some of the euphoria seep from her mood like air leaking from a balloon. He did not seem to be very happy.

"Is everything all right?" she asked. "No one's ill, are they?"

Jack's knife dug viciously into the mud. "Not as far as I know."

Rosie hesitated, then decided to seize the day. After all, if Jack had had bad news, her own news should cheer him up.

"I expect you heard the party was rather, um, *eventful*," she began gaily. "I wish you'd been there to see it."

Jack looked up sharply. His blue gaze hit her face like a Frisbee. "Would have been a bit in the way, wouldn't I?"

Rosie's smile widened to a grin. Here was her cue. "I hardly saw Mark, as it happens. He arrived before me, ignored me most of the time I was there, and then didn't come home afterward."

Jack said nothing. A slight increase in fervor could nonetheless be detected in his cleat scraping. Rosie took this as an encouraging sign. "As a matter of fact, we're going through a rocky patch at the moment," she admitted. Oh, what the hell. May as well tell him. "Actually, we've split up."

She wasn't sure what she had expected at this point. The surrounding animals to perform a can-can, perhaps, like the sheep on the Let Me Entertain Ewe card. At the very least, Jack leaping up, whirling her round the farmyard, and pressing her against the haystacks with a passionate kiss.

What was not in the script at all was for him to say, in a low, gruff voice, "I'm not surprised."

Rosie was puzzled. Had he not understood her? "You've heard then? About the row at the party? The things Mark said to me?" Oh, well. At least it saved her going through the whole thing.

As she smiled increasingly desperately at him, Rosie realized that he wasn't smiling back. On the contrary, his mouth was a flat, tight line in a face that looked as closed as a fist.

"You told me," Jack said, biting off each word he spoke, "that you weren't interested in me because you had a boyfriend already. I accepted that. I'd hate to make someone else suffer like I did when Catherine . . ." He paused, his throat working furiously. "I hoped you might change your mind—"

"Yes," said Rosie, half eager, half panicking. "That's what you said. *If you have a change of heart, let me know.* Well, as it happens . . ." She took a deep breath. Why wasn't he understanding what she was about to say?

"And the next thing I hear," Jack cut in, "is you left the party with some bloke who's just landed one on your boyfriend."

Rosie's knees wobbled. "What?" She could recall only a voice, the comforting press of a hand, a reassuring presence. But surely not. . . ?

"Yes," said Jack, bitterly attacking his boots again. "With Matt Locke."

Oh, God. Hadn't he left after the . . . attack? Had he really seen fit to hang around and get her in even deeper shit than she was already? Went home with her, to all intents and purposes. Rosie gave Jack an incredulous smile. "But I hardly even know him. I'd never met him before. I mean, he didn't even give me his real name."

"Ha!" Jack's laugh was rasping and humorless. "That's not what your boyfriend thought, I hear. And, bloody hell, do you think that makes it better? Running off with some bloke you've only just met?"

It was a bad dream. It was unbelievable. It got a million times worse with whatever she said. Rosie looked pleadingly at Jack. How could she get it through to him that of all of the ends of sticks to be got, this was the wrongest?

"Who have you been talking to?" Rosie wailed, realizing, as she did so, that she already knew. Duffy. She had, after all, had a pretty colorful version of events herself from the postman. Her head started to throb violently.

"Jack, please. None of this is true. I came to tell you that I changed my mind. That I was wrong to stick with Mark. That it's all over with him."

"Very convenient that. Now that he's dumped you."

"Dumped *me*?" Rosie fought to contain her temper, which was in danger of escaping through the splits now forcing her head apart. "That's not what happened. *I'm* leaving *him,* because I've had enough of his behavior. And because of you." She swallowed, aware of the danger of sounding desperate. "As I say, I've changed my mind. If you still want me."

"I was an idiot," Jack said, as if to himself. "A gullible fool. Fell for one city lass and got my fingers burned, only to do exactly the same with another. So," he said, lifting a set face to Rosie, "I'll be turning down your kind offer, if it's all the same to you. Besides," he added, his voice dropping, his eyes small and mean, "what do I want with another man's castoffs?"

"Castoffs?" Rosie finally saw red. A blaze of fury swept through her. "How fucking *dare* you!" she shouted. "You haven't the foggiest idea about what really happened at the party. Just whispers from that sodding postman. But you don't want to know the truth, do you? You're not interested in what's *real.* Only in comparing every woman you ever come across to your fucking wife who left you because all you ever do is moan about *this sodding farm.*"

Rosie paused for breath, reeling with the pain in her head, the blood thundering in her ears, and the irresistible force of her own anger. All the hurt, disappointment, and shame that had been festering for the past week came bursting out like a lanced boil.

Bella was absolutely right about Jack.

"Talk about farm here to eternity," Rosie echoed, casting a scornful glance around the chaotic yard. "The land of your fathers," she snapped. "Well, as far as I'm concerned, your fathers can fucking have it."

Jack's face paled at this. Had Catherine, she wondered, said the same thing when she left? Well, she had one more, entirely original, thought of her own by way of finale.

"And if you're so worried about getting your fucking fingers burned in the future," Rosie yelled, "why don't you go and get some sodding asbestos gloves?"

She had made it across the first field before the sob struggled out. More followed. After the storm in her heart, the rains fell thick and fast down her cheeks.

Later, calmer and having sluiced her eyes in cold water to address the swelling, if not the redness, Rosie decided she might as well face the music—or the football results, depending on what the radio was tuned to. Holding the white suit, she knocked on Mrs. Womersley's door.

Tightlipped, the old woman let her in and immediately scuttled back to the stove in the corner of the room where she was ostensibly making lunch. Warming himself, despite the sunshine outside, by the fire as usual, Mr. Womersley shifted awkwardly in his seat and flicked an unhappy glance Rosie's way.

"Are you both all right?" Rosie asked with a strong sense of déjà vu.

"*We're* all right," said Mrs. Womersley. The clear implication was that someone else wasn't.

"The suit," Rosie muttered, all fingers and thumbs as she scrabbled at the plastic supermarket bag Mrs. Womersley had originally given it to her in. "Everyone loved it."

"Yes, I heard it was much admired," said the old lady darkly.

Rosie flinched, but plowed on. "I've had it cleaned. There was a stain on the back—someone bumped into me with a sausage . . ."

"Aye," said Mrs. Womersley in freezing tones. "I heard *that* as well."

I have, thought Rosie, beating a hasty exit, been dumped by two men, one of whom I wasn't even having a relationship with. Furthermore, I made an exhibition of myself at a party with an international celebrity, my neighbors are barely speaking to me, and no doubt the entire surrounding area believes me to be a woman of low morals. Hardly how I imagined country life, really.

Reeling into the sitting room of Number 2, Rosie hurled herself on the sofa and gave way to tears again. Moving to the country had not been a wonderful new start, but a slow and painful end. And whose fault had that been? Hers? Mark's?

"Or Matt bloody Locke's?" Rosie howled, pounding the cushions with her fists so that clouds of dust exploded into the sunbeam-slanted air. Now, with hideous clarity, she recalled his mocking voice. "More's the pity." Well, he was too bloody right there. More's the pity, Rosie thought, I ever clapped eyes on him. It had been Matt, she now remembered quite clearly, who had walked her home, drunk and distressed, from the party. And straight into her career as the scarlet woman of Cinder Lane.

Feeling Mrs. Womersley's disapproval beaming through the dividing wall like a laser, Rosie decided to go out. The cottage and its contents were a constant reminder not only of what had ended but of what was yet to be resolved. She would have to leave the village, of course. She could not afford the cottage on her own, and the publisher's advance from *A Ewe in New York* would clearly not be enough to cover the mortgage for long. But what was there to stay for, in any case?

Yet the thought of going back to London was not a welcome one. The property boom in the capital having penetrated even the consciousness of one as vague as she, Rosie was aware that returning might mean not so much broom closet as shoe box. Matchbox, even.

She could move in with Bella—temporarily, of course—as Bella would insist Rosie did the moment she found out what had happened. There was a spare bedroom next to Ptolemy's suite. A port in a storm, Rosie supposed, even if sharing a landing with the Antichrist was a far from inviting prospect. But Bella need know nothing about what had happened. Yet.

By now, Rosie had reached the top of the hill. She gazed miserably at the village spread around and beneath her. Never had it looked so perfect. The pond on the green sparkled, the rose-towered church stood proud in the sunshine; even the roofs of Cinder Lane cottages running up behind it looked an adorably rickety huddle. Beyond the village, hills rose like green waves into the next valley, then the valley beyond, and beyond that until, finally, they flowed into the purple sea of the moors. Could she really leave all this behind? Did she have much choice?

Rosie jumped as someone suddenly appeared beside her. Someone with black hair and a great deal of eyeliner.

"Hey, there," drawled the girl from The Bottoms. "That's a bit of luck. I was just coming to check you out. We never introduced ourselves the other day." She stuck out a narrow hand heavy with silver rings. "Iseult. How's it going?"

"Rosie. And badly." One of the many recent decisions Rosie had made was to stop saying things were all right when they weren't.

The girl nodded. "Me, too. My stepmother's driving me crazy. I sing in a band called Thrilled Skinny, right, and she won't even let me play my goddamn demo tapes. Says that if that's the future of music she doesn't want to be alive. And I'm with her on that. I don't want her to be goddamn alive either. So"—Iseult looked Rosie swiftly up and down—"what's eating you? Man trouble, at a wild guess?"

"Among other things."

"Thought so. That boyfriend of yours seems to have moved in with us." Iseult fished out a cigarette pack and offered Rosie one.

Rosie shook her head vigorously. "He's *not* my boyfriend. Not any-more." Was this why Iseult had come to look for her? Mark had been in residence at The Bottoms for a week or so now; were the Grabsters already desperate to get rid of him?

"No?" Iseult's lighter clicked and she disappeared behind a cloud of smoke. "But you wigged out completely when you thought he'd handed in his lunch pail. Better dead than alive, was he, then?"

"Sort of."

Iseult drew on her cigarette sympathetically. "So what are the other things? That are wrong, I mean."

"Oh, just that I might soon be homeless as well. My boyfriend paid half the mortgage," said Rosie, resisting the temptation to add "some-times." "So I might have to move back to London."

"Far out." Iseult opened her blue eyes wide. "I mean, that's cool, isn't it? You'll be able to get out of this shithole and back to where the action is. I only wish *I* could."

Rosie looked at her in surprise. "But you've only just got here, haven't you? Rapturous reunion with your father and all that?"

"As soon as I persuade Dad to up sticks and come back to London, we're out of here," said Iseult decisively. "I'm here on a rescue mission, see. Dad can't stand the friggin' country. Hates it. Don't you?"

Rosie paused. In the adjacent field, a bird spilled a succession of high, pure notes on the air. "No," she said, her heart lifting as she recognized a lark, then lowering again as she remembered Mark's comment about fizzing noises and modems. How could she have lived with him for so long?

"But you can't possibly *want* to stay here."

"Actually," Rosie said as the realization crystallized, "I do."

Isuelt's brow knotted as it wrestled with what was obviously to her a conundrum of spectacular proportions. She inhaled again and blew out contemplatively. "Well, I suppose I can understand it in your case. You have pretty good reasons, after all."

Rosie was staring at the two collapsed dragons, just visible in the valley after the next one. Their crumpled tips shone in the sun. Warming their old bones, she thought, her mind suddenly full of Jack and the afternoon when they had eaten the cheese and, afterward, shared that amazing kiss—although in retrospect perhaps that was the wrong way round to do things. He'd been so charming then. Damn him.

"Matt Locke, for example," pursued Iseult.

Rosie came storming out of her reverie. Not this again. Had Duffy been spreading rumors to Iseult as well?

"Whatever you've heard, it's not true," she said hotly. "I don't even *know* Matt Locke. I'd never seen him before the party and I never want to see him again."

There was an astonished silence.

"Freaky," said Iseult, giving Rosie the sort of mixed fear and pity look usually accorded to the terminally insane. "Because Matt Locke sure wants to see *you* again."

"What?" Rosie was shocked. Then she seethed. Bastard. No doubt he wanted to hear firsthand what the results of his actions had been. No doubt, too, he would find the whole thing hilarious. What did the mess she was in matter to him, after all? He was rich, famous, invulnerable.

"I've been trying to call you, but you haven't been answering your phone. He came round to The Bottoms to find out where you lived. Fortunately," Iseult said, grinning, "Mark was in the garden with my stepmother at the time." Her eyes widened with wonder. "Oh, man, he's gorgeous."

"But what did he want?" As if I care, thought Rosie, tightlipped.

Matt Locke was emphatically not gorgeous. As far as she was concerned, he had all the charisma of a tax return.

"Your address. He has a message for you, although I got him to leave it with me." Iseult rummaged in her beaded bag, dragged out a crumpled envelope, and held it out. "Here."

"**D**on't you want to know what it *says*?" Iseult, still holding out the envelope, blinked her kohl-lined eyes in amazement. "A *megastar* has just sent you a letter. An *icon* is trying to communicate with you. Aren't you *interested*?"

"Not really." If it was Matt Locke, it was bound to be trouble. Rosie glanced suspiciously at the envelope, half expecting an evil green glow to be seeping from the sealed flap.

"Can *I* open it then?" Iseult was clearly hell-bent on liberating the contents of the envelope.

Rosie shrugged. "If you like."

Iseult ripped the envelope almost in half. "Bugger," she said ruefully. "That'll halve its value at Christie's." She scanned the piece of paper inside and gave a long, low whistle. "Wow."

Rosie said nothing.

"*Bloody hell,*" said Iseult, her eyes still glued to the paper while Rosie's eyes remained determinedly fixed on the landscape. "You've won the lottery."

Rosie's neck whirled round in amazement until she realized Iseult must be speaking figuratively. Matt Locke might be an influential person, but she doubted even he had a hotline to *National Lottery Live.*

"A lot of people would kill for this," Iseult added after a minute or so's silence.

"For *what*?" Rosie wondered how long the amateur dramatics would go on. From what she remembered of Dame Nancy and friends at the party, there was quite enough of that in Eight Mile Bottom as it was.

"But you're not interested." Iseult gave her a wicked look. "It *is* an amazing offer, though. You can't possibly not do it."

"*What*, for Christ's sake?" Rosie snapped. "Wants me to *sing* with him, does he?"

Iseult's eyes widened. "It's good, but it's not that good. Sing with him—that really would be a blast," she added wistfully.

"So what is it?" Rosie asked for the third time. Iseult seemed to have drifted off into a trance of some sort.

"Oh. Sorry. Matt wants you to do a painting."

"What of?" A watercolor of the village? Of Ladymead?

"Him."

"No way," said Rosie quickly.

"Well, according to this you discussed it at the party. Or maybe," Iseult added, her eyes an innocent blue, "the champagne did."

Rosie threw Iseult a furious look.

"He says here he'll pay you a *fortune*." Iseult then named a sum so staggering that Rosie's brows, which had contracted with irritation, shot apart in amazement. She could not only buy the cottage with that but probably the rest of Cinder Lane as well. Yet she was determined not to be bought.

"No," she insisted.

"Why the hell not?"

"Because Matt Locke is . . . a liar, he's laid waste to my entire life, he's single-handedly responsible for the fact that I have to leave the village, he's . . . Oh, I don't know." Rosie ran a hand through her hair and stared fiercely into the distance. "He's *horrible*."

"Horrible? But he won the Most Gorgeous Man in the Universe title two years running. Not to mention being Best Dressed Male and Most Intriguing Star." Iseult blushed. "OK, I admit it. I've visited his website."

Rosie shrugged. "I don't care."

"How can you be so stupid?" snapped Iseult, abandoning any lingering attempt at appearing laid-back. "Think about it. You're having to sell your cottage and you obviously don't want to. For some insane reason, you even want to stay in the countryside. Now listen to me. If you do this bloody painting, you could buy any house in this friggin' village. Except The Bottoms, of course, although someone's going to have to when Dad and I go back to town."

"They're getting divorced?" Rosie grabbed at the change of subject. Arguing with Iseult was not for the fainthearted. Beneath that frail exterior she had a will of steel and a juggernaut determination to get her way.

"That's the idea," Iseult said airily. "Well, *my* idea. But I think Dad's coming round to that one as well."

There was a silence. Rosie realized she was almost in awe of Iseult. "I'm off," she muttered. "Got some work to do."

"Bet it doesn't pay as well as Matt Locke."

Her face set, Rosie started to walk off.

"Here." Iseult, striding after her, shoved the letter into Rosie's pocket. "You're crazy, you know. I'd give anything to be asked to do anything by Matt Locke. Hell, I'll even do the picture for you. I could always learn to paint . . ."

I won't do it, I won't, I won't, Rosie repeated to herself. But her fingers inched toward the letter in her pocket. Round the corner, Iseult safely out of eyeshot, she tore it out and saw, eyes rounding with shock, that Iseult had not been exaggerating about the promised money. Hell, Matt Locke must be loaded. "Come round and we'll talk about it," the note invited in handwriting that was more carefully rounded and uncertain than the autograph slash she had imagined.

Rosie arrived back at Cinder Lane to discover that Mark had taken advantage of her absence to come round and remove his clothes, books, and records.

"He's left you, hasn't he?" shrieked Blathnat, who had returned as mysteriously as he had disappeared. As had everyone else. The row of clapped-out vehicles once again festooned the graveyard wall and Arthur's dreadlocked head was once again under the hood of his Transit. Just for good measure, Mr. Womersley was sitting outside his front door in the weak spring sunshine with his radio tuned to the local pop station. As a result, "I Feel Love" was pumping out. As Satchel roared by within inches of her on what was without doubt the noisiest, scrapiest, rattliest skateboard in existence, Rosie reflected that love was the last thing she felt at the moment.

She looked at Blathnat indignantly. "That's none of your business."

"Why not? My mum leaves my dad all the time. Although he's so pissed off with her at the moment he's threatening to throw *her* out. She was a waitress at this party, see, and—"

"Get inside, you little bugger," yelled Dungarees, coming suddenly round the corner with her breasts, for once, closed to public view.

When Rosie finally rang Bella, she had not intended to discuss the Matt Locke offer. But in the end it proved the only way of getting her off what was to her the intensely satisfying subject of Mark's unworthiness as a boyfriend and Jack's grumpiness. While managing to refrain from the exact words "I told you so," Bella, with the adroitness of a *Just a Minute* contestant, pressed practically every other euphemism into service. She also made the anticipated offer of the room next to Ptolemy in her house.

"You're very sweet," Rosie said, "but I want to stand on my own two feet."

Bella sounded amazed. "But, darling, what on earth would you want to do *that* for?"

When Rosie finally told her about the letter Iseult had given her, Bella was aghast at the idea of refusal. "But of course you must do it, darling, don't be silly. The money's more than enough for a deposit on a really nice property. Which is what you want, isn't it?"

"Ye-es." The question was—where? Rosie had not yet mustered the nerve to tell Bella, who had blithely assumed she would be returning immediately to the capital, that the only nice properties she was interested in looked out over fields and were hundreds of miles from a Tube station.

"Bel, I really don't want anything to do with him. Everything that's recently happened to me is Matt Locke's fault. Mark shouting at me;

Jack—" Rosie stopped, unable to bear going through the entire unsavory episode again.

"Jack what?"

"Oh, nothing. Well, everything. If Kevin—I mean Matt—hadn't kissed me and hadn't been talking to me when Mark saw me, and hadn't hit Mark, and if Jack hadn't gotten to hear about it from that wretched bloody postman . ..."

Bella whistled. "And you think that's all Matt Locke's fault?"

"Definitely," Rosie said emphatically. "Well, sort of . . ."

"Sort of nothing," Bella said briskly. "If you ask me, Matt Locke has done you the most enormous favor. Mark's a selfish, pigheaded bastard who's always treated you like shit, could you but see it, and Jack's macho pride has never gotten over his first wife pissing off and leaving him. Not that anyone in their right mind could blame her . . ." With what sounded like superhuman effort, Bella stopped herself.

"Hey, don't hold back," snapped Rosie. "Tell it like it is. Don't pussyfoot around on my account."

"Don't you *see*?" Bella urged. "Matt did nothing wrong at the party. On the contrary, from what you said, he saved you from some hideous lech. And you did nothing wrong, either. Apart from not realizing who Matt actually was, of course, which was a *bit* dim, darling, let's admit it. Honestly, Rosie, do people have to go around with flags on their heads saying 'I Am a Celebrity' before you—"

"But he hit Mark . . ."

"My point entirely, darling," Bella said heavily. "Personally I've wanted to hit Mark for years."

Rosie felt her foothold on the argument, already weakened by Iseult, begin to slip. Her eyes ached. She longed to put the phone down and just sleep. It was all too much to think about.

Bella, however, was determined not to let the subject drop. "This portrait is a once-in-a-lifetime opportunity," she said decisively. "Everything I've been saying from the start. Forget the heartbroken bloody farmer, go for the heartthrob rock star. He's been given to you on a plate, darling. He's stinking rich—he could probably get Lucian Freud if he wanted. But he wants you. *You,* Rosie. And think of the money. If you don't like him, just think of it as another commission. It doesn't have to be personal."

Rosie hesitated. There did seem to be a small grain of sense in this. Perhaps it was just possible to regard the portrait as routine work. Even if painting Matt Locke was as far removed as could be imagined from illustrating kumquats for magazine-food pages.

Rosie felt her resolve flag. The proposal, in any case, had a secret attraction for her. Having seen Ladymead so many times from the top of the hill, it would be fascinating to see inside the beautiful old place. As a sop to Bella, she mentioned this.

"Hate to disappoint you," was Bella's unexpected reaction, "but it'll be *beyond* hideous, darling. Believe me, I know what rock-star pads are like; I've done enough of them for *Insider*. Post-ironic ghastly, every last one of them. Swirly carpets, fish-tank walls, gold Trim-style phones and Parker Knolls covered in beige plastic."

"Are you sure?" Rosie recalled the romantic golden huddle of buildings on the moor. She'd imagined great halls, not fish-tank walls.

"Oh, absolutely. Table football, vending machines, and inflatable armchairs everywhere you look. Believe me, they're all the same. Just *horrid,* darling."

"Oh. That's a shame."

"But think of the money, darling."

The following afternoon, after thinking long and hard about the money—even more so after the car had failed to start—Rosie walked slowly up the long and twisting drive of Ladymead. Her legs ached. It had taken over an hour to make the journey from the cottage to the mansion, a period in which Rosie's dislike and distrust of her forthcoming commission had had time to harden. She was doing it for the money. This did not mean she had to like him.

It was difficult, however, not to like his estate. As she glimpsed acres of lush parkland between the fat trunks of the lime trees bordering the drive, Rosie tried not to be impressed.

Rounding the bend and facing the automatic black gates above and around which it was impossible to see, she struggled against feelings of intimidation. It was like something out of a Bond film.

"I've come to see, um, Mr. Locke," Rosie informed the juddering lens of a security camera. A click, a creak, and then the great gate swung back.

A fat tower of honey-colored stone stood before her, glittering with diamond-paned windows. Through the archway framed within a tumble of white roses, Rosie could see a paved courtyard; above, amid the riot of turrets and crenellations, a white flag bearing a rose tree and a lamb fluttered briskly in the breeze. It was, in short, the perfect medieval manor house. And at least ten times more beautiful than Rosie had imagined.

"It's *gorgeous,*" she breathed despite herself. It seemed incredible, not to say tragic, that a place with so gracious an exterior could be filled with ironic junk inside. Yet Bella had assured her it would be—and when, Rosie thought with a tinge of sourness, had she ever been wrong? Particularly recently.

As a tall man dressed in black shimmied into view, she jumped.

"My apologies if I alarmed you, madam. I'm Murgatroyd, Mr. Locke's butler," the apparition rumbled at her in dignified tones. "This way, please."

Rosie sighed as she followed. So Bella was right. A butler, no less. Matt *was* a rock-star cliché after all. "I didn't realize he had a butler," she remarked as Murgatroyd glided across the courtyard, his polished shoes almost silent on the smooth and ancient stones. Rosie stumbled after him, taking in a jumbled impression of mullions, roses, the flash of ancient glass and acres of weathered stone.

"Well, to be perfectly honest, madam, I don't think Mr. Locke did either, at first," Murgatroyd said.

Rosie frowned. What did he mean?

"What I intended to convey, madam," the butler added, evidently noticing her expression, "was that when Mr. Locke bought Ladymead, he very kindly took on all the existing staff. Very good of him, that was."

"Are there many staff?" Looking up at the ancient walls enclosing her, Rosie imagined an entire army of retainers hidden away.

"Only myself, madam. Sir Hadley, the former owner, had a much larger staff originally, but by the time Ladymead passed out of his hands, most of his requirements were being met by myself."

"You must have been a bit shocked when you heard Ladymead had been sold to a pop star," Rosie said provocatively, thinking this butler was too respectful for her liking. The tramplike, fisticuff-prone Matt Locke she had met bore little resemblance to the enlightened lord-of-the-manor figure whose praises were now being sung. Still, no doubt Matt's vandallike destruction of the fabric of her life was, as Bella predicted, reflected in his vandallike destruction of the fabric of Ladymead. "I expect," Rosie probed, "there have been all sorts of changes to the house." Surely now Murgatroyd would mention the fish tanks?

"As indeed there were, madam." Murgatroyd glided to a halt before a vast and ancient oak door. As his hand turned a massive iron-ring handle, worn and polished from centuries of use, Rosie braced herself for the swirly carpets.

"This," Murgatroyd announced, ushering her in, "is the great hall."

"But it looks as if nothing has been altered for centuries," Rosie said after a few minutes' amazed scrutiny. Around her, bare white walls of an antique thickness, sprouting here and there enormous pairs of antlers, stretched from the sisal floor to the hammerbeam ceiling. A fireplace the size of a bus dominated one wall, above which, Rosie noticed, cavorted a plaster representation of the same lamb and rose tree emblazoned on the flag. At the far end, a narrow refectory table ran almost the entire width of the hall, its polished surface glowing in the mellow light of a nearby leaded window.

"Indeed, madam. Mr. Locke embarked on an extensive program of restoration soon after he took possession."

"Really?"

"Absolutely, madam," said Murgatroyd. "Restoring the great hall to its former condition is entirely the inspiration of Mr. Locke."

"I didn't realize he was interested in antiques," muttered Rosie, confounded.

"Indeed he is, madam. In fact, one of his first acts on acquiring Ladymead was to trace all the pieces of furniture that Sir Hadley, a descendant of the noble family that had owned the house for generations, was obliged to sell over the years." Could she, Rosie wondered, detect a hint of freezing disapproval in the butler's tone? "Mr. Locke persuaded all the auction houses to alert him when a piece was coming up.

As most pieces were made for the house, they were easily identifiable by the Ladymead crest of a lamb and a rose tree, which you may have noticed on the panel above the fireplace over there."

Rosie goggled. "So the former owner just sold everything off?"

"Unfortunately, yes, madam." No doubt about the tone this time. "Sir Hadley was more interested in, ahem, bringing the house up-to-date, madam. In Sir Hadley's time, the walls of the great hall were covered in flock wallpaper and he used to keep his aquarium in it. This way, if you don't mind, madam."

Rosie followed as he glided on through a sequence of dark, paneled rooms. Eventually they emerged into an airy stone hall whose wide, shallow-treaded stone staircase rose the entire height of the building to a ceiling painted to represent Mount Olympus. Here, muscular gods reclined lasciviously alongside pert-breasted goddesses in skimpy lengths of rippling pastel silk.

At the top of the second flight of stairs, Murgatroyd pushed aside a heavy tapestry curtain. "The long gallery, madam. Generally considered to be one of Ladymead's finest rooms. Now that"—the butler permitted himself a gentle cough—"the snooker table and vending machines installed by Sir Hadley have been removed."

Rosie hardly heard him. Entranced, she was drinking in the details of the room that stretched before her like an amazingly long and ornate shoe box. One side was indented by lattice-windowed bays through which the sun poured in diamond patterns on the polished oak floorboards. Spread magnificently across the opposite wall were two marble fireplaces with vast and elaborate overmantels, again featuring the lamb and the rose, between which bristled hundreds of portraits in heavy and elaborate gold frames. In keeping with the splendor of their surroundings, the expressions on the faces were freezingly formal. Rosie stepped forward and examined the nearest, a haughty young woman with a very high forehead and skin the color of raw haddock. The intervening centuries had not reduced in the least the beady force of her stare.

"It's original," she muttered, tracing the fine brushwork with her eye.

"Indeed it is, madam." Murgatroyd sounded almost offended at the suggestion it could have been otherwise. "They all are. Mostly

seventeenth-century and dating from the time of Ladymead's main period of expansion and building. Although Mr. Locke is, I believe, planning to inaugurate a collection of twentieth—twenty-*first*-century, I
should say—portraits."

Rosie felt a shudder of shock and excitement. Surely Matt did not
intend her work to hang here—in this magnificent room, alongside
what looked suspiciously like a couple of Clouets and at least one
Kneller? And there, looming in a vast white gown out of the distance
at the gallery end, wasn't that a portrait of the Virgin Queen herself?
To be among such company was deeply flattering, but Rosie pushed
the thought firmly aside. It was just a job. She had not wanted to come
here. Even if it was one of the loveliest houses she had ever seen.

"Mr. Locke is on his way, madam," murmured Murgatroyd, showing her into one of the windowed bays where two battered but very
comfortable-looking leather armchairs had been placed opposite each
other. So the sitting was to take place in this room? As the butler moved
away, Rosie fished out her sketchpads and pencils, feeling, as she did
so, the inscrutable gaze of the portraits lining the wall. The silence and
the stillness sang in her ears.

She almost leaped out of her skin as a gloomy figure appeared in the
distance. It was, however, only Murgatroyd, reappearing with a tray
bearing a silver coffeepot, cups and saucers, and a plate of biscuits. "Mr.
Locke thought you might like some refreshments, madam."

"Thank you." Rosie realized she was starving. As soon as Murgatroyd disappeared, she fell on the plate of custard creams with a
vengeance. Then a slammed door at the distant end of the gallery
stopped her in midcrunch.

It was him. She could recognize his voice, advancing up the gallery,
shouting. As he approached, she realized he was carrying a mobile.

"I tell you, Geordie, I'm not delivering until I'm ready. I don't care
about their sodding schedules . . . I don't *care*, Geordie. If I handed it
over now, it would be a fucking disaster . . ."

As Matt came into view of Rosie's bay, he pointed to his mobile and
rolled his eyes. "Yeah, right. Well, that makes no odds to me . . . Anyway, look, I've got to shoot. A meeting . . . No, nothing you need to
know about." Matt snapped the mobile away and threw himself into

the chair opposite Rosie. She stiffened with dislike. At least with determination to show him that she disliked him.

"Sorry about that." He grinned at her and raked both hands through his disheveled hair. "Nice to see you again."

His open friendliness was the last thing she had expected. Charmed, despite herself, Rosie resisted the strong urge to grin back. She hated him, remember. She gave him a distant smile and noted that he was wearing the same hooded top and grubby cargo pants he had worn for Samantha's party.

"Bloody managers," Matt groaned, raising his eyes to the ornate ceiling. She had not noticed before how prominent his lips were. Or the way his eyes, long and green as blades of grass, smoldered. Not that this made any difference to her, of course. The sudden fizz in her feet was merely the delight of the artist preparing to sketch a particularly interesting face. Wasn't it?

"All managers care about is the sodding money." He was looking at her and smiling. "No matter if the bloody album goes down the bog. There'll be another just like me around the corner. Or so they think. And they're probably right."

Rosie, shifting uncomfortably in the spotlight of those green eyes, oddly piercing above their sleepy bags, shrugged. She knew nothing about managers, unless you counted the one in the supermarket.

"Sorry to rabbit on," Matt said. "I'm having a couple of problems with the new album. Well, a couple of hundred, actually. Just won't come together, for some reason." He pulled a wry face. "Between you and me, I'm shitting myself about it."

This was both unexpected and profoundly disarming. Despite herself, Rosie felt her lips part in a smile.

"I mean, I can see the reviews now," Matt muttered. " *'Can a performance this wooden give you splinters?'* Or how about: *'About as much impact as a tea towel falling on your foot. . . .'* "

His features twisted in a mixture of anger, misery, and resignation. Feeling a twinge of sympathy, Rosie immediately forced it down. Why, after all, should she feel sorry for him?

"Aren't you going to start?" Matt asked, snapping forcibly out of his mood. "Warts and all," he told her, flashing his perfect teeth. "I want you to do me as I am."

Rosie nodded, thinking that, now that she was really looking at him, she had never seen anyone as wart-free in her life. As free of blemish in general. Beneath the mass of uncombed dark hair were cheekbones you could hang-glide off of and a nose of Botticelli straightness. He had the careless confidence of the assuredly beautiful, the extravagant untendedness of a pile of couture dumped on the bedroom floor. Bedroom floor? Rosie stopped herself sharply.

There was silence for a few minutes. Rosie sketched away vigorously. The sooner she got the preliminary sketches finished, the sooner she could move on to canvas and get the whole thing over and done with. Matt, meanwhile, had lapsed deep into thought. His long hands plucked restlessly at each other. Obsessing about his album, Rosie imagined, her pencil tracing the fine curve of his jawbone. The jawbone suddenly moved.

"Look, I'm really sorry about the party," Matt burst out suddenly. "Hitting your boyfriend and all that."

"Ex-boyfriend," muttered Rosie, immediately wishing that she hadn't. No doubt it would amuse him to know how what he had started had finished. A blush began to spread about her face and neck.

"You must be pretty pissed off with me," Matt continued. The green eyes, she saw, looked almost anguished. "I'm really sorry. Gutted, in fact."

"I don't want to talk about it," Rosie said, drawing furiously. It was difficult to have an embarrassing conversation with someone whose face you were forced to stare at frequently. She focused on his mouth, noticing the contrast of his heavy lips to the delicate planes and shadows of the rest of his face.

"I understand," Matt said. "But I'd like to talk about it. I'd like to explain why I behaved the way I did. Calling myself Kevin and everything. Must have seemed pretty strange."

Just a bit, Rosie thought crossly, pressing her pencil hard into the paper. Yet, despite herself, she was surprised. She had been determined to avoid at all costs the subject of the party; in the unlikely event they ended up discussing it, she had been expecting aggression and defensiveness on Matt's part. Arrogant imperviousness, even. But apology? Never.

"It did seem strange," she admitted. "But," she added in a rush of fairness, "it must have seemed pretty odd that I didn't recognize you. I'm afraid I've no idea about famous people at all, you see. I don't know who anyone is. It used to drive my boyfriend mad. My ex-boyfriend, I mean . . ." She winced.

The bee-stung lips stretched in a broad smile. "To be honest, I was thrilled when you didn't know who I was. I didn't want to be recognized."

Thrilled? Didn't want to be *recognized?* And he a famous rock star. Was he making fun of her?

"Not very rock star of me, I know." Matt grinned, effortlessly reading her thoughts. "But I was *terrified* of going to that party. I'd planned to go in disguise, but Oakie wouldn't let me. So I dressed down. It was brilliant when that Grubster woman or whatever her name is thought I was a builder."

Rosie smiled faintly at the memory of them both standing apprehensively before the Tudor rose doorbell and half-timbered closed-circuit camera. Kevin/Matt had seemed perfectly all right then. That was before the world fell in.

"So why go at all?" she challenged.

She expected a bit of bluster at this, but instead Matt looked at her keenly. "Can I trust you? I feel that I can, but I'd hate to read what I'm about to tell you splashed over the *News of the World* or whatever."

Rosie hesitated, not wanting his confidences. "You don't have to tell me anything," she blurted out. The bleeding hearts of the famous or, failing that, their fridges, were more Mark's department. On the other hand, being the recipient of celebrity confidences—even if Mark was unaware of it—would give her a certain satisfaction, especially as they were the secrets of a star he had been desperate to interview. "Not if you don't want to," she added more reasonably.

"Well, I'd like to, if you can bear it. It would help me to talk." He paused for a few seconds before adding, in a rush, "I only went to the party because Oakie made me."

Rosie was frankly disappointed. As star revelations went, it was hardly seismic.

"Don't you want to know who Oakie is?"

Rosie looked up. "If you like."

"Oakie Cokie is my therapist." Matt searched her face for a reaction. She looked back at him blankly. What did he want her to say?

"I don't want to sound like an egomaniac or anything," he said, his eyes fixed on her in a mixture of amazement and amusement, "but I thought you might have heard I'd become, um, a bit of a recluse. I mean, I'm not trying to blow my own trumpet, but it was on the front page of all the papers and *OK!* did a special commemorative edition . . . Oh, my God, just listen to me." He let out what sounded suspiciously like a snort. His shoulders were shaking, Rosie saw.

"Yes, I did know that." She smiled at him uncertainly. Was he laughing?

"Want to know why?" His smile had switched itself abruptly off.

I know why, Rosie thought. Bella told me. Champagne D'Vyne broke your heart. "If you want to tell me," she muttered.

"Christ, I can't get over you. No one's ever said that before. People are usually right in there with the most personal fucking questions."

Rosie sketched on. His lashes, she saw, were the longest she had ever seen on a man.

"It was all to do with . . ." Matt began, addressing his knees, then paused. Rosie's pencil stopped, waiting for the first mention of Champagne's name. She felt, suddenly, intensely curious.

". . . the first two albums being such hits. You know the story. Or perhaps you don't?" As Matt flicked an amused, green glance up at her, Rosie blushed and shook her head. "OK, well, it was like this. One minute I was singing into my mother's hairbrush, then I was driving a van, doing church-hall concerts. No one had a fucking clue who I was. I was so underground I practically hit the water table. Next thing I knew, some A and R men saw me in a pub in Northampton and thought I was the hottest thing since vindaloo. Then Geordie was all over me like a rash, I hit Abbey Road and *Posh Totty* hit number one. Suddenly there I was. Playing more stadiums than David Beckham."

Rosie put her pencil down.

"At first"—Matt pushed a lock of hair out of one eye—"there was no stopping me. My second album, *What Did Your Last One Die Of?*, came out and was even bigger than the first. I could do no wrong. I thought I was God's gift. And of course it went straight to my head. Used to have two seats booked on every flight, one for me and one for my ego. I'd have the entire top floor of a hotel reserved because I didn't want anybody else near. All my hotel bills had at least ten thousand pounds extra on them for damages. I made it a point of honor to wreck the rooms, throw the TV sets out of the windows, and all that." He smiled mirthlessly, eyes roaming unhappily up and down the windows. "Harder than it sounds, by the way. TVs nowadays—well, you can't throw them out of windows anymore. They're all huge."

Matt's eyes narrowed. His lips twisted ruefully. "I was such a plonker. Refusing to sit anywhere but the very front of the Concorde because the engines were too noisy at the back. Ordering five Savile Row suits a week in materials more suited to soft furnishings than menswear. Going to the Met Bar so often I practically had my own bloody sofa. You ever been to the Met Bar?" he suddenly demanded.

Rosie shook her head. It had always sounded terrifying to her. Mark had gone there for some feature, she recalled. Having been deemed insufficiently cool to enter on his own merit, he had had to book a room to enter the hallowed portals of style as a hotel resident. The managing editor had been furious at the cost. But not as furious as Mark at the indignity. Her heart lifted slightly at the memory.

"Well, don't bother," Matt snapped. "You'll only meet people like me. Full of champagne and self-loathing. There I was, the boy who slapped the world's face, determined to knee it in the balls as well. There was nothing I wouldn't do; no one I wouldn't do it with. Girls?" His eyes shot to the ceiling. "My motto was the Four F's. Find 'em. Feel 'em. Fuck 'em. Forget 'em.'"

He shot a chastened glance at Rosie. "Sorry," he muttered. "But it happened. Hell, I even had a reputation for the number of pint glasses I could dangle off my cock."

Rosie, head lowered over her work again, hoped he was not going to ask her to guess how many. Why was he telling her all this? Who did he think she was, Susie Orbach?

There was a silence.

He had, she saw as she glanced up, withdrawn into himself again. His expression had darkened.

"Fame was fun at first. For about five minutes. Then I got sick of it. *Really* sick of it. Sick of the grungy greasefests in airport McDonald's, sick of the planes, sick of if-this-is-Monday-it-must-be-Milwaukee." He rubbed his eyes and looked at her desolately. "But, hey, what was my problem? My career had taken off like a rocket, I was working every hour of the day and traveling to countries I never even knew existed. But," he finished, his voice dropping an octave, "I was pretty confused and unhappy."

"But why?" asked Rosie, thinking irresistibly of Mark, who was confused and unhappy for precisely the opposite reasons. "When you had the world at your feet like that." Perhaps this was where Champagne D'Vyne came in.

Matt shot her a sardonic look. "Because I hated every minute. I was stressing obsessively and was completely fucking terrified about the future. The first album was huge and trying to beat it was impossible. Then when I did beat it I realized I was expected to do it again, four months later. The promotional stuff was manic. Every day it was 'You have a meet-and-greet here, then an interview there, then a TV show here,' and in the end, I just couldn't do it. The fans never left me alone. They even took soil from my garden. They cut bits of my hair off when I was in the supermarket. In the days when I still went to the supermarket." He paused. Rosie thought she had never seen anyone that wistful about Tesco. There was a silence. Then Matt spoke again. "I was all over the papers, all the time. My entire private life had been reduced to something that cost thirty-five pence. So I started to go off the rails. Took so much charlie my septum almost fell out. Got on the booze as well, for good measure—and I had a few of them, I can tell you. Half a bottle of sherry first thing in the morning. Hair of the dog, it was. But then I had the dog as well and in the end I opened an entire kennel." He groaned. "And there were other problems. Relationships and things . . ."

Relationships and things. Champagne D'Vyne, in other words, surely. No wonder he'd had a breakdown if he'd had to cope with her leaving him along with everything else. And what sort of a woman could she be, Rosie wondered, unceremoniously abandoning a lover already suffering to such an extravagant extent it made her own recent traumas over Jack and Mark look like a grazed knee.

"Sorry. I'm crapping on," Matt muttered, looking at her sheepishly. "You're wondering what all this has got to do with the party."

"Sort of," mumbled Rosie.

"After the breakdown," Matt told her, "my confidence was at an all-time low. I hid away here in Ladymead. I could barely get up, let alone write songs. I'm better at the getting up now, but the songs are still a struggle. And as for going onstage, well, I walked off a stage in L.A. a year ago and I haven't set foot on one since. Not that anyone saw me walk off. I was playing behind a wall of bricks meant to represent the alienation of the rock star." He flashed her a grin. "Pretentious, *moi*? I'd gone bonkers, basically." Silence again.

"I don't know what to say," Rosie said eventually, "except that I feel better than I have done for years about being totally poor and a complete failure at everything. I'd always imagined being rich and famous to be fun, you see."

Matt shot her a suspicious look, as if checking to see that she wasn't being sarcastic. Then he laughed.

"Of course it's bloody fun. It's the best fucking fun in the world. It's a dream come true. A privilege. My problem was that I couldn't see any of that. Spent all my time feeling sorry for myself." He twisted his lips. "How sad was I?"

"Well, relationship problems can sometimes affect you that way," Rosie said slowly, thinking of her own recent past and curious about the part Champagne D'Vyne had played in all this. Hadn't she been the real root cause of his breakdown? But he had not mentioned her. Had she hit him that hard then? That deep?

Matt was looking at her, blinking as if jolted from his train of thought. "Oh . . . yeah," he said. "Course they can. Listen, are you sure I'm not boring the arse off you? Only it's making me feel a lot better."

Rosie shook her head. Hearing about Champagne—Mark's replacement on the paper, after all—would be interesting. On the basis that any enemy of his was a friend of hers.

"Oakie's my latest therapist," Matt said, veering off the elusive subject once again. "I'd tried everyone under the sun before him. Every treatment imaginable from having crystals shoved up my sphincter to primal screaming."

Rosie giggled, thinking that having small, sharp things shoved up your bum probably would have that effect.

"Then I found Oakie, who told me that the only way to build my confidence up again and literally get my act together was to go out and meet people. Get used to contact again. Start with small-scale social events, like that bloody stupid fancy-dress party. I wanted to turn it down, but he wouldn't let me. It was him that made me go." Matt's eyes widened. "*On my own.* It was the first time I'd been out of Ladymead for *months.* By the time I met you, I was shitting myself. The thought of meeting other people was *terrifying.*"

He bent his head. "You were the first woman I'd spoken to for ages," he muttered, addressing the floor. "It wasn't as bad as I thought it would be."

Thanks, thought Rosie, suppressing a smile. Surely now he'd get on to the subject of his legendary girlfriend?

"And then when you mentioned you were an illustrator, I hit on the idea of the portrait."

Rosie looked over at the wall of paintings. Imagine. Her humble daub hanging next to those. "It's a great idea."

Matt looked pleased. "Glad you think so. Oakie said sitting opposite someone else for hours on end would be kill or cure. Although whether for me or you, I'm not sure. And the bonus, of course, is that there will hopefully be a nice picture at the end of it as well."

"Oh," said Rosie, deflated.

"Madam?"

"Yes?" It was Murgatroyd. The session had ended. At the large oak door on the way out, Rosie paused.

"Mr. Locke has asked me to ask you, before you leave, what your travel plans are."

"Travel plans?" repeated Rosie, before the penny dropped. Of course. No doubt Matt thought the entire world could fly off to Rome and Cap Ferrat on a whim, just as he could. He probably imagined she was hopping over to Capri that very weekend, in fact, and was worried about the effect her globetrotting would have on the sittings. "I'm not going anywhere," she said flatly. In any sense of the word, she reflected miserably.

Murgatroyd raised an eyebrow. "Mr. Locke means travel to La-dymead, madam. He wonders by what means you get here. He hasn't noticed a car or a bicycle."

"I walk. From the village." Rosie's heart was already sinking at the prospect of walking back.

"That's what he thought. He asked me to ask if you would mind if he sent the car for you."

"Not at all, I'd love it," said Rosie, amazed and delighted.

"He thought you might appreciate a lift home as well, madam," Murgatroyd continued. "If you'd just come this way, madam. You can tell me on the journey what time you'd like to be picked up in the morning."

Bella tried not to sound astonished at Rosie's account of Ladymead, delivered, as promised, the moment she arrived back at Cinder Lane. "Hmm," she said. "It's what you can't see that counts. Darling, you might mention *Insider* to Matt. I could do with something huge for the October issue." She paused. "How's it all going, anyway?"

"Oh, OK, I think," said Rosie doubtfully. "The first session seemed to go quite well." It was hard to work out how it was really going. Or what she thought about it. Matt was so very different from what she had expected. As was the fact that she had assumed the role of his confidante.

"I wasn't meaning the *work,* darling."

"Well, what else is there?"

"Darling," said Bella. Rosie pictured her fingers drumming impatiently on the Biedermeier console that supported the telephone. In fact, she could actually hear them. *Tap, tap, tap.* "Exclusive access to eligible rich bachelor and all that?" *Tap.*

"Matt's not interested in me. He's not even interested in having his portrait painted. It's part of his therapy, apparently."

Bella sniggered. *"That* old line."

Rosie was indignant. "It's true. He's had a nervous breakdown and now he wants to be back on his feet. The idea of the picture is that he practices human interaction while it's painted."

"Human interaction, eh? It gets better and better, darling."

"Oh, lay off, Bel," Rosie wailed. "You've got it completely wrong. And even if he was interested in me, *which he isn't,* I wouldn't touch him with a barge pole. He's not a very nice person." In her heart of hearts, however, she was no longer sure she still believed either of these things. The lift home in the Mercedes had smashed through the last of her defenses.

"And what the hell difference does that make?" demanded Bella. "He's rich, isn't he? And gorgeous. That's a bonus, darling, let me tell you." She was, Rosie could tell, thinking of Simon.

"Yes, but I've done gorgeous," Rosie said, thinking of Mark. "And I'm not sure it suits me. Matt's a business arrangement. Nothing else."

She had just put the phone down when Duffy burst in with the afternoon post. Which, Rosie saw in mingled exasperation and amusement, comprised nothing more than a flyer advertising the takeaway services of the Indian restaurant in Slapton.

"Boyfriend gone, has he?" Duffy's eyes were darting about. "I hear he's moved into The Bottoms. Odd business, that, isn't it?"

Rosie shrugged, determined not to be drawn into an explanation. "These things happen."

"Not round here they don't. Not usually, anyway. Nice for him, though, it's very posh there." Duffy flicked a disparaging glance around the kitchen whose messiness without Mark around to complain about it (yet fail to address it personally) had reached unprecedented levels. Still, Rosie thought, if it put the postman off, she had no intention of tidying it up.

She gave no further information and waited for Duffy to go away. She had not forgotten his role in the breakdown of her friendship with Jack, even if, with hindsight, she suspected he had done her a favor. Jack's rejection had been a shock but was preferable to spending the rest of her life being compared to some impossible ideal. Especially an ideal who had made off with a sheepnut salesman from Chesterfield. But it would have done no harm to remain friends, although, given some of her remarks—*all* of her remarks, actually—last time they had met, that seemed an unlikely prospect.

She ran some water over the pile of pots in the sink, hoping this would hint to Duffy that his presence was not desirable.

It did not. Or, if it did, he ignored it. Rosie realized Duffy had no intention of going until he had found out what he wanted.

"Is it true you're doing a painting of Matt Locke?"

"Possibly." Rosie, although too truthful to lie, was determined to confirm nothing.

"Dame Nancy used to do that. Stripped off for artists when she was a struggling actress and had no money. Then she realized she could strip off for directors and make lots of money. That's what she told me, anyway." Duffy sniggered.

"Matt Locke," Rosie said firmly. "is *not* stripping off."

Duffy looked triumphant. "So you *are* doing it then!"

Rosie took a defiant sip of coffee. "As I said. It's a possibility." Appallingly rude though it felt, she was determined not to offer Duffy any form of refreshment whatsoever.

"Nice, it must be," Duffy said, almost wistfully.

"What must be?" Rosie felt lacerating guilt about the coffee.

"Meeting people like Matt Locke. Becoming, ahem, good friends with them."

"I'm not good friends with him," snapped Rosie, exasperated. She wondered why Duffy had ever vacillated about journalism. He was wasted on the Royal Mail, when a brilliant career on a tabloid could so clearly have been his for the taking.

"More than that, is it then, eh? Thought so, after the party." He winked at her.

"No! Do you understand me? *No!*"

"Love to know a famous person, I would," Duffy said. "What decided me to become a postman in the first place was when I read that Julie Christie once went out with the bloke who delivered her fan letters."

"Really? Where did you find that out?" Despite her irritation, Rosie was finding it hard to keep a straight face.

"*Daily Mail,* of course," said Duffy. "I thought, Hang on a minute, I might get lucky as well. Not with Julie Christie, obviously."

"No," said Rosie. It was difficult to imagine the exquisite film star and the red-faced, roll-eyed postman as an item.

"Don't think she lives round here, for one thing," Duffy continued

blithely. "Anyway, it didn't work out with the postman. But she definitely had a thing about letters. Went out with Terence Stamp after that."

Duffy had just left when there was another knock at the door.

"Oh, hi," said Iseult, trying rather too hard to sound casual. "Just
passing."

Rosie was not naturally suspicious, but she thought this odd. Passing *where*, exactly? Cinder Lane led nowhere apart from Spitewinter
Farm, and it seemed unlikely Iseult was dropping in on Jack. Her dislike of farm animals seemed to be one of the few areas in which she had
anything in common with Samantha. Puzzled, Rosie struggled with the
bottom half of the stable door to let Iseult in.

"Who are you?" demanded a high, cheeky voice. Iseult turned to see
Satchel standing behind her, gawking with unfettered curiosity.

"An undercover cop," said Iseult, not batting a midnight-blue eyelid.

"*Can't* be," said Satchel triumphantly. "Police only came round to
our house last night."

Iseult looked at Rosie with a raised eyebrow. "There goes the neigh-
borhood," she drawled.

Rosie finally conquered the lock and let her in. "They used to drive
Mark mad, but I don't mind them. They're rather sweet, in a noisy, irritating sort of way."

Iseult raked the cottage with her sharp stare. She was clearly wondering how anyone in their right mind could live here. Rosie was, in
fact, beginning to wonder the same. She braced herself for reports of
her ex-boyfriend's bliss among the manifold comforts of The Bottoms.

"How's Mark?" she asked, assuming this was the reason for Iseult's
visit. Best to get it over with.

"Being driven slowly insane." Iseult grinned. "He and my stepmother spend all day in what Samantha calls the gaze-bow working on
some cheesy film script. At least Mark works on it. As far as I can make
out, Samantha loafs around with her feet up banging on about her glorious Hollywood past."

"Oh, of course. Her glorious Hollywood past." Rosie dimly remembered the *Punkawallah* conversation during the *Insider* shoot.

"But as far as I can make out, Hollywood totally passed on *her.* Her entire career is TV bit parts, a high spot doing a margarine ad, and a movie that went straight to airline."

"What's 'straight to airline'?"

"It's when the movie sucks too much even to go straight to video," said Iseult gleefully. "*Punkawallah,* it was called."

Rosie felt a smile pull hard at the corners of her mouth. "How's it all going for you, anyway?" she asked. "Your various plots and things?"

"OK. The dad one's going like a train. Almost literally—he's desperate to get back to London now. So desperate that I'm having to put the brakes on it a bit."

"But I thought you hated the countryside."

"I do." A guarded look rippled across Iseult's resolute features. "But it might do me some good to stay on the scene a bit longer. Now that *he's* here . . ."

"Who?" The possibility that she meant Mark suddenly burst on Rosie. She looked at Iseult in horror. Surely . . .

Iseult fumbled in her bead bag and produced a small plastic box. "Like, could you give my demo tape to Matt Locke?"

As Rosie left her cottage at the appointed hour the following morning, Satchel, Blathnat, Arthur, Guinever, and Dungarees were noisily trying to bump-start the still noisier VW camper van down the lane. Dirtier and rustier than ever, a dingy curtain hanging askew in its grubby back window and its interior crammed with broken furniture, the van, which exploded periodically in a cloud of filthy smoke, looked fit only for the least choosy of scrapyards. As it jerked hysterically past the church, something large, smooth, and shining purred alongside it. It was the Mercedes, with Murgatroyd at the wheel. Climbing into the gleaming vehicle, Rosie felt horribly self-conscious, all the more so when, as the big silver car pulled sleekly away, she caught a glimpse of Mrs. Womersley at the window. Lips pursed in disapproval, no doubt.

Matt was in the long gallery, pacing up and down and talking agitatedly into his mobile. "Look, Geordie, can't you tell them to get stuffed? I'll deliver when I'm ready, and I'm not ready yet . . . No, I told you, I'm not ruling out collaboration, but I'm *not* doing it with bloody

Posh Spice." Spotting Rosie, he raised an eyebrow, cut the conversation short, and shoved the phone in his pocket. His hand, Rosie noticed, was trembling.

The smile of welcome Matt gave her did not disguise how tired he looked. Or how miserable.

"What's wrong?" Rosie asked, taking out her pencils. The knowledge that the drawing sessions were entirely therapeutic was far from flattering but oddly relaxing. It clearly didn't matter how it turned out and she was being paid, anyway. And, as power play went, a nurse-patient situation was a lot easier than a rich-rock-star-and-poor-artist situation.

"Everything." Matt groaned. "Geordie's just called with the welcome news that my record company's threatening to drop me altogether if I don't finish the album soon. As if I give a fuck." From the despairing way he buried his head and sprawling, nervous fingers, however, it was obvious to Rosie that he did give a fuck. If not several.

"Why's it so difficult?" She realized immediately what a stupid question it was. What did she know about hit albums? Hit singles, even? The only singles she knew about were flops. Like herself.

"Same old sound, same old ideas." Matt rubbed his eyes again and looked blearily at her. "I need a shot in the arm, but fuck knows what. Apart from that, of course"—he rubbed his forearm meaningfully— "but I'm off that shit now." He looked broodingly out of the window, his lips pushed out in resentful, sultry fullness.

Watching him, Rosie thought she had never seen anyone so despairing look so good. Almost tenderly, she sketched in the long, stray tendrils of hair that flopped over his face and wondered whether she should show him her drawings. They were, after all, going surprisingly well. They might even cheer him up.

"I know it doesn't matter, but . . ." Rosie reached into her portfolio and fished out the work she had done so far, holding them up for Matt to see. "OK, they're only therapy, but—"

"But they're *great*," Matt cut in, staring at them with what looked to Rosie suspiciously like amazement. "Really, they are. You're *good*. Very good."

Rosie felt irrationally thrilled. Even at the beginning of their relationship Mark had never been as unreserved in his praise as this. Looking into Matt's eyes, green as the parkland outside and glowing in admiration, all her nerve endings tingled.

The door clicked at the end of the gallery.

"Hey, Murgatroyd," Matt called as the butler glided silently up with a tray of coffee and biscuits. "Come and cast your expert eye over these."

Murgatroyd carefully put the tray down. The biscuits, Rosie noted with interest, were shortbread—her favorite. Homemade, too. Double favorite. "Very lifelike, sir. If I may say so, I think they do you justice."

Matt whistled. "That's high praise from Murgatroyd," he said, grinning at Rosie. "He's very difficult to please. I've just had some photos done for the new album and he thinks they're all crap. Censored pretty much all of them, haven't you, Murgatroyd?"

"With respect, sir, I felt some of them were less than flattering."

"Murgatroyd has a very good eye," Matt enthused. "And a good ear, too. He's an old rock 'n' roller himself at heart. Used to play in a band called Fast Joe and the Accelerators. Supported the Beatles a few times, he tells me. Although even *he* can't quite come up with what's needed for this sodding album. Not just a case of banging it all back through the reverb, is it, Murgatroyd? We were up all night trying to crack it."

Rosie looked at the impassive butler in astonishment.

"We were indeed, sir," he murmured.

"Makes top shortbread, too," Matt added, his thick white teeth sinking into one of the biscuits. "Buttery and crumbly, just like it should be. What's your secret ingredient, Murgatroyd?"

"Rice flour, sir." Murgatroyd, Rosie saw, was red with pleasure.

"Oh, yes. I'd be up shit creek without Murgatroyd," Matt assured her. "My right-hand bloke he is. Brian Epstein and Jeeves all rolled into one. Even gets rid of the fans at the gate by telling them I've moved to Ireland for tax reasons and no one has any idea when I'm coming back. Oh, and not to take the soil because it's radioactive after Chernobyl. It works, too. Used to be coachloads of girls when I first moved here, but now you only get the odd Spaniard or German. *Very* odd they are, some of them." He grinned. "Stuffing their knickers in the postbox and everything. Bras, suspender belts, the lot. Mind you, it serves that nosy bastard of a postman right."

Rosie smiled. "Yes. Duffy certainly could be said to take an intense interest in the correspondence he delivers."

"And then some." Matt's spirits seemed to have risen like bubbles in champagne. Could it possibly have been the drawings?

"Let's go out to lunch," he suddenly urged. "You'll have lunch with me, won't you?"

Doubt and excitement coursed through Rosie before she realized the suggestion was hardly likely to be personal. No doubt Oakie had decreed that the next stage in his rehabilitation was the issuing of a social invitation.

"But *where*?" Matt asked himself fretfully. "Rome's been done to death, Paris is too girly, New York is boring, boring, boring. *I know*," he shouted, clapping his hands. "Let's go to Istanbul."

"Er . . ." stammered Rosie, her thoughts flying to her plants. Mrs. Womersley had not directed her helpful, all-watering hose over the garden wall recently.

"Or if I may make an alternative suggestion that may fit better with your schedule, sir," murmured Murgatroyd in silken tones. "I've got a very nice fish pie in the oven. It will be ready in half an hour."

Lunch was served in a tiny octagonal room in the tower. Dancing excitedly ahead of her up the stone spiral stairs, Matt explained to Rosie his plans to open Ladymead to the public eventually. "But this tower is all mine. Out of bounds to visitors. But not," he added, flashing her a smile that made her swallow hard, "for friends."

Seated at the circular oak table, the perfect size for an intimate lunch *à deux*, Rosie dug her fork into a fish pie that made even Ann's at the Barley Mow seem oddly lacking something. Matt launched immediately into a stream of music-business anecdotes that left her wide-eyed, open-mouthed, bent double with laughter, or, frequently, all three.

"You've never heard that before? But it was all over the papers," he exclaimed in amazement when Rosie professed complete ignorance of the drummer, the tadpoles, and the bath full of cleaning gel.

"Sorry, I don't read the papers," Rosie mumbled.

"Why be sorry about that?"

Rosie sighed. "It used to drive my boyfriend—*ex-boyfriend*—mad. He hated it that I couldn't have picked Sally Jesse Raphael out of a lineup. Or that I didn't know Pee-Wee Herman's real name."

"Or that you didn't know who I was. Although I suppose the problem there was that he thought you did."

"Hmm," said Rosie, reluctant to be drawn into discussing the matter.

For a moment Matt looked as if he were about to discuss it anyway. Then, to her relief, he bounced up and, lunch being over, offered to show her over the rest of Ladymead.

"Smart, isn't it?" he said proudly as they admired the goings-on of Mount Olympus painted on the ceiling above the staircase. "Took three years to finish. Apparently the artist put some of the Ladymead servants in as well. That toothless old crone in the corner is supposed to be the housekeeper and that fat bloke next to Zeus is the head gardener. He was massive on trompe l'oeil as well. . . . Oh, yes, I *can* pronounce it." He laughed at Rosie's stare of surprise.

Rosie blushed. Once again he had read her mind. But she was surprised that Matt seemed to know so much about his pictures. Enough to be irreverent about them.

"Not bad," he said when Rosie paused on the wide stone stairs to admire a classical landscape. "The main reason I bought it was because I thought the crapping dog at the front was funny."

Rosie peered. Sure enough, before the depiction of an ivied, crumbling Forum during a golden sunset was a patch of white, which, on close inspection, proved to be a very obviously defecating Jack Russell.

"Cross-looking Dutch people," he said, grinning when Rosie exclaimed at the workmanship on some seventeenth-century portraits from the Netherlands. "But you're right, they are exceptional," he added with quiet pride. Rosie looked at the pinched and disapproving faces above the starched white ruffs and was strongly reminded of Mrs. Womersley. Whom she had seen neither hide nor hair of—apart from twitches of Number 1's curtains—since returning the suit. It was tempting to conclude her neighbor was trying to avoid her.

This uncomfortable thought was soon dispelled by the joy of exploring Ladymead. Rushing around like an excited child, Matt pointed out everything from the hand-painted Japanese wallpaper in the salon to Queen Victoria's bed.

"Only she never slept in it," he told Rosie. "They did the whole place up for her visit, but then one of the kitchen maids got typhoid and she never came. Bummer or what?"

Rosie, her nostrils filled with smells of wood, furniture polish, dust, and age, hurried in Matt's wake as he disappeared down endless twisting corridors, his hands never still from drawing her attention to yet another Ladymead delight. He tapped at windows to point out the beveling, showed her the cast-iron detail of the door locks, gestured at a series of perfect vistas. They passed a wonderful trompe l'oeil hat, ribboned, flowered, and "hanging" in perfect eye-deceiving detail from the back of a door. "And see that enfilade of doors there? Each one framing the one after it. Top stuff, isn't it?"

He drew her attention to the wide and sweeping park, pointing out the landscaping, the crescent lake, the clump of three oak trees planted by two Bonsanquet sisters in memory of themselves and a third, who had died. "And see that little stone doorway over by the temple of Diana? That's the icehouse, which I've converted. It's my studio now. Bit on the nippy side, but the acoustics are phenomenal. And this is the pub." Matt grinned, taking her into a small sitting room whose every wall bristled with carved paneling in dark wood. Each panel, she saw, held the exquisitely rendered head of a stern-looking bearded gentleman. She looked round. There seemed no evidence of drink whatsoever.

"Why's it a pub?"

"One of the former owners bought this lot wholesale from a German monastery," Luke explained. "It's eighteenth century. But it always reminds me of the 'Elizabethan bar' in some pompous, provincial hotel. Believe me, I should know," he added ruefully. "I saw enough of them." Then he darted off again.

"And here's the chapel," he announced, opening a pair of double doors that stretched to the height of the ceiling at the end of a long corridor. Rosie had no idea where in the building they now were. Ladymead inside was every bit the warren the outside promised it would be.

"How incredible," she said, "to have your own chapel. A bit like owning God."

"I think that was more or less the idea."

The chapel was seventeenth century and very ornate. Although now almost sated with the variety and beauty of Ladymead, Rosie nonetheless found she had room for one last expanse of carved and gilded wood, another eye-tanglingly geometric marble checkered floor and a final explosion of garish painting behind a heavily decorated altar. All, not that she'd ever say it, just a trifle . . . *vulgar*?

"Bit Donald Trump, isn't it?" Matt grinned, reading her thoughts again. Finally he took her back to the tower.

"My sitting room," he declared, opening a linenfold paneled door to reveal an imposing but intimate room with a Tudor fireplace and vast, comfortable-looking sofas. "Not that I do all that much sitting in it. Except to watch the telly or a video," Matt said, revealing with a flick of a small, silver remote control how a huge, flat state-of-the-art TV was concealed behind a sliding panel in the wall. "And this," he added, disappearing up a further flight of narrow spiral stairs, "is my bedroom."

Rosie hesitated before following him up. Matt beckoned her with the disinterested enthusiasm of a stately home room steward, pointing out the plaster animals, birds, and flowers molded on the low ceiling and the rose tree and lamb panel over the fireplace, picked out in reds and golds. "Restored to their original colors," Matt said proudly. From the deep-silled latticed windows, their panes dimpled and curved with age, Rosie looked across the green and rolling valley to see, in the distance, the top of the spire of Eight Mile Bottom church.

"And this is my bed." As Rosie glanced hurriedly away from the huge four-poster, something between her navel and her pubic bone plunged downward while excitement mounted in her throat.

He was, she saw, looking at her, watchfully from narrowed eyes, his lips curved in a heavy, sultry smile.

"Look inside the canopy. It's carved there as well."

Striding over, he positioned her in front of him and pointed up inside the bed. His fingers, though holding her with an almost infinite lightness, scorched into her shoulders. It was with a mixture of excitement and fear that she saw the carvings were extremely explicit. Figures with enormous breasts and colossal penises; frequently both.

Quite suddenly he spun her round and kissed her. It happened almost before her brain registered it. Her body, on the other hand, had no such problems. Her lips burned and a feeling of urgent need began to build within her.

"Oh," she gasped.

She watched, heavy with longing, as the lips approached again. Contact was explosive; they pulled eagerly at her throat, her lips, her cheeks, her hair. Finally, his tongue still eagerly exploring her mouth, he pushed her closer to the four-poster and in one fluid, practiced movement laid her down. She blinked up at him, modestly averting her gaze from the priapic penises above his head. Although why, as he expertly slipped off her top and began licking her nipples, she had no idea. There was nothing modest about what he was doing.

"I fell in love with you the first time I saw you," Matt murmured, his dark, tousled head still busy with her breasts. "Standing outside the door of that stupid bloody house."

"In love with me?" Rosie giggled, arching her back with pleasure as his hand trailed liquid fire between her thighs. "But you can't be in love with me."

"Why not?"

She gasped, stiffening with pleasure as his sure fingers touched places Mark had hit but only intermittently. Places she had been too shy to show him. Places Matt knew apparently by instinct. "Because," she murmured, "you're, um . . ."

"What?" He raised himself on his elbow and traced her lips with his fingers.

"Er . . ." What was she trying to say, anyway? That she'd heard his heart was broken? "Too rich and famous," she finished flippantly.

He rolled his eyes and lowered his mouth on hers again.

"There you were, looking almost as scared as I was," he growled, coming up for air and removing the rest of their clothes. "Only a million times more beautiful. That suit was sensational. Gucci, was it?"

"No." The aching, longing cavern within her seemed to be expanding into infinity. Then, gloriously, sliding slowly into her, Matt filled it. Rosie pushed herself fiercely, rhythmically against him. She was floating, soaring, rising to join the gods in the sky above the staircase. And not the ones who looked like head gardeners at that. "Mrs. Womersley," she gasped as fireworks exploded behind her eyes.

Matt having finally, reluctantly, but apparently unavoidably disappeared into his icehouse studio, Rosie was driven home by Murgatroyd. She stared, unseeing, as the village reeled past the window. Had any of it really happened? Firmly in the yes camp were a certain lightheadedness and a throbbing rawness between her thighs. But had he *really* said he loved her as well? *"I fell in love with you the first time I saw you. . . ."* Rosie heaved a sigh of happiness so loud and prolonged that Murgatroyd flashed her a concerned glance in his mirror. Rosie blushed as she looked back at him, then smiled.

Passing The Bottoms, Rosie spotted Iseult wandering down the winding drive and crashed back to earth. She looked, Rosie thought, both bored and impatient. Guiltily, she remembered the demo tape still in her bag. She had completely forgotten to hand it to Matt, understandably enough, though, given the circumstances. There had been other matters in hand, after all. *Damn,* though. Iseult would be so disappointed.

Still, there was always tomorrow, Rosie thought happily. Or, there was always Murgatroyd. He seemed to sit in on the studio sessions, after all. She blushed as she looked at the back of his chauffeur's cap. The front, she had noticed, bore the Ladymead lamb. He drove smoothly along, not revealing through so much as a glance in the mirror what, if anything, he knew of the afternoon's activities.

Sliding her hand into her bag, Rosie closed her fingers round the plastic oblong. "Murgatroyd?"

"Yes, madam."

"Could I possibly give you a demo tape?"

"I wasn't aware that madam had singing ambitions."

Rosie laughed "Not me. It's a friend. She's very keen that Matt should listen to it. Could you slip it in somehow?" She looked down, blushing, and immediately regretting her choice of words.

Murgatroyd, however, did not miss a beat. "I'll try my best, madam, though slipping things in isn't as easy as you'd imagine with Mr. Locke."

Rosie stared, embarrassed, out the window. What exactly was the butler implying?

"People try all the time, though," Murgatroyd continued. "One chap trained as a stove repairman for the sole purpose of penetrating the country houses of people in the music business so he could give them his demo tape."

"Really? How amazing. What happened?"

"Unfortunately, it seemed he was better at fixing stoves than he was at writing songs, madam."

CHAPTER 23

Mark now found it impossible to believe that he had ever thought Samantha was attractive. Day after grinding day stuck with her in what was actually the gazebo but what she insisted on calling the film development unit had, far from stoking his lust with her proximity, almost driven him to contemplate murder. The fact that she insisted they occupy chairs with "Star" (hers) and "Director" (his) on the back had not improved matters. Worse even than this, though, was his increasing suspicion that her film connections might not be all she made them appear. There was something about the way she kept referring to Glynnis Paltrow and Brad Reeves that smacked of a less than intimate knowledge of the Hollywood scene, despite her constant Hollywood-ese references to actors as "talent" and frequently expressed desire to cast Matt Damon, Ben Affleck, and someone called Kevin Spacek in the film.

Then there was the matter of the first act of *Charlotte in Love* being an unmitigated disaster, mostly because Samantha, considering a rain-lashed northern village unglamorous, insisted on making the repressed daughter of Haworth Parsonage the party-throwing chatelaine of a villa in the South of France.

The writer's love life had also been found wanting. "We're never going to get Matt and Bill—I mean Ben—to play those," Samantha had snapped on the discovery that the main romantic events in Charlotte's life had been an unrequited passion for an aging Belgian schoolmaster and marriage to a curate called Arthur. Under duress, Mark changed them to what Samantha considered to be a more Hollywood-friendly womanizing duke and a randy field marshal. He squared it with his conscience by reflecting that all the Brontës had been great fans of the Duke of Wellington.

As if this were not enough, there was also Samantha's wretched soon-to-be-ex-stepdaughter to cope with. Although it now seemed official that Guy and Samantha were going to divorce, Iseult, who was apparently going to live with Guy in London, was still at The Bottoms, ostensibly because there were "things to sort out." This explanation did not entirely wash with Mark, especially now that Guy himself had disappeared to the capital on a practically permanent basis, but Mark was not interested enough to inquire. Nor did he want to encourage Iseult, who made no attempt to disguise the fact that she found his plight hilarious. She had dubbed the film project *Sunset Boulevard* and lost no opportunity to call in at the gazebo and mock it. Unfortunately for Mark, there were many such opportunities. When one day he finally asked Iseult why such an avowed country hater like herself didn't just go back to London, she smiled mysteriously and said she was waiting for something.

According to Iseult, Samantha had reacted well to Guy's request for a divorce, possibly because of his decision to hand her The Bottoms as her settlement. This news filled Mark with mixed relief and dread; Samantha was clearly going nowhere for the moment, which meant, of course, that he and *Charlotte* weren't either. A prisoner of her thespian ambitions and his own impecunious situation, Mark felt increasingly like a bird in a gilded cage, albeit a gilded, distempered, decoupaged, and beribboned cage lined with toile de Jouy. Full board and lodging at The Bottoms had long lost its glamour—the rioting pastoral prints all over his room gave him a permanent migraine, and the relentless low-fat nature of all food served was making him fear for his blood-sugar levels.

"How's *Sunset Boulevard* going?" Iseult asked as she dropped by that afternoon. "Where's Samantha?"

"Out getting her thighs electrocuted or her nipples repositioned or something." Mark sighed, adding that Samantha had, of late, indulged in at least two treatments a week with the ultimate goal of looking as polished as possible as she approached the Dorothy Chandler Pavilion.

"Is she having her lips puffed up?"

Mark shrugged.

"Hope not," Iseult said, screwing up her face. "I read somewhere that women with very thin mouths need more than collagen injections, and the lips have to be split, peeled back, and stuffed with fat from dead people's bodies."

"Yuck," said Mark, who thereafter experienced a wave of revulsion every time he looked at Samantha's mouth. Every time he looked at Samantha, in fact.

Her complete lack of talent ensured that the situation between them couldn't have been less like *Sunset Boulevard*. Much as Mark identified with William Holden's hapless screenwriter, Samantha was no Norma Desmond. She was not ready for her closeup and she never would be.

"What's my motivation?" she demanded in the final scene of the first act of the film.

Mark had envisaged this as a touching tableau in which Charlotte tremulously ties up the just-completed *Jane Eyre* before sending it off to try its luck with the publishers. "What's my motivation?" Mark repeated grimly to himself. He had painstakingly explained to Samantha how, at this point, Charlotte's whole literary future hangs in the balance as she silently, passionately, prays that her manuscript will be accepted. Shot through with hope, vulnerability, and ambition, the scene was, he thought, a powerful piece of cinema, even if its power was not apparent to all. "Your motivation," he snarled under his breath, "is money."

"What about this?" Samantha said now, craning her neck into profile and assuming a tragic air. "Perfect for the scene where Charlotte looks out to sea and watches the duke's ship disappearing over the horizon?"

"Great," said Mark heavily, reflecting that at least that scene didn't involve any speaking parts. Samantha's interpretation of Charlotte

Brontë as a breathy-voiced temptress with an epic cleavage set his teeth on edge. He groaned. Nothing about the project was remotely right, still less, as Samantha informed him the film jargon went, dead leather perfect. Still, he thought wearily, these things could surely be improved on. They would have to be.

"Haven't seen you up at Spitewinter much recently," Duffy remarked, casually dropping in to hand-deliver the pizza restaurant handout that made up the whole of Rosie's post that day.

Rosie glared, hoping this would distract him from the guilty look in her eye. Before he had burst in, as usual without knocking, she had been waiting for Murgatroyd and thinking with happy anticipation of the day ahead with Matt.

Having spent the night reliving their afternoon together, she had been awakened by a hungry throb between her legs. The exact time had been difficult to establish; the church clock had banged out first eleven, then fourteen an hour later. Rosie had finally been driven out of bed when it struck twenty-eight, only to find that it was, in fact, six. Awake, she had passed the early morning working on the final paintings for *A Ewe in New York*. Now that her sketches had been approved by the publishers, all that remained was to fill them in with color. Rosie was eager to finish them as soon as she could in order to spend as much time as possible on her new artistic project.

Duffy, however, had hit on the one cloud in the blue sky of her happiness. Rosie was nothing if not softhearted and, despite his treatment of her, with her new found luck had come the recurring question of how Jack was coping in comparison. She pictured him sitting lonely and embittered in the farmhouse with only Kate for company, brooding over Catherine and the intransigence of women. Her stomach twisted with guilt.

"Haven't been up there for a while, have you?" Duffy's tone was almost accusing.

In reply, Rosie gestured at the painting she had been working on that morning. "I've nearly finished my animal pictures. There's no need for me to go anymore."

There was a pause.

"Jack seems happy enough, anyway," Duffy said with elaborate casualness.

"Happy?" It was impossible not to betray her astonishment.

"Been writing off to that magazine. Lonely 'earts thing, you know."

"Lonely hearts?" Rosie tried, but failed, to visualize Jack sitting in the candlelit corner of a bistro watching the door with a rose in his teeth. *Northern farmer with burned fingers seeks reliable, nonurban woman with guaranteed lack of interest in pop stars or feed salesmen from Chesterfield.*

"Which magazine?" she asked.

"You know," said Duffy. "That thing that's been in all the papers— you must have seen it."

Rosie shook her head. "No."

"That country magazine that's worried about farmers being too isolated to find suitable women . . ." Duffy paused and flicked her an impudent glance.

"I don't know what you're talking about." Rosie was determined to rebut both meanings.

But Duffy, as ever, was impervious. "This glossy magazine, right, well, it's running a campaign to help these farmers. They're putting pictures of farmers needing wives into the magazine, along with a little interview, and women who want to meet them write in to the magazine. They set up meetings in restaurants, the farmers click with the women, and hey, presto, problem solved. Jammy buggers," he added ruefully. "Wish they'd do the same for country postmen."

"What, and they've put Jack in?" Rosie was astonished. Grumpy, obdurate Jack courting publicity, let alone advertising his lovelorn plight? Delivering himself into the hands of fickle fate via a magazine feature? "I can't believe it."

The postman's eyes slid toward the almost-empty biscuit package on the shelf. Rosie grasped it and pushed it at him.

"It was his auntie who put him up to it." Duffy, biscuit in hand, jerked a thumb at the wall that separated Rosie from the Womersleys. "Jack had some kind of bust-up recently with some woman old Mrs. W. had high hopes of . . ." He cleared his throat meaningfully. Rosie looked boldly back at him but blinked first. "And so Mrs. W. lost her rag. Told Jack to stop moaning about his luck with women and get his act together because moping around Spitewinter wasn't going to help things."

Duffy, thought Rosie, was extraordinarily well informed. It seemed very odd that Mrs. Womersley, who had always seemed to regard him with suspicion, would let the postman into her confidence to such an extent.

"So then she sent him this farmers' lonely 'earts thing she'd seen in the paper . . ."

Sent. Now that made sense. The source of Duffy's information was suddenly crystal clear.

". . . and told him to get the magazine and get on with it. He's receiving lots of letters. Some very racy ones from London, I must say."

Well, he won't be replying to them, it was on the tip of Rosie's tongue to say.

"And there's this one woman from some village in Yorkshire who's very keen. Has loads of ideas for going orgasmic."

"Orgasmic?" echoed Rosie. "What sort of a magazine did you say it was?"

"You *know*. Potatoes with dirt on, that sort of thing. Milk with bits of straw in it."

"Organic, you mean?"

"Organic, that's it. And she had lots of plans for opening bed-and-breakfasts and things. Sounded like a real live wire, even if the picture she sent wasn't what you'd call gorgeous."

Rosie said nothing but thought that, after the beautiful but un-governable Catherine and her obviously unsatisfactory self, a hard-working, plain woman would be the answer to Jack's prayers. Someone completely different, who could on no account be compared. And if she had ideas as well, so much the better.

"But Jack's not made his mind up. Still auditioning 'em all." Duffy grinned. "You should keep a look out—you'll probably see them going past the window on their way up to the farm. His auntie certainly does."

The excitement of the postman's visit had been such that only as he screeched off did Rosie notice Murgatroyd had not yet arrived. Odd, for someone so punctual. She opened the stable door to look out, but the big silver bonnet stubbornly failed to slide into view. Apart from Blathnat throwing stones at milk bottles, the lane was silent and empty. After half an hour had passed beyond the agreed pickup time, Rosie felt ill with concern. Had something happened? Had Geordie been putting the pressure on Matt again? Had Matt, driven back into the depths of depression and self-doubt, done anything *stupid*? Rosie's breath caught noisily in her throat. But he had seemed so happy yesterday. Had even told her that he . . .

Rosie was aroused from blissful memory by the telephone.

"Murgatroyd here. From Ladymead. Sorry to disturb you, madam."

"Oh, Murgatroyd. Where are you? Everything's all right, isn't it?"

"Yes, madam. But Mr. Locke is in bed."

"Oh, God." Rosie's hand flew to her throat. "Is he ill?"

"No, madam. Just very tired. Up all night again. I'm afraid, madam, that the session for today will have to be canceled. I'll pick you up tomorrow, madam."

Disappointment hit her like a fist. She wouldn't see Matt for a whole day. Twenty-four entire sixty-minute-long hours. They would, quite obviously, *never* pass. Rosie swallowed hard. "Fine," she croaked. "I'll see you tomorrow. And please give my . . . say hello to Mr. Locke for me."

"Indeed I will, madam." The line clicked and went dead.

Rosie wandered into the kitchen. Two minutes had probably passed since Murgatroyd had called. Twenty-three hours and fifty-eight minutes to go.

Duffy had by this time moved on to Mark. He had made it his business to separate Mark's post from Rosie's and deliver the former to the gazebo so that he could keep an eye on things. As Mark received, on the whole, even less post than Rosie, Duffy had been required to call on all his reserves of initiative to create some. Mark was now the recipient of an unrelenting stream of special-offer film development envelopes.

"Well, you're making a film, aren't you?" Duffy said innocently as

Mark communicated his irritation at being interrupted for the sake of a flier announcing a sale on Quarter Pounders at McDonald's.

"Not that sort of film," said Mark shortly, wishing he had been less free with the movie's prepublicity. His steady loss of faith in the project had not been helped by Iseult's informing him that morning that the closest Samantha had ever come to fame was on a low-budget TV miniseries where the director's secretary had gone by the name of Holly Wood. A story, she assured him, Guy had heard from the horse's mouth, though whether that meant Samantha or the secretary was not established.

Duffy grinned at him. "I suppose you've heard?"

"Heard what?" Mark asked irritably, trying to stem the flow of coffee that Duffy's sudden arrival had propelled over the scene he was writing. Samantha had gone to Dame Nancy's for lunch, so he had the gazebo to himself for a change. Yet for some reason this still had not helped the third redraft of the saucy exchange between Charlotte Brontë and the dashing duke. It just wouldn't gell. If he was honest, it was practically liquid.

"Filming in the village." Duffy's eyes were almost popping out of his head with excitement.

"Who is?" snapped Mark. "The Vicar of bloody Dibley?"

Duffy looked hurt at the suggestion that he would peddle such low-grade gossip. "Course not. Big American film company, apparently. Going to have lots of famous people in it—Julie Christie, so I've heard." His eyes gleamed with hope.

"Big American film company?" Mark felt as if a hair dryer had just dropped in his bath. He'd long since ceased believing in them, but had Samantha's claims of friends in Hollywood high places been true all along? Odd . . . but just about possible. Yet Samantha had said nothing about it. *Very* odd. Even weirder was the fact that now that she had literally cut Haworth out of the picture, *Charlotte* had no village scenes to film. All this notwithstanding, a wild hope clawed at his heart. Had *talent*—Christ, I'm sounding like her now, thought Mark—had a director, stars, and a film unit been found overnight?

Julie Christie seemed strange, though, as Samantha had firmly and repeatedly stated her intention that the rest of the cast apart from her-

self were to be unknowns. She had explained to Mark that this sprang
from her determination to give obscure actors a break, but he suspected
it sprang from her determination not to be upstaged by anybody better known than she was. Or known at all, come to that. The Holly
Wood anecdote had, after all, a ring of truth, and Mark had yet to meet
anyone who had ever heard of *Punkawallah*.

"It's some sort of country romp, apparently," Duffy went on eagerly.

"Historico-literary drama, you mean," corrected Mark, wondering
if there was in fact such a word. His bowels contracted in excitement.

"Don't think so. Set in the present day as far as I know. *Farm Fatale*
or something, it's called."

He'd staved it off for as long as he could, but the hideous suspicion they were talking at cross purposes finally began to dawn on
Mark.

"You sure it's not called *Charlotte*?" he demanded. Had Samantha
changed the title without asking him? Calling it *Farm Fatale* didn't
make much sense. But then nothing about this whole venture did.

"Well, there might be someone called Charlotte in it," said the postman doubtfully. "It's supposed to be a romantic comedy or something,
so they say."

Mark's heart sank. Even given his gift for inaccurate précis, it
seemed unlikely the postman had gotten things this wrong. He was
clearly talking about another film altogether. For, however sweeping,
gratuitous, and dramatic Samantha's additions to the story of the great
Victorian novelist had been, the one thing she hadn't put in was comedy. There was nothing remotely humorous about *Charlotte*. Not in-
tentionally, anyway.

Mark turned grumpily back to his script to find the heroine
where he had left her, laughing prettily at one of the dashing duke's
saucy sallies. Or did Charlotte Brontë, Mark wondered, have a dirty
laugh?

The postman had not moved. "Well, don't you think that's interesting?" he urged Mark. "About the film?"

"Nope." Mark derived a masochistic enjoyment from Duffy's disappointed tones. "Actually, I'm a bit busy," he added impatiently.

"But there's talk of us all getting parts in it," pressed the postman desperately. "They might make a fly-on-the-wall documentary about the filming of it."

Mark gave an elaborately uninterested grunt.

"And Champagne D'Vyne is in it, you know, that columnist from the newspapers? Posh blond woman. Used to go out with Matt Locke?"

Mark's hackles rose at the mere mention of the hated woman who had stolen his column. His upper lip curved in a sneer. Yet he revealed nothing of the violent emotion he felt.

"Star of it, she is. So they say. That'll be interesting, won't it? *Her* up here. Near to *him*. After him having that nervous breakdown after he left her and all that." Duffy sounded almost pleading now. "I would have thought the papers would be interested. Can't you write something about it? Give us all a mention?"

Mark turned in his chair and looked witheringly at Duffy. What did the bloody postman know about what papers would be interested in? As for writing something about it . . . Mark opened his mouth to blast this idea out of the water and then, remembering he had quite possibly neglected to inform Duffy that the paper had let him go, turned it into a yawn of apparent boredom instead.

"I'm busy," he repeated forcefully. Accepting defeat, the postman finally slunk out.

Films? thought Mark savagely. He was sick of them.

Minutes after Duffy had left, Mark's mobile phone rang. The instrument was not technically his, belonging as it did to the paper. However, despite his summary dismissal from employment, they had not yet asked for it back. Given the editor's legendary meanness, it seemed incredible it had been forgotten, but given the editor's cruelty, particularly over his severance pay, Mark had no hesitation in keeping it. It remained in his pocket, a means of outside communication and the one thing, apart from an adaptor to charge it up with, that he didn't have to rely on Samantha for.

Cursing at another interruption, Mark fished it out and stabbed at the buttons. To his complete amazement, it was the newspaper. His immediate thought was that they were calling about the mobile. The voice was, after all, that of the features secretary, a woman with an asphyxiating stranglehold on the stationery cupboard.

"I'll send it straightaway," he said.

The voice at the other end sounded surprised. "Well, that's very professional, I must say."

"No problem," said Mark. "I'd have sent it before, only—"

"Only that you didn't realize the story was going to get even bigger," soothed the voice. "Now that Brad Bergspiel's directing, Champagne D'Vyne's in the film, and they're apparently doing some of the filming at Ladymead, where Matt Locke lives, it's all gone up a gear. We want a behind-the-scenes inside track. Including, of course, lots of speculation as to whether Matt and Champagne will get back together. Two thousand words, by the end of tomorrow."

"Right," said Mark, swallowing. "No problem. Matter of fact, I was already on to it. It's a great story."

"Lucky for you it dropped right into your patch, eh?"

"Guess so," said Mark, trying hard to sound casual. "But I was on the case anyway."

"Be the front-page splash if you get it right. Editor's *very* keen on it."

Mark closed his eyes ecstatically and imagined the moment. *His* story on the front of several million newspapers. What a relaunch to his career that would be. With the renaissance of Mark Green, *Über-reporter*, the ignominy of the past months would be obliterated.

"You still there?" demanded the voice, sounding puzzled by the long silence.

Mark jerked abruptly out of his daydream. A thought had struck him. "Hang on a minute. I don't want to be rude, but didn't you used to be the features secretary? How come you're commissioning news stories?"

"I'm doubling up," said the voice. "Features secretary half the time, news editor the rest. Cuts, you see."

Mark clicked off the mobile and staggered to his feet. His legs felt quite weak with the magnitude of the opportunity. If he could pull *this* off, not only would the paper welcome him back with open arms, but also he could finally tell Samantha to get stuffed. It was difficult to decide which would give him the most pleasure, and so Mark decided to devote what remained of the afternoon to pondering this delightful conundrum.

There was not, in the end, much time for contemplation. The door of the gazebo was suddenly wrenched open and Samantha, eyes flashing and nostrils flaring, burst in. "I have never known such *humiliation*," she screeched.

The memory of the party still fresh in his mind, Mark found this hard to believe. "What's the matter?" he asked guardedly.

"*Farm* bloody *Fatale,* that's what," spat Samantha.

Mark's ears pricked up as he recalled his assignment. Did she know something useful about it? "Oh, yes," he said casually. "I've heard a bit about that. What is it?"

Samantha flung him a glance of contemptuous amazement. "*What is it?*" she squawked. "Only something practically everyone I met at lunch has parts in. Nancy, obviously, and every single one of those appalling old queens." Samantha's voice hit a pitch that could shatter glass. "And I knew nothing about it. *Nothing!*" She seemed about to explode with volcanic fury. "Why didn't *you* know about it?"

"Well, you're the one with the film contacts," Mark fired back, emboldened by the prospect of escape proferred by the paper. "Didn't Brad Bergspiel mention it the last time he called?"

Samantha's saurian eyes glittered. "How *dare* you?" she hissed. "How bloody *dare* you? Get out there and get me a part *now.*"

"Oh, piss off!" bellowed Mark, storming out and slamming the fragile gazebo door hard in his wake. Now to work, he thought. Round up my sources. Where the hell had that bloody postman gone?

"Put it this way," Bella said when she called that evening. "It definitely put the rain in Mediterranean. Poured down all weekend."

Bella, who had been testing a new South of France spa for *Insider* magazine, had not yet been brought up-to-date on events at Ladymead. Hugging her secret excitedly to her, Rosie wondered whether to tell Bella now, later, or ever. Was it like a wish, liable to disappear if spoken of?

"Darling, *please.*" Bella, two hundred and fifty miles away, took the receiver away from her mouth to negotiate with Ptolemy. "Eat your tomatoes, darling. Yes, I know the silly nanny's not sliced them sideways as you like, but . . . *Jesus*," she groaned to Rosie, her mouth returning to the phone. "*Children*. Don't have them."

Rosie's mouth dropped open in astonishment. Could this really be Bella speaking? A woman who had previously worshiped every inch of the hand-rubbed beech floor her son's handmade shoes had walked on, every Biedermeier chair they had kicked and scraped against?

"What's happened?" she asked. Had something occurred to force the realization that Ptolemy was considerably less than perfect? Rosie was amazed to find that the answer was yes. Ptolemy, it transpired, had been to the opticians and had been unable to see the test board, let alone read out the fourth row from the top.

"It's a nightmare," moaned Bella. "It's all my fault."

"How can it be?" demanded Rosie crossly, determined, in her new happiness, to put a stop to Ptolemy's reign of filial terror. "Honestly, Bel. If you start feeling guilty about his eyesight, where's it all going to end?"

"But it *is* my fault," insisted Bella. "Apparently it's all because of his nursery. All the sisal and plain walls, and the fact that I wouldn't allow any ghastly patterns. It turns out he's never really been able to focus." She sounded anguished.

Wanting to comfort her friend, but still deliciously delaying the moment of truth, Rosie switched the conversation to the spa weekend.

"Wonderful." Bella sounded considerably more cheerful. "I had my bottom buffed."

Rosie giggled. "Had what?"

"Darling, it's wonderful, I tell you. They rub your wobbly bits with an exfoliating scrub until after five minutes you feel as if you've been flayed alive."

"But you don't have any wobbly bits," Rosie said, thinking it sounded considerably less fun than what Matt had done to her own nether regions.

"*Everyone* has wobbly bits," said Bella firmly. "That's the one great universal truth, darling. Anyway, as I was saying, they scrub you and then they rub you with aromatherapy oil right down to your ankles to remove the cellulite."

"But no one has cellulite on their ankles."

"No-o," Bella conceded. "But it's best to be on the safe side. Anyway, after this they cover you in detoxifying seaweed and wrap you in cellophane so you feel like a prepacked vine leaf. Result, a bottom softer than a one-hundred-percent cashmere pashmina."

"Amazing," said Rosie, tuning out of the conversation to watch a capable-looking woman, apparently bound for Spitewinter Farm, striding past the cottage window. She looked as if she could wrestle a bull to the ground. Was this, Rosie wondered, the woman Duffy had mentioned? The orgasmic candidate from Yorkshire?

"So I really think you should try some of these treatments," Bella was saying as Rosie tuned back in. "I mean, you can't keep going up to Ladymead looking like you do."

Thanks, thought Rosie. On the other hand, it hadn't seemed to bother Matt. Her clothes had presented no obstacle to him at all. But was Bella right? Should she make more of an effort?

"You don't need to do much, not with a pretty face like yours and all that lovely blond hair. Although it *might* be a good idea to brush it now and then. Just smarten yourself up a bit. Wear a skirt even. And remember, the shorter and tighter, the better."

"But I hate skirts. Especially ones that are too short."

"There's no such thing as a skirt that's too short—another great universal truth for you, darling. Anyway, remember, Matt's been out with some pretty glamorous women. You've got stiff competition. In every sense of the word, I would think."

"Champagne D'Vyne, you mean?" A chill, slight but definite, suddenly swept through Rosie. The society blonde Matt had loved and lost. But if it had been such a tragedy, why hadn't he mentioned her? He'd mentioned practically everything else. The four F's, even the pint-glasses-on-the-penis trick. So why hold back?

"You got it, baby. Supposed to have been the whole reason he became a recluse, remember. Never got over being dumped by her and all that."

"But that's rubbish," Rosie burst out. "His breakdown was about being too famous too quickly. He told me."

"Well, he would say that, darling, wouldn't he?" drawled Bella.

"He never said anything about Champagne," Rosie insisted, remembering, suddenly and uneasily, Matt's reference to relationship problems. When she had tried to draw him out, he had resisted. But that could have meant anything. Geordie, Murgatroyd, anyone.

"Not something he wants to boast about, I imagine," Bella returned to Rosie's growing annoyance. Why was she playing devil's advocate? Well, if she thought Rosie was going to tell her everything about her afternoon with Matt after this, she had another think coming.

"Anyway, darling," Bella said with every ounce of the wisdom of Solomon, "there are certain things, and people, one never gets over. Your farmer and his wife, for example—"

"Thanks for reminding me," snapped Rosie.

"Just pointing out a few stately home truths, darling. You need to be tough if you're going into this game. No point having your legs open if your eyes are tightly shut."

"I don't know what you're talking about."

"Yes, you do."

"No, I don't."

"Yes, you do." There was a laugh in Bella's voice.

Rosie blinked first. "How did you guess?"

"It's in your voice, darling. You've obviously had the shag of your life. But the real clue was that you never denied it when I said you had stiff competition. Normally you'd have slapped me down instantly. Was it as good as it sounds, anyway?"

"Better," breathed Rosie, tingling all over at the thought of it.

"Good. But if you want more where that came from, you must listen to your aunt Bella. The difference between a one-night shag and a relationship is some serious grooming."

Rosie's stomach twisted with irritation. "Doesn't it have something to do with liking the other person, a shared sense of humor, respect, and all that sort of thing?"

Bella snorted. "Oh, sure. In the case of Champagne D'Vyne, it also had something to do with being posh and blond with tits. Seriously, Rose, Matt had a nervous breakdown after she dumped him. She's pretty gorgeous, you know—if you like that sort of thing," she added loyally. "Personally, I find her looks a bit obvious."

But weren't everyone's looks obvious? Rosie thought. Obviously good or obviously bad. "A pretty hard act to follow however you look at it," Bella concluded.

Nervously, Rosie scrolled back through her memory. Had she missed something? *Had* Matt mentioned Champagne directly? Oh, God, he *had*. At the party. "*What my ex-girlfriend called MTF,*" he had said about Guy Grabster. *"Must Touch Flesh."* But she could remember neither his expression nor the tone of voice in which he had said it. At the time, it hadn't seemed important.

CHAPTER 24

Rosie spent a troubled night in which fitful dozes were alternately dominated by blond women with enormous breasts and Matt himself. Looming ever closer, a wicked expression in his long green eyes, his heavy lips twisted with malicious intent. As the church clock struck seventeen, she climbed out of bed exhausted. More bushy-eyed than bushy-tailed, she thought, examining the black smudges of sleeplessness in a mirror whose lack of a recent clean did not improve things greatly. Nonetheless, as soon as the silver hood of the Mercedes slid up to the window, Rosie was out of the cottage like a ferret out of a trap.

Or like a ferret out of Arthur's house. The lane outside rang with the shrieks of Satchel, Blathnat, and a clutch of other children with equally well-developed lungs. "The ferret's escaped," Satchel screeched excitedly, attempting to run past Rosie into her cottage.

"Well, it's not in there," Rosie told him firmly as she locked the door and climbed into the back of the Mercedes. It rolled off, to the assembled whoops and jeers of the children.

"Is Matt feeling better today?" she asked Murgatroyd eagerly.

"Mildly so, madam. Unfortunately, he was up all night again."

At this evidence that the album was still going badly, Rosie's spirits sank slightly. She decided not to inquire further.

Piled up on the backseat of the car were a number of newspapers.

Murgatroyd, it seemed, had bought the daily press on his way to pick her up; obviously his way of killing two household birds with one stone. And birds, Rosie saw, was right. The front page of the topmost tabloid was almost completely dominated by a huge photograph of a leggy, big-breasted blonde leaning forward into the camera with a rapacious and red-lipsticked grin. "Champagne's Fatale Attraction," proclaimed the headline.

So this is what Champagne D'Vyne looks like, Rosie thought, reading the caption and taking in the pale blond hair, perfect teeth, expensive skin, and breasts that rose triumphantly from the dress with no visible means of support. She stared at the picture, trying to suppress the drumbeat of dread that had struck up within her. Bella was right. Champagne was a hard act to follow. Only, Rosie thought determinedly, I'm not trying to follow her.

"Model, journalist, and aspiring actress Champagne D'Vyne," gushed the accompanying paragraph, *is on a role—literally. The blond society beauty, as famous for her string of celebrity boyfriends as for her well-known social column, is to star in the forthcoming multimillion-dollar "rustic romp"* Farm Fatale. *See page 8 for full story.*

Feeling oddly numb, Rosie obeyed and read on. *"It's my first starring role and I'm ecstatic," purrs D'Vyne, who beat off stiff competition—rumored to include Cate Blanchett, Kate Winslet, and Gwyneth Paltrow—to land the part. "I've no idea how I did it." She dimples. "I simply put my best front forward."* Farm Fatale *is being directed by acclaimed U.S. director Brad Bergspiel, 85, who also happens to be D'Vyne's boyfriend. Bergspiel's recent hits include the Oscar-winning supermarket love story* Aisle Always Love You *in which Meg Ryan's portrayal of a ditzy blond checkout assistant landed her the Best Actress statuette, and last year's box-office-buster, the gritty gymnastics comedy* Arse over Tit, *which starred Gene Hackman as an inspirational sports teacher and was hailed as* The Full Monty *with parallel bars. As Bergspiel is currently in the hospital in the U.S., D'Vyne has taken over and is currently scouting for locations in the British countryside. D'Vyne, 26, whose previous escorts include singer Matt Locke . . .*

Rosie hurriedly put the paper down. She felt a sudden chill in the air. Had Murgatroyd turned up the air conditioning? Staring at the impassive back of his head, she was suddenly seized with the panicked urge to find out what, if anything, the butler knew about the woman who had once figured so largely in Matt's life.

"Amazing, isn't it?" Trying to sound amused, Rosie grabbed the paper and held up the front page so that Murgatroyd could see it in his rearview mirror. "Wouldn't have had her down as the rural type, would you?"

She waited, coiled like a spring, as, beneath his peaked cap, the reflected Murgatroyd raised an eyebrow. "If I may say so, madam, I have to disagree."

"Really?"

"Indeed, madam. From what I can gather, Miss D'Vyne was very skilled at making hay while the sun shone."

Rosie had no idea how to convert this gnomic remark into a full explanation of what the relationship with Champagne D'Vyne had meant to Matt. Not least because Murgatroyd's mouth looked determinedly clamped shut. Silence descended in the Mercedes' interior. Oh, well. Why was she worrying about it, anyway? As Rosie looked out at the fields romping away to the horizon, her heart soared at the thought of what lay ahead. Matt had told her he loved her, hadn't he? Too good to be true it may have seemed. But it had been true and— Rosie glowed at the memory—it had *definitely* been good.

Murgatroyd stopped in front of the archway beneath Matt's tower and murmured that it being such a lovely morning, Madam might like to wait in the courtyard for five minutes while he parked the Mercedes. Rosie happily assented and climbed out of the car, looking up at the ancient stones, golden against a sky as blue as a Madonna's robe. It *was* a lovely morning, but then it would have been were it pouring. She breathed in the cool, fresh air, quietly ecstatic at the thought of seeing Matt again at last. Only a few minutes to go now.

"Play to your strengths, darling," Bella had instructed. "Show your lovely teeth. Give him a big smile when you see him."

"AEIOU," Rosie mouthed obediently, stretching her mouth about in order to warm up the muscles of her face as Bella had advised. She was thus occupied, grimacing extravagantly at the sky, when an imperious voice rang out in the silence like a gunshot.

"And who the hell are you?"

It was like being hit in the face. Standing in the archway, the sun from the courtyard behind streaming through her ice-blond hair, thin, braceleted arms tightly folded, and slender brown legs planted aggressively apart, was the most exquisitely lovely woman Rosie had ever seen. Although she had seen her before, a mere ten minutes ago, in fact, on the front page of Murgatroyd's newspaper. But even if she hadn't, there would have been no doubt that this was the legendary Champagne D'Vyne.

Rosie stared at her feet first. Slim and tanned they were, Rosie recognized, and the other end of the pedicurial universe from her own unloved toes, shoved unceremoniously into the unvarying trainers. Champagne, by contrast, swayed atop a pair of killer-heeled magenta mules festooned with flowers and sequins.

Rosie raised her eyes to Champagne's legs. Legs that, with their smooth, caramel, elegantly oval kneecaps and thighs set so far apart you could drive a bus through them, positively shouted of the benefits of exfoliating, tanning, and waxing, not to mention godlike genes. Helplessly, Rosie recalled her own gray and whiskery calves. A glimpse of Champagne's skirt, a mere slip of lace-edged ice-blue satin, set Bella's voice booming in her head: "There's no such thing as a skirt that's too short. Another universal truth for you."

Above the universal truth, Champagne's slim hips curved into a tiny waist. Above this a feather-trimmed fuchsia cardigan barely contained her famous breasts. Miserably, Rosie recalled her own arrested buds beneath the inevitable fleece. The only similarity she had with the goddess before her was hair color, yet Rosie knew her own unruly, strawlike mass bore, in truth, little resemblance to the shining river of white fire flowing over Champagne's straight and shapely shoulders.

During the nervous nanosecond she dared to look directly into Champagne's face, Rosie registered a straight and perfect nose, slanted green eyes, and inflatable lips oddly suggestive of Matt's. Oddly suggestive all around, in fact. The woman before her positively thrummed with sex. Again in stark contrast to herself.

Champagne, she recognized, wasn't just the kind of woman who

stopped traffic. She was the kind of woman who made planes fall out
of the sky. And men fall head over heels. And *never* get over it.

"Who did you say you were?" Champagne repeated, obviously satisfied with the impression she had made.

"A friend of Matt's." Rosie tried to sound as unfazed as her hysterically chattering teeth would permit.

"A *friend*?" Champagne's exquisite lip curled in contempt. She
raised a perfect arc of eyebrow and swept Rosie with a glare like a green
laser. "He didn't say he was expecting any friends."

Rosie's heart thundered with panic. What was she doing here?
Bella's voice again: "He had a nervous breakdown when she left him."
And now she was at Ladymead, lounging against the tower wall as if
she owned the place. As if . . . Rosie's throat contracted. Her palms
began to sweat. Had she and Matt . . . could they have . . . There was,
of course, no point wondering why. One glance at this sublime creature and it was obvious.

As for when, that, too, was obvious. She had not seen Matt yester-
day. He had been in bed all day. He had been up all night last night.
With . . . ? Well, it was staring her in the face, wasn't it? Or rather
Champagne was. Smirking nastily.

Rosie swallowed hard. "Er . . . I've come to do Matt's picture," she
stammered, horribly aware, before this paragon, of her own sartorial
shortcomings. *Why hadn't she listened to Bella?* Then again, nothing
short of plastic surgery, a personal shopper, and a limitless platinum
card would have brought her anywhere near the style, taste, and perfection of the vision in front of her.

"Picture?" The vision snorted. The sun caught several large jewels
on her long, thin fingers as she beat them irritably against her folded
arms. Unlike her own digits, Rosie noticed, they were completely free
of paint stains, scalpel cuts, and garden dirt under the nails. "Oh, I
see," Champagne said sneeringly. "You *work* for Mattster. Well, I'm
afraid the session for today is canceled."

Mattster. "Canceled?" Rosie croaked, her mouth dry. "Did he . . . I
mean, did he ask you—"

"To come and meet you and tell you? Yeah," snapped Champagne,
her voice fast and irritated. "Couldn't come himself—he's frightfully

busy. With a picture, too, as it happens. One with *me* in it. He's terribly excited that we're filming *Farm Fatale* here. . . ."

Rosie's legs had turned to stone. Her bowels felt dangerously wobbly.

Filming? She recalled the newspaper report—"D'Vyne is currently scouting for locations in the English countryside." "But . . ." Rosie's brain pushed feebly, trying to make sense of it. "But why did Murgatroyd come to pick me up?"

"Because Matt's been too bloody busy to tell him not to, obviously," snapped Champagne. "You're hardly at the top of his list of priorities, you know." She stuck her brown globes of breast forward, shooting Rosie a mocking glance from beneath suggestively lowered lids. "Now I suggested you toddle off home, yeah?" She yawned. "Mattster's not going to be requiring your, ahem, services anymore. Not while I'm at Ladymead, at any rate. And who knows how long *that* might be?"

Watching her turn on her foot-high heels and, with the graceful, spindly lurch of a colt, click-clack back across the cobblestones, Rosie felt the world fall in. She reeled as the ground rushed up to meet her, catching herself just in time. As she staggered down the Ladymead drive, snatches of conversation surfaced and stung her brain.

Not while I'm at Ladymead, at any rate. And who knows how long that *might be? Because Matt's probably been too bloody busy to tell him not to . . . to meet you and tell you . . .*

Rosie raised her eyes and stared hard at the heavens, which, appropriately enough, had begun to cloud over. How could Matt *do* this? Had it all meant nothing to him? After all he had said? She was swallowing back the sobs so hard her throat hurt. She'd been a quick shag, nothing more. A one-day dalliance to be dumped as soon as the real love of his life came back to him, hair and breasts flowing. A woman who made even Bella look plain.

Bella, of course, had been right about Champagne. Matt, like Jack, had never got over the One That Got Away. Another widower grieving inconsolably over a dead relationship. Except that this one was all too alive. Champagne's hair, her skin, even her narrow and spiteful eyes, had all been bursting with vitality. Her cardigan, in particular, had been bursting.

"Mattster's not going to be requiring your, ahem, services anymore." Matt must have *told* Champagne about the afternoon they had spent in bed. Cringing, Rosie recalled the mocking green gaze, the curved, curled lip. She shut her eyes tightly and immediately saw Matt and Champagne lying, sated, a tangle of elegant limbs, in the four-poster bed. "But did you have to fuck her, darling?" she could hear Champagne's bored drawl. "I mean, not really fair, was it?"

"Rosie?" The twentieth time the phone rang, she finally picked it up. The faint hope that it was Matt had finally triumphed over the strong fear that it was Bella.

In any event, it was neither.

"Mark." Rosie swallowed hard, unwilling for him, of all people, to realize she had been crying.

"Well, don't sound quite so embarrassingly thrilled to hear from me."

Rosie, head whirling, could barely understand what he was saying. Why should she be thrilled to hear from him? Her mind still churning with Champagne and Matt, she was struggling even to remember who he was.

"Everything all right?" breezed Mark.

"Fine."

"Been managing with the, um, mortgage?"

Mortgage? What was that? "Er . . ."

"Good," said Mark briskly. "Now, listen, Rosie, I want you to help me. I'm on the verge of a big break here. Biggest of my life, probably. Working on a massive story about, ahem, your friend Matt Locke . . ."

"He's *not* my friend," Rosie snapped, vehemently enough to stop her voice from shaking.

"Well, whatever he is. Now you know this film, *Farm Fatale*— Champagne D'Vyne is filming it at Ladymead and all that."

The walk home had been as long as it had been painful and the one conclusion Rosie had drawn was that nothing was now more dead to her than Ladymead and its inhabitant. Or inhabitants. Blanking them out altogether was the only way she could cope. "What makes you think I know anything about it?"

"Well, the postman mentioned having seen you going up there."

"So?"

"So I need help, Rosie," said Mark urgently. "Come on. Spill the beans. 'Fess up. Sing. Tell me what happening with those two. You know. I *know* you know."

Oh, I know, thought Rosie, screwing up her face tightly against tears. I know, all right. In the back room of her brain, she realized what Mark was asking. For the dirt on Champagne and Matt. The gossip, tickled up with a spot of speculation. To give him this would, she reflected bitterly, be a neat enough revenge for Matt's treatment of her and for Champagne's arrogance. It would be a slap back, a salve for being told to toddle home, yeah, as her services were not required.

"Rosie? You still there?"

Rosie looked out of the window, her mind whirring and clicking with the possibilities. For she could give Mark even more than he bargained for. Much more. Everything Matt had told her about his past, for instance. His Rock-Star Hell. Well, it would certainly help with Her Rejected-and-Used Hell.

"*Lots* of money involved, Rosie," Mark whispered, trying not to think about the budget costs.

Rosie wavered. In ordinary circumstances, she would have slammed the phone down instantly, but these were not ordinary circumstances. Of course, it wasn't the kind of thing a nice girl like her did. But hadn't that been the problem all along? Too nice. Too understanding. Too romantic. Too gullible. She'd been too easy. Too lacking in self-respect. The desire for revenge rose within her. Matt had used and abused her unforgivably. What was stopping her from doing the same to him? No more Miss Nice Girl, thought Rosie, as the blood rushed noisily to her head. Looking at the receiver, she saw her knuckles were clenched white.

"Think of the power you have, Rosie . . ." Mark's persuasive whisper slithered, serpentlike, into the fast, red, whirling center of her thoughts. *Power*. Now *she* had the power. Matt had had power over her. He had made her love him. He had abused her. And *now* . . .

"For old times' sake, Rosie," wheedled Mark, scenting closure.

In Rosie's nearly persuaded brain, something snapped. The whirling stopped.

"What did you say?" she gasped.

"Old times' sake," repeated Mark easily. "You know, the life we shared, hopes and dreams and all that."

Rosie's thoughts came slowly but very sharply into focus. Hopes and dreams? Yes, well, *she* had had hopes and dreams. The countryside, the cottage, a new life. And Mark had gone along with that. Not to please her, heaven forfend. Not because he loved her, for God's sake. But because it fitted with his ambitions at the time. That sodding column.

And now, again for career reasons, he had the cheek to invoke the memory of a relationship he had put up with only because it had suited him. He, too, had thrown her over when it didn't. Hold on, Rosie thought. Just w*ho* is being gullible here? Being used?

"Old times' sake?" she screeched into the receiver. "Old bloody times' sake? Are you joking? I'd do it for practically anything. But I won't do it for that."

"Come on, Rosie—"

"No comment," Rosie yelled as she hurled the phone down. "No bloody comment."

Shouting at Mark made her feel marginally better. A dull calm descended, relief from the stinging pain of earlier. Her head felt oddly clear.

Dully, she realized she had to leave the cottage. And the village. Eight Mile Bottom was finally over for her. Cinder Lane was finished.

Coming out of the door and looking up the street, she saw she was not far wrong. The Muzzles had dragged out what seemed like the entire contents of their sitting room onto the road. Blathnat and Satchel were bouncing manically up and down on a sunken floral sofa. A broken armchair slumped nearby, and another child Rosie did not recognize was riding a coffee table up and down the lane. Its castors roared against the tarmac.

"We're going to have a painting party," Satchel yelled. "We're doing up the lounge. It's going to go on all night."

Of all Rosie's regrets concerning Cinder Lane, the keenest, just then, was that Mark was not present to witness the truly fearsome sight of all the Muzzle furniture on the street. Arthur and Guinever's sofa would, she knew, have driven him into a rage; the ambulant coffee table possibly to a nervous breakdown.

As the only destination up the lane was Spitewinter, Rosie turned sharply down it, almost colliding as she did so with a tall, vague-looking woman wandering up in a billowing floral dress. She wore a straw hat festooned with flowers and ribbons; surely, Rosie thought, not someone going to the Muzzles' painting party? As she turned the corner, Rosie looked back and watched the woman float dreamily through the assorted shattered soft furnishings and head up the lane to the farm.

Then Rosie realized. Of course. Another glossy country-magazine reader who had written to Jack. And someone, Rosie thought sardonically, watching the receding frills and florals, with an even more romantic idea of the countryside than hers had originally been. A thousand million years ago. Passing Mrs. Womersley's windows and noticing the old lady standing there, purse-lipped and scribbling vigorously into a notebook, Rosie's suspicions were confirmed. She was amazed to see Mrs. Womersley wave at her. Still, thought Rosie, I'm probably imagining things now. As if to confirm this, the church clock, showing two, struck a wobbly nine.

It had reached twenty-one as Rosie marched, head down, firmly up the High Street and quickly past The Bottoms lest Iseult spot her. She had no idea where she was going. Just that she had to go.

"Hello there." As she passed the Barley Mow, a cheery voice broke through the haze like sunshine. Alan the landlord was sitting on the paved terrace at the front of the pub enjoying a late and delicious-looking lunch of fish pie, peas, and chips. Rosie's stomach rumbled as she tried to work out how long it had been since she had eaten.

"Coming to Talent Night?" Alan called. "Everyone in the village is taking part. Going to be a good 'un."

Rosie, forcing a smile, shook her head. "Don't think so. I don't have any talent."

"Don't be daft, you're an artist, aren't you?" Alan rubbed his chin, his brows contracting. "Then again, difficult to do that on a stage, I suppose. Can you sing though? Or play anything? Your chance to be a rock star, this is."

Rosie flinched. "Don't think I'm that type."

"Rubbish. Everyone's got a rock star in them."

But not me, thought Rosie, torn between tears and laughter and opting for a watery smile. Not anymore.

"We've got the headmistress on the organ and the local school inspector in drag singing Marilyn Monroe," Alan continued. "I've put them next to each other in the running order, so that should be interesting. You know they don't get on, don't you?"

"Something about a cat, wasn't it?"

Alan nodded, his cheek bulging with chips. "We've got the plumber doing Lionel Ritchie," he added, waving his fork. "The milkman's playing the triangle and the postman's on the tin whistle. Oh, and the builder's doing 'Another Brick in the Wall.' "

Rosie smiled, remembering Bella reading out the results of the last Talent Night in the village newsletter. Her smile faded as she remembered that directly after that had come the fatal conversation in which Bella had encouraged her, nay, *insisted,* she go after Matt. What a great idea *that* had been.

"Plenty of opportunity for latecomers to sign up," persisted Alan. "You any good on maracas?"

Weeding furiously in the garden later that afternoon, Rosie wondered why she was bothering. It wasn't as if she would be here to see the results of her labors. Who knew where she would be when next year's bulbs came poking out of the dark earth like the blades of green knives? As soon as the weekend was over, she planned to go to see Nigel at Kane, Birch & Spankie and put Number 2 Cinder Lane back on the market.

Lost in thought and the tearing of dandelion stems, Rosie thought she could hear a voice. Was it speaking to her? She looked up to see Dora Womersley peering over the wall.

The old lady was smiling and holding a tomato plant rather nervously. "Thought you might like this," she said, stretching out her liver-spotted hand with its bundle of leaves and earth.

Rosie hesitated, then took it. Might as well let bygones be bygones. Everything would be bygones soon. "Thanks," she said. "Everything all right?" she added.

"Oh, yes." Mrs. Womersley nodded vigorously, her postparty frozen manner apparently evaporated. Blinking agitatedly, she cast an eye at the heavily clouded sky. "Black as t'inside of a cow up there though. It'll be raining tin 'ats later. I can feel it in my plastic hip."

"Oh, dear," said Rosie, who had spent the last half hour lugging watering cans from the protracted dribble otherwise known as the cold tap. What a waste of effort.

Mrs. Womersley hesitated. There was obviously something she wanted to say. "We're going to a wedding soon," she blurted out.

"How lovely," Rosie said automatically. "Who's getting married?" A split second later, she realized. "Not Jack?"

Mrs. Womersley nodded so hard her spectacles almost flew off. "Yes. I've only just found out meself. I know it seems a bit previous, but they didn't want to waste any *more* time . . . any *time,* I mean." The old lady paused and blushed. "She's a nice, sensible girl from Yorkshire called Susan. Bit older than Jack. But very capable. Got lots of ideas for the farm. Wants to open a bed-and-breakfast, start a garden center, sell cheese and jam, oh, there's no end to it."

"Well, that's great." Rosie was surprised to find she really did feel glad. Relieved, certainly. Thank God *someone* had come out of the whole mess with something to show for it. "She sounds perfect farmer's wife material."

Flower Hat, then, had failed to make an impression. Probably failed to find the farm, given the vague way she'd been weaving up the lane.

"Do send Jack my, um, love. Tell him I hope they'll both be very happy."

The old lady nodded violently. "I will that. Don't you worry. Thank you." Mrs. Womersley's glasses finally shot off her nose and swung drunkenly about on their plastic chains.

Just then Rosie's ear caught what sounded like a violent assault on the front of the cottage. Or could it be someone at the door?

"Excuse me," she said to Mrs. Womersley. "I think it's the postman."

"I'd stay here in that case," said the old lady with a wry smile.

Bang bang bang bang. The noise as she hurried through the kitchen was terrifying. Duffy never made a row like this. Or knocked at all, come to think of it. Satchel? Possible, though even he usually stopped short of a din of this proportion. The Muzzles and a collection of friends were all inside their house anyway, wielding brushes with more enthusiasm than skill. Arthur was an early casualty; Rosie had spotted him on her return home, his dreadlocks plastered with primer. "If you think this is bad, you should see my bongos," he had muttered. "They'll be a write-off for Talent Night."

The banging went on. As Rosie reached the sitting room, she froze with shock. Crashing his fist against the window, shouting her name, a deranged expression on his face was . . . Matt.

Rosie fell back against the wall.

His blows redoubled in force as he saw her. "Let me in, Rosie. Let me in!" Behind him, Rosie could see Blathnat and Satchel, their mouths wide open in admiration. Even Guinevere never got up a head of steam like this.

Rosie hesitated. The glass was about to crack. For God's sake, hadn't this man done enough to her? Not content with breaking her heart, he had to come to smash her house up into the bargain. She half turned on her heel.

"Rosie!" screamed Matt, his voice a raw howl.

For once the latch slid easily back in its socket. Matt shot in like a bullet from a gun, slammed the door behind him, and dragged her with him into the kitchen. It was a wise precaution. Thrilled by the drama, every child in the street now had his or her nostrils flush to the sitting-room window.

Rosie shrank against the kitchen sink, confused, angry, and terrified. Matt, his eyes spitting sparks, his chest heaving, his breath rasping, was clearly almost deranged with fury.

"I found out," he snarled at her. "I heard all about it. I had no idea. *No idea at all.*"

"About what?" Rosie's hands clutched the edge of the steel draining board. Did he mean Jack? Ancient history—and so what, anyway?

"The bloody film, of course," bellowed Matt, banging his fists against the wall so that the plaster fell in a shower from the ceiling.

"Film?" Yes, they were filming at Ladymead. She knew that; so did he. So what was he talking about?

"*Farm Fatale,* or whatever it's bloody called. The rustic romp. The one with"—he paused, apparently struggling to get the word out— "*Champagne* in it."

Despite flinching at the name, Rosie spoke calmly. "Yes. I know, I met her. She told me all about it. How excited you were she was filming at Ladymead and so on—"

"Well, she had no bloody right to," Matt roared. "I never gave her any sodding permission. She's *not* filming at Ladymead. I told her to piss off."

"You told . . . her . . . to piss off," repeated Rosie incredulously.

"Well, of *course* I bloody did." Matt smashed what must have been already bruised fists against the kitchen table for emphasis. "I can't believe she had the cheek to come anywhere near me. But then she always did have plenty of that."

Rosie gaped, then frowned. Something about this wasn't quite right. Wasn't he desperately in love with Champagne?

"Turns out the sodding film unit's been going around the village for days saying I'd agreed," Matt snarled, pacing up and down in the kitchen. "Been casting bloody everyone from the vicar to the sodding district nurse as extras. Before they'd even talked to *me*. Champagne told them all of it would be no problem filming at Ladymead." His brows knit furiously. "*No problem*. As it happens, it's a fucking *massive* problem."

"Is it?" whispered Rosie, still clinging to the draining board.

"Of course it bloody is. Let me tell you," he added, eyes hard as diamonds, "about Champagne."

Rosie braced herself. Here it came. The love, the betrayal, the pain. The incomparable love.

"Champagne," said Matt, his voice caressing the syllables. "She walked into my life in a skirt so short it was like a novelette with a happy ending . . ."

Just as she had imagined, Rosie thought. Why was she listening to this shit? "I heard you never got over her," she muttered miserably.

"Too right I never bloody got over her. But not quite in the way she liked to make out. When we split, she told everyone I was destroyed by her dumping me."

Rosie drew a sharp breath. Here they went.

"I was destroyed all right. And her dumping me was the only thing that saved me. Except that she didn't dump me. It was me who dumped *her*."

"You . . . ?"

"Of course I bloody did." Matt snorted. "The woman's a *monster*. I wouldn't have her within a hundred miles of Ladymead. Being with her was the worst time of my life. Never got over her, too bloody right. I'm probably damaged for life. She was a *nightmare*."

"Nightmare?"

"Nightmare," repeated Matt. "Champagne's the most spoiled and feckless woman on the planet. You must have read the stories . . ."

Rosie looked down. The kitchen seemed to be whirling about her.

"You haven't? But of course you haven't. You don't read papers. Very sensible of you. But let me tell you, anyway. I once had to book an entire penthouse suite at the Savoy because Champagne wanted a cup of coffee. She wouldn't even get on a Gulfstream unless it was the same color as her nail polish. Drove me fucking bananas."

A feeling of calm began to spread through Rosie.

"And, Christ, she was thick." Matt rocked back on his heels agitatedly. "The only deep thing about her was her cleavage. And most of that was fake. I never saw what her real face was like, it was so plastered in makeup. Her arse, by contrast, was on permanent public view."

Rosie closed her eyes.

"Financially, she almost finished me. Went through my money like water. Once gave six hundred pounds to a beach attendant just for putting a parasol up and bringing her a Sea Breeze. She used to bloody live on caviar. Millionarie's Marmite, she called it." Matt paused. "Amazing I had enough left to buy Ladymead in the end," he continued. " 'Get yourself a tame bank manager and a stockbroker with inside information,' everyone said when I hit the big time. It was only once Champagne started raiding my accounts that I realized my bank manager was barely house-trained and my stockbroker was keeping all his insider information to himself." Matt smacked his palm hard against his forehead.

He continued, eyes slightly watering. "It was her that drove me to drink. After she'd finished with me I wasn't just a songwriter with an alcohol problem, I was an alcoholic with a songwriting problem. I thought I was just drinking socially, whereas in fact the tabloids were regularly reporting that I was drinking very antisocially indeed. She drove me so close to the edge that I thought I might go over it. I looked into the abyss, and the abyss looked back into me . . ." He paused, rubbed his eyes, and gave Rosie a mirthless smile. "Enough already. I sound like an outtake on one of my own albums."

"But I thought—"

"Yes, I know what *you* bloody thought. She met you in the archway and told you to sod off because she was filming and we were getting back together. Didn't she? *Didn't she?*"

Rosie nodded, tears pricking at her eyes.

"Well, that was a bloody lie. Everything she told you was a bloody lie. She was jealous. One look at you and she would have guessed what was going on."

Going on? Was anything, Rosie wondered dully, going on?

"I only realized when Murgatroyd marched her into the studio. Found her trespassing on the property, he said. When she told me what she'd said to you, I almost . . ." Matt swallowed hard. "I came straight round," he whispered, wild-eyed.

"I thought you had gone back to her," Rosie murmured in a monotone. "I thought everything she said was true. *I thought . . .*"

"Rosie," Matt said, speaking to her from across the miles between the sink and the kitchen table. "I was *desperate* to see you. I knew what you would think and that you wouldn't want to see me. I was going to write to you and explain everything." He paused. "Then rather fortunately, Murgatroyd reminded me there was a slight problem with the postman."

Rosie smiled.

"I love *you*," Matt said, his voice bubbling and echoing as if through water. "Not Champagne. Champagne means nothing to me. Not anymore. I fell in love with you the minute I saw you, wearing that gorgeous suit and looking at me with big, scared eyes outside the door of that house. It helped me so much being with you. I felt so much better. You're so gentle, so encouraging, such a good listener . . ."

Rosie strained to catch the words, but her ears seemed to be filled with cotton wool. His voice loomed and faded, as if he was speaking underwater.

"You've helped me more than you can ever know," the watery voice continued. "Even with the album. That tape you gave to Murgatroyd is *fantastic*. Amazing stuff. Just what I needed. I got that girl Iseult in to help me on a few tracks. Her voice is unbelievable. *Incredible.* We're going to perform together soon—just a little thing to help me get my stage boots back on." His eyes flashed with joy. "Oh, Rosie. Say you'll forgive me. Say you'll marry me. I'm so bloody sorry . . . *Rosie?*"

Rosie's elbow suddenly gave way beneath her. The kitchen floor came toward her face. A stray piece of penne by the sink came clearly into focus. Then everything went black.

"Now then," Alan boomed, wielding his crackling microphone and calling the noisy barroom to attention. "The next act needs a bit of encouragement. We've got Keith here on the bass, Les on lead, and Ann on the drums. They're going to try to play 'Apache,' and I want you to clap every time they hit the right note . . ."

Guy, sitting beside Rosie at the table next to the window, guffawed. When a few minutes after the performance had begun, no one had yet put their hands together, he guffawed still louder.

"Apache?" He snorted. "Bloody patchy, I'd say."

The sweet-faced, dark-haired woman sitting opposite him put her finger to her lips. "Don't be so horrible."

"Practicing all night in the village hall they were last night," Alan told him chidingly over the microphone. "It's not their fault they haven't played it through yet. They kept having to stop for the bingo."

The musicians, fortunately, seemed oblivious to criticism. Ann, a Native American headdress of retina-frying neon feathers crammed over her helmet of blond hair and crushed in the corner behind what even Rosie recognized as a distinctly ad hoc–looking drum kit, pawed away with her jazz brushes, brow furrowed in concentration. In front of her, the barroom shouted encouragement.

"Dum der der dum der der dum der der dum der der DER DER," boomed Alan triumphantly. "Ladeezandgennelmen, I think you'll agree they hit the right notes there. Round of applause, please."

After much laughter and even more effort, "Apache" limped to its end. The two subsequent acts, the headmistress on the organ followed by the Ofsted inspector, put up a creditable show, although remembering the cold war that existed over the "Ofsted" feline, the headmistress's choice of "What's New, Pussycat?" seemed a tad injudicious to Rosie.

She looked around again. Still no sign of Matt. Where was he? She'd turned up at the time he had suggested. He had spent the afternoon bringing her cups of tea in bed and telling her how much he loved her before finally going back to Ladymead. Had he gotten cold feet at the prospect of appearing in public, even if it was just for a drink at the village pub? It was depressingly possible.

"Knickersplitter?" Guy, beside her, was heaving himself up to go to the bar. Rosie shook her head. Her stomach was fizzing as if crammed with Alka-Seltzer.

"Lezgennelmen." Alan's voice boomed from the crackling mike. "Our next act is very special. A last-minute entry—announced they'd be playing only an hour ago, in fact. But no less special for that. Very special, indeed."

"What is it then?" yelled someone at the back. "Mrs. Womersley on spoons?"

Alan's eyes twinkled, but he shook his head. "This is an *exclusive,*" he said in tremendous tones. "Even by the Barley Mow's own high professional standards."

"Gerronwithit," called someone else at the back.

"I'll say no more," Alan said, clearly intending to do just the opposite. "Except that it's someone you're all going to recognize. He's been away for a while, but now he's making a comeback, and we're privileged to be the chosen venue. Not Madison Square Garden, lezgennelmen, not Wembley Arena, but the Barley Mow, Eight Mile Bottom."

Everyone laughed again.

"Cut the crap, Alan," shouted a white-haired man in a tweed jacket. Alan cut the crap. "Lezgennelmen, I give you . . . *Ma-att Locke.*"

Rosie gasped. The shouting and applause died away into a shocked silence, punctuated by a few nervous titters. As the pub door opened and Matt's tall, slender figure appeared silhouetted against the night sky, carrying his electric guitar above his head, Rosie's heart bounced hard and fierce against her ribs like a squash ball. This was impossible. There was no doubt now that she was imagining things.

Matt was performing. In the Barley Mow. She vaguely recalled him saying something about getting his stage boots back on. But surely *this* wasn't what he had meant. Watching him push his way through a huddle of farmers to the stage, Rosie's eye caught the signs surrounding the menu. Not only were Mr. Womersley's onions still enjoying pride of place, but the ferret sign had gone up again.

"In order to make his first public appearance for some time," Alan boomed excitedly as Matt struggled through a crowd of large ladies clutching pint glasses, "Matt Locke, the internationally famous rock star, our very own local legend, lezgennelmen, has chosen not to go unplugged in a room at the BBC before an exclusive celebrity gathering, nor has he been tempted by one of the lesser stages at Glastonbury. He has chosen *you*, lezgennelmen. *Us.* The Barley Mow. Eight Mile Bottom."

"Eeh, 'e's not bad, is 'e? Very lifelike. Same hair and everything," muttered a thick-set man with a dark mustache to his wife, who peered at Matt through her bifocals as he climbed slowly onto the pile of curtain-covered pallets constituting the stage.

"Looks just like 'im," the wife pronounced. "Them big lips and everything. Should go on *Star Search,* he should. Looks a bit nervous though, don't he?"

This, Rosie saw, was the understatement of the century. Matt's face was white with panic as he eyed the eighty or so people crowded in front of him. He was clinging to his guitar like a drowning man to a raft, his bloodless fingers pressed tightly to the strings. Even if his road crew alone was normally bigger than this audience, being here was obviously costing him unimaginable effort. Through the thick atmosphere Rosie could feel him battling his demons, wrestling desperately with the urge to dash out of the door and run back to the safe prison of Ladymead. Come on, Matt, she silently urged him. *You can do it.*

But could he? His eyes had retreated behind his brows; he pulled strands of hair nervously over his face and swallowed violently and repeatedly, his Adam's apple traveling up and down his long neck like a turbocharged lift. Chewing his lips, he looked wildly around him. Oh, God, Rosie thought, he's going to run. She jumped up and down to catch his eye, finally succeeded and, crossing her fingers, put her whole heart into her smile back at him. At that moment, Matt seemed to relax.

Skimming his elegant fingers across his guitar strings, he smiled unsteadily at the audience. "This is a new song I just wrote," he muttered.

"For my, um, new album." His voice cracked slightly. The feedback screeched like a banshee. Alan winced. *Go on, Matt,* urged Rosie, everything crossed.

The noise of chatter died down. Even the clink of glasses behind the bar was silenced. The entire barroom listened intently as, after a few soft chords, the familiar raw, sleepy voice, shaky at first, then more confident, filled the smoky air. As he hit the chorus, Rosie felt tears spring to her eyes; heard, too, a few powerful sniffs from behind her in the audience. After a few minutes, Rosie glanced at the *Star Search* couple. They seemed in no doubt now to whom they were listening. Matt's final chord fell like a drop of water into a silent pool. After a few seconds of absolute quiet, the pub rose to its feet and erupted into a frenzy of raucous applause.

The bifocaled woman clamped a tissue to her nose while Alan, Rosie noticed, was looking decidedly moist around the tear ducts. And there, at the back by the door, was none other than Murgatroyd, scraping at his eye with a white handkerchief and cheering like a football supporter.

Stamping her feet furiously into the flowered red carpet, Rosie alternately cheered, wept, and hammered her ecstatic fists hard on Guy's shoulder. "He's done it. He's done it!"

Matt, grinning broadly, eyes shining with relief, suddenly murmured something through the microphone. The room fell instantly silent once more. "Thank you very much," he said softly. "You don't know what it means to me to hear you react like that. I haven't heard that sound in a long while. Hell, I might even start performing in public again." As everyone laughed, Rosie saw that she was the only person who thought he wasn't joking. Or who guessed how much had really been riding on their reaction. "I'm very proud of the new album," Matt added, wincing slightly at the screeching feedback. "But I haven't worked on it alone. I've had some help from someone very special. Someone I've only met lately . . ."

Rosie shrank into Guy. *Oh, please.* Matt wasn't going to mention *her* . . .

"Ladies and gentlemen, Iseult Mahoney."

The door of the pub burst open, hitting Murgatroyd hard on the arm and provoking from him a most un-Jeeves-like curse. The crowd parted like the Red Sea as Iseult danced in, hair flowing, and strode to the stage as if she'd been doing it all her life. Her huge eyes shone with stuck-on sequins and excitement, while her barely there pink T-shirt, bearing the diamanté legend F*** ME, I'M FAMOUS, struck Guy as rather familiar. One of Samantha's? Yes—and abandoned, he was sure, because no one had ever recognized her in it. Or in anything, come to that. Iseult grinned happily at the audience, slipped a hand heavy with silver skulls round the microphone, and as Matt slashed away at his guitar, ripped into a number that practically blew the dust off the rafters. Her voice was sweet, rich, and powerful and, when Matt joined her for the chorus, combined perfectly with his own smoky rawness.

Soon the entire pub was dancing. Ann, still wearing her feather headdress, slipped back behind the drum kit while Alan dived behind the bar and reemerged with an accordion. The headmistress wrested the maracas from the Ofsted inspector's grasp and shook them provocatively in his face. To Rosie's surprise, he smiled. Duffy, meanwhile, was cavorting with a tambourine and a large lady in purple who was looking adoringly into his eyes. "You can stuff my envelope anytime," Rosie heard her growl as they waltzed past, Duffy's face as red as his Royal Mail van.

To judge from the numbers arriving, word was apparently spreading not only around the village but down into Slapton, too. As more and more people arrived in the pub, it seemed the thick-walled building would burst with the pressure of numbers.

Hours later, a perspiring Matt and Iseult played their last encore to a stamping, cheering crowd. Looking slightly abashed, Murgatroyd quietly slipped back to Ann the headdress he had spent the last hour leaping about in and melted away to get the Mercedes. "Do you do special delivery?" Duffy's admirer was asking as, arm thrust firmly through his, she levered him past Rosie and out of the pub door.

Matt shot Rosie a mock-desperate look through the masses now pressing him and Iseult to autograph bar towels, beer mats, and even a bottom. "Please don't tell me you'll never wash it again," said Matt, grinning and crossing the *T*'s with a flourish.

Rosie leaned over to Guy. "Iseult's fantastic. What a voice. You must be very proud."

"We are," Guy said, sliding his hand into that of the sweet-faced brunette. "Despite the fact that she's obviously decided the family name lacks star quality. *Mahoney* indeed."

"It *is* family. My mother was Irish." The brunette sniffed. Her eyes, Rosie noticed, were shining with tears.

"At least no one took their knickers off." Matt grinned as, eventually, he and Iseult signed the last cigarette pack and struggled through to Rosie, Guy, and the brunette by now established as Iseult's mother, Marina.

"You got off lightly then," said Guy, snorting, and the memory of Mrs. Womersley's Harvest Festivals sprang irresistibly to Rosie's mind.

"But I *have* been asked to open the Eight Mile Bottom carnival," Matt added. "They desperately need a celebrity, apparently."

"Congratulations," said Alan, swooping in on the conversation. "That's a great honor, that is. Last year it was the local wildlife artist that opened it, and the year before it was a presenter from Radio Cobchester."

Rosie looked closely at Alan. As usual, it was difficult to tell whether he was joking.

"I said I'd think about it. Can't see how I can refuse, though," Matt said, rubbing his hair and grinning devastatingly at Rosie through the tousled strands. "It turns out they're being lobbied night and day by some nutcase actress in the village who fancies herself as the lady of the manor as well as the most famous person since God and is desperate to open it. Apparently I'm the only person who could stop her getting her way."

"Can't imagine who *that* could be," drawled Iseult, while Guy noisily cleared his throat and Marina bit back a smile. "Still, she needs something to do now that Mark's gone back to London and the film's gone tits-up."

Mark's gone back to London. Rosie felt a slow wave of relief course through her. Now, perhaps, life could begin again. She looked at Matt, who was listening to Alen.

"I take it that they didn't tell you about the curse of the carnival, then?" the landlord was saying in an undertone.

Matt shook his head. "Curse?"

"Oh, yes." Alan grinned. "Notorious for trouble the carnival is. Last year the brass band crashed on the motorway on the way here, we couldn't get anyone to be the carnival queen, not even a man, and there weren't any floats because the farmers needed all their trailers for hay-making. And a couple of years before that the person opening it—some singer, I think—had a heart attack that morning."

Matt's brow furrowed. "Sounds a bit risky. I've only just got myself back on the straight and narrow as it is." He flashed Rosie a grateful glance that went straight to her groin. "Do you think they'd want me to be the carnival entertainment instead?" he asked Alan. "I could do a concert. For free, obviously."

Rosie looked at the landlord, expecting delight. But Alan was sucking his teeth and looking doubtful. "Difficult one, that. They've booked Norman Billy for the evening, you see. Plumber from Slapton and very popular—people round here arrange their weddings around whether he's available or not. Very good cover versions he does. Mostly yours, as it happens."

Matt shrugged his shoulders and smiled. "No contest, in that case. You don't want me spoiling the fun and performing my own stuff. Suppose I'd better practice my ribbon-cutting then." He slid an arm around Rosie. "Come on. We'd better be off. I'll see you at Abbey Road then, Iz. Time we started laying a few tracks down. Nine-thirty next Tuesday morning, be there or be square."

At this, Marina burst into tears. "Abbey Road," she sobbed into Guy's chest. "My little baby's going to be recording at Abbey Road!" In reply, Guy kissed the top of her head.

Iseult rolled exasperated eyes at Matt and Rosie. "Ridiculous, isn't it?" she hissed in a stage whisper. "My parents are divorced. And now they're having an affair with each other. *An affair.* Grown-ups are so bloody stupid."

Matt grinned at Rosie as he humped a guitar case out of the door. "Back in a minute. Just sticking this in the back of the Merc." He paused and cleared his throat. "Don't go away," he added nervously, searching her face with serious eyes. "I've got something to ask you.

Something to give you. Had to wait and see if the gig went well first. But it's all OK now."

It's all OK now, Rosie repeated silently, exultingly, watching him disappear. *It's all OK now.* It was then that she noticed, with a jolt of the heart, a familiar hulking figure at the back of the emptying room. By his side, a short, round, dark-haired woman was talking animatedly to Ann.

There was no way she could avoid him. "Jack," Rosie said, walking up to him, glad of the gloom hiding her blushes as she remembered their last furious exchange. "I've never seen you in here before."

"Aye, well, I've never been a big fan of this pub."

Rosie could have bitten her tongue out. Of course. It was in the Barley Mow that he had met Catherine. Please, she thought, don't let him start banging on about all that again.

"But Susan thinks I should get out more. Great concert, wasn't it? Matt's pretty good, I reckon."

Rosie nodded, trying not to look amazed. "It was. He is. And thanks for saying so."

Jack's teeth shone in the gloaming. "Maybe I'll get some of his CDs. You get sick of Jennifer Lopez . . . This is Susan," he added suddenly as the dark-haired woman, having finished her conversation with Ann, turned bright, inquiring eyes on Rosie. "My fiancée."

"Congratulations," said Rosie, meaning it. From the way Susan was beaming at him with mingled love and pride, it was obvious Jack would have no trouble from the woman he was with in the Barley Mow tonight.

"Rosie's an, um, illustrator," said Jack, shifting uncomfortably from foot to foot. He was, Rosie noticed with astonishment, wearing shoes, not wellies. Moreover, the shoes were new.

Susan's face lit up. "Wonderful. I need someone to do some drawings for the brochures I'm planning for Spitewinter. Advertising bed-and-breakfast, farm-fresh produce, and so on. Would you be interested? When we get back from our honeymoon, that is?"

"Of course. I'd love to." Rosie was about to add that she'd done quite a few Spitewinter sheep and cows already but thought better of it.

"Thanks." Jack grinned as Susan disappeared to retrieve her coat.

"We're getting married on a beach in the Seychelles. Susan thinks I need a break from the farm."

"She's right. Have a great time."

"We will."

Rosie screwed up her courage and looked directly into his eyes. "Be happy, Jack. You deserve it."

"So do you. You be happy, too."

"I will." Spotting Susan returning and Matt coming back in, Rosie crossed her fingers behind her back. Was the something he had to ask her what she hoped it was? Or was he merely wondering if she'd seen his guitar pick?

"Oh, and if you're thinking of buying us a wedding present . . ." Jack added.

"Yes?" Matt and Susan were getting closer. Rosie did not want to be discussing toasters when he reached her.

"Forget the asbestos gloves. I don't think I'll be needing them after all."

Susan, overhearing, shot Jack a puzzled glance. Matt, meanwhile, was rummaging hard in his pocket.

"I will." Rosie smiled at Jack, hoping that she wouldn't be needing them either.

"You've answered my question," murmured Matt, sliding the pale blue Tiffany ring box into her hand.

Also by the
"absolutely fabulous"*
WENDY HOLDEN

The New Yorker

INTERNATIONAL BESTSELLER

A NOVEL

"WICKEDLY WITTY."
—ESQUIRE (LONDON)

INTERNATIONAL BESTSELLER

A NOVEL

"PERFECT"
—THE TIMES (LONDON)

SIMPLY DIVINE

WENDY HOLDEN

BAD HEIR DAY

WENDY HOLDEN

SIMPLY DIVINE

Jane is a struggling twenty-something writer who has just been handed her worst nightmare of an assignment: ghostwriting the life and times of bedazzling blond socialite Champagne D'Vyne. "Delightful," says *Entertainment Weekly*.

BAD HEIR DAY

After being dumped by her rich, gorgeous boyfriend, Anna vows to give up men forever—that is, until she meets Jamie, the dashing heir to a castle in Scotland . . . but is he too good to be true? "Perfect," says *The Times* (London).

Available from Plume